Dear Reader:

I'm delighted to present to you the first books in the HarperMonogram imprint. This is a new imprint dedicated to publishing quality women's fiction and we believe it has all the makings of a surefire hit. From contemporary fiction to historical tales, to page-turning suspense thrillers, our goal at HarperMonogram is to publish romantic stories that will have you coming back for more.

Each month HarperMonogram will feature some of your favorite bestselling authors and introduce you to the most talented new writers around. We hope you enjoy this Monogram and all the HarperMonograms to come.

We'd love to know what you think. If you have any comments or suggestions please write to me at the address below:

HarperMonogram
10 East 53rd Street
New York, NY 10022

Karen Solem
Editor-in-chief

INTO THE NIGHT

"I have to go," Blade said finally.

"Now?"

"Yes. I need to talk to Sheriff Cameron."

"It's cold and dark outside. And there are crooks out there," Ruth said.

"Are you actually worried about me?"

She reached over and touched his shirt just below the pulse point in his neck. "Yes. I don't want you hurt."

He was suddenly humbled. "Thank you. But I'll be all right." He stood and pulled her along with him. With his arm around her waist, he led her down the hall.

"Where are you taking me?" she asked, trying to keep the anxiety out of her voice.

Blade entered her room, lifted her onto the bed, leaned down, and brushed his lips over hers in a feather touch. Then he tugged the covers up to her chin. "Next time I'll wish that you reach up and pull me in with you."

He shut the door, delighting in her shocked expression.

Harper
Monogram

One Man's Treasure

CATRIONA FLYNT

HarperPaperbacks
A Division of HarperCollinsPublishers

HarperPaperbacks   *A Division of* HarperCollins*Publishers*
10 East 53rd Street, New York, N.Y. 10022

Cover illustration by Jean Restivo Monte

First printing: December 1992

Printed in the United States of America

HarperPaperbacks, HarperMonogram, and colophon are trademarks of HarperCollins*Publishers*

❖ 10 9 8 7 6 5 4 3 2 1

For Chris and Rory

ACKNOWLEDGMENTS

Our sincere thanks for all the assistance we received from the helpful people at the Flagstaff Chamber of Commerce who found advertisements and maps for 1897, which made writing this book much easier and more historically accurate. And a tremendous thanks to the people at the Sunset Peak Visitor's Center who told us about the bean fields.

Also, to our friends in Flagstaff, Holbrook and Winslow— thank you for believing in us.

ACKNOWLEDGMENTS

Prologue

San Francisco
November 1895

"There's nothing I like better on a cold foggy night than a nice warm whorehouse."

"It's called a gentlemen's club, Poppa," sputtered Gladius Blade, choking on his fine Napoleon brandy.

A rude snort was his father's only reply. Seamus Augustus Blade was anything but a gentlemen. Looking ever so much like a debauched leprechaun, the elder Blade prided himself on his earthy origins, almost as much as he did in his enormous fortune. "Call it anything you want, boy-o," he muttered in a voice as thick as Irish peat, "club or cathouse, it's still the same thing, whether it be up on Snob Hill or down on the Barbary Coast, and the gents be here to rut the same as us common folks."

His son shook his head in amused tolerance, having

learned many years ago the futility of arguing with the incorrigible old reprobate. Gladius pointed to a table on the other side of the near-empty barroom. "Let's sit over by the fire and relax a bit. It's been a hell of a day."

"Ah, laddie, you're never gonna be a banker." Seamus picked up his glass and the fancy Waterford decanter and walked across the ornate room, his bearing ramrod straight.

In the parlor, on the other side of the tall, elegant house, the piano man stroked the ivories and a soprano began the first strains of a sad watery ballad. Gladius paid them no mind. The old man's comment rankled, as it always did—as it was meant to do. The ornery old bastard knew how to twist the knife.

The younger Blade wasn't a banker, never had been, never wanted to be. Drawing was his passion, his true talent, his life. To Seamus, picture drawing was a damned fool thing for a big hulk of a man to be doing with his time. He often wondered why Gladius couldn't be a financial wizard like his youngest brother, Cornelius. Seamus himself had made his fortune wresting gold from stubborn Colorado rock and a second one from investing and speculating. There was simply no precedent for an artist in the family.

Gladius sighed, pulling out a heavy, dark olive-green leather, upholstered captain's chair, and sat down. It was an ancient argument between them, never to be solved, and he sure as hell wasn't going to waste time worrying about it tonight. Father and son were as different as night and day. And that was that.

A soft glow from the gaslight chandelier and wall

sconces filtered down over them, highlighting their one common physical characteristic—red hair. Seamus's bright orange curls had faded and thinned to a respectable sandy red, while his son's thick wavy mane was deep auburn. Otherwise, Gladius was tall and massive, an oak of a man, while Seamus was a runty willow. Physically, emotionally, in every other way, the men were opposites who often clashed.

Behind the rosewood bar, Chauncey, the bespectacled bartender, quietly went about his business, cleaning the spotless mirror, polishing the gleaming brass. He smiled to himself. This was a fine place to work, clean working conditions, decent wages, good food, a little music, and a few upstairs benefits thrown in. It was Chauncey's idea of heaven.

The soprano had just finished her first set, and the piano man stepped in for a beer when two of the girls and a client emerged from the parlor. The man, holding a girl in each arm, looked very pleased with himself.

"I thought we were the only ones foolish enough to come out on a night as miserable as this," Gladius said.

A puckish twinkle lit Seamus's blue eyes. "Many a man would brave a bit of fog for an evening in this fine place."

Behind them the barkeep hurried across the green oriental carpet to wait upon the other client and his companions. They'd seated themselves at a table near the door, whispering and laughing, the girls obviously amused at a naughty story the dark-haired gent was telling.

Donal Phelan couldn't have been in a finer mood. He'd waited a long time and had traveled a long way for this moment. He thought he deserved a little celebration.

"Champagne," he ordered. "These ladies want your finest French champagne."

The "ladies" trilled their agreement in titters and giggles, and exchanged congratulatory glances. For once they were in luck. Not only was this fellow handsome, with his raven black hair and China blue eyes, and free with his cash and coin, but he'd bathed before he arrived. Now if he wasn't mean or peculiar, they'd have a splendid night. Even if it wasn't a busy one.

The champagne cork popped and bubbles sparkled in the gaslight. The heavily ornamented green and gold decor seemed exactly right for this party. Green and gold—for money.

"Here's to the most beautiful city in the world," Phelan stood up and toasted. He looked at the women beside him. Suzette, the dark one with the scarlet ostrich feathers and the daring emerald velvet bodice, probably had been quite attractive several years and pounds ago. Still, her milk-white breasts begged for his attention. And Monique—why did all whores have such absurd names?—was the blonde in pink silk and worn lace, with wicked blue eyes and long slender limbs. Too bad her teeth were so crooked. But what the hell, all women looked good in candlelight. "And here's to the city's most beautiful women," he finished, and took a long drink of the sparkling wine.

Gladius glanced over at the table where the women emptied their glasses and then held them out for more. His hard eyes met the other man's as they took each other's measure. Blade was rugged looking, while the other fellow was tall, fined boned and conventionally handsome. An even match, each man decided. They looked away.

"Only two other things could make my life more perfect than it is right now." Phelan looked directly at the leaded mirror above the bar. He had an excellent view of the men near the fire from where he stood.

"What's that, darlin'?" Suzette asked, leaning forward to expose even more of her fabulous breasts.

Phelan almost forgot what he was after. Almost. He might be randy as a goat tonight, but to him business always came before pleasure.

"I need to find a rich investor, love. A man with the money and the stones to stake me to a treasure hunt."

"What kind of treasure?" Suzette's interest was piqued.

"Have you ever heard of Coronado?"

Suzette shook her head. She didn't think he was a regular at the club.

"He was a Spanish explorer, and he came to this country looking for gold."

"Like the forty-niners?" Even Suzette knew about the California gold rush.

Phelan nodded slightly and walked to the windows that looked out onto the foggy street. He closed the lace curtain, certain he had the attention of every soul in the bar, and continued. The soprano in the parlor started singing again, but she was no match for Donal Phelan. He had a magnificent speaking voice, and he used it to his best advantage.

"Coronado led a band of explorers into the American southwest in a search for the fabled seven cities of gold. But he didn't come to dig for it as the forty-niners did. He believed the Indians knew the location, and he told them he had a sickness of the heart and would die if they didn't bring him gold."

"Did he find the gold?" Suzette asked, her heart palpitating .

"He traveled west to the Grand Canyon and east to the prairies of Kansas, but he didn't find the seven cities. Actually, he just didn't travel quite far enough." Phelan paused and looked around the room. "But I know where he should have looked."

"Are you a miner?" Seamus Blade asked.

Gladius groaned. Gold dust ran through the old man's veins. If ever there was talk of the yellow metal, Seamus Blade couldn't stay out of the conversation.

"Not a miner, sir," Phelan answered respectfully, "although I dig in the earth. I'm an archaeologist. And I'm in the city to hunt up some financial backing for my latest expedition."

"Did this Coronado fellow really exist?" Seamus whispered to his son. He'd had little education him-self, but insisted all of his children have the best schooling.

Gladius nodded. "His story is more or less correct."

"Fine."

Gladius knew in his gut the old man was hooked. It was a hell of a coincidence: a man looking for an investor ending up in the same brothel, on one of the city's most miserable fog-bound evenings of the year, with a wealthy and slightly crazy financier. Unfortu-nately, Gladius didn't believe in coincidence. And even more unfortunate, he had no influence over his father whatsoever.

"My glass is empty," Suzette simpered, annoyed at being ignored. All this serious talk bored her.

Monique merely watched the men. She was far more intelligent than her counterpart and she knew that something important was about to happen. Her mind began to calculate how she could make the most of the situation.

"Are you gentlemen from the city?" Phelan asked casually as he refilled the tall glasses and motioned for another bottle.

"Denver," Seamus answered. "We're here on business."

"What's the second thing that will make your life perfect?" Monique asked, in her cool husky voice.

"An artist," Phelan proclaimed. "I need an artist to record every step of the dig and document our findings. The colored drawings will go in the manuscript I'll write afterward."

"Holy saints in heaven!" Seamus crowed as he jumped to his feet and introduced himself. "This is your lucky day, man." He pointed to his scowling son. "That's my eldest, Gladius, but he hates the name. He's the finest artist in the state of Colorado. And I am an investor who loves treasure hunts—the wilder the better."

The younger Blade watched Phelan's look of incredulity turn to innocent joy, and he almost applauded. The man was good, damned good.

He rose to his feet to join the toasting and backslapping, knowing nothing would change his father's mind.

Eventually, Phelan sought him out.

"Welcome to the expedition." He held out his hand.

Gladius took the aristocratic hand in his own massive paw, smiling inwardly at Phelan's momentary look of surprise. He didn't grind Phelan's hand as a lesser man would have done.

"I'm coming along to watch my father's money," he replied in a deadly undertone. "If you cheat him in any way, I'll break your bloody neck."

1

**Flagstaff, Arizona Territory
March 1897**

Ruth McKenna lurched to her feet before the train rumbled to a halt. She knew there was little time to lose. Reaching across the seat to pick up her black leather satchel, she steeled herself for the inevitable argument with the conductor, and stepped into the aisle.

Years of traveling had seasoned her to the hazards of train trips, particularly the sloppiness of baggage handlers. On this trip she wasn't leaving anything to chance. Everything she owned was on this train and she meant to have it off at the Flagstaff depot in decent condition.

The conductor had disappeared, just when she needed him. Ruth sniffed in disgust. The lazy, whey-faced man was, in her humble opinion, the poorest excuse for a railroad conductor she'd ever encountered. From what she'd observed, all he did was tell off-color stories and ogle women's breasts.

In the last seat of the car was a forgotten cane. A look of pure devilment flashed in Ruth's blue eyes as she reached for it. At the far end of the car, she saw the conductor sneaking away.He was a fast little bugger—probably he'd had years of experience avoiding eastern ladies with notions about their luggage, but Ruth was determined. She caught his arm with the crook of the cane just as he started down the steps and brought him to a stand still.

"I need your help," she said. "I'll thank you to wait for me."

Resignation crossed his face. He'd known this one was trouble the first minute he'd looked at her. He could always tell the starchy ones, they never failed to make his work difficult. But he did her bidding. Otherwise, he was certain he'd feel the rap of the cane.

Ruth plunged forward, ready to take on the next problem, the baggage handler. Action, she found, reduced her fear. She didn't want to think of why a normally sane, responsible woman of twenty-eight would make a cross-country journey all alone without telling a soul of her plans. And why she was so nervous now that she'd reached her destination.

She'd not only traveled to the Arizona Territory without warning Donal of her arrival, but she'd also brought along all her worldly possessions. She hoped he wouldn't force her to return to St. Louis once he saw the mountain of belongings she'd shipped with her. Now, in Flagstaff, she wondered at her faulty reasoning. The man had no conscience. And nobody knew that better than she. Would he send her away, knowing full well she had little money and no place else to go?

Despite a shiver of fear down her spine, Ruth banished the unthinkable from her mind. She stepped out onto the platform, conductor in tow, issuing orders like a calvary sergeant. The bracing mountain air revived her sagging spirits, and instantly she felt ready to handle any challenge. After all, she'd quartermastered for whole archaeological expeditions before she turned twenty-one. A few boxes of china should be a simple matter.

Determination could have been called the family strength, or the family weakness. Donal carried it to impossible lengths, of course, as he did everything else. In Ruth's opinion, she had a healthy amount of the trait, while his was absurd. A mule was positively weak-willed compared to her brother.

Donal Phelan was stubborn as stone. Standing there beside the railway baggage car, she thought of the last time she'd seen him four years ago. That night in St. Louis, he'd been the Devil himself.

It had been raining. Funny how she remembered that little detail, when the other more important events had changed her life so completely. The dark streets glimmered wetly beneath the gaslights, and Ruth had been quaking in fear as she stood up to him, telling him that she was leaving with Farley McKenna.

Donal responded like a maniac! Dark and handsome as sin, and raving mad, swearing at the top of his mighty voice, he accused her of all types of whoredom and betrayal. He'd actually accused Farley of stealing his research and publishing it, which had hurt Farley terribly. Consequently, the men never spoke again.

And because Ruth had argued in her new husband's defense, Donal hadn't communicated with her in any way since that fateful night.

Her heart felt lacerated by the whip of his nasty tongue. But she left him anyway. She was twenty-four years old, a grown woman with her own mind and her own life. She left with the man she'd married an hour before.

The side door of the baggage car rumbled open and a humped-back man of forty began shoving boxes negligently to the opening.

"Watch that!" she called, keeping a sharp eye on the shabby youth who'd slouched up to the door to assist. Determined to get her carefully crated Remington off the train in working order, she bore down on the boy. The disgruntled conductor trudged along slowly in her wake.

Normally the conductor would have tried to ignore her. A number of city women rode the A&P to Flagstaff to take the Grand Canyon tour, so he was accustomed to bossy females having tizzy fits over hatboxes and the like, but this young woman was different. Somehow she managed to command more authority than most men.

As soon as he saw the girl had everything under control, the conductor quietly drifted off, thinking he'd rather hear a little local gossip than supervise baggage. And he didn't quite trust her not to blow up and use the cane on his balding head.

Out of the corner of her eye, Ruth saw him sneak off to the warmth of the depot. What a worthless boob! Her previous case of jitters over Donal's unknown reception swiftly evolved into anger at the conductor, and then at men in general. She squawked like a seared chicken when the grimy boy started to kick the Remington crate aside.

"What's in the box?" the boy asked curiously. He'd been unloading boxes since he was twelve and he was so accustomed to being yelled at that he hardly noticed. "Ya got glass eggs in here, lady?" he teased good-naturedly, certain he'd made a splendid joke.

Ruth took a deep breath of the cool mountain air and pulled the navy blue serge macintosh cape straight, allowing time for her normally good disposition to return. There was no sense taking her annoyance with the conductor out on the lad. After all, he'd done exactly what she'd instructed and the Remington was safely off the train. It had survived the journey undamaged, perhaps in better shape than she.

"It's a typing machine," she said quietly, "a fine Remington typing machine."

The youth stared at her in amazement. Was it possible, could this be . . . ? He'd heard rumors about women joining the workplace, but he had never seen a working woman except hashers and whores. And those didn't count.

"Are you a typewriter?" the boy asked, unable to keep the awe out of his voice. He wanted to make sure he had the facts straight before he began bragging around town.

"Indeed I am," Ruth answered proudly. Her typing skill, as well as her grammatical and spelling abilities, was remarkable. Most typewriters, like most clerks, were male, but few, if any, had Ruth's expertise. Farley McKenna raved about her skills and kept her constantly busy. He'd been so pleased with her, he'd gone so far as to dedicate his book to her. She still felt a thrill, remembering those words: to my wife and helpmate.

Ruth sighed quietly at the sudden thought of Farley. He'd sworn his colleagues were violently jealous of him because his wife had such marvelous skills while they had to pay typewriters to work for them. Ruth figured that was the truth; Farley wasn't a man to fawn and flatter.

How her life had changed since those comfortable days! She often thanked God fervently for the Remington. Farley had purchased it as a birthday gift for her— the most costly gift he ever gave her—and he'd told her they would produce many fine books together. At the time, though she'd been delighted with the gift, she hadn't realized just how valuable the little machine would be to her future.

If anything had the power to soothe Donal Phelan's wrath at his younger sister for running off with his arch rival, it was the Remington. Donal was a brilliant scientist, one of the country's foremost archaeologists. In her heart, Ruth considered him the best, though out of loyalty to her husband she never said so aloud. But the man was an utter slob. Somehow he had the power to create havoc wherever he went. Within minutes he wrecked the most carefully set-up workroom, losing valuable artifacts, notes, reference books, and, more often than not, his supper.

Surely Ruth was his salvation! She'd sort and file. With the aid of her Remington, she'd whip that nightmare of scrawled notes into an orderly, scholarly manuscript fit for the academic world within weeks. Donal Phelan needed her.

A soft smile touched her lips. Vile creature that he was, he needed her.

"Is somebody comin' ta getcha, ma'am?" the youth asked as he pulled the two-wheel baggage cart toward the large stone building.

"No. I need to hire a cab or wagon." She opened her handbag to consult her pocket watch and frowned. It was late. If the ranch house Donal occupied was many miles out, she wouldn't arrive till after he'd retired for the night. She considered staying in a hotel room she could ill afford, since the only thing she could imagine being worse than surprising her surly brother was awakening him from a warm bed.

"Git! Git outta the way, ya little varmits! The lady don't want none of that trashy stuff. Go on home. Go on or I'll take a broom to ya!"

Ruth looked around to see the baggage boy waving his arm at two tattered Indian children standing forlornly on the rough boards of the platform holding what appeared to be small rugs. They slunk back into the shadows as the baggage handler pulled the cart past. Ruth fished around in her pocketbook for a couple of coins.

"What are they selling?" she asked the youth as the coins fell innocently to the platform. She didn't have to look to know the ragged children had dived for the fallen money.

"Trash," he answered disgustedly. "Them two is the worst. Old woman's a drunk, old man's gone. I get danged sick a seein' 'em here at the depot. Always beggin' money. Little varmits."

"I see," Ruth said evenly, holding her annoyance in check. She'd spent too many years with archaeologists and scholars not to understand some of the shameful treatment of the native inhabitants of America. Obviously these small children were so poor and hungry they'd braved the cold and darkness to meet the train. She could imagine how her brother would have cursed the bag boy.

At that moment, the conductor came cheerily out of the depot, having caught up on all the local gossip, and checked on his minion's progress. "When you finish up, Natty, go on home. Train's leaving early tonight. Nobody's getting aboard. Engineer's gonna try to make up a little time."

The boy nodded. "Lady needs a wagon for all her stuff. Where ya goin', ma'am?"

"To my brother's place," Ruth answered. "I'm not exactly sure of the directions. Outside of town. It's a little northeast, I believe, near some Indian ruins. He's Donal Phelan, the head of the archaeological expedition. That's not too far away, is it? I'd like to be there before he goes to sleep." Her voice trailed off as she realized how startled her audience looked. Or was it the flickering light from inside the depot window? She saw the two exchange a glance and knew she hadn't been mistaken. What on earth had Donal Phelan done this time?

"Natty, tell Juan to run up to Grand Canyon Stables and hire the lady a wagon." The conductor tipped his hat to Ruth and began to back away. "Well, I'm off." He walked into the night, leaving Ruth speechless.

"Wait here, ma'am," Natty mumbled. "I'll rustle up old Juan to help ya. Only be a minute." And he, too, was gone.

Ruth glanced around the platform. Even the tattered Indian children had disappeared into the darkness. She wondered what she'd said to clear an entire train station in a matter of moments. The engine began to hiss and snort, making ready for a hasty departure. She felt suddenly like an abandoned child. Had she offended everyone, or had Donal? The question was absurd. Of course, Donal had committed the offense.

All of a sudden she longed for a cup of tea. Travel weary, she thought she must be imagining problems where none existed. A steaming cup of tea would be just the thing.

Within minutes she'd left word with the toothless man inside the depot and set out across the train yard in search of a repast. Toothy Thompson, as he introduced himself, recommended she try the Yellow Canary right across Railroad Avenue. He assured her all her luggage would be safe on the baggage cart till the delivery wagon arrived from the stable and it could be unloaded.

"This here's a law 'biding town," Toothy told her. "No crime a'tall . . .'cepting a murder or two." Then he gave her a gummy laugh, delighted with his own hilarious joke.

Railroad Avenue was dark and empty. Ruth was thankful it wasn't knee-deep in mud as some wild West towns often were. The navy blue serge macintosh cape flapped around her in the breeze off the mountains. The soft scent of pines teased her sensitive nostrils, and she inhaled with pleasure, looking forward to seeing the scenery in the daylight. A sharp gust of wind tossed her cape back. The macintosh outfit had been quite practical for train travel but Ruth realized now it lacked the proper warmth for this high mountain elevation. She hurried across the rest of the road and stepped quickly up the wooden steps to the boardwalk.

Suddenly the dark form of a creature shot out in front of her.

Giving a startled cry of alarm, Ruth stumbled backward to the dirt road. It was only luck she didn't fall.

A larger animal tore after the first, barking. From some place down the road an angry cat let out a squall, and then the dog began to yip and howl.

Ruth chuckled. Not wild beasts at all.

It wasn't difficult locating the Yellow Canary even in the dark, since it was the only establishment on the block open for business. Down on the next block soft tinkling piano music identified several saloons.

THE YELLOW CANARY RESTAURANT AND BAKERY had been elaborately painted on the cafe window along with a couple of singing birds and a corner sign that read MEALS 50 CENTS. Yellow and white starched gingham curtains hung in the windows, giving the place a cheerful appearance. Ruth opened the door and was pleased to see how well lighted and pleasantly clean the restaurant looked. A faint aroma of baked bread and spices hung in the air, reminding her she'd skipped supper.

Half a dozen men occupied the small oilcloth-covered tables despite the lateness of the hour. Several stood near the stove watching a checker game, one was eating an enormous bloody steak, and the others clutched coffee cups. The moment Ruth opened the door, every eye in the place turned to stare at her. Astonishment was the only word for their expression, astonishment at discovering a lovely stranger in their midst.

It wasn't especially unusual for unknown women to come to Flagstaff, at least now that the railroad was finished. Women were often in the groups of hardy individuals arriving to take the scenic stage tour to the

Grand Canyon of the Colorado River, but such females stayed near the hotel and never ventured out alone at night.

Ruth was a most diverting oddity. Tall for a woman, and very well dressed, with shiny brown hair and features so perfect they could have graced a ladies' magazine, she appeared to be a walking dream. Several seconds passed before any of the men found their manners and looked away to return to what they'd been doing.

Walking quickly to an empty table near the bakery counter, Ruth seated herself with as much poise as she could muster. She removed the slate mocharette gloves with care, clasping her chilled hands beneath the yellow-checked oilcloth. She dearly wanted a cup of tea.

"Goddamn, I set myself afire! I sure as hell did. Almost blistered my ass off."

One of the men, a long-jawed cowboy with a beaky nose and narrow shoulders, hopped away from the stove, nearly upturning the checkerboard, and began frantically rubbing the back of his grimy denims. "Son of a bitch!"

"Hanks, watch your mouth. There's a lady present." The older man issuing the order never raised his eyes from the checkerboard. He was winning.

"Goddamn," Hanks whined. But he sat down and said no more.

The faint odor of scorched fabric assaulted Ruth's nostrils. She lifted her chin and ignored the scowling cowboy. She was in the West now, and she had to adjust.

To the men in the Yellow Canary she had as much dignity as a queen. Ruth would have laughed heartily at the description, exhausted as she was from the stress of the trip. The afternoon meal she'd purchased in Winslow had been a greasy, overspiced concoction of beans and meat she'd barely touched. Sitting in the pleasant-smelling cafe, she considered trying a little food with the tea.

As seconds ticked past and no one emerged from the kitchen to take her order, Ruth grew very uncomfortable with the whispers and glances from the men. She frowned, wondering if the oafs had never seen a stranger before, and quelled the urge to ask them just that.

That she was a lady, these men had no doubt. Being more accustomed to women who weren't, they could spot a real lady a mile off. The serviceable all-weather navy blue serge macintosh suit Ruth deemed so ordinary looked to them like it came straight from Paris. Even in the 1890s, women of Ruth's caliber and breeding were still a rarity in the Arizona Territory. It was the unspoken consensus of the men in the cafe that this unattached female was the most beautiful creature ever to walk the wooden sidewalks of Flagstaff. They'd fight any man who argued the point.

Had she known their thoughts, Ruth would have been shocked, for she never considered herself a beauty. She didn't have that round delicate prettiness fashion deemed so desirable. She wasn't fragile or foolish or awed by men. Her features were too strong, her eyes too wide, blue and direct, and she was too opinionated by half. She'd had to be to survive as Donal Phelan's younger sister. Actually Donal had all the looks in the family. Ruth was the first to admit she was less spectacular in every way than her magnificent brother, like a peahen to a peacock.

Ruth might not have the superior looks, but without a doubt she had a nicer temperament. Farley told her that repeatedly. He'd never been one to flatter her unduly, and he certainly didn't bother to prattle on about her physical beauty even in their most intimate moments, but he did give her a word of praise from time to time about her strong body, nimble mind, and good sense. So that's how she saw herself, as a plain, capable woman who possessed a strong constitution and common sense.

But the lonely men in the Yellow Canary wouldn't have agreed with her matter-of-fact assessment. The smoky brown hair beneath the navy blue tam-o'-shanter made a man's hands itch to dive into its satiny thickness. And her deep blue eyes held a haunting quality, a touch of undiscovered passion.

At that moment a stout, heavily corseted woman in turkey red taffeta rustled in from the kitchen and spied Ruth, who'd nearly decided to forgo the tea and leave. After a startled blink at the well-dressed stranger, the woman turned back to the kitchen and hollered, "Myrtle—you gotta customer."

Ruth felt her cheeks flush with embarrassment as all the men again stopped talking and turned to stare. She sincerely wished she'd stayed at the depot and waited with her belongings for the delivery wagon.

"Sorry for the wait, girlie," the stout woman bellowed. "Didn't hear ya come in." She scowled at the men. "Why didn't one of you danged fools speak up! And quit gawkin' at the girl. Cain't ya see you're shaming her?"

Ruth's cheeks blazed. Clenching her teeth against a strong impulse to run, she told herself sternly to order the tea very strong.

A shabby, sullen girl of thirteen or so shuffled in from the back to take her order. Ruth noticed the soles of the child's shoes had come apart and one flapped as she walked. She stopped to wait silently at Ruth's elbow for the order.

"I'd like a piece of toasted bread, with butter and honey. And some tea."

The child glanced fearfully at the stout woman. At her nod, the girl shuffled and flapped back to the kitchen.

"Is that all you want?" the older woman yelled. It appeared she didn't know how to speak in anything softer than a shout.

"All I want is tea and toasted bread. And a chance to rest quietly before I make the last part of my journey."

The stout woman shrugged. Then she walked from behind the counter and stood boldly by Ruth's table. "Who did you say you came here to see?" she asked, covering a belch with her pudgy hand.

Ruth felt an unholy inclination to tell the nosy, rude woman to mind her own blasted business—that's what Donal would have done in no uncertain terms—yet she thought better of it. As politely as she could manage, she answered sweetly through tightly clenched teeth, "I'm visiting my brother."

The young girl plunked a heavy white china plate of unevenly cut but nicely toasted bread down on the table and reached for the china teapot.

The woman's disgusting curiosity still wasn't satisfied. "Who's your brother?"

Ruth blue eyes began to glitter at the obnoxious woman's nerve. Still, her voice was steady and polite when she answered, "Donal Phelan. The archaeologist."

The teapot crashed to the table, sloshing its scalding contents onto the tray and splashing the girl's fingers. She shrieked loudly, and ran howling back to the kitchen. The older woman chased behind, cursing the girl loudly for her clumsiness and stupidity.

Only luck and quick reflexes prevented Ruth from being burned by the steaming liquid. Flinging herself backward, Ruth tipped the chair precariously. A man nearby caught the chair and prevented her from toppling to the floor.

The sounds of violent slaps and screams burst from the kitchen, along with a new string of curses. Seeing the ruins of toasted bread floating soggily on the china plate, Ruth rose to her feet. She'd had enough! Maybe Donal would have tea at his place. Surely the show he'd put on wouldn't be any worse than this.

As she turned to leave she glanced at the man who'd caught her falling chair. He was a rough-looking sort, bearded and weathered, his denims faded, his hat stained, his duster and boots worn with age. He nodded awkwardly, and then remembering his manners, hauled the hat from his head.

"Thank you for your assistance," Ruth murmured politely. Then on an impulse she asked, "Do you know my brother? The archaeologist?"

The fellow seemed embarrassed she'd spoken. His leathery cheeks flushed. "Heard of him," he answered hoarsely. Then he cleared his throat and shrugged. "Heard he found himself a treasure t'other day."

Ruth's cheery laughter filled the silent room. Nobody ever understood the sort of treasure Donal Phelan dug for. "Oh, I'm sure he found a wonderful treasure," she agreed, feeling positively giddy, and she opened the door and walked hurriedly into the night.

To her relief a heavy wagon loaded with her belongings waited near the depot house. She smiled in satisfaction at how well her possessions had been packed, and went looking for the driver.

Inside the depot, Juan, a wizened old Mexican, greeted her and told her the driver would return shortly. Toothy Thompson was nowhere to be seen.

Juan was pouring himself some coffee from a gray metal pot. "Coffee, senora?"

Ruth breathed a sigh. "That would be wonderful. Thank you." She took a sip as she settled herself on a wooden chair.

Juan walked over to where she sat and held out a round piece of flat white bread on a worn linen napkin. "This is a tortilla. Eat. She is good."

The coffee was black and strong enough to dissolve a spoon but she drank it thankfully. Then she took a cautious bite of the flat bread, smiling at the old man because she knew he'd given her part of his supper. The door opened just then and in walked an Indian. Ruth managed to swallow her startled gasp just as old Juan greeted the young man with great enthusiasm. She felt ashamed. She'd seen other native inhabitants before, she probably knew more about native cultures than most people. Still, this was the first time she'd been West, and she'd read so many lurid tales about Indians in the Arizona Territory.

Ruth gave herself a mental lecture while Juan talked to the Indian in Spanish. If she was going to live with her brother, she'd never disgrace him by showing ignorance. The days of the wild West were over. Even

Geronimo, the Apache renegade, had surrendered several years ago. It was time to put away her silly eastern notions and learn the truth about Arizona's natives.

Over the rim of her coffee cup Ruth studied the Indian. He was quite young, she realized, in his late teens at the most, well formed and thin as whipcord. His clothes were similar to those worn by the men in the cafe. A red calico shirt fit snugly over broad shoulders and black denims were tucked into heavy leather boots. Around his forehead, above his long black braids, he'd twisted a scarf of scarlet silk.

He answered Juan's fluid Spanish in clipped phrases, his ebony eyes darting to her once. Ruth decided his eyes were like the jet buttons on her mourning dress.

The old man spoke to her. "He asks where's your man?"

Ruth looked directly at the Indian who was watching her passively. "I have no man," she said. "I'm a widow. My husband died nearly a year ago." That still sounded strange to her, Farley being dead. It had been so sudden. One minute he'd been standing before the fire telling her to order more coal, one hand absently stroking the quilted, wine satin lapel of his velvet smoking jacket, and the next minute he'd been crumpled on the floor, dead. "I'm going to live with my brother, Donal Phelan, the archaeologist. He's expecting me."

Ruth felt no guilt about the lie. There was no reason for her to explain her alienation from her brother to strangers. All she wanted was to hasten her journey to its conclusion.

The young Indian watched her a minute, then walked to the stove and poured himself some coffee.

He said something terse to the old man. She thought she recognized the word "blade."

Old Juan looked her way and nodded.

"What is he saying?" she asked.

"He says you can trust Blade."

"Is that his name?"

"No. His name is Che Nez."

"I don't understand."

"You will, senora. Remember, trust Blade."

The Indian put down his cup and started for the door.

"He's going," Juan said. "You get in the wagon now."

"He's my driver?" Ruth was incredulous. It hadn't dawned on her the young Indian was the driver she'd hired.

"It's good, senora. Che is good Indian. Get in the wagon."

Telling herself this was turning into quite an adventure, Ruth marched stoically outside. Wouldn't her eastern acquaintances think her utterly mad for driving off into the night with an Indian?

Old Juan helped her into the wagon and wished her Godspeed.

"Take this. You'll need it to keep warm."

The low male voice startled her. With wide eyes she turned to Che Nez, surprised to hear him speak clear concise English. He held out a thick woolen blanket, which she wrapped around herself.

The faint city lights soon faded away as the wagon rolled northeast along the wide, rutted dirt road. Weariness overtook her and her head began to nod. The seductive combination of the rocking wagon, the clip-clop of horses hooves, the jingle of the harnesses, and the pine scented air lulled Ruth to sleep. Once she began to list sideways and a hand reached out for the wool blanket and gently tugged her in the other direction. She sighed quietly and rested her head against the wide shoulder beside her.

2

Gladius Blade rubbed his long fingers over his weary eyes and looked at the amber-colored rye whiskey on the table in front of him. It was his second, and the evening had barely begun. Where the hell was Phelan?

Blade wasn't much of a drinking man, at least he no longer was. In the dark days after his faithless wife deserted him, he'd seldom known a sober moment. He remembered little about those days, and what he could recall shamed him deeply. He'd made a fool of himself with booze and whores. Her death in a carriage wreck in Baton Rouge and his subsequent arrest for her murder—he'd followed her and her scrawny lover in a mood of self-righteous indignation—abruptly ended his binge. A jury found him innocent, which indeed he was, and he'd gone back to his home in Denver and started life anew. Even after he'd sold the Denver house and moved on he led a quiet life.

Yet here he was in a Flagstaff saloon drinking, waiting for a man best described as a liar and a cheat. Blade took out his solid-gold Bunn Special pocket watch—a gift from his father who believed the Illinois Watch Company's railroad watch was the finest timepiece ever made and, therefore, a status symbol other men would notice and appreciate—and assured himself Phelan was very late. What the hell could have detained him?

The door of the Woodbine Saloon swung open and the undertaker walked in.

"Cold out there tonight, Frank," said the owner of the hotel up the street.

"Damn cold," he said to the hotel owner. "An' I gotta go pick up Sam Waverly out at his brother's place east a' here. Jaspar Bird foreclosed on his business last night, and he went an' shot himself. Blew his head clean off."

"Son of a bitch!" the hotel owner said. "Bird couldn't wait, could he! Sam had a buyer for his store."

"Bird's got a heart o' stone and no conscience a'tall. He's already down at Sam's place going through his stock. I seen him when I passed the store." The men nearby murmured appropriately. "Now I gotta go get Sam. He's shot up so bad his brother couldn't touch him."

Gladius Blade felt his stomach turn. What the hell kind of business was worth dying over? He'd lived too long in his father's world of high-pressure finance, he'd seen too many men die for money and property. His own brother-in-law succumbed to heart failure right after the recent bank panic, leaving a widow and two orphan sons.

No, high finance, or any type of business dealings,

was not Blade's cup of poison. Maybe he had too much of a conscience to be a cutthroat. Or maybe, as his father complained, he was simply too damned lazy. Whichever, he'd taken the easy way out and hired on as an artist with Donal Phelan.

The new Woodbine Saloon on Railroad Avenue catered to the business and professional men of Flagstaff. Few cowboys and drifters wandered in, and when they did they wandered out again quickly to the livelier, bawdier establishments down the block. The Woodbine's elegant mahogany bar, gleaming brass rail, and enormous plate-glass mirror reflected a gentlemen's club where professional men could unwind and converse. In a way it reminded Blade of Denver. Or San Francisco, where he'd fallen into Phelan's scheme in the first place.

Donal Phelan strode through the door at that moment and a gust of cold winter air blew in with him. Everyone in the room turned to look at him. That didn't faze Phelan at all; he expected people's attention. He relished it.

Phelan was an arrogant bastard with a disposition that rivaled a viper, and he was a genius to boot. Most folks were intimidated by him, and few people liked him. But Blade tolerated him with something akin to fond amusement. He didn't trust Phelan worth spit, but working for the mad archaeologist was never dull.

"I found it!" Phelan boomed in a voice that would have been the envy of any stage performer. "A veritable treasure, my lad. Wealth beyond gold!"

Blade shook his head and sighed audibly. He'd been through this before. The last time, his father sunk more gold into Phelan's scheme than he'd ever manage to recover. But what the hell, the old man was loaded, and he deserved a little chastisement once in a while. "Sit down and have a drink, Donal." He signaled to the bartender to bring the bottle. "This is a gentlemen's club. Sit down before they throw us out."

"Oh bullshit, boy. They won't throw me out. They want to hear about the treasure."

Blade shrugged his massive shoulders and grinned at his boss. Phelan was in rare form tonight, there was no doubt about that. Obviously nothing was going to shut him up, so Blade might as well let him way eloquent. Treasure, indeed. It was a bloody wonder the fool hadn't been robbed and his head split wide open with his wild crazy stories about treasure. This genius had little sense about what information should be shared and what should be kept under his hat.

"I found a crystal cave," Phelan said in a stage whisper which would have reached the back row of any theater, as he downed the first glass of rye and poured himself another. "One of nature's miracles, Blade. It looks like a million glistening diamonds. So beautiful it makes your heart ache. And it's full, laddie, full of the most magnificent treasure since the tombs were opened in Egypt."

Blade felt the sudden tension in the saloon. All of the quiet chatter had ceased, and Phelan had everybody's attention. He looked up to see the bartender polishing a glass, his back to them but his narrow eyes on the mirror, scanning the whole room. A shiver went down Blade's spine then. He hoped it wasn't a premonition. Phelan damned well better be careful.

And Blade told him so in a low voice. "These men

will think you found Coronado's legendary gold." That was the story Phelan had used nearly two years ago to get Blade's father to finance the archaeological expedition when his other backers walked out on him. It worked fine then. In fact, old Seamus Blade still thought the seven cities of gold rested somewhere near Flagstaff. Maybe some of these men did, too.

"Watch your step, Phelan," he cautioned.

Phelan waved the warning aside dramatically. "I'm buying these men a drink," he told the barkeep. "Here's to the successful completion of my expedition, gentlemen. It will put the Arizona Territory on the map. I've found a treasure more valuable than gold."

The men drank eagerly, trying to discover exactly what Phelan had found. They all agreed that he was a crazy, overeducated crackpot, but maybe this time he had actually found something of value. Few of them understood, truly understood, what an archaeologist was and what he dug in the earth for; few of them actually cared. But treasure was something they did understand, and they wondered what—if anything—could be more valuable than gold.

The door opened again, ushering in a stiff breeze and Jaspar Bird. The talk immediately ceased. By their silent censure the occupants of the Woodbine Saloon expressed their outrage at Bird's callous treatment of poor, weak Sam Waverly. Unfortunately, Jaspar Bird was too thick-skinned to notice. He sauntered up to the bar and called for his bottle.

"Have another drink," Phelan said to Blade as he poured his own glass to the rim.

"No. I want to go over to the hotel and get a steak."

"Aw, c'mon, have one more and then I'll go over

with you. I want to send off a telegram to have a woman come next week. I'm randy as hell."

Blade wasn't surprised. Donal Phelan had a monumental sexual appetite. He was as obsessive about sex as he was about work.

"Why don't you hire someone from around here, instead of bringing some doxy in on the train?"

"Because, my friend, the local whores are a bit too scabby for my tastes, and frankly there aren't enough of them anyway. Besides, I'm scared shitless of the good women—they're looking for husbands. Can't you just imagine me hitched to some heifer?"

Blade nearly choked on his drink. "You'd be the worst husband imaginable, Donal. Worse even than me."

Phelan looked at him with knowing eyes, then grinned and looked down at his glass. "Come on. Let's finish and go over to the hotel. I'm starved. I'll send off my telegram before we eat. And then we'll order champagne. This is a night to celebrate!"

"What are you celebrating, Mister Phelan?" Jaspar Bird asked as they rose to leave.

"Treasure, my little man," Phelan said arrogantly. "Ancient treasure resting in a bed of diamonds!"

The parlor was unearthly quiet, and almost dark. Only the candles flickering at the four corners of the table gave off any light. Gladius Blade sat in the corner with his arms folded across his chest, his thoughts as glum as the room.

A letter delivered today from Tucson had brought bad news from Blade's brother Cornelius. Usually, the brothers had nothing much to talk about. Sadly, they did now. Their father, Seamus Augustus Blade, had suffered a mild stroke the previous week. It apparently wasn't severe enough to permanently impair the old man's health, but he was deeply depressed by his present lack of mobility. Neel suggested that some good news from Blade about the treasure might just be the thing to raise their father's spirits.

Blade sighed in the gloom. The one time the old man needed his help, really needed something only Blade could provide, he had nothing to give. The treasure hunt, he suspected, had come to an end. Blade guessed at this point that Phelan hardly cared.

Again he sighed and watched the light of the big white candles reflecting off the brass handles on the coffin.

The lateness of the hour, his lack of sleep, the stress of the past two days, and the difficulties in his own life all weighed heavily on Blade and soon his eyes closed and his head drooped down on his chest. He began to breathe rhythmically, heavily, as a deep, dreamless sleep overtook him. The candles on the corners of the table continued to flicker, giving the room a faint golden glow.

It was the silence that roused Ruth. The wagon had come to a halt at some time, so the rumbling of the iron wheels had ceased, the gentle creaking sway of the sprung seat had stopped, and the horses with their jingling harnesses were oddly quiet.

"Che?" Ruth turned to her driver, then quickly realized she was on the wagon seat in the misty silver of darkness, cocooned in a thick wool blanket, totally alone. "Che!" she demanded.

One of the horses snorted, and she jumped at the noise, momentarily panicked. The other horse swished his tail and shook his head, causing the harnesses to jangle in the darkness. What on earth had happened to Che? And where exactly was she?

A faint glimmer caught her eye as she looked around for the young Navajo. Ruth swung awkwardly toward the light, the blanket hindering her mobility, and gasped when the enormous silhouette of a house loomed before her as if it had suddenly appeared from nowhere.

A weak chuckle bubbled in her throat, and she took a deep breath to slow the rapid thump of her heart. She had arrived. At least her driver had gotten her where she'd paid him to go, even if he'd taken off in the dark and hadn't bothered to wake her. She looked cautiously at the dim outline of the house. In the faint glimmer of the cloud-covered moon it looked huge.

A pale flame danced behind one downstairs window. It took Ruth a second to realize it was candlelight instead of a lamp. Again her breathing grew shallow, her heart thudded, and her palms grew damp. Someone obviously was home. Her brother.

Ruth tried to quiet her screaming nerves. She was here. Now she had to face him. Despite her bravado she was afraid of Donal.

After the long, tiring trip her emotions were traitorously close to the surface. Her defenses were down. She needed to regain some of the ironclad control she normally maintained, which had slipped enough to allow her to own up to the weakness of fear.

But she *was* afraid he'd cruelly throw her out when she had no place else to go. And she was equally afraid he'd make her stay.

She whirled as the sudden sound of footsteps penetrated her thoughts. Then she gasped as, dimly through the darkness, she saw the forms of two men.

It was far too dark to see who they were. Ruth survived several anxious moments before they were close enough for her to recognize Che. The other man appeared to be an Indian also. Swiftly, silently, without a greeting, they opened the wagon gate and unloaded the trunk and boxes, carrying them up the steep stairs to the front porch of the house.

An owl called hauntingly into the night sky and was answered by an icy blast of pine-tinged wind off the mountain.

When the wagon was empty and the tailgate closed, Che lifted her to the ground, wool blanket and all. "I'm going now."

"No!" she cried, hating the panic in her voice but unable to prevent it. "All my things must go inside the house." That wasn't the reason she wanted him to stay, of course, but she wasn't able to speak of her concerns. Che was a familiar person, even though she'd only known him a short time. "I'll pay extra."

"No."

"Why?"

"Tsosi won't go in Phelan's house."

Ruth looked to find the other man had vanished into the night. Che was her only hope. Clearing her throat nervously, she decided to tell him the truth. "I want you to stay because I might need a ride back to Flagstaff. I didn't tell my brother I was coming. We were angry the last time we saw each other—he might ask me to leave. I want you to wait till I find out." To her own ears, her voice sounded weak and tearful.

"You'll stay. Blade will help." He disappeared into the night, leaving her alone at the foot of the steep stairs.

Ruth knew there was no arguing. She straightened her shoulders and faced the stone steps with quiet determination. Behind her in the darkness she heard Che Nez get into the wagon and pull away. She bit back a frantic call, chiding herself sternly for being a coward, lifted her serge skirts, and determinedly climbed the stairs to the porch.

Concealing her agitation, she pounded on the heavy wooden door with far more force than necessary. The banging startled her. She knocked again, and waited. After what seemed an eternity, she tried the doorknob and discovered it opened with little effort. A faint misty light filled the wide entrance hall.

"Donal," she called, but the word emitted was barely a hoarse croak in her dry throat.

Hugging the warm blanket, she waited on the doorstep. Nobody stirred. She called again, then pushed the door wider and entered, closing the heavy door against the cold breeze behind her.

A naughty idea teased her tired brain. Why not walk in and find a comfortable chair for the night and face the wrath of the mighty Phelan in the morning? Perhaps he'd be in better spirits if he'd slept the night through. In any event, Ruth knew she'd feel a lot better in morning's welcoming light.

A flickering glow from the room to her right caught her eye. Like a beacon it grew brighter and bade her to come closer.

Suddenly she knew without question that her brother was in there.

She stood completely still in the doorway of a large elaborate dining room. At the far end of the room, against a wall papered with pink cabbage roses, stood a tall china closet with etched glass in the doors. Beneath the window was a matching buffet with a tall silver and glass epergne on top.

A heavy mahogany table nearly filled the room because it had been extended to its longest length. At each corner of the table stood a tall brass candlestick holding a white candle. And atop the table, which had been polished to a high sheen, between the four spikes of flame rested a large, open, brass-handled coffin.

The blanket that had kept Ruth warm during the long cold ride suddenly threatened to stifle her; she let it slip unnoticed to the floor as she moved forward with halting steps, as though she was being pushed by some unseen force.

She did not see the shadowy figure slumped on an upholstered chair in the corner. All she saw was a partial view of the body in the huge walnut coffin. Folded hands, the waxy profile of a face, and black, black hair.

"No!" she groaned, but the word stuck in her parched throat. If possible, this scene was more terrifying for her than when she'd watched her husband fall dead to the floor.

A final quaking step told her what she knew but couldn't admit, what she'd guessed in her heart from the moment she saw the coffin. In the box of gleaming wood and brass rested the body of her brother, Donal Phelan. Dead and gone before his fortieth year.

"No!" she sobbed in bitter anguish. It was impossible to comprehend that a man bigger than life could ever die.

Ruth still did not see the man in the corner, although her cry had awakened him from a sound sleep and he'd started to rise from the chair.

The strain of the trip finally overcame her, and her knees buckled beneath her, her slender body crumpling. Out of the shadows a pair of steely hands reached out to catch her. Ruth screamed in mindless fear and fainted dead away.

Blade wasn't a man to believe in ghosts, but his first groggy sight of the slim, uncanny apparition floating toward Phelan's fancy coffin chilled him to his bones. Her undisguised grief woke him to the fact she was very human. He'd risen from the chair to comfort her, to let her know someone had been with Phelan since his shocking death, to somehow lessen her raving sobs. Certainly he hadn't meant to frighten her.

Blade had forgotten she was coming, forgotten Phelan had sent a wire for her to join him for a few days of debauchery. The man's sudden and mysterious demise had knocked every other thought from Blade's mind.

As he lowered the woman to the floor to try to revive her, Blade noticed two things. She was not the doxy who generally serviced Phelan. What was her name? Monique. The sly, skinny one Phelan had with him in San Francisco the night he met Blade. This one was lovely, even in the stillness of a faint.

Somehow Blade managed to haul her limp body down the pitch-black hall and into the downstairs bedroom. He groped his way across the dark room and found the bed, laying her down gently. Then he lit the lamp and removed her cape and hat, tossing them carelessly onto a nearby chair.

The woman did not stir. She lay there looking as still as poor Phelan in his coffin.

"Now what do I do?" Blade asked. This was one situation he'd never been in before with a woman. He unbuttoned her shoes and removed them, then chaffed her cold feet and her hands. Nothing. In desperation he walked into the bathroom and drew a basin of water, thankful it was still reasonably warm, and went back to the bedroom.

Kneeling by the bed he soaked a rough cloth in the warm water, squeezed out the excess and began to bath her face. Even as pale as she was, he found her beautiful. Blade ran the cloth down her neck, opening the top buttons of her shirtwaist as he worked to prevent the collar from getting soaked. Water trickled inside the blouse, so he unhooked several more buttons.

It seemed strange to him how plain her traveling clothes were. While he wasn't the roué Phelan had been, or his own father, either, for that matter, Blade had known his share of scarlet women, and he'd never known one of them to outfit herself in such austere clothes.

Before he realized what he'd done, Blade had completely unbuttoned the shirtwaist and had started to tug it out of the waistband of her skirt. The skirt button came next. It wasn't until his hands came into contact with the rigid form of her corset under a perfectly scandalous pink-flowered corset-cover that he stopped to think what he was doing.

He glanced up at her face. It was still as a statue and as white and cold as alabaster. "What the hell," he mumbled to himself. "No wonder she's out cold, with this damned thing on." After unbuttoning the frilly cover, it seemed the sensible thing to do to unsnap the steel-boned contraption and allow her to breathe. "Why the hell do women wear these things?"

Her heavy serge skirt came next, whisked over on the chair with her cape, and then several fancy lace-trimmed petticoats. This made him smile, the first since Phelan's horrible death. Whoever this jade was, she wore lovely undergarments. And they were scrupulously clean. She smelled faintly of flowers on a rainy afternoon. Blade inhaled her scent and gazed at her. Her full bosom, outlined by the thin material of her chemise, was what nature supplied, not padded with heavy ruffles as some women's were.

Blade poured the tepid water in the slop jar and replaced it with more warm water from the gasoline water heater in the bathroom. Then he returned to the bedroom. The woman lay silently on the bed, clothed only in cambric pantalettes, the embroidered chemise, and silk stockings.

"Miss," he said again. "Wake up. You have to wake up and tell me who you are."

The dark-haired young woman did not respond in any way. He tried shaking her gently but to no avail. Blade began to worry.

He sponged her arms and hands, then started to remove the blue silk stockings so he could sponge her legs and feet. The woman stirred, a tiny whimpering sound escaping her pale lips.

Blade jumped like he'd been shot. Quickly he tossed a blanket over her and began to put her clothes away. He hurried out to the hall and spied her leather satchel.

There were no smelling salts inside. He clenched his fists and groaned in frustration. Then he went back to the bed and began to talk to her.

"You've got to wake up. I need to find out who you are and send you back where you belong. I'll pay you, of course. Whatever Phelan promised. But you can't stay here. Not now. Not with him dead."

With brisk efficiency he threw back the blankets covering the girl, unbuttoned the top of the soft chemise and slipped it over her head. God she was beautiful! He tightened his jaw and forced his eyes away. He was a man with a mission, helping a woman in distress.

With his entire being clenched against his lusty instincts, he finished removing the stockings and pantalettes. Then he washed her body, front and back, talking to her softly all the while. He was actually wondering if he should ride back to Flagstaff for the doctor when she finally stirred.

Smoothing the cloth over her back, he drew repeated circles where her small waist tapered inward and larger circles where her smooth hips flared. She moaned suddenly, and he stiffened, fearing she'd awaken screaming when she discovered a stranger bathing her. But she only sighed and was silent again as he continued to nurse her with loving concentration.

When he dried her body carefully with the linen towel, she stirred restlessly as he trailed the towel down her long slender thighs. This time he talked to her in his normal tone of voice, hoping she'd awaken. She moved her lips slightly and made small animal sounds. But that was all.

Holding her with one arm, he pulled down the bedclothes and slid her between the sheets, pulling the blankets over her. But he continued to rub her arms and legs beneath the covers and to talk to her. Eventually she answered him but refused to open her eyes.

"Look at me, damn it. I want to be sure you're all right."

She shook her head. "Go 'way. I'm tired." Her long lashes remained closed tight against her pale cheeks.

Blade ran a hand through his wavy hair. "Okay. You can sleep. But if you need anything, just give a yell. I'll be down the hall with the . . . uh, I'll be down the hall."

"Mmmmmff."

After a final look at her, Blade piled on a couple more quilts, turned down the lamp, and returned to his post in the parlor. He did not sleep the rest of the night, but the body he thought about was not the one in Donal Phelan's coffin.

3

"Who are you?" Ruth's cold white hand clasped the lapel of the soft blue woolen dressing gown tightly to her throat. Frightened by the big brawny man who stood in the kitchen doorway, she'd nearly screamed when the door burst open. Her heart thumped a staccato beat. Silently she cursed her foolishness for venturing about in a strange house without getting fully dressed. It had been so cold in the bedroom, but a bit of frigid air was no excuse for lax behavior.

"Good, you're up. Are you feeling better this morning?" He nudged the door shut with his shoulder and quickly dumped the armload of firewood he carried into the woodbox. Then he took off the heavy green jacket, seemingly unaware of the splinters and chips that fell to the wooden floor. "Are you ready for breakfast?"

"I'd like some tea." Her voice was as icy as the blast of air that had come in the open door.

"Not coffee? Everybody here swills the stuff. The pot's always on. Thick as mud, generally." He gave her a quick grin. "Let me think, where did I see the tea tin?" He moved the softly hissing kettle onto the stove top, and turned toward the elaborately tooled tin-fronted cupboard. "What about breakfast?" He began to rummage in the cupboard, carelessly destroying all sense of order.

"I don't think I could eat much, thanks." She noticed with a grimace that he hadn't bothered to shave. Bright red whiskers bristled his face.

Ruth started toward the cupboard for a teacup but, struck by a momentary wave of dizziness, stopped dead still. But she had no intention of falling over on this man. For once she'd sit and let someone wait on her. He seemed anxious enough to do so, whoever he was. The handyman or gardener, she supposed, surely not one of the archaeologists.

Goodness, he was big! Burly with an incredible mane of thick auburn waves that hung well over his shirt collar.

"Ah ha," his deep voice boomed. "Tea!" He plunked the red tea tin down on the wooden counter, rattled around until he found a teapot and cup, and busied himself with the brew.

The man annoyed her. Ruth considered herself a charitable woman, but something about him grated on her nerves. He seemed to fill the room completely with his size and his voice and his disgustingly good disposition. She wished he'd disappear, and probably would have told him so with very little compunction if she hadn't wondered if he just might not be the owner of the house. He was so crude-looking in his unbuttoned green and brown plaid shirt that showed a faded butternut union suit at the neck and sleeves and a bit of curly auburn hair where the underwear failed to completely cover his chest. That plus his worn denims and heavy boots made her think of Paul Bunyan. She pursed her lips in disgust. Mountain man. Man of the West.

Ruth's years with Farley McKenna had accustomed her to a more refined sort of man, genteel, urbane, elegant. She sniffed, her perfect nose held high in the air.

Gladius Blade turned, teapot in hand, in time to see her delicate nostrils twitch as if she'd encountered a bad smell and his coffee-brown eyes narrowed. Who the hell was this doxy to turn her fine nose up at him? And he had no doubt that's exactly what she was doing. He'd spent too many years in the company of society women not to understand that look of disdain. His lips hardened. She'd obviously judged him by his unshaven face and work clothes. So the little snob couldn't see the man beneath the clothes.

"Your tea, fair lady." He carefully poured the weak tea into the heavy white china mug and set the pot in front of her.

"Sugar?" she asked loftily.

"We're out of it."

Ruth sipped the hot tea, prepared to be critical, but it was wonderful, even unsweetened.

It wasn't until the eggs were ready—whipped, fluffy and light, that he remembered the biscuits he'd put into the oven before he went out for wood. "Oh shit!"

Ruth's eyes widened in horror at the vulgarity, and her hand went to her shocked mouth. She didn't realize that the movement pulled the blue dressing gown askew, and that it gaped open exposing a tantalizing view of ivory skin and Irish lace with fawn ribbons.

Blade wasn't looking at her cleavage, he was too busy saving his biscuits. They were only a little bit browner than he'd intended but he reached in the oven with his bare hand, burnt his fingers, and cussed eloquently. Then he dumped the lot into a basket and plunged his hand beneath the water pump.

"Are you hurt?"

"Yes."

"May I help?"

"No."

Blade took a deep breath and removed his hand from the bowl beneath the pump. Without another word, he grabbed up dishes and utensils, plopped them on the table along with the biscuits, the skillet of eggs, a jelly jar, and the butter dish. "Let's eat."

Ruth intended to refuse. His churlish manners deserved that. But her mouth began to water, and she reached for the serving spoon.

Ruth was accustomed to silent meals. Farley had often pushed food around on his plate, too preoccupied with his work to make fascinating dinner conversation; and Donal, too, often was so lost in his thoughts that he wolfed down his food without a word. She didn't understand why this man's boorish behavior chaffed her nerves so.

"Do you have a suitable dress?"

His words startled her and she crushed the half biscuit she was about to bite, sending crumbs all down her front. "Pardon me?"

"A proper dress? Do you have one?"

"Of course I have a proper dress. All my clothes are

proper. Oh"—she swallowed the scathing remark she was about to make when she realized what he was talking about—"a mourning dress." She looked down at her plate, trying to hide the sudden tears that filled her eyes. "Yes, I have a mourning dress. Quite new, actually. My husband died a year ago."

A wave of shame hit Blade in the gut. He had no right to treat this woman badly. However she behaved, she was still Phelan's woman and her man was stone stiff in his coffin. Blade guessed she had a right to be unfriendly, or any other damned way she wanted to be.

"Sorry," he said gruffly. "About your husband. About Phelan, too. It was a real shock."

Ruth took a deep breath that sounded suspiciously like a sob, and closed her eyes until her emotions were firmly under control. She never cried, never in front of others, at least. "You couldn't have known." Her voice was strained. "About my husband, I mean. It was very sudden. One minute he was telling me to order some more coal because winter wasn't over, the next minute he was dead on the floor." She took another shaky breath. "But life goes on. People adjust. I did. I was coming here to live with Donal." She clenched her jaw and put her hand tight to her mouth, but all her defenses crumbled. A solitary tear slid out beneath her long black lashes.

Blade was out of his chair and around to her in seconds. Normally tears didn't faze him, he'd known too many women to use them as a weapon. His late wife, for instance. But, to his confusion, this slender bundle of starchy manners and French undergarments made him both angry and protective. He pulled her from the chair into his arms.

Ruth had never felt anything as solid and comforting as the iron muscles of this man's chest. After several luxourious seconds, she straightened her spine and pulled away.

"I'm sorry," she said woodenly. "I never behave that way."

"It's perfectly understandable."

"Not for me."

Blade didn't know what to say. He was silent a minute, as disconcerted by her strange behavior as he was by his own desire to protect her. "If you have a dress, I can take it to Marie to press. She said she'd do that if she didn't have to come in the house while—" He shrugged, then continued. "Marie is the housekeeper. She's an Indian woman, and because of her Navajo beliefs she doesn't want to be in the house as long as the body is in here." He waited, tense with expectation. He knew that most people thought Indian beliefs were pagan.

"I understand," Ruth told him. "The dress is in the big olive-green bureau trunk. The driver wouldn't bring it in last night."

"I brought the trunks in this morning."

"Thank you." Her smile was genuine.

She was lovely. Blade had the urge to pick her up in his arms and twirl her around the room, but he resisted. She was too prim and proper. Oh hell, what was he thinking? She might act like some tight-laced eastern schoolmarm, but he knew she was Phelan's paramour. What stuck in his craw was his own craving for her. Since he'd helped her into the guest room last night to try to revive her, he'd thought of little else. Damn it, he should have left her flopped on the floor beside the coffin!

"Are there any services planned?" she asked.

"This afternoon. Some people are coming in from Flagstaff with the preacher. He's to be buried in a private plot near here."

She nodded, then continued to look at Blade questioningly. "I don't understand what happened to him. Had . . . had he been sick?"

"I sincerely apologize. I thought you knew. Didn't someone in town tell you?"

"As a matter of fact, nobody in town had the courtesy to mention a thing about Donal's death." Her voice was bitter. "They acted quite odd, I admit, but I thought that might just be western manners. I didn't realize he was . . . gone until I saw his body in the coffin."

Rage shot through Blade. How could people have been so stupid or so cruel? "No wonder you fainted."

She didn't bother to comment.

"Let's go get the dress. Marie will do a careful job pressing it."

Ruth nodded and followed him to the storage closet. Fortunately, the big bureau trunk was in the front, and could be gotten to with little trouble. Blade watched as she opened the trunk, a veritable traveling chiffonier, and began sorting through the drawers and compartments with efficient ease. In no time she had extracted a heavy black wool cape, soft kid shoes, and a modest velvet hat with a lightweight veil and three rosettes on the side.

"Here," she said, handing him a brown paper-wrapped parcel, "hold this. I'd forgotten all about this—I want to look at it later." Then she opened the largest drawer and shook out a simple dulled silk and

Henrietta mourning dress with jet buttons that ran from neck to hem. Despite careful packing, it definitely needed pressing.

Blade glanced down at the parcel and saw the name RUTH EVELYN MCKENNA printed in large letters on the front. He realized with a start that until now he did not know her name. Nor did she know his.

Is there anything else you'll be needing in the next hour or so, Mrs. McKenna?"

Ruth was so preoccupied she didn't notice it was the first time he called her by name. "No, I don't think so. Wait, there is one thing. Do you think there's enough water for me to take a bath in the tub?"

Blade almost groaned aloud at the images that floated through his mind. No woman her age could say such things to a man without expecting to get some reaction out of him. Still, she looked so innocent. What a wonderful ploy for a wanton. He knew then that as soon as Phelan's funeral was over, he was going to make her an offer. There was no doubt in his mind she'd accept. As she said she'd brought all her things and she'd come to live. He suspected she had no place else to go and little money to live on. Any sensible woman would jump at a second chance. After the services, he told himself. It would be crude to do so before.

"I'll make sure there's hot water."

"Oh, wonderful! I do so want to take a real bath in that big deep tub. I know the housekeeper washed my face when she put me to bed last night because I saw the dirty water in the bowl on the bureau, but it's not the same thing as a good hot soak."

"Let me check on the water," he growled as he put down her clothes on the carved table in the hallway and beat a hasty retreat before he said something he'd later regret. Within a minute he came out of the bathroom and retrieved her things. "I refilled the water heater and lighted it. The water will be ready in no time."

He turned to leave, then changed his mind. "There's something you should know, Ruth McKenna, so there won't be any misunderstandings sometime in the future. As I said before, Marie won't come into the house as long as the coffin is in here. I'm the one who put you to bed last night when you fainted. And I'm the one who washed you." He clenched his jaw to keep from telling her how much he'd enjoyed the task, and how his body hadn't known a moment's peace since. In spite of her negative thoughts toward him, he was a man of honor.

Shame flushed her face crimson, then shock washed the color away. "Th-that's impossible," she gasped. "I don't even know your name!"

He inclined his head slightly. A self-mocking smile hovered near his wide mouth.

"My name is Blade. Gladius Blade." He turned and walked from the house.

To Ruth the rest of the day was like a dream, unreal and tinged with fear. A bracing wind blew off the snowcapped San Francisco Peaks, chilling her in spite of the heavy wool cloak and the lap robe Blade tucked around her before he climbed into the buggy.

Now clean shaven and respectably clad in a handsome black suit, Blade bore almost no resemblence to the red-whiskered ruffian she'd met earlier that morning. He was attractive in a solid way, big and sturdy and very much alive.

Donal Phelan was dead. Yet the sun shone brightly on the weed-filled flower bed with its center sundial as they drove from the yard behind the velvet-draped hearse.

Phelan's earthly remains, now photographed for posterity, were being carted ahead of a procession of strangers to be laid to rest in some hillside burial plot belonging to the Phillips family who owned the house he leased. For Ruth, his only kin, it was all a ghastly nightmare she expected to awaken from at any moment, because Donal Phelan was too vital a man to be struck down in his prime.

"I made the decision to bury him here," Blade explained, breaking the silence. "He was excited by this land—the majesty of it, the vast wild beauty. He told me once he'd like to stay forever."

When she did not comment, he continued. "Donal Phelan's spirit is too big to be confined to a crowded city cemetery. He belongs to the rich land he explored. He deserves to be one with the Ancients."

Ruth nodded, her eyes glistening with unshed tears. "Thank you for knowing that," she whispered.

The stately funeral wagon moved sedately across the open meadow, into the edge of a pine thicket and back out in the sunlight. The sun beamed crystal rainbows off the sparkling windows. Finally the hearse lumbered up the slow gradual assient of the rocky knoll to the grave site. A winter-stripped aspen grove hugged one side of the hill beside the tall wrought-iron fence that stood stark and alone against a magnificent backdrop of distant coppery mesas, vast lavender emptiness, and the endless winter blue sky. The Arizona Territory was truly a fitting place for Phelan's final rest.

Just at that instant Ruth woke up from her dream-like trance, knowing with the first shaft of pain that she must complete her brother's work. If Donal's ghost had been perched on her shoulder whispering in her ear to finish it and get it published, she couldn't have been more convinced.

The sight of the brown gaping hole in the earth brought her up short, and she gasped. This was too soon after Farley's death for her to be dealing with another loss. She began to tremble as the wind off the mountains swirled her black cape away from her body. Almost immediately, Blade's strong arm came protectively around her shoulder and eased her against the warmth of his body. The trembling and general weakness fled as she mutely accepted his comfort and strength.

The funeral service began.

Ruth's attention drifted, and she leaned closer into Blade's muscular warmth, absorbing his strength and kindness. He seemed to understand, not looking at her but giving her arm a gentle squeeze. And he held her steady as the wooden coffin sank into the open grave.

The raucous scream of a raven penetrated the cotton wool of her brain.

"Earth to earth, ashes to ashes, dust to dust; in sure and certain hope of resurrection..."

The shovel rasped as it dug deeply into the gritty dirt. Another scoop of sandy soil was flung into the grave, resounding like thunder as it struck the wood coffin. Ruth flinched, and stared as though mesmerized as each succeeding shovelful plummeted downward.

She wondered if the day would come when she smelled damp earth and wouldn't think of death.

Within moments the grave was filled . The minister stopped to speak to Ruth, explaining he hadn't known Donal well.

Coming out of her reverie, Ruth almost laughed. How could this aesthetic-looking man ever have hoped to know her brother well? Donal would never countenance any religion that had not been dead and gone five hundred years at least. But she managed to accept his condolences with a murmur of thanks.

"Your brother was a fine man," the preacher said. "A servant of humanity in the finest sense. This is not only a personal loss for you and his friends, it's the world's loss."

Ruth winced as Blade's fingers cut through the cloth of her cloak into her shoulder. Glancing quickly toward his face, she noted his features were stiff with shock and amazement. Evidently he had known Donal quite well indeed.

The three men huddled together near the beer keg that Dilman, the brewer, had provided, pretending to be a part of the mourners.

"Did you find the papers?" the nervous one with the gray beard asked the man in the shabby mail-order suit and heavy work shoes.

"I didn't even get in the house," Shabby Suit said with a whine.

"Can't you do just one thing right?" Gray Beard demanded loudly.

The third man, a businessman of some success by

the look of his attire and the emerald fob he wore on the gold watch chain hanging over his round belly, narrowed his eyes.

"Keep your voices down, you fools! Do you want the world to hear? Why don't you tell me the reason you couldn't get in," he said in a deadly quiet voice. "And the excuse better be good."

Shabby Suit felt the hair on the back of his neck lift. The threat in Emerald Fob's velvet voice scared him a hell of a lot more than Gray Beard's blustering.

Shabby Suit wet his lips. "Blade was in the house all night," he complained. "About the time I figured he'd be asleep, the woman arrived in the wagon. You shoulda heard her screaming! Then, when things got quiet again and I was ready to sneak in, I saw Blade walking around in the kitchen. It musta been after three. I don't think he went to bed at all, the damned fool. Did he think the body was gonna get up and walk off?"

"That's an Irish custom called waking the dead . . . "

Gray Beard giggled. "How can you wake up a dead man?"

His laughter stopped abruptly as he saw the violence in Emerald Fob's eye.

"What about when everybody went to the grave site?" Emerald Fob asked, "You had plenty of time. Why didn't you go inside then?"

"Hell, them damned Indians was watchin' me the whole time you was gone." Shabby Suit nodded toward the six or seven Navajos who loitered nearby. "I'd be on one side a the house, and one of 'em was there. Then I'd wander to the back an' three of 'em was spyin' on me. I damn near wore myself out trotting back and forth."

"Well, why didn't you just wear a goddamn sign that

says, 'I'm trying to rob this house'?" Emerald Fob asked sarcastically, his voice rising for the first time. "Now I want those papers, and I don't care what you have to do to get them. I mean to have that treasure."

"Why don't you just ask Blade for them?" Gray Beard suggested. "He don't need 'em no more. Not with Phelan dead."

"You dumb shit!" Shabby Suit exploded. "Blade won't give you those papers because he wants them hisself. And if you go asking for 'em he's damned sure gonna wonder if old Phelan really passed on nice and natural-like."

"Well, didn't he?" Gray Beard asked.

Emerald Fob smiled a slow smile that didn't reach his pale eyes. "As far as I know he died a natural death. And a very convenient one."

Hertha Bird, the stout proprietress of the Yellow Canary, swept into the parlor like a mourning ship in full sail. Her black silk faille dress with its voluminous skirt was topped by a full cape of black wool trimmed in gray fur. On her head sat the most unusual hat Ruth had ever seen.

Made of black velvetta, it dipped slightly in the front and back, which unfortunately emphasized Hertha's jawline. It sported a black parrot with sweeping aigrettes and was topped with two large ostrich feathers. Ruth tried hard not to shudder.

She hadn't thought of the older woman since their unfortunate interchange at the cafe the night Ruth arrived. It didn't take her long, however, to realize she'd seen Hertha Bird at her best that night.

As Hertha began to babble loudly about "poor dear Phelan," Ruth murmured a conventional response and hoped the woman would move on.

A smallish man with a droopy mustache and slightly receding chin entered the room. He wore an exquisitely tailored suit, but unfortunately the coat hugged his round belly and made him look silly instead of impressive. He was carrying a large, deep basket on each arm. Hertha, who was several inches taller and a good fifty pounds heavier, reached out suddenly and grabbed him, hauling him bodily over to where Ruth stood.

"This is my brother, Jaspar Bird," she announced with a wheeze, her corsets creaking ominously from her exertions. She took a deep breath before she could continue. "I make the best pies and bread in the country, Miz McKenna. Your dear brother swore to me he couldn't make it through the week without my baked goods. One of the baskets has pies, the other bread."

Ruth smiled stiffly. The woman's voice grated on her already fragile nerves.

"Go put the pies on the table, Jaspar," Hertha ordered. As he walked off, she continued, "My brother is the most important businessman in Flagstaff. I imagine poor dear Phelan told you about him."

Ruth was spared answering when a sweet gentle voice from behind her interrupted, "Excuse me, Miss Bird. Granny Higgins is asking for you. She's sitting out in the kitchen. She's interested in the spices you put in your mince pie."

Hertha sailed off in an aura of self-importance, leaving the two younger women in her wake.

"I do apologize for interrupting," the small woman said, her eyes twinkling brightly. "I'm Myra Bemish. My husband, Joseph, and I are so sorry about your brother. He was such a brilliant man. Joseph teaches over at the Emerson School and he loved to talk to your brother."

"Thank you," Ruth said with complete sincerity.

Myra's gentle, soothing voice matched her sweet face. She was Ruth's age, or perhaps a year or two older. As they spoke together, Ruth noticed how stylishly Mrs. Bemish dressed. Perched on her shiny brown hair was a small black English felt hat with one silver blue ostrich plume.

"Joseph and I were horrified when we heard no one in town told you of your brother's death the night you arrived. What a ghastly shock it must have been."

Tears sprung to Ruth's eyes.

Mrs. Bemish laid a small hand on Ruth's arm in silent comfort. "Please don't think badly of the townsfolk. We have some ruffians, naturally. This is the wild West. But most of our citizens are wonderful and caring people. All I can think of is that the ones you saw assumed you already knew."

Ruth wasn't so certain. The conductor, for one, was definitely aware of her ignorance about Donal's death. But the man had already proved himself to be a slackard and a coward. Surely she couldn't expect a noble gesture from the likes of him. But aloud she said, "I'm sure you're right. I don't blame anyone."

"Good. Now, would you like to get something to eat?" Myra gestured toward the dining room where the table was laden with food contributed by the mourners.

The thought of eating anything off that table where Donal's coffin had so recently rested made Ruth's stomach heave. "No," she said quickly. "I could use a breath of air, though."

Alarmed at how pale Ruth had suddenly become, Myra grasped her arm and steered her quickly out the front door, avoiding all the other well-wishers who wanted to chat.

"Thank you," Ruth said after a few minutes of breathing the cool, clean air. "I appreciate your kindness."

Myra smiled understandingly. "The West is mainly inhabited by men. We women have to stick together."

Ruth's head was throbbing when the townspeople finally left the house late in the afternoon. She'd never been so thankful to see people go in her life. She changed out of her mourning dress into a simple pongee shirtwaist and rose-brown wool skirt, and went to the bathroom to sponge her face.

Blade had gone out to the cabins to take some of the food the women from Flagstaff had left. He'd told Ruth he'd probably stay for a while, the Indians were going to have a ceremony.

"I don't care if he stays away all night," she told herself as she washed her face in the cozy bathroom. She'd never minded being alone. She'd been alone most of her life. "When a man is around he always needs attention. He's hungry or thirsty, or he's misplaced his glasses. A woman needs time alone."

Tonight, however, wasn't one of those nights. In spite of what she told herself, she'd wanted to ask Blade to come back quickly and keep her company, though naturally she didn't. And why should she? Really she didn't know a thing about him.

"Men," she muttered disgustedly as she walked back into the kitchen, "always keeping women in a turmoil."

She spied a bottle of sherry on the kitchen table and poured herself a glass. It seeped warmly into her veins. She pulled a kitchen chair near the stove and closed her eyes, shutting out the light and the hurt of the day.

The drums began to beat just as she drifted into the misty world of sleep, and a song as ancient as the land itself lifted up to the gods of the great stony mountains. The rhythm of the drumbeats woke her, and without even a conscious thought, she rose and lighted a lamp, carrying it up the stairs to the second floor where Donal had his office. The room was exactly as she'd expected, a horrendous mess of books, papers, maps, and odd pieces of clothes. Ruth felt exhilarated. Here, at last, was her chance to organize Donal Phelan.

Outside, Gladius Blade watched the blazing fire and the people who sang and danced, but his mind was on the grieving woman in the house. Phelan's sister. Ruth McKenna, Phelan's young, beautiful, recently widowed sister.

Damn the bastard to hell and back for never even mentioning he had a sister!

Now, Blade wondered, what was he going to do with her? Her identity clearly changed his original intentions. Far from being the trull he'd thought her to be, Ruth McKenna was a respectable widow. He couldn't very well offer to set her up as his mistress. But the fact of the matter was he still desired her with every fiber in his body. And she was here, his responsibility until she decided to leave.

She was also Phelan's heir. That fact put his own future in jeopardy. Blade frowned, wondering what he was going to do next.

Beyond the house, toward the eastern part of the

ranch, Ruth heard the Indians singing their ancient rites to their gods, seeking to walk in perfect harmony with the world. The chanted rhythm held her captive as she gazed over the chaos her brother had created. Only a genius could have created this hell. How had the man ever found anything amid all this clutter? She longed to escape, but she knew she had to mend the rift between Donal and herself.

"I'm going to have this place sparkling. Then I'm going to finish his manuscript, though it might take months. Then and only then can I go on with the rest of my life."

Resisting the urge to toss lamp oil on the mess and set it ablaze, she studied the office and poked at the desk. Nothing alive jumped out and bit her, so she decided to clear off the desk top. Reasoning that at least some of the papers scattered across the desk had to be extremely valuable, she carefully stacked up everything so she could go through them later, separating the wheat from the chaff. Then she went on a search mission.

The office opened onto another room which, judging from the scattered piles of clothes, was the bedroom. Two more rooms stood across the hallway. After rummaging through clothes, tossing most of them on the bed, Ruth located Donal's old safe beneath a velvet smoking jacket and a moth-eaten overcoat not fit for a dog to sleep on. The safe had belonged to their father and Ruth knew the combination as well as Donal. She opened it and smiled. It was empty, naturally. Donal Phelan never bothered to put anything in it even though he hauled it with him everywhere. She stuffed the huge pile of papers she had garnered from the desk top into the safe and spun the dial. She'd worry about them another day.

On her way back to the office, she peeked into one of the other rooms. Evidently it was occupied. But unlike Donal's quarters, the plain golden oak furnishings were neatly dusted, the bed was made, and whatever clothing belonged to the occupant had been hung in the wardrobe. A photograph stood on the bureau. Feeling a bit daring, she walked over and held the lamp near the frame. A large family, stiffly posed for a photographer, was illuminated by the light: father, mother, and five youngsters. A rawboned adolescent Gladius Blade stared back at her from the group.

Ruth stepped back, startled to realize that Blade lived in the house with Donal. Her brother must have considered him important to the job, far more so than a field worker. The thought both pleased and disconcerted her. She turned and went back to the office.

After dusting the desk with a rag she found in the windowsill, she breathed a sign of satisfaction. The desk was a perfect place to set her Remington and begin her work. Her headache had lessened, the drumbeats outside no longer thumped in her temples. She actually thought she might like something to eat. Then to bed—she craved a good refreshing sleep.

Walking over to pick up her lamp, she noticed one of the desk drawers hadn't closed completely. She didn't notice the shadow in the hall.

The drawer refused to open as stubbornly as it refused to close. She gave it a sharp tug. A heavy paper folder had jammed itself up at the top of the drawer. Putting her fingers beneath the folder she managed to wiggle it free.

Outside a wild cry was raised to the gods and the drums rolled. Ruth was about to return the folder to the drawer when a word scrawled across the front in Donal's arrogant writing caught her attention. BLADE. Closing the drawer with the toe of her shoe, Ruth sat in the old desk chair, curious about what Donal knew of the big man who'd been so kind to her.

The chair rolled backward and bumped the bookcase behind it. The bookcase, like everything else Phelan possessed, was cluttered and crammed with things that belonged elsewhere. Books were piled atop papers, pottery shards, and rocks. Vials of dirt lay next to archaeological tomes, notes, bones, maps, and scraps of half-eaten food. The collision of the heavy old chair with the jumbled bookcase started an avalanche of massive proportions.

Ruth didn't have a chance to move. Books, papers, rocks, orange peelings, bread crusts, bones, baskets, cinders, pottery, and maps all began raining down on her head. Caught in an instant of stunned disbelief, she didn't see the large volume of medical facts fall until it hit her squarely in the temple.

With a faint moan, she slumped forward and slipped to the floor in a heap. From out of nowhere a big hand plucked the folder marked BLADE out of her cold fingers. Then strong arms lifted her up. Several minutes later she was dumped unceremoniously on the neatly made, golden oak bed down the hall.

"Just one time, woman, I'd like to have you conscious when I put you to bed."

4

Blade rose early. And after checking on Ruth, who slept soundly beneath a pile of quilts on his neatly made bed, he wandered barefoot down the steep wooden stairs and started a fire in the kitchen stove. Coffee was the first order of the day.

He'd dressed himself in the same clothes he'd worn the night before and he badly need a shave, but his mood was so dismal he didn't feel like making the effort. He sat for a long while with his socks in his hand and stared at the stove. The coffee slowly began to perk.

The impact of Donal Phelan's death hit him like a brick on the head.

"Damn it to hell!" Blade slapped the thick woolen socks against the table top in a fury. He realized Phelan's untimely passing had jolted him more than the death of his own wife. At least Phelan's life had been filled with a purpose beyond self-indulgence and greed.

"The crazy bastard had so much to live for," he murmured. It disturbed him that his own father's reason to live was tied so closely to Phelan's.

Blade slowly pulled on his socks and boots, all the while considering his life, Phelan's life, life in general.

So what the hell was he going to do now?

After a couple cups of strong coffee, and a slice of chocolate cake, he tucked some food in his pocket and rode out to the dig site.

The morning wind off the San Francisco Peaks bit at Blade's ears and nose as the big roan gelding clomped along. The air smelled damp and fragrant as it blew though the tall, slender, widely spaced Ponderosa pines. The clouds hung low, heavy, and threatening. Blade decided it wasn't cold enough to snow, but it damned sure wasn't the sort of morning any sane man would have chosen for a horseback ride.

Yet he felt he had little choice. He either took care of the problem on the job site or he took care of the problem at the house. Somehow old bones seemed safer than the ones slumbering in his bed.

At the moment he was in charge of the dig, at least as much as anybody was, and he reckoned it necessary to be on the job. Whether or not Donal Phelan's demise was natural, strange and peculiar things were in the wind. Blade could feel it in his gut. And he was too Irish not to heed those instincts.

Phelan, in his grandiose way, had definitely stirred up something.

So here Blade was, riding out to the site of an ancient Indian village in frigid weather, just so he could prevent treasure hunters from destroying all Phelan's meticulous work.

He also wanted to think. About what had been in that damned folder he'd retrieved from Ruth McKenna's fingers. About what to do next on the dig. If he was ever going to recover a fraction of the money his father had sunk into this star-crossed expedition, he must locate Phelan's alleged treasure.

Whatever the hell that was.

Blade had no faith that he'd find gold, ancient or otherwise, since Phelan's only interest in gold of any kind was to fund further expeditions. No, Blade hoped to locate some ancient temple, or polychrome pot, or whatever discovery Phelan considered a treasure. If he found something—anything—and could publish illustrations with an accompanying story, the expedition might not be a total loss.

And the old man would be satisfied. One more crazy treasure hunt would have paid off.

After leaving the clearing where the house sat, the horse picked his way carefully up an incline, through stones, lava rock, pine needles, bushes, weed clumps, and small prickly cactus. He skirted a few snowdrifts leftover from the last storm, as well as soggy wet bogs, and steadfastly headed to where the trees thinned out. To the north, Sunset Crater, a magnificent half mountain of mahogany red peppered with ebony cinders, jutted upward and disappeared into the winter clouds.

Farther northeast, between the pine-covered hills, the vast openness of the Navajo lands and the sandstone mesas inhabited by the Hopis, sat the ruins of the village of the Stone Age people who had lived there hundreds of years earlier.

A dozen or so wild turkeys darted in front of the gelding, causing him to shy violently. The turkeys blended into the camouflage of a pile of weathered lava. Blade calmed the horse, then urged him forward, down the gentle slope to the dig site. He wondered if any place had ever looked so bleak.

No one was at the site. Most of the field workers were students who had returned to the university, and the few seasonal hands hadn't worked after the first snow. The winter had been quite mild, a surprise after nearly a decade of devastatingly severe winters. But Phelan had decided not to rehire the men until spring. He and Blade had done all the work themselves.

Blade felt relieved that no one was there. At this point, he felt he couldn't afford any employees. He suspected finances were one reason Phelan chose to spend the winter without help.

Dismounted, Blade tethered the roan near a rock pile, then hurried to the wood stack and within minutes had a small fire burning. He tossed pinecones onto the flame until it blazed and then added several large limbs. After warming his hands, he refilled the battered, smoke-blackened coffeepot from the water barrel. Then he set himself to do some serious thinking.

"Phelan, you mangy son-of-a-sea-pup, where did you find that lousy treasure?"

Up the incline, behind a scurvy juniper, Sheriff Rand Cameron sat his horse and contemplated Blade. The big redhead hugged the fire. No one else was in sight. Sheriff Cameron had counted on the site being empty when he decided to ride out. He was surprised to see

Gladius Blade. He waited patiently but Blade did no more than blanket his horse and make coffee. It was the coffee smell, strong and tantalizing, that decided Cameron. He urged his mount forward.

"Hello, the fire," Cameron called as he descended the slope.

Blade scalded his tongue on the bitter coffee. He hadn't expected anyone to visit the site on such a dismal day. He turned toward the approaching horse and recognized the rider immediately. His stomach gave a sickening twist.

"I thought I was the only one fool enough to be out on a day like this," he said as the sheriff dismounted.

"You got another cup?"

Blade handed him a gray tin cup. Stream rose in a silent swirl as Cameron held the hot container in his gloved hands.

"I guess it's foolish to ask what you're doing this far from your office on such a cold day," Blade said.

"No more foolish than me asking you."

Blade nodded. "I was afraid someone would destroy this"—he gestured toward the partially uncovered dwellings of layered sandstone—"looking for buried treasure."

"Have any idea what Phelan was bragging about the other night?"

"I wish to hell I did."

"Tell me exactly what he said. I've heard about a dozen different versions. Most of them were about gold."

"I've run this through my head so may times my brains have curdled." Blade sighed. "To the best of my recollection he said he found a treasure in something he called a crystal cave. Any idea where that is?"

"I don't even know *what* that is. It sure as hell isn't in this ugly old pile of rocks." He gestured toward the rust-colored stones carefully piled one upon another.

"You can't tell for sure, Cameron. Phelan also called this structure a treasure. One time I remember he found a handful of red speckled beans in a clay pot and he danced around like a kid and called it a treasure."

"Crazy son of a bitch! So he found a bloody cave. That was all?"

"No." Blade reached for the coffeepot and refilled their cups. "He told me the cave contained a treasure equal to any Egyptian's tomb."

"Ke-rist! You think that's true?"

"The investors would be delighted." Blade kicked at a small stone, then bent to add another log to the fire. "Hell, Cameron, I'm just the site artist. I've made drawings of everything Phelan found. He was meticulous about keeping records. Determined to regain his reputation."

"I never thought Phelan gave a fiddler's fugh about his reputation." Cameron took off his hat and scratched his head. "Not with all the tarts that came to visit."

"I think he meant his academic reputation. One time he mentioned a colleague stole some of his work."

Cameron replaced his hat and straightened it. "What work?"

"Can't remember. We were both well oiled at the time. But I think Phelan blasted the colleague, only people believe the other guy." Blade laughed. "He did have a grand talent for annoying folks. Oh, yes, I remember Jaspar Bird came in the Woodbine that night just as we were leaving, and Phelan told him he'd discovered a fabulous treasure on a bed of diamonds."

"Damned fool."

"Bird and his sister really irked Phelan. More than anybody else he knew here. I guess because they're ignorant and crass. But whatever the reason, they sure as hell managed to bring out the worst in him. He would tease and ridicule, and be utterly outrageous, loathing them all the while because they weren't sharp enough to understand he was mocking them."

"I heard Hertha Bird was sorta sweet on Phelan."

Blade snorted in surprise and burst into laughter. "My God, Sheriff, she's at least ten years older than Phelan, and thirty pounds heavier. And she's more dog-faced than her brother!"

Cameron chuckled at Blade's reaction.

Blade just shook his head and groaned. "That lantern-jawed old bat smells like yesterday's fried meat, her corset creaks when she walks, and when she isn't hollering at somebody, she's stuffing something in her mouth. Phelan might have been a randy bastard, but he was never that hard up."

"I never said she was a beauty. Just that she had eyes for Phelan and was real upset over his death."

"As far as I know, the only thing Phelan got from Hertha Bird was her breads and pastries. Che Nez brought out a big order from town every week—meat, fruit and vegetables, beer, as well as baked goods. I don't think Phelan ever even went to the Yellow Canary himself."

"Hell, you know how folks gossip."

"So what are folks saying about Phelan's death?"

"Everything from Indian curses to strangulation. Doc Brennan maintains Phelan succumbed to heart failure."

"And you're out here freezing your nuts off just because you wanted some of my coffee."

Cameron chuckled. "What Brennan is questioning is, what caused the heart failure?"

"He thinks it was something other than a natural cause?"

"Let's just say he's a very curious man."

Cameron's statement stuck in Blade's mind long after the sheriff had ridden away. He, too, was curious. It did not set right that Donal Phelan would simply crumple over in a heap as he walked through the woods.

It was early in the day for most customers of the San Juan Saloon, but one table at the far end of the bar near the stove was already occupied. A man with an emerald-colored fob hanging from his watch chain sat with his back to Quincy, the bartender, who worked the day shift, and drank in silence.

Quincy was an affable gent. He was keen on the ladies and spent most of his free time in the company of one or another. That is, when he wasn't bathing or shaving or brushing his hair. No man who frequented the San Juan managed to look as dapper as the daytime bartender.

The door opened and Quincy looked up from his glass polishing to see a slender fellow on the shy side of forty. Quincy winced at the man's clothes. The obvious mail-order suit looked as if the guy had slept in it all the way from New York City. Quincy had never been to New York, but to him it was the farthest place in the world from the Arizona Territory.

"Good morning, sir," Quincy said pleasantly.

The man in the wrinkled suit merely wet his lips nervously and peered across the room.

A gust of wind disturbed Quincy's carefully brushed hair. "Come in and shut the door," he said with a touch of annoyance.

After a second or two the fellow stepped into the warm saloon and reached for the door.

"What'll it be today?" Quincy asked when the man reached the bar.

"Beer." He put some pocket change on the bar.

"One beer coming right up." When Quincy set the mug on the bar, he noticed how bloodless the man's lips were, although he kept licking them, and how shaky the hand that reached for the beer. There was no doubt in Quincy's mind how this one had spent the night.

The man downed half the beer in a single swallow, his red-rimmed eyes closed in thanksgiving. He silenced a belch, then said to Quincy, "I'll be over at that table. Bring me another. He'll pay for it." He gestured toward the man with the emerald fob.

The chair squeaked on the wooden floor as he pulled it out from the table. "My stomach was a bit queasy this morning—"

The man with the emerald fob cut him off sharply, "Goddamn it! I bought you that meal ticket at the restaurant so this wouldn't happen. Can't you stay sober long enough to get the job done?"

Hatred flashed through the younger man's eyes and

quickly disappeared. He didn't bother to answer. Instead, he sipped sullenly from his mug and waited for the shakes to stop.

"Where is Sholes?"

The younger man shrugged.

"I asked you a question, Grover."

The words were so deadly quiet they made Grover's stomach clinch. He forced himself to meet the almost colorless eyes that threatened to pin him like a bug. He realized with a jolt the reason his body shook now had little to do with last night's binge. This man terrified him. He cleared his throat. "I haven't seen Sholes. Maybe he's still eating."

"What a couple of losers! Why the hell do I bother with you two?"

"Because nobody else likes you?"

Grover's life was saved from immediate extinction by the saloon door banging open. The way his head throbbed, he wasn't sure that was a blessing.

A big man with a long, gray-streaked beard lumbered up to the table.

"Mornin', Mister Vanderdam. Grover."

"You're late."

"I was eatin'. Don't wanta waste that there meal ticket ya bought me. Ain't et so good in a long spell."

It was rumored around Flagstaff that Theobald Vanderdam had been an up-and-coming lawyer someplace back East before his wife died, and grief-stricken, he'd come west to forget his pain. Of course Quincy didn't pay much mind to rumors. But he was aware Vanderdam spent more mornings in the San Juan Saloon with a bottle of Barbancourt Haitian Rum than he did in his Gold Avenue office. And when he did meet with people, they were more often than not ruffians, thugs, and other nasties.

Quincy delivered Grover's second beer to the table. Grover looked a little more human now, in spite of his shabby appearance. "Can I get you something this morning, Mr. Sholes?"

"It's mighty cold out there this morning."

Quincy gave an inward sigh. They'd gone through this same performance a couple days ago. Supposedly, Cecil Sholes was part of some authoritarian religious community that forbade drinking and dancing and other forms of joy.

"Maybe a little coffee? It'll warm you up. I made it for myself because it's so ugly out."

"Well, I'm not supposed to drink coffee . . . but I'm sure cold."

"Get him the coffee," Vanderdam snarled. "I haven't got all day to wait on these fools."

"I have something to tell you," Sholes said defensively. "That's why I was late."

Vanderdam poured himself another glass of rum.

"I heard something at the Yellow Canary."

The older man merely raised a brow.

Sholes pulled a chair around to sit down. Unfortunately, Vanderdam made him more nervous than he normally was, and his foot hit the table leg. Vanderdam's glass wobbled dangerously, and rum sloshed over the rim. Sholes lurched forward intending to catch the glass but instead knocked it over with his large callused paw.

Quincy walked up just as Sholes pulled a torn handkerchief from his pocket and attempted to sop up the mess. Ignoring the clumsy, apologetic Sholes and the livid Vanderdam, Quincy instantly righted the matter with a clean counter towel and another glass.

Within minutes, Quincy's calm, efficient manner of seeing to their needs unruffled the feathers of the three men. Sholes drank his syrupy coffee, Vanderdam his fancy rum, and Grover—a gleam of feral pleasure in his eyes—sipped his beer.

"I heard something at the Yellow Canary," Sholes began again. He stroked his gray beard nervously.

"What?" Grover asked.

"Phelan's sister arrived on the train two days ago . . ."

"And you just found out?" Grover taunted.

"I ain't finished!" Belligerence rang out in Sholes's voice.

"I'm waiting." Vanderdam almost sounded patient.

"Folks is sayin' Phelan sent all the way to Saint Louie fer her 'cause she can use that there typin' machine."

The dangerous light left Vanderdam's pale eyes as something more frightening entered. Pleasure. Oddly, Theobald Vanderdam was delighted with Sholes's tidbit of gossip.

"Yes, I remember hearing him tell Blade he was sending the telegram. It was to his sister, of course. Just before they went off to celebrate finding the treasure. My God," he whispered, "this must be bigger than I imagined."

"I ain't done yet." Sholes felt indignant at being interrupted in his tale.

"I'm sorry, Cecil. Finish your story. Please."

* * *

With a scowl Blade threw the rest of his coffee into the fire and watched it steam and sizzle. He tried to concentrate on his own problems. What happened next with this archaeological expedition? Was he even the man to decide? But if not him, then who else?

He swore in frustration.

Unfortunately, too many of his thoughts centered on Ruth McKenna instead of the more pressing problem of what to do about the job. He couldn't seem to get her out of his mind. Last night after he had carried her into his bedroom and laid her down on the bed, he stood looking at her for the longest while.

In a way he was vastly relieved she was not some doxy Phelan shipped in for his wicked pleasure. Ruth appeared too clean, too fresh, too lovely to be the sort of experienced jade Phelan favored. Yet in a way Blade felt bitterly disappointed.

He desired her. With every cell of his being he yearned to bed her. Had she been the libidinous floozy he first thought her to be, Blade would already have claimed her. Now all he could do was ache. Ache, and hope like hell she would continue with her travels damned quick.

His stomach growled loudly, and he realized it had been hours since he ate his bachelor's breakfast of cake and coffee. Turning toward his horse, he fished his lunch out of the saddlebag. Then he walked back to the fire and began to eat. "I wonder why the sheriff really came out here?" he asked himself.

A piece of one of the ham sandwiches broke off suddenly and tumbled into the ashes near the fire. Blade scowled as he caught a second hunk of bread as it hit the dirt. He tossed it out into the clearing.

A big raven which had watched him eat with hungry interest swooped down on the dirty bread.

"Be gone, you lousy scavenger," Blade yelled. "I've barely enough for a midget as it is. I won't be sharing with the likes of you."

"Folks says his sister come out here to write a book about him finding Colorado's gold . . ." Grover said, sipping another beer.

"Coronado," Vanderdam corrected.

Sholes shrugged and continued, " . . . now he's dead and she's gone and inherited his papers—and the gold."

Vanderdam thought a minute. "She can't inherit what she can't find."

"What are you saying, Mister Vanderdam?" Grover asked.

"We need those papers. Now more than ever. No skirt-twitching woman is going to snatch this away from me. Us. Not after what we've already done to get that treasure."

Shortly after Blade had consumed his scanty lunch and drank a cup of the mudlike coffee, it began to drizzle.

"Swell," he snarled. "This makes my day perfect."

He moved quickly underneath a tarp and shivered, scowling at the smoldering fire. The blaze was too small to radiate much heat.

"This is stupid! Freezing out here in a pile of rocks while you've got a nice warm fire at home."

And a nice warm woman, his brain taunted.

Blade snorted at the thought. "Maybe you better cool it off just a while longer."

An hour later rain and sleet began in earnest and he gave up his troubled thoughts and sought the shelter of the big house. The slow, wet ride from the expedition site back into the forest left him feeling mean and mangy. Nothing was worth such discomfort.

From now on, Blade promised himself, he'd keep his thoughts above his belt buckle. After all, she was just another woman. No sense getting in such a lather. He'd just finish the job and leave, and he'd go to some fine big town where there were plenty of lovely women.

When the ugly stone house finally came into view at the edge of the clearing, Blade groaned in pleasure. He'd never been so glad to see the place since he'd moved here. He nudged the horse to move a little faster.

As he approached the house Blade realized it looked dark and unoccupied.

He felt a shiver of alarm. It looked as silent and dreary as when he'd left that morning. What if Ruth's head injury had been more serious than he thought? What if she, too, was dead?

His stomach twisted sickeningly at the thought. He urged the horse forward, dismounting on a run before he reached the back door. He nearly tore the door off its hinges in his rush to get inside.

The smell of chicken simmering in a rich gravy assaulted him the moment he burst into the room. The kitchen was as dark as the rest of the house, but a small fire burned in the cookstove beneath the black Dutch oven. Potatoes simmered in another pot. A quick check showed him corn bread in the warming oven under a cloth as well as sliced braised carrots.

Blade lit the lamp and set it on the kitchen table next to the cruet set. The table had been completely laid out for supper. He wondered absently where Ruth found silver napkin holders.

"There must be a cook around here someplace," he said, trying to hide his relief. "Ruth? Mrs. McKenna? Are you here?"

She met him in the hallway, looking half asleep and sweetly disheveled. The dress she wore was a bit rumpled, as if she'd slept in it, and the fashionable twist on the top of her head appeared in danger of falling down.

The first thought that slammed into Blade's mind was how she looked like she'd recently been made love to. He nearly groaned aloud.

"Mister Blade. I'm sorry. I don't know what's gotten into me. I never nap during the day, but this afternoon I just couldn't keep awake."

In the shadowy light she looked fragile to Blade. Young and fragile and forlorn. His desire fought with the urge to protect her, to gather her close and shield her from the world. Apparently six hours in the frigid wilderness wasn't enough. He was still thinking like a fool.

"Perfectly understandable, Mrs. McKenna. It takes a while to get used to this elevation," he said more briskly than was polite, and started to pass her by. Instead, like a cloddish lout, he bumped against her shoulder.

"Oh, you're all wet!" Ruth's hand went from her wet sleeve to his.

"It's raining. I need a change of clothes." Again he started past her.

"You need a hot tub," she told him matter-of-factly. "I'll light the water heater while you fetch dry clothes. Strip out of those wet ones immediately!"

It wasn't until she was in the cozy bathroom that she realized the shocking intimacy of their conversation. She'd spent a good part of the day agonizing over the fact he'd undressed her the night she arrived. Now she sounded like she could barely wait to disrobe him.

"What in heaven's name has come over me?"

Nothing, she told herself silently, she had simply treated Blade the same way she would have treated her husband, or her brother, ordering him to strip off his wet clothes. "For no other reason than to prevent him from taking sick."

But Gladius Blade was neither husband nor brother. He was a total stranger with whom she was suddenly alone and sharing a house. A stranger who had stripped her naked, who had seen what no other man had ever witnessed, not even her husband. And she had behaved as casually as . . . well, frankly she didn't know what she'd behaved as. She was certain it was someone very common. The thought left her stunned.

Ruth returned to the kitchen and stood by the stove violently mashing potatoes when Blade walked in. Her drooping hairdo had been neatly repinned, and she wore a big green plaid apron over her simple navy blue wool dress with lace collar and cuffs. She didn't glance up at Blade, but instead added a dollop of butter and a shake of salt and continued to beat out lumps with great intensity. Only the telltale sign of deep rose tinting her cheeks indicated she knew of Blade's presence.

He tried not to look at her. Instead he shrugged into a rain slicker and went to the door. "I need to stable my horse and feed him. How much time do I have before you put the food on the table?"

A stab of misplaced annoyance hit Ruth like a brick. "You should have done that before you bathed," she said tartly, raising her head to glare at him.

Blade's mouth thinned. "I came here first because I didn't see a light. I was worried."

Crimson flooded Ruth's face, and her eyes dropped in shame. Why was she behaving like a child? She was far too sensible a woman to let petty irritations rile her. "I was rude. I apologize."

"Don't." His voice was cold. "I need to take care of the horse."

She nodded. "Supper can wait till you're ready."

"Fine."

He started to leave, then stuck his head back in the door. "How's your head? I walked in the office last night just as the avalanche started."

"It's sore. But my headache is gone. And so is the lump. I guess I'm lucky I didn't get buried alive in the rubble."

Guilt nipped at Blade's conscience. He slammed the door harder than necessary.

"This is worse than all the dreadful things I imagined. What am I going to do?" She tasted the potatoes and added a pinch more salt.

"I'll just speak to him," she said as she peeked in at the chicken. "I need to know what's going to happen next." She took a deep breath and let it out in a sigh. "I can handle anything . . . except not knowing." And she began to dish up the food.

Sharing a meal with Gladius Blade remained a unique experience. The man's size filled the room.

Ruth could not recall knowing a man so tall and muscular, so vital. He ate the way he did everything else, with relish. A surge of pleasure washed over her at his obvious enjoyment of the meal she'd prepared. The feeling both surprised and disconcerted her. She had no right to feel anything about Blade, at least until she knew his intentions.

Complimenting her lavishly, he refilled his plate. "You'll think I haven't eaten in a month."

"You're just cold and hungry, Mister Blade," Ruth answered reasonably. She wondered when she'd last known a man with such a healthy appetite. "Would you like some coffee?"

"Stay put. I'll make tea. Let me wait on you this time."

Ruth couldn't contain her astonishment. Never in her life had a man waited on her, even when she was sick, and for the life of her she didn't know how to behave. Tears welled up and she blinked them away furiously, lest he see, and sat staring at her cold fingers knotted in her lap.

"Here you are, beautiful lady," Blade said in a decent imitation of a carnival barker as he plopped the heavy teapot on the table with a thump, "the very best, no, the absolute finest pot of English tea in the Arizona Territory."

Ruth couldn't help herself. She giggled.

His answering smile lit up his dark brown eyes. He was a magnificent-looking man, a true man of the West. How could she have ever thought him uncouth or barbaric? Was that only yesterday? She lowered her eyes as her wayward thoughts threatened to confuse her and busily poured the steaming tea into the clean cup he offered.

Blade sat back down in the chair. For a second she'd been so spontaneous, so alive, so unbearably beautiful he wanted to catch her in his arms and twirl her around.

"We need to talk, Mister Blade."

"Yes, we do." That much was certain. And after that he needed to get her the hell back on the train to someplace else.

"We're in a very awkward position."

"How so?"

Ruth wrapped her fingers around the teacup. She wished Blade would look at her. Instead he seemed to be concentrating on the flowered sugar bowl.

"Well," she said crisply, "you and I are here, together . . . alone."

His brown eyes met hers squarely. "Interesting."

Ruth's composure slipped a notch. The high color had returned to her cheeks. "You know how people talk . . ."

"Our neighbors?" He gave a short laugh. "We don't have any neighbors. Oh, there are a few Navajos around here, but basically they don't care a fig what you and I do together alone in this barn of a house." He poured more tea in his cup.

"Mister Blade." Her tone was one of exaggerated patience. "I came all the way out here unchaperoned from Saint Louis . . ."

"I've been meaning to ask you about that. Exactly why did you come out here without benefit of a chaperone or companion? I know it's modern times, but that's a long trip for an unaccompanied lady."

Ruth wet her lips, then straightened her back and met his gaze. "I had no one."

"No maid? No friend? No relative?"

"Donal was my only kin."

"Why didn't he pay for a companion? What about your maid?"

Ruth chose to ignore the first question for the moment. "I didn't have a maid. Farley didn't believe in having servants. He felt it was far more democratic, more American, to wait upon and clean up after ourselves."

Blade's eyes narrowed. "I assume that means you waited upon and cleaned up after Farley, not vice versa."

Ruth jumped to her feet. "Mister Blade, that was uncalled for and unspeakably rude!"

"Yes it was," Blade agreed after the briefest pause. "And I apologize." His tone sounded anything but apologetic. "Now sit down again so we can finish this discussion about our problem of being here together, alone."

Reluctantly she sat.

"Did you want any dessert?" Blade asked.

"Not right now. I had some cobbler with lunch. I think there's a pie left from yesterday, but most of the cake is gone. What do you want? I'll get it."

"No," he growled. "I want it, I can get it out of the pie safe. I can even get you some, too, if you want."

"I didn't mean to offend you, Mister Blade," she said stiffly. This conversation was not going the way she had rehearsed it.

"You didn't offend me, Mrs. McKenna." This time he sounded contrite. "I was raised to care for my own needs. "My father insisted on that from all of us."

"I can't remember not caring for others." She looked down at her hands and frowned. Talking to Blade was maddening. They were way off the subject.

"If we're going to live together, we'll have to be understanding with one another."

"Are we going to live together?" she asked in a strangled voice.

If she was surprised at his statement, he was even more. Until that very second, he had every intention of placing her bodily on the next train out of town. "Do you have another place to go?"

"No, I don't."

"What about Saint Louis? Do you have a house there? Friends?"

Blade thought she gave her answer considerable preparation. He cut himself a large slice of dried apricot pie and took a bite. Obviously it had come from the Yellow Canary. Nobody made a pie like Hertha Bird.

"It never occurred to me Farley could possibly die so young. Apparently it hadn't occurred to him either, for his affairs were definitely not in order. There was barely enough money from the sale of the house to cover his debts." There was no bitterness in her voice, although she had suffered from her husband's neglect.

She twisted the garnet ring on her right hand, the only gift her brother had ever given her. "I've lived in a single room over a bakery for the past year, sharing a kitchen and bath with another widow. I've managed to keep myself from starving because I'm an excellent typewriter. A few of the insurance companies were willing to hire me from time to time."

"Didn't Phelan send you the money for your train fare?" As he swallowed the last bite of pie, the truth slowly dawned on him. Could it be that Phelan had had no idea Ruth was coming to live with him?

Ruth hesitated. "No. I sold my furniture and Farley's books. And my mother's pearls. I did manage to keep the few pieces of jewelry with the greatest sentimental value, but beyond that . . ." She let the sentence trail off into silence. She was afraid to confide the whole story to Blade, afraid he'd use the truth against her and send her away.

"It must have been tough for you. I mean, my sister's husband died a couple months back. My father and brother took care of everything. They even accompanied her out to San Diego so she could recover in a resort by the sea."

"How lucky for her to have someone." Ruth's eyes held a faraway expression and her voice was wistful.

Blade wondered if she was thinking about telling him the rest of her story. He wished she would. When she made no move to do so, he decided, with a nudge of unexpected disappointment, that there were still to be secrets between them.

"I plan to stay here and wrap up the expedition. That should be by early summer. I believe the lease on the house is up then." He took a deep breath and plunged ahead, wondering all the while if he was making the mistake of a lifetime, "It's all right with me if you stay till then."

Ruth nodded, lowering her eyes so he wouldn't see the tears of relief. "Thank you," she whispered.

Blade was deeply moved. Obviously she had absolutely no place else to go. He picked up the teapot and filled her cup, determined to act as if his decision was perfectly rational and businesslike. "First of all, I need to contact the investors about Phelan's death."

"I can type the letters for you."

"That would be a big help," Blade said. "I'm a better artist than a businessman."

"Artist? Is that what you do?"

Blade felt the defensiveness rise swiftly. He took a deep breath and forced himself to relax. "Field artist for the expedition."

"Oh, wonderful! You must be good if Donal let you live at the house."

"I'm the only one who could stand him." As soon as the words were out Blade realized how horrible they were, under the circumstances. Blood rushed to his face.

Ruth chuckled, in spite of herself. "I understand. I truly do."

"I'm sorry. That was unforgivable."

"Oh, I forgive you." She gave him a beautiful smile. "And I want to type more than the letters. I can read my brother's handwriting. I want to finish his manuscript. I want to prepare it for publication."

This was better than he'd hoped, and worse. Ruth could make sense of Phelan's chaos, but she would also learn that Blade was more than a simple artist. He didn't want her to learn about his father's investment. Or his own. Not yet, at least.

"Perhaps we should wait on what the investors decide."

The stubborn set of her mouth told Blade she'd have her own way. One way or another.

"We do need to talk about our living arrangements. As you pointed out earlier, we're here alone together. And eventually someone beyond our nearby neighbors will notice, and comment. My reputation won't suffer much because I'm a man, but, people being what they are, I suspect you might be accused of immoral behavior."

She looked straight at him, her blue eyes stubborn. "I'm staying."

"I wasn't suggesting you leave."

"Good, because I won't. You need me."

Blade shook his head in consternation. He could see more than one trait that resembled her brother. "All I'm trying to say is that we'll need someone to come and live at the house as a chaperone."

"Fine."

"The problem is that Marie is sick. Tsosi told me so when I went out to the barn. So for a couple more days it seems we'll be by ourselves."

"That's no problem, Mister Blade. I'll make a great effort to behave myself."

5

She was sick. Dreadfully, horribly sick. Her head throbbed, her bones ached, and a weakness heretofore unknown held her a complete prisoner in her bed. Marie Manyhorses struggled desperately to rouse herself from the sweat-soaked sheets, but a wave of dizziness hit her full square, and she fell backward with a groan.

"Mama, aren't you up?"

Marie heard her son call from the main room of the cabin, but she could only manage a croaking answer. She knew she was expected at the big house. She'd promised Blade. Again she made the effort to move. She couldn't remember feeling so awful, so frighteningly weak. She wondered if she was dying. Even that required too much effort to think about, so she lay back and closed her eyes.

* * *

"Marie generally comes over about eight." Blade helped himself to more apple butter. Ruth had surprised him this morning by cooking breakfast. He showed his appreciation by eating well.

"Fine. I want to get started on Donal's papers."

"I have a better idea. It looks as if the storm blew over last night. How would you like to drive out to the dig?"

"Oh, could we?" Her eyes sparkled with interest. "I'd love to get out of the house!" She looked startled at her own vehemence.

"I understand. A day outside will put the color back in your cheeks." Blade noticed a faint bloom touch her skin.

"I need to get my bearings," she said self-consciously. "I'll do a better job with the notes if I have some idea about the countryside."

"Right." He glanced up at the pressed-oak Waterbury clock hanging on the kitchen wall. "I wonder where Marie is?"

"Has Marie always worked here?"

"She was here when I came. I understand she and her husband had land out on the reservation and a large herd of horses. Did well for a while."

"What happened?"

"The weather has been bad the past few years. Harsh winters, drought in the summer. Many Navajo ranchers have lost their herds. A number have been forced to seek work off the reservation. Marie's husband died three years ago, so she and her son came here. The boy is a fine stockman. One of the best I've ever seen. And she's adequate as a housekeeper, but not much of a cook. It didn't take Phelan and me long to decide to buy most of our food already cooked from town. There are some good cooks in Flagstaff. And what we didn't purchase already prepared, we cooked ourselves."

"You must mean you did the cooking. I can't imagine Donal around a pot that wasn't steeped in history."

"You underestimated the man. He could do anything he had to do. I admit he was a bit heavy-handed with spices, but he did his share of the cooking."

An hour later Gladius Blade pounded at the door of the small cabin, now genuinely concerned about his housekeeper's absence. He glanced up at the sky as he waited for someone to open the door. The day had begun chilly and damp, but the sun shone bright and the clouds had blown eastward toward Santa Fe.

"Looks like a fine day," he muttered. He was looking forward to showing Ruth her brother's dig site.

Marie Manyhorses told Blade yesterday she'd return to work today, and he'd never known her to shirk her duties. Worried something might have happened to her, he waited with growing impatience.

"Blade, I'm glad you came," Tsosi said as he pulled open the cabin door, his youthful voice shaking with alarm. "My mother is sick. She fell. Can you help me get her off the floor?"

Blade rushed into the cabin behind the boy. His heart throbbed when he saw the frail gray-haired woman on the floor. Oh, God, not her, too, he thought.

Moments later he dashed out the door and raced toward the stable. Marie was alive but out of her head with delirium. He needed to bring the doctor out from town immediately.

"Go tell Mrs. McKenna I'm going to town for the doc," Blade told Tsosi when he saw the teenager had followed him into the stable. "Then go back and stay with your mother. Keep her in bed and covered. I'll be back in a couple hours."

"What about the white lady? Who will stay with her?"

"Mrs. McKenna is a strong woman. She can take care of herself. Just tell her I've gone to town."

"What about a housekeeper?"

Blade threw the saddle on his roan and tightened the cinch. "We'll have to do without one till your mother is well."

"I have a cousin in town," Tsosi told him. "Tell her to come. She can work for the white lady, and she can take care of my mother, too."

"What's her name and where do I find her?"

"She is called Jennie Begay. She works for Miss Bird. At the house."

"Oh, great. All I need is that old blister mad at me." He urged the horse forward, then whirled it back around to face Tsosi. "Tell Mrs. McKenna I'm sorry about our trip out to the dig. We'll go tomorrow."

It was later that morning before Blade finished talking to Doc Brannen about Marie.

"It might be the influenza," Doc said. "It's going around. Some folks get real sick with it. I'll go out and take a look at her. You riding back?"

"Not just yet. I need to collect Tsosi's cousin to stay with Mrs. McKenna."

"Mrs. McKenna is a handsome woman."

"Yes. And intelligent, too."

"Like her brother?"

Blade snorted. "Much nicer. But determined, though. She wants to stay here awhile to go through Phelan's papers. She's hoping her brother wrote down enough about the dig that some publisher might be interested."

Doc nodded. "I understand that. There must be something salvageable in his notes. It would be a damned shame to let several years of his work die along with him." He got his worn leather bag and started for the door. "I imagine the situation could get awkward."

Blade felt himself tense. He didn't want to discuss what he felt about Ruth with the doctor or anybody else, so he chose to misunderstand Doc's comment. "I think Tsosi's cousin will rectify the situation. With her living at the house, nobody will dare gossip."

Doc Brannen turned his head toward Blade. His brows raised a fraction but not a hint of a smile touched his mouth. "We wouldn't want gossip," he said mildly. "How long do you think it will take her to read Phelan's notes?"

"Spring, maybe. That's not far away. The lease is up on the house this summer, so I'll need to wrap things up by then."

"Where will you go after that?"

"I'm going back to Denver." In all honesty, he'd given no thought to his plans. It was safe to mention Denver, since his father still had a house there. Maybe he would go back.

"What about Mrs. McKenna? "

The thought made Blade's gut tighten. What would

happen to Ruth after she finished her brother's work?
"I don't know. She hasn't said."

Blade rode away to find Jennie Begay. He suspected
it wouldn't require too much convincing to get her to
leave Hertha Bird. Hertha had trouble keeping girls.

In spite of the reason for his trip to town, Blade
enjoyed the ride. The elevation and types of vegetation
growing in the area reminded him of Denver, as did the
clean, crisp air. Both cities had been built in mountain
foothills, and both had progressive-thinking residents.
He grew a bit nostalgic thinking of his childhood home.
Nobody in the family lived in the house anymore except
his youngest sister, Celestine, and several family servants. He doubted if the place was much like the home
in which he'd grown up.

He'd read that western visitors often compared
Flagstaff with San Francisco. Blade could see the similarities in how the town spread up into the graceful
hills. But he doubted if Flagstaff would ever grow into
such a magnificent lady as the California city by the
bay, or as wild and willful a town. But he could certainly envision Flagstaff growing. People were already living farther up in the hills, away from downtown.

The horse ambled north on San Francisco Avenue
past the two-storied Babbitt Bros. Wholesale and Retail
Establishment and onward until he saw the handsome
ocher-colored sandstone courthouse with its clock
tower,

"A horse!" he muttered to himself. "She'll need a
horse."

He turned west on Birch and then south on Gold,

hurrying the horse along till he reached the Grand Canyon Stables on Aspen.

Once he'd rented a serviceable but far from handsome animal for the girl to ride out to the ranch, he mounted the roan and headed north on Beaver to Hertha Bird's house.

He wondered why a woman of her girth had chosen to build so far up the hill, since she wouldn't ride a horse and didn't own a buggy. The house was located some distance from the closest house, perched on the crest of a hill, like a ghastly wart. It was truly a Victorian nightmare. His artistic soul shuddered. Every possible thing that could have been decorated, had been—in gingerbread, geegaws, and folderol. The yard was littered with birdhouses, bird feeders, and birdbaths, and the iron gate had a bird welded on the front.

Blade twisted the doorbell with more force than necessary, and a shabby woman in her early twenties answered. Her eyes were so badly crossed, Blade wondered how she could see.

"I need to see Jennie Begay."

She looked at him a minute with her head slightly tilted. "I'll get her."

When the woman walked away, Blade noticed she limped, as if one leg was considerably shorter than the other.

The first thing that struck Blade was how very young Jennie Begay looked. At the most she was fifteen. He also noticed, with some surprise, was how pretty she was—Hertha Bird was notorious for hiring only homely, backward women, or unfortunate ones like the one who'd answered the door.

Perhaps Jennie appeared so young because she was

quite small. Less than five foot tall, Blade guessed. Only her well-rounded figure attested to the fact she was not a child.

Like the rest of the girls who worked for Miss Bird, Jennie dressed shabbily in a thin cotton skirt and blouse, and she wore no coat, just a ragged wool blanket. Her small hands showed the signs of hard work and improper care, but her soft dark eyes gleamed with intelligence.

"Your cousin Tsosi Manyhorses asked me to come see you. His mother is quite ill. He suggested you might be willing to work as a housekeeper at the Phillips Ranch for Mrs. McKenna and myself while his mother is unwell." Blade noted the shadow of a smile on her face.

She simply nodded.

"Will you come?"

"I'll come," she said in a voice as soft as cotton fluff. "I'll get my things."

"Good. I'll pay you well," he said as an afterthought, watching her scurry back into the house.

She quickly returned, carrying a sack in her hand. Another Indian girl peered out the parlor window.

Anger for this tiny overworked girl surged through Blade when he saw the worn flour sack she clutched which held her meager possessions. Blade felt as if he was absconding with an ill-treated slave instead of an upstairs maid.

"Are you ready?" he asked.

"Yes," she answered shyly.

Blade had hoped to make their escape before Jennie's loudmouthed employer noticed they were gone, but luck was not with him.

"Where the hell are you agoin' with my girl?" snapped Hertha, as Blade secured Jennie's paltry hoard of treasures onto the horse.

"Good afternoon, Miss Bird." Blade tried very hard to recall a few of the manners his mother insisted he learn, and tipped his hat. "Today turned out real nice, didn't it? Kind of surprising, after yesterday's storm."

Hertha stormed up to Blade, her corsets creaking as she moved, and gave him a shove.

Astonished, he stumbled backward into Jennie's rented horse. The old plug was accustomed to all sorts of peculiar human behavior and simply stepped aside, totally unperturbed. Blade managed to catch his balance before he flopped to the ground.

"You mangy son of a bitch! What the hell you mean by taking my girl?"

"I explained that to you in my note, Miss Bird, when I stopped by the Yellow Canary. Her aunt got sick and needs her."

"Your note, huh? Ain't you got the rocks to talk to me face-to-face?"

Phelan had once told Blade that meeting Hertha Bird on the street was like encountering a steam engine on a sudden incline. The moment you saw her, Blade thought to himself, you knew you were going to be run down.

"I tried to talk to you, Miss Bird, but Myrtle said you were gone."

"Myrtle's an idiot!"

While Blade privately agreed with her assessment of Myrtle, he stuck to his point. "You weren't in the Canary when I stopped."

"I was out back attending to nature's call."

Realizing this conversation was going nowhere in a big hurry, Blade stepped over to where Jennie waited in her tattered blanket. He grasped her by the waist and lifted her up into the saddle. "Ride on out to the ranch. They need you. I'll catch up."

Hertha gave an angry squawk. "What the hell are you doing, shitbag? That girl belongs to me."

"That girl doesn't belong to anybody but herself." Blade felt his control begin to slip. "Maybe she did work for you, but she just quit." With that he swung up into his own saddle, turned the gelding toward the edge of town and galloped away. He could hear Hertha screaming at him three blocks down the road.

"No wonder she never got a husband," he muttered. "Even with women being scarce in the West, no man alive was ever that hard up."

Jaspar Bird watched Gladius Blade ride after the little Indian girl.

"Looks like Blade is occupied for a while," he said to his empty room. "This just might be a right fine day for a ride in the country. Maybe out to Phelan's dig. While the cat is away, the mice will play." He giggled loudly.

Jaspar Bird wasn't the only one who decided to take a ride in the woods. Several other men who had been loitering in front of the San Juan Saloon had also noticed Blade ride into town. They didn't waste any time. Before Blade had ridden another block, they were mounted and hightailing it down the road. They weren't going to the archaeological site, however. They made a beeline toward Phelan's house.

A man could wander through the woods for years

and never find that damned treasure. But with a map, a smart man could locate the loot within hours.

Blade caught up with Jennie before she reached the outskirts of Flagstaff. He tried to explain why he and Ruth McKenna needed a housekeeper to live at the house.

"People who aren't married don't live in the same house," he told her as they rode together. "Other people would talk about them. If you stay at the big house with Mrs. McKenna and me, everything will be fine."

Jennie gave him a blank look and refrained from comment. Sometimes the ways of the white man were incomprehensible to her. "If my auntie is all right, I'll stay at the house."

"Good. We'd appreciate that." Blade glanced toward the San Francisco Peaks. A white oval cloud hung over the top like an inverted bowl. "By the way, Mrs. McKenna is a nice woman. She'll treat you much better than Miss Bird did." His eyes strayed to Jennie's chapped hands. "She won't yell, and she won't strike you. And she'll see that you're warm and well fed."

The girl simply nodded.

"I don't recollect this field being so big." Cecil Sholes sat dejectedly upon his tired horse and peered through the trees at the big stone house.

"Let's go on over." Grover wasn't in the mood for any discussion. Vanderdam had chewed his ass this morning about being drunk again. He decided he didn't much like the fancy lawyer. He only wanted his share of the treasure and to get the hell out of town.

"Somebody will see us coming."

"Who cares."

"I care. I don't want somebody ta shoot me afore I get a chance ta break in and find the map."

"Nobody's gonna shoot you, ya big coward."

Sholes exploded. He grabbed Grover and hauled him out of the saddle. "Listen, you shithead, I'll cut your throat if ya call me that agin! I ain't stupid. If we ride across that meadow an' somebody sees us, they'll know we's up to sompthin'. We needs ta think."

"That'll be a new experience for you."

Blade and Jennie were halfway back to the ranch house when they met Doc Brannen on the road heading back to town.

"How is Marie?" Blade asked.

"Sick."

"Is that the best your medical opinion can do? I knew she was sick when I road into town."

"I wish you knew what her ailment was then, because I sure don't. Let me know if anybody else gets sick."

"Okay. What will that mean?"

"It's contagious."

"Thanks."

"You can pay my bill the next time you're in town. Better yet, I'll send it out with Che Nez."

Blade looked perplexed. "Che? I haven't ordered anything from town lately. Why would Che ride out to the ranch unless I did?"

Doc Brannen glanced sideways at Jennie. "You've been out in the woods too long, Blade. Everybody knows Che is sweet on Jennie."

The girl studied her chapped hands on the worn leather reins. "Miss Bird didn't allow," she whispered.

"Allow what?" Blade asked.

"Anything!" Doc said. "Hertha threatened to shoot Che on sight if he came within a block of her house."

A tiny dimple that appeared at the corner of Jennie's mouth told Blade the handsome young Navajo had managed somehow to court the girl in spite of Hertha's threats.

Jennie nudged her horse, and Blade started to follow, nodding good-bye to the doctor.

"Wait a minute. I want to talk to you alone for a moment," Doc Brannen said.

"What about?" Blade felt a chill touch his skin.

"Rand Cameron came out here yesterday."

"I saw him." Blade noticed how blue the San Francisco Mountains seemed as the afternoon sun edged toward the western sky.

"Did you ever notice Phelan being peaked or sickly? Complaining about shortness of breath or digestion problems? Anything like that?"

"Donal Phelan was the healthiest man I ever saw. He never even had the sniffles."

Doc thought for a minute. "If a man is shot or stabbed, it's easy to establish a crime. And in the West, that's how most criminals do away with their victims."

"So you think Phelan was the victim of a crime?"

"Donal Phelan died of a heart attack. I'm just not completely certain that he didn't have a little outside help."

"What?"

"Poison, maybe. Certain weeds. Things that over-stimulate the heart."

"So why haven't you and the sheriff called it murder?"

"It's not real simple proving a case of poisoning here in the Arizona Territory. There's no scientific laboratory available. Sheriff Cameron thinks it's better to let things stand for the time being. Maybe somebody will get sloppy. Maybe they'll try again."

"Great."

"You're a suspect, you know."

"Thanks a lot, Doc," Blade growled.

"Cameron thinks you have a motive."

"I had the best motive in the world for keeping Phelan alive. Money! My company sunk a bunch of money into this expedition and so far we haven't got a cent back out. Not even any glory."

"What about the treasure he bragged about?"

"Christ, you don't believe that any more than I do. He probably found a clay pigeon. Or a stone knife. He did handstands one time over projectile points."

Doc Brannen chuckled. "So, tell me. What about this good-looking sister? You think it's coincidence she showed up when she did?"

"More like bad luck. For her and me. I'm breaking my ass trying to locate some unknown treasure that only Phelan would find valuable while every frigging cutthroat in the territory is hunting gold. And up pops Phelan's sister." In his tirade, Blade nearly told the doc that he hadn't known Ruth existed, but he thought better of it. Right now Doc didn't need to know that little tidbit. Nobody did.

"She's a fine woman."

Blade grinned. "That's another piece of bad luck. She's a woman of high morals and fine virtue."

Doc Brannen was beset with a fit of coughing.

"What I need is silence, and nobody else pawing through the notes. And especially nobody looking beautiful at the breakfast table."

Jaspar Bird was in a foul mood when he climbed stiffly off his horse and tied it to a broken plow handle by the door of the rundown hogan. He felt mean and ugly.

Jaspar hadn't been a joyful creature for any full day of his entire life, but this day he was more contentious than usual. Nothing had gone as he'd anticipated today. His malicious streak lurking not far from the surface began to simmer.

He kicked at his horse with his thick-soled shoes.

He hated animals, and they hated him. The horse he owned, a dour mud-brown nag with knobby knees, tried to bite him at least once on every ride they endured together. Jaspar would have shot her in the blink of an eyelash except that the horse was small and relatively placid compared to the beasts other men rode.

So Jaspar suffered the mare and she tolerated him with mutual loathing. Today the ride had been long and the terrain rocky. After Jaspar spied other men skulking in the woods, he'd abandoned his original idea of going to the dig and decided instead to visit the ranch house. After all, the dig was a number of miles farther east and he had no idea what to look for there.

He was certain the other men must know something

more about the treasure than he did. Something, he decided, that centered on the house. After more than an hour of trying to sneak up to the Phillips Ranch and always seeing people around the yard, Jaspar had another idea. Unfortunately, it required more miles in the saddle. Neither he nor the mare was pleased.

It was nearly dark now and Bird was cold and hungry. His buttocks hurt and his back ached, his bowed legs felt bloodless. He still had the long ride back to Flagstaff ahead of him and that thought made him downright spiteful.

He thrust back the heavy quilt at the door of the hogan and stepped into the room without waiting for an invitation.

Moses Bigboy raised his rheumy eyes from the bowl of mutton stew he was eating and stared at the blurry figure of Jaspar Bird. Even if he hadn't recognized Jaspar from his bottle-green checked suit and derby hat, the old Navajo would have known him from the Eau de Quinine hair tonic he'd doused himself with. The strong scent overpowered all other odors in the smoky mud and log dwelling.

"Fix me some food."

A gust of wind blew down the smoke hole and ashes twirled in the flames.

Moses ignored Jaspar's command and kept on chewing the tough mutton.

"I'm talking to you, ya mangy old fart!" Jaspar kicked viciously toward the gaunt figure, his leather shoe flinging dirt from the earthen floor into the bowl of stew.

Moses Bigboy sat stone still.

He had known many white men in his life. He'd

made the long walk with his people when the white soldiers overran the Navajo land, killing and conquering the people, destroying their lives and their pride. Years later he'd returned to his homeland and had prospered as many Navajos had. And like many of his people, he'd suffered over the past decade from the cruel hand of nature. He owned little now except his hogan, his stew pot, and his soul.

When Jaspar Bird stepped uninvited into his hogan, Moses Bigboy felt his soul cringe. Of all the white men Moses had known in his lifetime, Jaspar Bird was one of the worst. An enemy. An evil man.

Moses waited with the patience of age, his frail body still, his dark eyes expressionless.

Jaspar peered around the dimly lit hogan and spotted a metal bowl. He grabbed it and rushed to the fire ring, brushing the old man aside as he lunged toward the stew and filled the bowl to overflowing.

In silence Moses sat cross-legged while Jaspar noisily gulped down the food, using the serving ladle as a spoon, reminding the old man of a pig at a trough.

Jaspar belched loudly and tossed the bowl in the dirt. Then he picked up a woolen blanket and inspected it for vermin. Once he had decided the blanket was pest free, he threw it to the floor and flopped on it. The warm fire felt good and he considered stretching out for the night even though the place did smell like an Indian. But he didn't. He was here for a purpose other than bodily comfort.

"Tell Marie Manyhorses the ghosts are after her."

Moses didn't even blink.

The snap of the fire was the only sound in the room.

"Did you hear me, old fool?"

After a long moment Moses turned his head in Jaspar's direction and fixed his black eyes on him.

The silence stretched out and Jaspar became uncomfortable. Hell, he was the white man, the superior man, yet this bony, half-naked old savage made him feel like a pile of dung. Without speaking one damned word.

"Phelan's ghost!" he said loudly. The words seemed to echo off the many walls of the hogan.

Moses continued to look at him.

Jaspar licked his rubbery lips. "Phelan's ghost is in the big house. Because he dug up your ancestors. Tell Marie Manyhorses. Tell her Blade and that woman at the house are the enemy. Her enemy. Tsosi's enemy. Because they still dig." He took a deep breath. "Tell her to run them off. Scare them away. Or kill them."

Moses reached out and tossed a stick on the fire. "I will pray about it," he said after considerable thought.

Jaspar couldn't contain his degenerate smile.

"I pray," Moses said again. "You go."

Reluctantly Jaspar rose from the warmth of the fire. He hated to face the long ride back to Flagstaff in the chilly darkness, but he realized his plan would fail if he insisted on staying. Still he was fuming at the old Indian's lack of hospitality when he left.

"Ignorant savage!" he said as he stomped toward his horse. "Ya ain't no better than a dirty animal." He turned around and urinated all over the quilt that covered the hogan door.

Ruth sipped her tea and stared at the fire burning low in the fireplace. She didn't want to admit it, but she was disappointed when Blade declined to have his after-dinner coffee in the parlor with her. Her day had been a lonely one and she'd looked forward to his company for the evening.

Suddenly restless, she stood and began to prowl around the large, elaborately decorated Victorian parlor. Now that she gave it her attention, she admitted the room was as lavish as anything she'd seen in the East.

In front of the wide fireplace sat a large sofa, an armed chair, and a rocker, plus two parlor chairs on either side of the fireplace. The entire suite had been upholstered in a three-tone maroon and was deeply fringed with fancy binding, chord, and tassels. The sofa was bracketed on either side by end tables, each holding a cerise banquet lamp. A hand-painted papier-mâché box sat on one table beside a pink Bristol glass vase enameled with flowers, and several small framed photographs. The other end table was cluttered with odd candlesticks of various sizes, an enameled matchbox with a hinged lid, and an end-of-day paperweight.

Ruth lifted it up and set it down again. The night loomed endlessly ahead of her. An uncharacteristic gloom settled over her, one she couldn't seem to dispel.

She walked to the window and reached for the lace curtain. It was foolish to look out. There was nothing beyond the house but darkness. A book lay on the table, and she picked it up, settling into a chair.

The book was a leather-bound version of *The Poetic Works of John Milton*, and it wasn't long before Ruth found her mind wandering. She moved her leg, instantly and painfully barking her ankle on the richly carved leg of the chair. She closed the book and, after replacing it, stood and looked balefully at the chair, wondering if she'd ever walk normally again.

She limped across the room, unable to take her eyes off the furniture and decor. Truly it was so grotesque it was fascinating.

She'd spent the sunny day in her brother's office mulling over his notes. His handwriting had not improved over the years, she noticed. For more than an hour she'd tried to put some order to the scrawls and scratches. And finally in sheer desperation, she hauled out the typing machine.

It would be far easier to make sense of the neat typewritten pages than Donal's illegible scribbles.

Blade had been distracted at dinner. She knew he was worried about Marie Manyhorses, as well as the fact that Marie's niece, Jennie, had decided to spend the night at the cabin instead of the house. But Ruth understood the girl's concern about her aunt.

"Who will know where she slept?" she'd asked Blade. "None of us is going to announce it in church."

Blade had laughed, but he was insistent about Jennie staying at the house. "We'll get her moved into the little room by the kitchen in the morning."

Ruth went back to the sofa and forced herself to settle down. She took a sip of tea and frowned to find it tepid. She felt lonely and wanted to talk to Blade, needing to ask him about the expedition, about her brother's discoveries.

Exactly what had Donal Phelan been searching for? And what had he found?

She looked over at the rich bookcase/secretary that sat against the wall. Unlike the other pieces of furniture in the parlor, the bookcase was a handsome piece. It stood over six feet tall and was nearly as long. The center section had a plate-glass mirror and three drawers as well as a hidden desk. She thought about writing a letter. Then she realized she had no one left to whom she could write.

It was a sobering thought and she quickly turned her mind back to her brother and what he'd found at his dig.

Upstairs at his simple golden oak writing desk, Blade also pondered Donal Phelan's findings. Before him lay the thick ivory sheets of his own brother's elegant copperplate writing. Nobody in the family could match Neel's handwriting. Certainly not Blade.

The appeal in the letter touched him deeply. Neel needed some assurance about the dig to lift the old man's dejected spirits, to help him recover from his stroke. Never before had his brother or his father needed him.

And what the hell could he give them?

When they were desperate, he had nothing. Nothing but a dead man and a hat full of rumors.

Blade stretched his big hands out in front of him.

Rumors were something.

He took a piece of blank paper from the desk drawer and dipped the smooth onyx-handled pen in the silver inkwell. He wouldn't lie to Neel. He'd explain about Phelan's demise and the weather-related shutdown of the field work at the dig site. He'd predict there would be no rehire in the spring. He'd say the money had run out.

But he'd mention the rumors. He'd write about Phelan's excitement just before his death and how his sister had come out to assist with the manuscript. And he'd use Phelan's words to describe the treasure. That's right, he'd call it a treasure, just as Phelan had.

He'd say he'd look for the treasure himself and that he thought there might be a map.

Hell, rumor would do fine. The old man thrived on it! Rumor would give him hope.

6

The men moved stealthily across the clearing, slinking nearer and nearer to the big stone house. It was very dark. The moon hung lopsided in the midnight sky, giving off only the faintest glimmer of light. A coyote's song cut through the cold night air. Then there was silence.

Several Ponderosa pine trees stood near the back door. They were fairly tall and filled the darkness with a pungent fragrance. Grover took a deep refreshing breath.

Sholes, for some unknown reason, proceeded to walk right square into the biggest tree, hitting it with an ominous thud that reverberated through the night.

He damned near knocked himself unconscious.

"Ughhhh."

"Shhhh!"

Sholes slid gracelessly to the dirt.

"Get up, you idiot."

All Sholes did was mumble.

It took a good five minutes before Grover got the bigger man back on his feet. Sholes didn't seem to be quite right in the head, but Grover suspected Sholes was never quite right. Whatever he was at the moment would have to do.

"I'm bleeding," he whimpered.

"Oh for godsake, come on. It will be daylight before we get in the house."

"What if the door ain't open?"

Through the darkness came a snarling, strangling sound. Not exactly animal, but not quite human either. The gnashing of teeth resounded in the shadowy gloom.

"Well, what if it ain't?"

Grover marched angrily up to the back door, grabbed the brass doorknob, and gave a lusty turn. The door flew open, banging against the wall with an awful racket, and knocked Grover onto his knees.

Ruth woke with a start, her heart pounding madly.

Over the blood thrumming in her ears and the maddening gasps of her breath, she strained to listen. Seconds passed. She heard nothing.

"Only a dream," she breathed as she pulled the quilt around her face against the chilly darkness. The soft scent of rose and lavender potpourri touched her delicate nostrils as she settled back into the dreamy state of nothingness.

The scrape of a kitchen chair against the wood floor jarred her out of her languorous snooze.

"Blade," she mumbled. "Eating again."

She'd never known a man with such a tremendous appetite.

She closed her eyes. A chair scraped. And another. No, she decided, it must be the same one moving about. Who else but Blade would be in the kitchen in the depths of night? Plates clanked. Cupboards closed. Voices whispered.

Voices?

Ruth's hand stole up from the warmth beneath the sheets and pulled the quilt down below her neck. Her entire body tightened with anxiety. Of course it was Blade. And somebody else. Tsosi, perhaps. Jennie, the new maid. Maybe one of the field hands. Or a woman.

There was no reason it shouldn't be a woman. He was as virile as any man she'd ever known. Her ears fairly ached trying to listen—she was completely awake.

Out in the kitchen Grover and Sholes had decided to take advantage of the plentiful supply of food in the pantry before they delved through Phelan's papers in search of the treasure map, finely drawn and specifically locating the treasure. All they had to do was find it. But first, food.

"Kin you read?" Sholes asked as he shoved a fat Cornish pastie into his mouth. Crumbs flaked down to collect in his stringy beard along with the refuse from several other meals.

"Course I can read! Can't you?"

"Well, ah, sure. Everybody kin read. Some. I jist cain't read everythin'."

"Like what?" Grover had discovered the bottle of sherry on the pantry shelf and was bent on emptying it while he munched on cold chicken he'd discovered in the icebox.

Realizing he'd nearly let out a secret that would make Vanderdam extremely angry if he knew, Sholes grew bristly and defensive, raising his voice in order to intimidate the smaller man. "Writin'," he blustered. "Sometimes I cain't make out writin'."

"Oh," Grover said as he drained the bottle of sherry in a final swallow. "If script is poor I have a little trouble m'self." He stifled a belch.

In her bedroom, Ruth decided the only way to satisfy her bursting curiosity was to get out of bed and take a peek in the kitchen. She rummaged around for her warm woolen wrapper and and found one slipper. Blade obviously had a guest. The last snatches of conversation suggested it was another man, but instead of being pleased it wasn't some woman, she somehow experienced a sense of uneasiness. And she wasn't sure why.

Suddenly, she heard a torrent of cuss words foul enough to peel the paint off the wall. She realized someone had run into the cast-iron urn in the hallway. The knee-high vessel stuck out in the pathway of any unsuspecting person walking past.

"Shut your goddamn mouth!"

"I broke my friggin' ankle on some rock."

Ruth froze where she stood. A shaky hand rose to her lips, as if quelling the call rising in her throat.

The voices in the hall were loud enough for her to hear distinctly. Neither belonged to Gladius Blade.

The angry muttering just beyond Ruth's bedroom door stopped and footsteps started again. Stealthily moving forward. Where? The staircase?

Holding her breath, Ruth took one silent step across the rug, then another. She nearly let out a squawk of terror when her bare foot encountered a soft unexpected object on the carpet.

Her other slipper.

She pushed her foot into the felt and wiggled the footwear in place. Beyond the door she heard a loud creak as someone stepped on the defective third step on the staircase.

Unable to contain herself any longer, she moved quickly to the open doorway and peered toward the stairs.

Suddenly there was light!

The wide landing at the top of the stairs had been abruptly illuminated. The light cascaded down the steps and into the hallway.

"Oh shit!"

Ruth heard the piercing obscenity but when her startled gaze sought the source of the flare, she saw Gladius Blade on the stairway landing, holding a kerosene lamp in his hand. Ruth's stunned brain could barely function. She had never seen such a sight as Blade naked to the waist and covered only to the knees in a pair of fleece drawers which fitted his muscular form like his own skin. Ruth tried to swallow, but her mouth had gone mysteriously dry.

"Run, you peckerhead!"

The place exploded into motion.

Ruth turned away from Blade and saw two unknown men falling over one another to run back down the steps. Without thinking, she rushed out into the hallway to intercept them. She didn't get far.

The smaller of the two men shoved a flattened hand into the center of her chest as he dashed past her and sent her tumbling crazily on her rump. Her long woolen robe tangled around her legs and feet. She gave an angry cry as she tried to get up, then bounced backward rolling on the floor.

At the head of the stairs, Blade carefully set the lamp upon the rounded lamp stand above the newel post at the top of the balustrade and ran down the steep flight, leaping over the handrail before he reached the bottom. Racing after the intruders, he barely missed knocking Ruth over a second time as she struggled to stand.

In spite of his superior physical condition, Blade had little chance of catching the men. They were too far ahead, and too determined to escape. They pulled open the heavy front door, thundered down the stone steps, and disappeared into the blackness of the night. Blade stood in the doorway, oblivious of the winter air, and scrutinized the inky darkness.

"No sense going after them," he said. "I can't see a thing out there. It's black as the devil's hind end."

"Did you recognize them?"

He started at the sound of Ruth's voice in back of him. Slowly he closed the door and turned.

In the shadowy light she appeared very young. Hardly more than a girl. Her hair tumbled down like a Gypsy's, and the tie strings on her robe were askew, allowing him a peek at her pink nightgown.

Her face glowed with excitement and her eyes fairly sparkled. Blade felt the impulse to haul her into his arms, whirl her around till she was dizzy, tumble her to the carpet, and kiss her senseless.

He wanted her hot and hungry with desire for him.

She stopped, lips parted breathlessly, and stared at him. One quick glance at his bare chest left her face full of confusion.

With that glance Blade realized he was standing there in only his tight blue drawers which clearly revealed his erotic thoughts. He turned abruptly and walked into the parlor, tossing a chunk of wood on the flickering fire. His body alerted him to Ruth's presence behind him.

"If you're not too tired," he said, "you can make us some tea while I put some clothes on. I need to know what you saw so I can tell the sheriff."

"I'm not at all tired now."

"I'll be right back down." He left the room as quickly as he could.

Ruth wandered into the kitchen, wishing Jennie Begay hadn't chosen to stay with her aunt.

I'll feel better, she told herself, with another woman in the house.

Then she let out a horrified scream. The kitchen was in shambles!

From the back door, open to the night, across the room to the doorway where she stood, the floor was strewn with bones, brown paper wrappers, bread crusts, fruit peelings, empty bottles, and dirty dishes.

"I guess they had a little snack before robbing the place. Filthy beggers."

She grabbed the broom, stopping only a minute to set the tea kettle on the stove.

Within a short time the wooden floor was swept clean, the rugs had been shaken out, and all the refuse dumped into a barrel outside the door. Then she primly straightened her robe, ran her hands over her mussed hair and took a deep satisfied breath.

The tea kettle shrieked its readiness.

"Well, Mister Blade, I hope you're ready."

Ruth had arranged the teapot, cups, and a plate of buttered bread on a tray when Blade returned to the parlor.

She saw instantly that he'd pulled on his black trousers, but his forest green wool shirt hung open to the waist revealing a mat of thick auburn hair that formed a line, disappearing into his pants. She tried to keep her eyes from straying to the thatch. She wasn't surprised to see her fingers trembling as she poured the steaming tea.

From the moment she'd witnessed Blade at the top of the stairway with the lamp held high, casting a golden glow around his magnificent male body, she'd been mesmerized. Her body, her entire being, had yearned toward him. She understood what she desired. She'd been a married woman, after all. And yet she craved something more. Something beyond her experience.

She'd never seen a naked man in her entire life. Certainly Farley McKenna had never bared himself to her gaze. And even though he had not done so, Ruth recognized the vast differences between a man of Blade's brawny stature and Farley's slighter build. She perceived a certain disloyalty toward her late husband, accompanied by a sense of guilt and shame, but the unflattering comparison was there all the same.

The mere sight of Blade's body had agitated her more than she knew how to cope with. She'd wanted to scream at him to cover himself and get out of her sight almost as much as she wanted to throw herself into his arms and feel his muscular warmth.

"Do you want some jam on this bread?" she asked, proud that her voice escaped her quavering throat.

"No, thanks. Are you warm enough?"

"I'm fine."

She didn't sound fine to him. She sounded as distraught as he felt. He nearly convinced himself it was the fault of the prowlers. But the tension in the air held something more elemental than fear.

Blade settled himself down beside her on the sofa and instantly cursed himself for yielding to the temptation to sit so close. He felt her tremble.

Clenching his hands into knotted fists to keep them from reaching over and pulling her hard against him, Blade tried without much success to cool the blood pulsating through his body. He managed to pick up a teacup without dumping it and lifted it to his lips.

With fingers as icy as stone, Ruth mimicked his actions. She wondered if he realized how uncomfortable his nearness made her feel.

"Did you get a good look at those men?"

"Not really. The light was dim down where they were . . ." Her voice trailed off as once again she visualized the splendor of Blade's body on the landing. She cleared her throat and licked her lips. "I guess I was too dumbfounded to pay attention. I thought it was you."

"What?" He turned his body to face her, his knee moving onto the sofa. It touched her thigh.

"I heard noises in the kitchen." Ruth could barely breathe. Had he purposely placed his leg against hers? "I thought you were fixing yourself something to eat. It never occurred to me housebreakers would have a meal before they prowled the rest of the house!"

"They ate our food?" Blade wondered if his voice sounded normal. Was it his perverted imagination, or did their blood pulse with the same rhythm?

"Lots of it. Most of it, in fact. And made a disgusting mess in the process."

"Well, I'll be damned. Maybe all they wanted was some food."

"Do you think so?" Her voice was hopeful.

"No," he answered softly. There were already too many lies on his conscience. He wouldn't be guilty of another.

Not with what was happening between them. He wondered if she knew. Surely she knew. He suspected she had little experience in spite of several years of marriage. Yet unless she was dead inside, she surely detected the taut sexual tension between them.

Flames danced sinuously in the stone fireplace. Scarlet and yellow fingers blazed wild and hot. Blade watched for a time before he spoke.

"I'm going to ride to town and talk to Sheriff Cameron."

"You think those men were burglars?"

"Probably. This place is too remote to be visited by a couple of bums just looking for something to eat. That sort of thing goes on by the railroad tracks, but not out here."

"Is there anything here of value?" Ruth pulled herself into the corner of the sofa.

Blade shrugged. Mrs. Phillips, the lady who leased the house to Phelan, owned good furniture and many fine ornaments; but Blade knew that none of those things had tempted the intruders.

The fire popped and a rainbow of sparks flared for an instant.

He decided Ruth needed to know the facts, at least

the important ones. "Your brother talked a lot about finding treasure."

"Oh sure." She chuckled. "Dirt, bones, broken pottery." Then she gasped. "My God, somebody asked me about treasure the night I arrived in Flagstaff."

"Where was that?"

"At the Birdcage . . . ah, the Yellow Bird . . ." She groped for the right name. "The cafe."

"The Yellow Canary. Hertha Bird's place."

"Yes. Some cowboy asked me."

"What did you answer?"

"I laughed, I think. And told him of course Donal found a treasure. Does someone really believe his treasure was something of value to more than a scholar?"

"He believed his treasures were of value to mankind."

"I know that, Blade. I listened to his theories for most of my life. But did somebody finally believe him?"

"Not about the pot shards and skeletal remains. But somehow people got the idea your brother was digging for Coronado's gold."

"Coronado the explorer? As in the Seven Cities of Gold? Who is that naive?"

"Quite a few people, I gather. Our midnight prowlers."

"Where on earth did folks get such an absurd idea?"

Blade looked over at the fire. The blaze had died down a little so he got up from the sofa and added more wood, pushing the fuel onto the pile with his foot. He stood with his arm resting against the mantel enjoying the warmth as it heated his flat belly. He wondered what he should tell her. The whole truth showed her brother in a bad light.

"Blade, did Donal tell the people of Flagstaff he was looking for Coronado's gold?"

"Not exactly."

She was off the sofa in a flash and jerking him around to face her before either of them could think what was happening.

"Don't lie to me," she yelled. "I'm sick of men lying to me. And don't give me any nonsense about trying to protect me. All my life I've suffered because men thought I was soft and frail. And female. What in the devil did my brother do?"

Blade couldn't have been more stunned if she'd picked up a stick of firewood and beaten him with it. She was so damn prim and proper on the outside but a veritable tornado of emotions beneath the surface. He wanted to shout with joy and laugh at the same time, but he knew she'd murder him if he so much as cracked a smile. He decided to try a little honesty.

"Phelan told various people various stories." Blade took a deep breath. He could feel the logs ignite behind his legs. His denim pants grew hot against his skin. "Your brother manipulated people when it suited him. Not everybody understood what he did, what his work stood for. If someone like that could help his cause, he simply concocted a story that suited the listener."

She lowered her gaze for a moment to his open shirt and the flatness of his stomach beneath it. He could feel her thoughts and his stomach clenched automatically. He wanted to lower her to the rug right there in front of the fire and ignite her with his lovemaking. But he spoke to her of Phelan instead.

"A couple years ago your brother ran out of money. Some of his financial backers had reneged on their promises and pulled out of the expedition. Phelan was left with a lot of debts and a dream he wanted to fulfill."

"And he bamboozled another backer using the old Seven Cities of Gold legend," she finished. "How convenient that Coronado tromped somewhere near the site of the excavation."

Blade reached out and touched her hair. It was soft and silky. He tangled his fingers in its thickness and smelled her light flower-in-the-rain scent. With an undisguised groan he stepped toward her.

"It's not right!" she snapped and turned from him, stopping when he twisted his hand tight against the back of her neck. His thumb caressed the tender skin.

"Ruth, I know you feel this, too."

"It's not right."

Blade dropped his hand, and sighed. She moved back to the edge of the sofa. Away from temptation.

"I wish he hadn't flimflammed people."

"I suspect he felt he had no other choice."

She turned to study him gravely. "You agreed with his atrocious conduct? You think it's all right to lie and cheat? To assume the end justifies the means?"

Blade gave a short laugh. He couldn't believe he was defending Phelan's behavior. Not after what it had cost him and his father. "Hell no! He was an arrogant bastard, and he used people whenever he needed to. But I understand some of his motives. And I understand his genius."

She shook her head, wondering how many times she'd excused unscrupulous behavior on Donal's part because of his genius.

"And sometimes I even liked him."

"Did he cheat you? Or string you along with tales of gold and glory as he did the others?"

Blade sensed her sadness. He wished he had the power to alleviate her pain, but he honestly did not. "No," he answered. "I'm not as naive as some. And not as greedy as others."

"Then why did you come here? It couldn't have been for what he paid you."

He grinned his agreement. It certainly hadn't been the pay that had lured him out to the excavation site. "Some things are more important to a man than money. Such as the opportunity to do something you're very good at. Also the opportunity to contribute something important that few others have the ability to do. For me, this was a chance to show the world—my world—how good I really am, and that what I love to do is worthwhile."

"So Donal didn't swindle you."

"Look at me, Ruth. I'm the biggest ox in the territory. I may have a gentle soul, but most men don't know that. Your brother included. He didn't dare swindle me. I'm big enough to break a man's neck and not even breathe hard doing it."

A scandalous thrill shot through her. She lifted her chin and dared him. The danger made her heart pound.

"What about a woman?" she whispered.

A shaft of fire hit him in the gut. Little witch. Tossing a dagger into a game she was scared to play.

"Damn you, Ruth." His voice was liquid velvet.

Her cheeks flamed and she turned her body away, ashamed at her wanton behavior. What on earth had come over her? Why she'd practically thrown herself on the carpet and tossed her skirt over her head. Dear Lord, had she gone mad?

"I'm sorry."

Blade came up behind her and placed both hands on her shoulders, holding her a gentle prisoner. "Don't apologize. I asked you before if you felt it, too. The attraction between us. Now I know without question you do."

"It's not right."

"Right or wrong, it's there, lady."

"Nothing can come of it."

He gave a soft chuckle, and leaned down to nuzzle the tendrils curling at the back of her neck. "Ruth. Relax. You're perfectly safe with me."

She stood stiff as a fence post, poised to flee.

"Relax. I'm not going to hurt you. That's the last thing I want to do."

"That girl . . . Jennie. I want her to move in tomorrow."

Exasperated, Blade forced her to turn and look at him.

"Woman, listen to me. I won't hurt you. Do you understand?"

His finger beneath her chin compelled her to look at his face. "You trust me?"

"Yes."

"This time say it like you mean it."

Her head flew back and she glared at him, her mouth pursed in anger, her eyes openly defiant.

"Mister Blade, I trust you," she spat at him.

He nearly laughed. Witch. "Mrs. McKenna, if I had been going to have my wicked way with you, I would have done it the other night when I undressed you."

"Ohhh!"

"I had plenty of time. You didn't seem to care at all.

I just kept taking layers of clothes off and you went right on snoring. I could have done anything evil I wanted, if I'd been so inclined."

She punched him in the chest as hard as she could.

"Ouch! Damn, that hurt." He was laughing, teasing her more. He grabbed both her hands in one big paw and twisted so both of them fell to the sofa. She lay across his lap with her hands stretched above her head.

"Damn it, Ruth. Behave yourself." Blade tried to ignore the erotic picture she made.

"I hate you, Gladius Blade."

He didn't laugh. Instead he reached over and straightened her gapping robe. Then he let her hands fall.

He watched as she fought for composure.

"I won't hurt you, Ruth. Not ever."

She nodded, closing her eyes so he couldn't see her emotions.

"Truce?"

Again she nodded.

"I need to ride into town and see the sheriff. Do you remember anything about our visitors? The glare of the lamplight altered my vision. I didn't see much."

"It all happened so fast I only got a glimpse of them. The taller, skinny one had a ratty gray beard. The little guy was shorter than I. He's the one who hit me."

"What?" Blade sat up straight and nearly bounced her off his lap. His arm snaked around her waist and held her still. She made no effort to move.

"He hit me right here when he ran past." She indicated her breastbone. "I think he bruised me."

Blade's free hand lifted to the front of her robe, parted the lapels and fingered the top button. Slowly he opened it and moved down to the next. Ruth watched his face and concentrated on breathing.

When he unfastened the third button, he parted the sides of the nightgown and looked at her. Although her skin appeared a bit reddened, there was no sign of bruising. With a sureness of hand he did not feel, he rebuttoned the gown to the neck. Only then did he look at her face.

What he saw there threatened to slay all his good intentions. Lips parted, nostrils flared, skin flushed with heat. Had ever a woman beckoned her lover more? And her eyes, deep lake blue, said more than words ever could. They spoke of a hunger never sated, passion long untouched.

And of fear.

He broke the spell. "I have to go," he said finally.

"Now?"

"Yes. I told you I was taking you out to the dig tomorrow. I need to talk to Sheriff Cameron first."

"It's cold and dark outside. And those crooks are out there."

"Are you actually worried about me?"

She reached her hand over and touched his shirt just below the pulse point in his neck. "Yes. I don't want you hurt."

He was suddenly humbled. "Thank you. But I'll be all right. If I leave now, I can see Cameron and be back here in time for us to ride out to the dig. You do ride a horse, don't you?"

"Well enough not to fall off."

He shifted her in his arms then and stood up, pulling her along with him. With his arm around her waist, he led her down the hall.

"Where are you taking me?" she asked, trying hard to keep the anxiety out of her voice.

"To bed," he answered. "I made a wish the other night and I'm about to make it come true."

"What wish?"

Blade entered her bedroom, lifted her onto the bed, and leaned down, and brushed his lips over hers in a feather touch. Then he tugged the covers up to her chin.

"I wished that you would be conscious the next I put you in bed." He walked to the door. "I think my next wish will be more selfish. I'll wish that you reach up and pull me into bed with you."

He shut the door, delighting in her shocked expression.

7

Ruth balanced herself on one foot as she pushed the other into the rugged brown leather boot and tugged it over her stocking and up the leg of her underwear. She was breathing hard when she finished.

She straightened, glancing at her slender figure in the wardrobe mirror, trying for the first time in her life to see herself as a man might see her.

The mirror reflected a rather serious woman in her underwear and work boots. The blue gray Australian worsted union suit fitted her neatly. She didn't have a perfect body, she decided after a moment's consideration. Although her waist was naturally slender, her hips weren't nearly wide enough for fashion. And her legs were too long. Her bosom, however, perked high and full against the knitted garment without aid of any of the rubberized deceivers some other woman used.

Her nipples jutted shockingly outward against the

soft union suit. She wondered what Blade would think if he witnessed her posturing before the mirror.

"Dear God, what an awful thought!" Her cheeks colored in the lamplight.

Without further foolishness she shrugged into a plain white chemise and knickers, smoothing them over the union suit and picked up a simple corset, fastening it quickly before she opened the wardrobe door.

"We really shouldn't go today," she said as she thrust her arm into a shirtsleeve. "Not after Blade's ride into town. He should stay home and get some rest."

If truth be told, she hadn't slept much herself after he left for town. Her mind was too troubled.

While she argued with herself about the sanity of riding out to the excavation, she nonetheless prepared for the trip. Blade was a stubborn man.

She stepped into the snuff-colored, brown canvas divided skirt, dragging the coarse, closely woven material over her hips to button snugly at her waist. Finally she slipped the matching vest over a soft rose shirtwaist, fastening it down the front. She looked ready to conquer the world.

She'd had the durable brown riding outfit made especially to survive the rigors of an archaeological expedition many years before—the first time, in fact, that she'd spent the entire summer in the field with her brother. The first time she'd met Farley McKenna.

She remembered her brother's amusement when she told him she'd been forced to buy boy's work boots because no woman's footwear was sturdy enough. She also recalled Farley's look of distaste. Later, of course, Farley realized just how valuable a companion she was on a dig, but at first he'd argued against Donal's decision to bring her along.

In those days Farley had been a bit of a chauvinist, believing a lady belonged in the parlor to flutter and flirt while a man owned the world. She wondered what Blade thought of women.

"Ruth! I'm back," he said suddenly outside her door. The bedroom door flung open and his enormous form filled the opening.

She caught her breath, trying to still her pounding heart.

His craggy face was ruddy from the morning ride. "Let me wash up while I have a cup of coffee. Then we can go. Hey, you look great! What is that you're wearing?"

"A riding costume," she answered, turning around so he could view it. "Actually, it's an archaeological costume, designed especially to tromp around the digs. I've had it for years." She picked up the matching brown canvas jacket and brushed past him. "I've packed a big lunch. I'll be ready to go when you are."

While she waited, she poured some vinegar over a dish of canned salmon and set the covered dish in the icebox to chill. It would make a fine supper when they returned.

Blade checked to see if Tsosi had taken care of the horse he'd ridden into town. He needn't have worried. The young Navajo had unsaddled the big black stallion and rubbed him down, and was now measuring out a good portion of grain.

The black pranced in anticipation.

"Pour him out an extra ration," Blade said. "He deserves it this morning."

"Did Sheriff Cameron know who came here last night?" Tsosi asked as he finished feeding the horse. He gave its nose a special rub and set a fresh bucket of water nearby before he turned his attention to the other horses.

In an area where a man's life sometimes depended on the animal he rode, it was not only being kind to the beasts to make sure they were well taken care of, it was smart. The horses at the ranch were very well cared for. Tsosi was one of the best wranglers in the territory.

"No idea at all. How about you? Any idea why somebody would want to break in and eat our grub?"

"Nope. I didn't hear nothing, either." He brought Phelan's chestnut mare out of her stall and saddled her.

Ginger, the mare, was docile and well behaved. Phelan hadn't been the best horseman in the country, and he had a curious habit of dismounting and wandering off to look at something that caught his attention. Other horses had taken off and left him stranded. Ginger stood quietly and waited for the man while he studied flora or fauna, or lost himself in wonder over what had occurred centuries before.

Blade saddled his own gelding. He'd ridden the stallion to town because the black was fast on the open road. The roan had a better temperament and was more surefooted in the wilderness.

A few moments later Blade led both horses out of the stable. Tsosi stood talking to the stallion, who was his favorite. He looked moody and forlorn.

As Blade walked up to the back door Ruth emerged from the kitchen with a bountiful lunch she'd stowed in two flour sacks knotted together.

"Ready," she said as she locked the back door and handed him the key. She turned toward Ginger.

To her surprise, Blade bent down and handed her up. Neither Donal nor Farley had ever bothered, assuming rightly if she wanted to go along she'd fend for herself. She swung lightly into the saddle.

Blade watched her without comment. She had a lot of pluck. Not many women could have handled the situation she was in with so much sense and spirit.

The West was a rough place, and often city-bred women couldn't adjust. She'd not only endured the loss of a husband and subsequent drop in finances, she'd also lost her brother, her one hope for security. And here she was ready to take on a rigorous trail ride with the same cheerful attitude other women had for attending a party.

Blade's initial respect grew in that moment, along with an a somewhat unsettling fondness.

"Is something amiss?" she asked. "You're looking at me strangely."

"No," he answered quickly. "I was just . . . ah, admiring your riding costume." He waved, taking in the brown canvas outfit, tan felt boater, and high boots. "It looks quite serviceable." It looked like something he'd like to strip off her. The vision of Ruth as Lady Godiva, wearing nothing but her long silky hair, flashed through his mind.

Quickly he swung into his own saddle and led the way northeast, past the stable and the cabin, across the end of the large clearing and up an incline into tall Ponderosa pines.

He'd deliberately refrained from describing any of the areas they would be passing. It would be interesting to see if her initial reaction mirrored his own when she saw the natural wonders just ahead. And so he led them through the trees, circling a bit south and then north again to emerge suddenly upon a cindered landscape more kindred to the moon than to earth.

"Oh my word!" Ruth's eyes widened as she pulled Ginger to a halt. She sat still in the saddle, turning her head in wonder. "Black sand dunes. And the mountain!"

Ebony black dunes, round, smooth with only a few wind ripples, rose straight ahead of their path, and to the left of the trail, jutting a thousand feet up to the cloudless sky, stood a mountain black at the bottom and red on top. Snow dusted the top.

"The dunes are volcanic cinders. They're not nearly as smooth as sand, but more like fine gravel. The mountain over there is an enormous cinder cone. A volcano."

"It was so sudden . . . like it popped out of nowhere."

"Impressive, isn't it? Every time I see it I'm enthralled. I'll bet I've drawn it a dozen times, in different seasons and at different times of the day." He looked startled at mentioning his drawing to her. Over the years he'd learned to curb his enthusiasm for art in public. "The cone was named Sunset Peak by John Wesley Powell when he came through in eighty-five doing a geological survey."

"The red top against all that stark black is amazing."

"Powell thought so, too. The last volcanic eruption was red, while the others obviously were black. The contrast is so great that Powell said when he first saw the mountain from a distance the peak seemed to be on fire."

"I wish I could see it that way. It must be wonderful."

"Maybe someday we'll find you a place to look at it from a distance. By the time we get all of your brother's affairs squared away it will be summer, and we can take a trip and see what Powell meant."

Blade nudged the roan and they continued on up the trail, around the cinder mountain until they came upon a primal tangle of furious jagged rock extending as far as Ruth could see. It was as if some raging river from hell suddenly froze in its rampage to destroy everything in its path.

Once again Ruth stopped her horse and stared in awe at the ruthlessly barren landscape nature had wrought.

"What an incredible force it must have been to create this!"

"The locals estimate the lava flow might go as deep as a hundred feet."

"Amazing."

"The river of lava cooled first on the bottom right next to the ground, and then on the top where the air hit it. But inside it was still hot and flowing. Lava tubes—or ice caves, as the folks hereabout call them— formed when the hot lava inside drained from the hard outer cores."

"Why ice caves, Blade?"

"Because ice forms inside the hollow core and it lasts all year round. That's where everybody hereabouts gets their ice. The hotels, restaurants, saloons— even the ice in our own icebox comes from the ice caves."

"I'll have to study the ice in our icebox when I get home."

He chuckled, remembering that Phelan said he had done just that when he found out about the lava tubes.

"I can't imagine how Donal managed to contain his excitement. He was probably racing from one end of the area to the other, trying to take it all in."

"He was still doing that when I met him." Blade noticed her enthusiasm, experiencing something akin to jealousy—though he refused to admit it. If he was going to be jealous of a dead man it should have been her husband, not her brother.

"You loved him very much." His voice was soft.

"I adored him!" She laughed. "Every brilliant, difficult, delightful, impossible atom of him. He was the most wonderful and horrible older brother any little girl could have. He raised me, you know."

"No, I didn't."

"I imagine our mother has turned in her grave many times at the way he did it. Mother was such a proper lady." She chuckled naughtily. "I mentioned that to him one time, and he flashed that devastating smile of his and said everybody needed a new perspective now and again. Even Mama."

"Were you very young when your mother died?" Blade couldn't imagine Phelan being in charge of a young child. Dear Lord, the man could well have forgotten her for days on end!

"Almost nine. Mama and Papa were taking a trip down the Mississippi to New Orleans—I was staying with family friends and Donal was off on some summer college excursion. I remember getting a letter saying they were having a wonderful visit and returning soon. Mama wrote she'd bought me a special French doll. On the way upriver there was an explosion . . ." She didn't continue.

"You don't have to talk about it. I apologize for my rudeness in asking."

Ruth shook her head. "The worst part was there was no way to get word to Donal. He'd graduated from Harvard in June and was somewhere in the wilderness with some of his professors. It was more than a month before he got back."

Blade thought of his own mother's death. What would he have done if the whole family hadn't supported one another?

"I thought he was dead, too. I was just a silly little kid and I was certain he was gone and I was an orphan." She was silent a moment. "I guess that's how I feel now."

He nodded. She was coping quite well considering her whole safe world had been destroyed over the last year. "Did you continue to stay with friends after Phelan came back?"

"Only about two weeks. Donal was very close to my parents and when he discovered their deaths he went wild with grief. It was awful. He actually disappeared for a few days. Looking back, I suppose he got very drunk, but at the time his absence terrified me. Then he came back, sold the family house, and liquidated most of my father's assets. It was all done in an incredible whirlwind fashion. The next thing I knew, I was whisked off to Boston and plunked in a good boarding school."

She studied the landscape for a moment. "Donal continued his studies at Harvard. I got a fine education with the nuns. And summertimes I spent with Donal. At first he would take me back to Saint Louis where I would stay with Mama's cousin, and he would see me as often as he could; but as soon as I was old enough I'd accompany him on whatever dig he was working on."

"That's how you learned to read his handwriting?"

She nodded. "I became very knowledgeable about archaeological sites and expeditions. After I left school I lived with him full time, and I became his right arm. It was because of him I learned to use the typing machine."

Blade saw a look of sorrow pass through her eyes. He thought it was because of her loss.

"Unfortunately," she continued, "right after that everything fell apart. Within a couple of weeks, as a matter of fact. Farley asked me to marry him. Donal absolutely forbade it. He said Farley was much too old for me, and not the sort of man I needed anyway. And Farley said Donal was just mad because his workhorse was running off. It was rather sudden, I guess, and Donal did depend on me to care for him . . ." She shook her head, still not understanding the explosion that followed. "Anyway, Farley convinced me to elope. A big wedding, he said, was a very public way of announcing a very private matter."

Blade ground his teeth. He wondered if Farley McKenna had every done one thing for Ruth's sake.

"So we eloped. Donal met us at the train station. He was like a crazy man. He accused me of all sorts of harlotry, and Farley of being a thief. Of stealing some journal he'd written on that last expedition we'd all been on together. And of publishing a scientific paper using Donal's theories. Frankly, I was astonished—I never expected Donal Phelan to be so petty."

"That surprises me, too. The whole affair sounds

foolish. What man in his right mind would expect his sister to stay with him forever? Especially when the sister is as lovely as you?"

Ruth flushed in embarrassment. "Especially a sister who is twenty-four years old," she said forthrightly.

"It doesn't make sense," Blade went on. "Surely he had to know that sooner or later some man would spirit you away. Certainly Phelan understood the ways of the flesh!" He gasped in astonishment at his own outburst, but Ruth apparently didn't notice.

The horses continued to pick their way carefully around the volcanic rubble.

She wondered if Blade did find her attractive. There were times she saw things in his look that confused and excited her. She'd had so little experience with suitors—Donal had made short work of most of them—she honestly didn't know what Blade thought.

And her feelings for him? She didn't lie to herself. She didn't deny her attraction to him, especially after seeing him bare-chested on the landing last night. And she didn't deny her need for his emotional support. But that was it in a nutshell—she was vulnerable. Not since the death of her parents had she been so defenseless, so completely susceptible to the kindness of another.

"I wish we had worked out the problems," she said with a sigh. "I tried writing to him. Several times. And I know Farley sent him a copy of his book when it came out. I thought that was very big of Farley because Donal's accusations cut him to the quick." She paused, looking quite forlorn. "Naturally, I wrote when Farley died. But my brother never communicated with me once after that fight at the train depot. It was as if I didn't exist anymore."

Blade frowned. Somehow that didn't sound like Phelan. Granted he was a law unto himself. But he had his own brand of honor and integrity. It didn't fit with ignoring his sister when she needed him or abandoning her to destitution.

"I always believed Donal was destined to be great. I wish I could have shared this expedition with him. Maybe I still can by putting his notes and your drawings in a book. It's his last chance at greatness."

Blade was still pondering Phelan's cavalier treatment of Ruth. He'd known the archaeologist over two years and never guessed he had a sister. He'd mentioned his father and occasionally his mother—her strict insistence upon proper manners. But never Ruth. Perhaps she was right when she said she'd ceased to exist for Phelan that night at the train station. How could he have been such a bastard?

"You know better than anybody else, Blade. What had he actually found at this dig?"

"A lot of nothing."

Ruth jerked her head around at the sharpness of Blade's tone. "Donal Phelan would not spend more than two years of his life in an area that was producing nothing!"

"Sorry." Blade said. "I didn't mean to offend you. Phelan has worked hard, and often without finances, but nothing he's come up with so far makes much sense."

"How so?"

"He told me that what brought him here originally were the journals of Lieutenant Lorenzo Sitgreaves. Sitgreaves had been given the assignment of finding overland transportation routes through the recently acquired New Mexico Territory. When his party probed west of the Little Colorado River in 1851, they climbed up an old trail and found themselves among a landscape of ruins."

He thought a moment, recalling what Phelan said was in the journal.

"Sitgreaves wrote that he saw broken pottery everywhere. Stone dwellings occupied all the prominent points of land—some of them as big as three stories tall."

"Three stories? That's incredible!"

"There was no sign of life, so Sitgreaves concluded the houses had been abandoned long ago. Due to lack of water, he thought. But he had the field artist who was with him make drawings of the ruins he found."

"And that's what attracted Donal's attention," Ruth finished. "He was adamant about pictorial documentation. Even when he was young. Aren't there some multilevel stone houses north of here?"

"Northeast. And a considerable distance if I remember correctly."

"Donal was enthusiastic about them even before I left. He called the people the Ancient Ones."

Blade nodded. "He spent some time there, but said he just couldn't forget the drawings in Sitgreaves's journal. So he hotfooted it down here."

"And decided here he must stay."

"Not exactly. At first he didn't find much. Then somebody told him about a prospector who had a homestead out this way and who had a lot of artifacts."

"Oh, dear. I suppose Donal made a complete jackass out of himself. He always did get livid at the thought of people removing any little artifact from a historical site before the artifact and the location were documented. Context is one of the archaeologist's most important tools in drawing conclusions about prehistoric people."

"I've heard this lecture before, Ruth." he said dryly. "More than once."

"Sorry."

"It boggles the mind that a man who was so demanding about complete and thorough documentation could have lived like a pig."

"Doesn't it? So, did he throttle the prospector?"

"He hired him."

"I don't believe it!"

"Hired him as a guide. The fellow led him to the ruins Sitgreaves wrote about."

"Then what?"

"Once your brother saw the value of the site, he charged off to find financial backers. And apparently the other guy went back to his hunt for Spanish gold."

"Oh no, not Spanish gold."

Blade chuckled. "There have been rumors of Spanish gold since white men first came out here."

"So the site we're going to is the ruins Lieutenant Sitgreaves wrote about."

"No. Those ruins are about forty miles northeast of Flagstaff. The original plan was to bring a crew to Flagstaff, taking permanent hotel rooms and moving back and forth between the site and town. But the money he expected never materialized."

"Why? He never had trouble raising money before."

Blade wondered if he should tell her about the ugly accusations that had blemished Phelan's scholarly reputation. He decided he'd wait. She was enjoying herself. Why spoil her day?

"Who knows?" he answered. "Anyway, he came out here with a skeleton crew and leased the Phillips ranch. It hadn't been available when he was here earlier. But Mrs. Phillips had recently lost her husband, shortly after the deaths of her mother and two children, and she was anxious to leave. The ranch became the base of operation." Blade halted the gelding and dismounted. "Let's take a breather."

"Fine with me." She hadn't expected help in dismounting, but Blade swung her down.

"When did you get here?" Ruth stretched and walked over to study the view.

"Later. That first summer there wasn't money to pay a field artist. Phelan hired a photographer to come out for a couple weeks and photograph the site. Then he and the students mapped out the area and wrote up a fairly impressive description of the site. They even excavated one sandstone crypt and found a woman buried with some beautiful pottery and some fine jewelry with turquoise mosaics."

"Exciting!"

"Apparently the backers didn't think so. They withdrew their support in the fall of ninety-four. Phelan had a long lease on the ranch, so he stayed and worked by himself for a while. But the winter was severe and more often than not he was snowed in. Eventually he came to San Francisco looking for backers. . . ."

"And conned some poor unsuspecting fool into thinking think he was after Coronado's gold," Ruth finished. "How like him!"

They walked along leading the horses.

It rankled when Blade thought how gullible his father had been. Yet, he supposed old Seamus would always be a treasure hunter. At least Phelan believed in the treasures he sought.

"I guess the backers of archaeological expeditions are a strange breed. They're willing to put down hard money for the thrill of being in on the discovery of something new and exciting. Maybe it's a way of buying immortality. Maybe just a highbrow way to gamble. At least with Phelan they got something for their money. Even if one man's treasure is another man's junk."

The sun had reached its midmorning position when Moses Bigboy appeared out of nowhere and slowly approached the cabin of Marie Manyhorses. He'd given much thought to the words of Jaspar Bird, and though he disliked the white man, he felt himself at the mercy of Bird's whims. The land on which Moses lived in his comfortable hogan belonged to Bird.

Moses was an old man who had lived many years and walked many miles with adversity. Right now his life was comfortable. He had a warm hogan, plenty of firewood, a nearby spring for water, and enough food to last till the weather got warm. He didn't want to leave his home. Yet he was a proud man with a keen sense of honor. He thought long about the words he would say to the people he visited.

It wasn't good that Jaspar Bird ordered him to lie about Donal Phelan's ghost. Jaspar Bird was not a good man.

But it wasn't a good thing either that Donal Phelan unearthed the bones of the Ancient Ones, forcing their ghosts to walk among the living, scattering all sorts of mischief and sickness.

Could it be that Phelan died of ghost sickness?

Moses pondered that chilling thought.

Tsosi saw the old man as he approached and called for his mother. Marie walked out into the morning sun. She appeared thin but was recovering from the strange malady that felled her. She waved a greeting to Moses, who was her late husband's relative, and waited for him to approach.

Jennie also came out of the cabin and watched the old man.

They sat in the yard and talked for a spell, and Jennie fixed them food. Moses spoke of many things, and they listened politely, waiting for him to reach the reason for his visit. It would have been impolite for anyone to rush him.

He took a stick from the small fire that burned where they sat and poked it at a beetle that crawled from a burning log.

"People are talking about the white man who died," he said at last.

"Donal Phelan," Tsosi said.

The old man nodded. "I've heard talk that his ghost walks."

Donal Phelan's ruin was an island of red sandstone surrounded by a wash of black cinders. Centuries of winds and rains had stripped the site, exposing the underlying stone structure, leaving it standing like a fortress against the sky.

The walls of cut, squared, and smoothed rock rose to a height of three stories, but it was hard to tell where the walls began and the bedrock ended. The ruin appeared to have grown from the very rock itself.

The dwelling had nine small rooms, the largest of which appeared never to have been roofed.

"Phelan thought this was a work area or community patio," Blade said.

"Since these other rooms are so small and dark," Ruth said, "the people must have lived outdoors most of the time."

She stopped to examine a fire pit with a deflector rock mounted between it and the ventilating hole in the wall.

In one room the builders had joined walls to some already standing. The seam was obvious because the building stones of the new room couldn't be interlocked with those of the old. Parts of the new wall had collapsed and fallen intact.

To Ruth's practiced eye, it was obvious that the sloping ground along one side of the ruin was a rubbish heap.

"I'm surprised Donal didn't excavate the trash pile."

"He was more interested in digging out the rooms first. Perhaps in hopes he'd find something to excite the investors."

"Did he?"

"Mostly odds and ends. Stuff that fascinates scholars but not the backers." He walked over to one of the rooms. "In here he found seven infant burials in slab-lined pits."

"How grim."

"Your brother found out that the Hopi Indians, a tribe that lives near here, has a belief about the spirit of the deceased child being reborn in the next baby. He speculated that the ancient people shared a similar belief."

"I don't imagine the financial wizards were thrilled with that finding."

"I doubt if they were told. Dead babies don't make good publicity."

She looked around some more. "Why was this structure abandoned?"

"No one knows for certain. Phelan had some theories."

Ruth's laughter peeled out. "He had an abundance of theories."

Blade grinned in agreement. Seeing her so enthusiastic about the place where he'd labored for two years made him feel good. He'd worried so much lately about his father's health and his investment that he forgot the importance of the expedition.

"Come here. Let me show you." He led her to one of the outer rooms which had a door leading outside—a door much larger than the others. "Phelan called this the tragedy room."

Ruth looked around the bare, empty space. There was an oppressive aura to the room. She dreaded the answer to the question she was about to ask? "Why?"

"This is the only room in which Phelan uncovered any evidence of violence. Here he found the skeletal remains of a young woman whose left leg had been wrenched from the socket, either at the time of her death or shortly after. And that leg had been deliberately broken in two places."

"How gruesome."

"Two other bodies—one baby and one adult—had crushed skulls, and all the long bones had been broken."

"Did Donal have any idea why?"

Blade shrugged. "He had three theories: a raid by some nomadic tribe, violence among tribe members themselves, or some form of tribal justice."

"That makes sense."

"Phelan felt certain that whatever the reason for the tragic deaths, those deaths were linked to the abandonment of the pueblo."

He saw her questioning look and answered. "The bodies were never buried. They were simply dumped and left. Apparently the rest of the people walked away and never returned."

Blade turned and walked out of the ruin. "I need something to eat." He walked down the incline and headed toward the horses. When he had spread the blanket neatly and set out the lunch, he took a sketch pad and began to draw. With a few swift strokes he captured Ruth as she poked among the ruins, her awe and delight, her intelligent curiosity, her exquisite face.

"Boyo, you're in sad shape," he muttered as he studied the picture. "A big fellow like you mooning over a pencil drawing."

Ruth walked around to the other side of the ruin, which faced out over the edge of a collapsed earth crack forming vertical rock faces six to twenty feet high. She stood on an outcropping and surveyed the landscape to the east of the excavation site. Even in the midday sun there was a hazy quality to the seemingly endless expanse of purple-hued land, rusty mesas, and cloudless blue sky. A raven flew in and perched on the ruin behind her, helping her keep the watch.

"Woman, I'm about to faint from hunger."

She simply laughed. "Go away. I'm communing with nature."

"It's my nature I'm worried about. Come on over. I have your picnic all spread out on the blanket and ready for sumptuous dining. And I have a hunger in me for the food you packed."

"I'll be right there. Just as soon as I crawl back over these rocks."

"Wait! Stay right there. It will take less time if I help you down."

When he appeared below her, she sat down, thrust herself forward and slipped toward him. For a second she thought she was falling and gave a startled cry, but instantly his steely hands caught her thighs and she was jerked against him.

Blade stumbled backward a few steps but righted himself and stood still, lowering her slowly down the length of his body, his hands moving up her hips.

Hard, slow beats drummed in her chest.

It's the excitement, she told herself. The excitement of jumping. And the danger.

And partly she was correct.

It was dangerous—being hugged against him.

He was dangerous.

She smelled the sunshine on his auburn hair, and felt the rock-hard muscles of his shoulders.She heard the sharp intake of his breath as he lowered her down, and saw his brown eyes heat with fire. And she wanted to taste him. Wanted his hot mouth on hers.

Her blood pounded so hard she feared he might hear it. Somehow she stopped her downward slide to the earth. His hands tightened as they slipped up to her waist, ending her descent to the ground. He held her level with his own face.

She opened her mouth to protest, but forgot what she planned to say as soon as she met his eyes. The tip of her pink tongue slipped out and moistened a tiny spot in the middle of her bottom lip.

A groan tore from Blade's throat.

Heat coiled through her body. Anticipation teased her brain.

"Ruth," he whispered. He lowered her a few inches, savoring the softness of her body as it rested against his. Her arms tightened around his neck. She leaned her face close.

"Blade?"

He gently kissed her forehead, then one closed eye and the other. He moved to the corner of her mouth and over to the other. Then ever so slowly he ran the tip of his tongue over the very spot hers had so recently moistened.

Then abruptly he set her on the ground and dropped his arms. Ruth nearly fell over.

She opened her eyes to watch Blade marching down the incline and across the stony flat to where he'd laid out the picnic.

She had no idea what to do next. Obviously she'd misread the situation.

She stood there, scarlet with mortification, on the verge of weeping. She who seldom shed a tear.

"Come on and get some lunch." His voice was as cold as the sudden gust of wind off the San Francisco Peaks.

Lunch! The last thing on earth she wanted was a chopped meat sandwich.

She took a deep breath and started down the incline. Her legs shook so badly she wouldn't have been surprised if she'd toppled over. When she reached the spot where Blade had spread the picnic blanket, she settled herself down in haughty silence and reached for an orange.

Blade watched her without comment, a half-eaten sandwich in his hand. He didn't know what to say, how to begin to explain his behavior. Hell, he didn't even understand it himself.

One minute he'd looked into her eyes and seen the blaze of desire that equaled his own, and all he could think about was dragging her down to the blanket and stripping off her skirt.

The next minute he remembered the men who invaded the safety of his house. Men who might still be lurking around, might be following him. Now, all he could think of was protecting her from their prying eyes.

He tossed the unwanted sandwich away and reached out to take the orange from her cold fingers.

"Look at me."

"Leave me alone."

"I can't." He captured her hand.

She sniffed sarcastically.

"A lot of men are looking for the treasure, Ruth."

"There is no treasure."

"They think there is, and they're crawling around these hills looking for it."

"So?"

"I'm not going to make love to you in front of half the scum in the Arizona Territory."

"You're not going to make love to me at all!" She tried to pull her hand out of his.

He didn't let her go. Instead, he began to rub the pad of his thumb back and forth over the tender inner skin of her wrist.

"We will. But not here. Not today."

"Not ever!"

"It wouldn't do us much good to bring Jennie out to the house to protect our sterling reputations, and then make love in the open for any passerby to talk about in the saloons. But you ache for me as badly as I ache for you. And one day it's going to happen."

"That's a lie!"

"Don't tempt me to prove it, Ruth."

"You couldn't." She jerked her hand out of his and jumped to her feet. "I've seen all I want to see out here. Thank you for the guided tour, Mister Blade. It's been an interesting experience. I'm going home."

He watched in silence as she marched to her horse and hauled herself into the saddle.

"You are one cantankerous woman, Ruth McKenna." He watched her trot away. "So what in the hell am I going to do with you?" He picked up the sketch pad and looked at her wonderful face. "I guess I'll follow you."

He caught up with her fifteen minutes later, after he'd picked up their lunch and folded the blanket. She spurred her horse the moment she heard him approach, and he let her go, watching her from a few yards back in case she got into trouble.

After the fiasco of his marriage, he'd sworn off any serious commitment to a woman. It was a lot easier to cope with women who expected nothing more than a good tumble and a ruby bracelet. The decision suited his life, and he'd been comfortable with it.

So why had he started to think about what would happen when the lease was up on the Phillips house? Where Ruth would go? Why did so many of his thoughts begin and end with Ruth?

"Damn it. I sure don't need this now!"

8

"*I'm taking the buggy* into town today. We're running low on food thanks to our unexpected guests, and I need to check on the boots I ordered. And maybe get a haircut. I thought you might like to ride along."

"No, thank you. I have typing to do."

She was so polite he wanted to shake her.

"I'm not going to beg, Ruth. And I'm not going to apologize for what I said yesterday because it was the truth."

When she didn't reply, he continued, "I just thought you might like to ride in to Flagstaff with me and visit Mrs. Bemish while I take care of my business. I know she invited you to stop by. We can have dinner at the hotel before we come home. Unless we have more problems out here, I won't go back to town for several weeks."

"I really liked Mrs. Bemish," Ruth admitted. She

wasn't ready to let go of her anger with him, but the prospect of spending the whole day and evening by herself didn't appeal at all.

"If you want to go, I'll be ready about ten."

"I'll think about it."

She dressed carefully in a French plaid skirt of dark purple and gray, worn with a pearl gray silk Basque waist and a steel gray Eton jacket. She knew some people would be shocked that she wouldn't wear mourning clothes for Donal a full six months, but she only had one black dress and no money with which to buy more clothes.

She had sold most of the mourning garments she'd worn for Farley after she'd been left destitute and forced to seek work. Full mourning wasn't suitable to the working environment, and some employers even had a prejudice about hiring married women or widows.

Fortunately, Elizabeth Malcolm, her elderly neighbor in the room above the bakery in St. Louis was a former seamstress who delighted in sewing for Ruth in exchange for a few pennies and an evening meal. They'd gotten on quite well till the old woman's death a month before. That, more than anything else, had convinced Ruth to seek her brother.

She sighed wistfully. How drastically her life had changed.

Hardly more than a year ago she'd been content as a married woman, satisfied to be working alongside her scholarly husband to advance his career. Now she was an impoverished widow, without any family, living in an alien world with a man she barely knew. A man she knew little about. A man, she admitted, who bewildered her and challenged all her values.

Ruth, who was eternally practical, found herself drawn inadvertently to a man she suspected was more of a dreamer than even her brother had been. She'd discovered a book of Blade's sketches on the bookshelf in Donal's office, and she'd marveled at the man whose creativity stunned her. A man who drew pictures of Indians and children. Of buildings and city streets. Even of old wrinkled drunks. An artist who appeared to have no other means of support, despite his obvious talent.

A man who promised to bed her at the first opportunity, but mentioned nothing of the future.

Why did he make her feel so alive?

"What's going to happen to me?" she asked herself as she pinned on her hat. "Where do I go from here?"

The door to the bedroom opened and Blade looked in. "Are you coming with me?"

"Yes," she said, feeling it somehow was the answer to her own question.

He'd replaced the rough work clothes he'd worn earlier that morning with a stylish three-piece suit and a shirt of fine unbleached linen. His tie was copper color, only a shade lighter than his hair. He held his hat in one hand and carried a heavy brown overcoat over his arm. Ruth noted the quality of his clothing with some wonder. Who exactly was Gladius Blade?

Blade helped her into her long coat and handed her up into the buggy, a strong, well-sprung mountain wagon without frills designed to withstand the rigors of rural travel. While it didn't compare to some of the elaborate vehicles she'd seen in St. Louis or Boston, Ruth had to admit that the wide seat and fully paneled back were as comfortable as most, and the leather top shielded her from the sun. She couldn't ask for more.

The pleasant weather of the previous day continued to grace the area, though a wisp or two of clouds adorned the sky. The air was fresh and clean with a bare hint of breeze.

Blade drove down the slight incline which led into town at a gentle clip. This was a view he always enjoyed.

Flagstaff lay before them like a jewel at the base of the snowcapped San Francisco Peaks.

"Oh my, it's so beautiful."

"I forgot, it was after dark when your train got into Flagstaff. It is a pretty town, isn't it?"

She breathed in her excitement. "Lovely."

"Local legend says the peaks got their name because if a man stands on the very top, he can see the city of San Francisco."

"That sounds similar to the story of Coronado's gold."

Blade chuckled. "Another exaggeration, I'm afraid."

"Okay. So where *did* the peaks get their name?"

"They were named for the Franciscan Fathers who'd been in the area years before."

The peaks loomed above the town, enormous and breathtaking, capped with a crust of snow. A cloud of fog shrouded the upper reaches and rolled down into the high valleys like an avalanche.

To Blade, who was mountain born and bred, that particular type of cloud indicated a pressure drop, a weather change. He cast a wary eye at the mountains, wondering when the change would come and if it meant snow. A person who lived in the high country had to be aware of such things. A drastic weather change could come in a matter of hours at this elevation. To be unprepared in the mountains was to invite disaster.

Blade stopped by the newspaper office on Aspen Avenue and bought a copy of the *Sun-Democrat,* then drove up past the handsome sandstone Coconino County Court House, which had been built about two years earlier from the native ocher-colored sandstone.

Blade wanted to show Ruth several houses that were under construction. It was obvious to Ruth that the town of Flagstaff was growing rapidly. One house was the same ocher-colored sandstone as the courthouse, a plain, unadorned structure with a darker slate roof and mullioned windows. It was sturdy, like the Phillips house, and equally uninspired.

Ruth commented on a Victorian house of two and a half stories. "All those curves and billowed appurtenances are quite interesting."

"I'd like to draw a pictorial history of western architecture—buildings and houses," Blade told her.

"When?"

The buggy passed a house that was being built of stone on the lower half and timbered above, similar to the Tudor style he'd seen in other parts of the country.

Her question caught him completely by surprise. He was so accustomed to people arguing with him or sitting in tolerant silence, he didn't exactly know how to answer. Could she really be interested in his artwork?

"Someday," he answered lamely.

"Why not begin when this project is finished? Unless

you have another job. Say, I wonder what sort of mortar that stonemason is using on that house with the Elizabethan look? Those stones appear quite heavy."

"I think the stone is basaltic. Lava. Yes, it's heavy. I'll find out about the mortar." He glanced at her. "I didn't know you were interested in such things."

"I've lived around scientists all my life. I'm interested in everything."

From there they drove over to the Bemish house on Gold Avenue.

The little white house with turquoise trim appealed to Ruth so much more than the huge sandstone building at the Phillips ranch. Right from the first the Phillips house reminded her of a cold, lonely castle.

"This is so pretty." Ruth sighed. It looked like the type of house she'd always longed for ever since Donal sold their family home in St. Louis. She didn't recall too much about the house except her own room, the huge summer porch, and the forget-me-not wallpaper in the parlor. And she remembered her mother had grown roses. It was the homey atmosphere that haunted her. She'd never lived in another house as pleasant or as pretty as the family home. Certainly not Farley's house. Archaeologists seemed fonder of hearths hundreds of years old than of their own.

"What color are the roses, Blade?" The stalks were nude and spindly without their summer greenery and fragrant flowers.

"Pink," Blade answered. "I think. What I really remember is catching my hair in the foliage. If I ever have a rose arbor, I'll have the framework built eight feet high."

"Picky, picky."

He smiled to himself. Apparently the drive in the fresh air had improved her disposition. He wished his own problems could be so easily solved, but as he pulled the buggy to a stop in front of the Bemish house his most sincere wish was for Ruth to have a nice visit with Myra Bemish.

His mother had always told him women needed the companionship of other women. Especially in the West. Life was hard and women were scarce. Loneliness had driven more than one woman away, unless they had gone mad first.

And God knew Ruth had had enough hardships and burdens in her young life without adding loneliness to the lot. Blade was certain Myra Bemish would make her feel very welcome.

At that moment the front door opened and Myra stuck her head out. "Come on in," she called. "I'm just taking coffee cake out of the oven. I'll be right back." Then the door shut with a snap and she disappeared back in the house.

Blade helped Ruth down, smiling, holding on to her waist just a fraction longer than was absolutely necessary. "I'll be awhile, so you'll have plenty of time to visit."

"Where are you going?"

"Kilpatrick's for groceries. Do you want anything?"

"You might pick up a few yards of material for Jennie. Her clothes are practically rags. And some gloves, or yarn and knitting needles. Her poor hands are almost raw."

"All right, if you trust my taste. Then I'm going to get some oysters from Richards—his are the best in town—and check on his selection of fruit. Do you think I need a haircut?"

The first time she'd seen him she'd found his shoulder-length auburn waves annoying, almost barbaric. Now she thought his hair was beautiful. "You could go a couple more weeks."

He nodded. "I'm planning on taking you over to the dining room of the new Bank Hotel this evening. The food is superb. I think you'll enjoy yourself."

Her whole face lit up. "Oh, wonderful! I can't remember how long it's been since I ate in a fine restaurant . . . a very long time."

A muscle in Blade's jaw tightened in annoyance. "I'll see you later," he said gruffly. "Tell Myra hello."

Blade climbed back into the buggy, started the horses, then raised a hand in salute to Ruth as he drove away. She watched him a moment, then walked toward the door lost in thought.

"You certainly have given me something to think about," Ruth said as she sipped her tea. "No, thanks. No more coffee cake. The lunch was wonderful."

"I'll give you Wayne's address if you want to write to him. And Joseph can write as well. As I said, Joseph and his brothers are all progressive thinkers, but Wayne is in a position to put his beliefs to work. He already has women working in his company. And not just as charwomen. With your skills, I'm sure he would snap you up."

"I am going to have to find work to support myself when I finish here. I hadn't given any thought to going out to California, but to tell you the truth, I hadn't thought about going anywhere. I'm still reeling from Donal's death. Coming so soon after my husband's passing, it really knocked me for a loop. But you're right. I do have to think about my future. I believe I *would* like your brother-in-law's address." She pushed her chair away from the table.

"Ruth, I am so glad you dropped by," Myra said as they cleared the luncheon dishes from the table. "And I wish you'd reconsider going to the dance with us tonight."

Ruth shook her head adamantly. "No, it would be unseemly."

"You wouldn't have to dance, just meet folks and talk to them."

Ruth touched the smaller woman's hand. "Thank you for inviting me. I would like to go, but it is still too soon. People would not understand." She smiled sadly. "Donal wouldn't have agreed, of course. He'd have said the devil take them, and gone anyway. And he'd have gotten away with it. But the rules are still different for women, whether we like it or not. There aren't enough progressive thinkers around."

"Out here things aren't as strict as back East," Myra argued.

"They're strict enough. And I do have to live here until I finish the manuscript on Donal's expedition."

"I think preparing that manuscript is a wonderful project for you."

Ruth sighed. "It's the last thing I can do for him, so I'm giving it my best."

"I'm sure Joseph would read it over for you when you're finished."

"Would he? That would be such a help to me."

"He'd love to, Ruth. He always enjoyed the nights your brother and Blade came for supper. They'd talk late. Joseph misses the company of scholarly men."

Ruth thought a moment. "Would you answer a very indelicate question truthfully?"

"I think so." Myra looked quite impish. "What is it?"

"Is there much gossip in town about me staying out at the ranch with Blade?"

Myra's cheeks colored a bit. She cleared her throat. "Truthfully? I'm afraid so. A little bit, anyway. Even with Jennie Begay out there. But you know how some people are?"

"Unfortunately I do."

Ruth looked at the gold watch pinned to her jacket. "Speaking of Mister Blade, my so-called partner in illicit crime, I wonder where he is. He should have been here by now."

Myra waved away Ruth's concern. "He probably ran into someone. Men are much worse gossips than women." She giggled lightly. "They just won't admit it."

Ruth laughed. "I intend to use Blade's tardiness as an excuse to walk downtown."

"Oh, you don't have to go so soon!"

"I know you're planning to take some coffee cakes to the dance tonight. And we devoured one already. If you're going to bake and get pretty for the dance, you don't need to be entertaining me. I'll stop around the next time I'm in town."

"You're sure?"

"Yes. I want to explore the town—you can't do that with a man, because he's always in a hurry. At least my husband was like that." She didn't notice the odd look Myra shot her way.

"Why don't you and Joseph ride out to the ranch next Sunday and have dinner with us?" Ruth added. "It would be so nice to dine with someone I like—my husband's business associates were such dry old sticks."

"I'll talk to Joseph. Unless the weather turns bad, I'm sure he'll say yes. I'll send word to you with Che Nez. I hear he spends quite a bit of time out your way."

They both laughed—nothing was secret in a small town.

Ruth walked briskly down Gold Avenue and turned east on Aspen, thinking how much she liked Myra Bemish. Being with her reminded Ruth of how much she missed Elizabeth Malcolm, her neighbor in the room above the bakery in St. Louis. It was their camaraderie that had helped Ruth through the hardships of the first awful months of widowhood.

Elizabeth had not only advised Ruth on matters of fashion in which she was definitely an expert, but she also gave her lessons in finance and affairs of the heart. It was Elizabeth Malcolm who convinced Ruth to seek out Donal, insisting blood ties were forever—nothing was worth being cut off from a loved one. Love was too precious, and too fragile. She herself was old and alone; she didn't want Ruth to end up in a similar situation. She was adamant about Ruth forgiving Donal for the horrible way he'd treated her.

Only I found my brother too late, Ruth thought. Pride, both his and mine, injured us both. I won't ever let that happen to me again.

She looked up and saw one of the good women of Flagstaff who had come to the house after Donal's funeral. She was a gaunt woman with a worn-out look to her despite her stylish biscuit-colored suit with red trim and hat.

For the life of her, Ruth could not recall the woman's name although she did remember her statement that she was a member of the Women's Christian Temperance Union. Ruth smiled cheerfully at the other woman and raised her hand in a wave. The purse-mouthed female turned her head, gathered her skirts in her hands, and crossed the street. She was in such a rush she nearly collided with a lumber wagon.

Stunned at the public snub, Ruth nonetheless held her head high as she proceeded down the street. Evidently some people didn't think having an Indian girl living in the house was enough of a chaperone. Ruth surmised that strong spirits wasn't the only thing the thin-lipped woman hated.

A pox on her, Ruth thought wickedly, and marched proudly on.

She glanced at three Indians who were riding slowly toward her, probably from the Commercial Building where they traded. They were all bundled in coats and heavy blankets, although the afternoon was quite warm. So she didn't see the man coming out of the candy store till he barreled into her.

He was tall and lanky, with a scruffy beard. Ruth thought he looked familiar—was he at Donal's funeral?—but he didn't speak, not even to apologize. He stomped past her with a scowl. She looked after him, amazed at his rudeness.

As she approached the entrance to Babbitts, she saw Jaspar Bird coming out. He was wearing a mulberry-colored suit that fit as badly as the one he wore to

Donal's funeral. His sister, resplendent in a fitted suit of ox heart red, puffed closely behind him.

"Jaspar, you have a man down at the Yellow Canary before sundown to put that window in," Hertha huffed as she tried to catch up with Jaspar. "It's a damned disgrace I have to pay these prices for new glass, and I'm not about to pay to have it installed."

Bird gave no indication of having heard her. But unless he'd been stricken deaf, he couldn't have missed hearing her tirade.

"It was bad enough they smashed my greenhouse. All my herbs froze before I saw the damage! Are you payin' attention?" She caught him by the arm and swung him around. "Now they're attackin' my bakery! And why? Because you foreclosed on Sam Waverly! And the damned fool blew his head off. I didn't do nothin'! I ask you, is that fair?"

Jaspar scowled fiercely. There were some days he just plain hated Hertha. Sister or not, she'd been a thorn in his hide as long as he could recollect.

At that moment he looked up into the blue eyes of Ruth McKenna and imagined she was sniggering at him just like all the other folks. Suddenly he hated her, too. She was another dame who plagued his life, who kept him from getting what he wanted.

"Go home, Widow Woman!" he snarled. "Go back where you belong!"

Ruth couldn't have been more astonished.

Hertha immediately cuffed him on the shoulder, sending him staggering. "Whatcha mean talkin' to a lady like that, you fool? An' where the hell should she go? She brought a ton a' stuff with her. I think she's meanin' to stay."

"Where exactly do you expect me to go, Mister Bird?" Ruth inquired in a cool, polite voice.

Jaspar admitted to himself he'd taken the wrong tack. He might be able to buffalo the McKenna woman, but he didn't stand a chance with Hertha. "Well . . ." he sputtered. "What I mean is . . . ahem— I'm just worried about yer safety. This bein' a wild town an' all. Ya shouldn't be out walkin' the streets . . . unescorted, ya know."

"Ah, hell," his sister bellowed. "You ain't got the brains God gave a turnip. Unescorted, my arse! This is Flagstaff, not some hick shoot-'em-up town. Women are safe walking alone. I do it all the time." She peered at Ruth. "You goin' to the dance tonight, girlie?"

Ruth couldn't think of a name she loathed as much as "girlie," but she supposed it didn't matter. Undoubt-edly she wouldn't see Hertha Bird more than a time or two before she finished the manuscript and left town. "No," she answered. "I'm about to meet Mister Blade and we're going back to the ranch."

Jaspar saw his chance to escape and hurried away.

"Excuse me," Ruth finished. "I believe I just saw Blade leave Babbitts. I don't want to miss him. Good-bye."

Hertha's attention was on her brother. She didn't bother to answer Ruth. "You little weasel! Come back here! I want my window fixed! I know you can hear me, Jaspar Bird! Shit!" She stormed down San Francis-co, her feet pounding on the sidewalk. "Men! The only earthly thing they're good fer is ruttin', and some of 'em ain't even good fer that!"

*   *   *

She saw them the moment they walked in the door. She'd stopped about halfway down the wide staircase to repin the hat she wore which had suddenly felt loose and wobbly. As she thrust in the hatpin, she spotted the tall, broad-shouldered, redheaded man stride across the lobby.

What luck!

Only when he stopped did Monique notice the tall woman with him. They made a handsome couple, so she supposed she would have noticed them even if she hadn't known Blade.

But she did know him, of course, ever since that night in San Francisco. And it definitely was an acquaintance she planned to pursue. His size and bearing had always intrigued her, not to mention his money. She could hardly believe he was an artist, but Phelan swore he was one of the best. Not that she'd cared about art. It was his other talents that interested her.

For some reason he'd always ignored her. She figured it was because Phelan was his boss and he didn't want trouble between them. Still, she had a hankering for him, an itch she yearned to have satisfied.

She waited in the lobby until they'd been seated in the elegant dining room, preening before one of the beveled mirrors that was lighted by an electric chandelier. She straightened the drapes on her salmon pink dress.

She frowned momentarily when she saw the crow's-feet near her eyes illuminated by the electric light. A girl looked better by candlelight. Then she composed herself and waited. The plain woman accompanying Blade, with her pallid complexion and her dull, unadorned style of dress, was no competition for her.

Monique made it her business to know what attracted men in droves and kept them panting. A plain little peahen like that one didn't stand a chance.

"Hungry?" he asked, as they waited to be escorted into the dining room. A boyish smile lighted his face.

"I didn't think I could be after the luncheon Myra Bemish fixed for me, but I'm famished . . ."

Ruth's voice trailed off as the man who'd been sitting in the lobby when they walked in strolled past them. Where had she seen him before? She knew it had been some place other than Flagstaff.

The second glance told her he was older than she'd first thought, his thinning blond hair was liberally mixed with gray, and his expression was somewhat pinched as if he squinted to see. He walked over to a dining table and seated himself. Glancing at him again, she decided she didn't know the scrawny balding man at all. But it was strange that he looked familiar to her, since she normally had an excellent memory for faces.

"I'm excited about this dinner," she continued. "My husband didn't like to go out to eat."

Blade frowned. It rankled to hear her mention yet another so-called frivolity that Farley McKenna didn't believe in. Blade couldn't imagine a woman as beautiful and full of life as Ruth shackling herself to a wet blanket like old Farley. Even Phelan treated his women better!

As far as Blade could see, Farley McKenna had married Ruth—who at twenty-four had naturally expected love and romance—and had treated her like his personal slave. Blade had a glimmer of why Donal Phelan had opposed the marriage.

The black-clad maître d'hôtel led them to a quiet table in the elegant cream and rose dining room, assuring them the cuisine and service in the new Bank Hotel was as fine as could be found in any first-class western city.

The dining room was crowded with townspeople who were dressed up to attend the Saturday night dance. Ruth glanced around, noticing how fancy some of the women were dressed. Her own suit looked very ordinary in comparison. Blade, too, looked over the room. He knew without a doubt he was escorting the loveliest woman in town.

The tables were situated between huge planters of green palms and tall Grecian pillars holding large beribboned floral arrangements. Ruth was charmed. Even before their waiter brought the drinks, she relaxed. The thin man was out of her sight, and out of her mind.

"Gladius Blade, as I live and breathe!"

Ruth turned her head to the loud female voice, as did everyone else in the dining room.

"You remember me, honey? Monique. From Mrs. Wells's Gentlemen's Club in San Francisco? And recently the fair city of Los Angeles."

Until that moment, Blade could have said with complete sincerity he was too old to be embarrassed. Monique changed his mind. Heat climbed from beneath his tight shirt collar up his cheeks, all the way to his hairline.

"I forgot you were coming," he mumbled.

She leaned forward and wagged her finger at him. "Shame on you, you naughty thing." The words dragged seductively, accompanied by a practiced pout on her painted lips.

Ruth fought her astonishment that such a tawdry tramp had been allowed in the room. The woman was a fright! Not only was the sleazy sateen dress ornamented with cheap green velvet ribbon which had shrunk at some washing, but also bunches of sateen roses that cascaded from the shoulder to the tight waist pulled the draped neckline even lower.

Monique might not have a large bosom, but everything she had was exposed to view when she bent over to wag her finger at Blade. Ruth gasped aloud when she saw the floozy's undergarment—a black corset that pushed her small breasts up and out at an unbelievable angle!

Blade glared at Monique. "Kindly lower your voice, or leave. This is not a saloon."

"I know what this establishment is, Blade." She pouted a bit but lowered her voice. "I've stayed here before." She flounced into a chair beside him.

Blade knew she'd make a bigger scene than she already was if he didn't handle her carefully. Above all, he didn't want Ruth embarrassed any more than could be prevented.

He'd honestly forgotten about Monique. Had he remembered, he'd have wired her about Phelan and sent her fee to Los Angeles. That would have been a cheap way of preventing Ruth from discovering her existence. Now he simply had to figure out how to get rid of her quick.

But why was she acting like there was something between them?

"So. Where is the boss-man, sweetie? I've been waiting, breathlessly."

Blade paused before he answered. He was trying not to strangle her.

The hesitation was a mistake.

"I know I'm a few days late. But I had previous . . . ah, commitments. I expected Phelan to be waiting at the depot with his pants unbuttoned, and his flag-staff waving at me. Don't tell me he's buried out there in that damned old Indian ruin, and he forgot he sent for me?"

Ruth sprang to her feet. It was all she could do to keep from slapping the woman. "Will you please leave!"

"Oh, do sit down, honeycakes," Monique drawled. "No sense in getting your bloomers in a knot. Every-body knows Phelan belongs to me. And even if he didn't, he wouldn't look twice at a drab like you."

Blade's face mottled with fury. He scrapped his chair backward, preparing to toss the harlot out into the street. Ruth laid her hand on his arm.

"For your information, honeycakes," she said, look-ing down her straight nose at Monique, "Donal Phelan was my brother. And, yes, he is buried out in the hills. He died last week."

Monique looked stunned. Then she let out a loud screech. She probably would have attempted a faint, but the maître d'hôtel, two waiters, and the bouncer from the bar whisked her out into the lobby in nothing flat.

"Mister Blade, I am so sorry!" their waiter said. "Things like that never happen here. I didn't know what to do."

"I'm sorry, too, Louie." Blade reached for his wallet and removed an indiscreet number of bills. "Would you ask the front desk to put this in an envelope and give it to . . . her when she leaves? I'll cover the hotel bill, too.

And if you could get her on tonight's train, I'd be forever grateful."

"Yes, sir. Right away."

"I apologize for that," Blade told Ruth when the waiter left. The words seemed inadequate, but he didn't know what else to say.

"It wasn't your fault. You didn't send for her. Apparently Donal did. He had such vulgar taste in female companions. Did she say you met her in San Francisco?"

Blade squirmed. He had no intention of telling her the truth. There were some things a gentleman just didn't discuss with a lady of Ruth's quality, even if he did want to be honest. "I was having a drink with . . . ah . . . a business associate in . . . ah . . . a club." He took a sip of rye and cleared his throat. "Your brother and . . . Monique came in."

Ruth quickly filled in the stammers and pauses. It didn't take a genius to guess the sort of place Monique worked.

"That's how you met Donal?"

"Yes. It was a foggy evening, so we sat around the fire and talked. As the conversation went along, I discovered he needed a field artist. And as luck would have it, I needed a job. We both came back here."

"People didn't always understand him. I'm glad he had one friend."

The waiter, having rid himself of Monique, came back to take their order.

To be truthful, Ruth's appetite had fled at the onset of Monique's histrionics. All she really wanted now was to go home and pull the covers over her head. But she would be double damned if she would allow a creature of that persuasion to demolish a lovely day.

"Is the trout fresh?" Ruth asked.

"Caught just this morning, ma'am."

"All right, I'll have trout, a roasted potato, and a broiled tomato."

"No dessert?" Blade asked. "I thought you said you were hungry." He wasn't hungry himself. He'd prefer a quart or two of rye and no witnesses. But he wanted to make Ruth happy. He'd eat if it choked him.

"I'll have the lemon sponge with custard sauce for dessert."

"And you, sir?"

"I'll have the elk brisket in an onion sauce, corn pudding, turnips in cream, spinach, a baked apple, glazed sweet potatoes, brown bread, and a tipsy squire trifle for dessert. And bring me another drink when you have a moment."

"Yes, sir. I'll have that drink as soon as I give your order to the chef."

Within moments the waiter had returned with steaming bowls of vegetable soup, wafer crackers, and a tray loaded with small bowls of preserves and jams, chow-chow, gingered pears, spiced plums, and three kinds of pickles.

In spite of how it began, they both enjoyed the meal, and ate with gusto.

Music filled the night air as they left the warmth of the hotel.

Blade tucked the lap robe around her, and climbed in the buggy.

"Would you like to go to the dance, Ruth?"

"Not tonight. Let's just drive home. There will be other dances. I simply don't think I could cope with another crisis tonight." And as they drove away from the town and the music, she told him about her day.

9

Ruth yawned, stretching her weary body. She couldn't remember when she'd been so tired. It was nearly two o'clock in the morning, and she was about to drop in a heap from exhaustion. The day in Flagstaff had been long and busy, and she'd hardly slept the night before.

While nothing had actually been settled between herself and Blade—at least anything that mattered— the journey had proven enjoyable and enlightening, perhaps more so than any other time they'd been together. That was certainly something to be thankful for.

She slipped off her wool suit, hanging it carefully in the mirrored wardrobe, and placed her plumed hat in its pink and white-striped hatbox on the upper shelf. After removing her shoes and petticoats, she stood with her small gold earrings in her hand, poised near the dainty, scrolled box containing her few meager pieces of jewelry. It occurred to her that it was important she settle her differences with Blade.

He was important.

The thought made her frown. She didn't want him to be important to her.

It wasn't that she hadn't given some thought to meeting another man, and perhaps marrying again. But the timing simply couldn't have been worse. Her life was a mess! She who had always been so levelheaded, seemed overloaded with emotions and bankrupt on sense.

All of a sudden she could think of nothing but being in Blade's arms as she had been yesterday. She wanted nothing more than that. Not a new job as a typewriter, not a new home in another city. Not a future for herself.

She wanted to be in Blade's arms.

To feel his power, the texture of his mouth, his body against hers, to lose herself in his kisses, his caresses.

Like a silly schoolgirl with her first crush, she could think of nothing else, despite her advanced age of twenty-eight.

She could still feel the strength of his formidable chest, and the thunder of his heartbeat. She could feel the sensation of his warm breath on her hot cheeks, and the softness of his wide mouth as it touched her wet, waiting lips. Petal soft. Summer breeze soft.

She ached to have him touch her again.

Without knowing exactly why, she was certain there were additional pleasures to intimacy than what she'd ever experienced. Even old Mrs. Malcolm, who'd shared her evening meals for nearly a year in the apartment above the bakery, and who'd sewed her a fine working wardrobe, had hinted that marital relations could be glorious.

Ruth wanted the glory.

She wanted it with Blade, though the very thought scared her silly.

Frowning, she shoved the earrings into the box, stuck it in the dresser drawer, and walked to her bed.

What she saw as she flipped the sheets back made her blood curdle. A scream of terror tore from her throat.

There in the middle of the sheets was a coiled snake. Fat, ugly, and deadly as sin.

A shudder of revulsion racked her slender frame, and she backed away from the bed in horror. Another scream rent the air.

Her door burst open with a tremendous clatter.

"What the hell . . ." Blade's gaze followed her horrified stare. "God!"

Pushing her behind him he stared at the snake, then reached for a parasol from the ceramic umbrella stand. Standing back, well out of striking distance, he gingerly poked the snake.

It did nothing.

Blade knew most reptiles were in hibernation this time of the year, particularly in the high country, but he was taking no chances. Especially with a rattler.

He nudged and poked its head and body repeatedly but got no response. It lay coiled but torpid, the deadly fangs concealed, the frightening rattles silent.

Blade let his breath out in a rush. "It's okay. The snake is dead."

Ruth nodded. She heard his words but they didn't

actually register in her shocked brain. "Get it out of here!"

"It's okay, Ruth, honest," he said roughly. Then he noticed that she was quaking like an aspen, her body shuddering with fear. She suddenly looked fragile in her lace-trimmed pantalettes, chemise, and stockings. Fragile, vulnerable, and terrified.

He picked her up and carried her from the room without thinking. All he knew was that he had to get her away from what frightened her—to take her to safety. And he had to do it immediately.

Ruth gratefully buried her face against his warm throat, her lips resting against the pulse that beat there.

Her voice quavered as she asked, "The snake. How did it get there?"

Blade wondered that himself. The reptile sure as hell hadn't crawled between her linen sheets and expired from exhaustion. Who in the name of God had been in the house while they were gone? Since the break-in, they'd been locking up whenever they left.

He'd have to talk to Tsosi as soon as he got her settled. Maybe the young Navajo had seen someone near the house.

What he couldn't comprehend was why somebody wanted to scare Ruth in the first place. Did this have something to do with the break-in? Or was it a personal attack against Ruth?

She was still shaking when he laid her on his neatly made bed. She sat up quickly and looked around. "How can you be sure there aren't snakes under your covers, too?" Her voice became shrill as she fought off hysteria.

Blade realized Ruth's fear of snakes was more than

an ordinary human response, though she was actually right. He didn't know for certain he didn't have an uninvited guest, and he couldn't reassure her again unless he looked. Without a word he turned back the covers on his bed, one by one, proving to them both no reptiles lurked beneath them. He glanced at her, checking to see if she watched.

Then he swooped her up and plunked her back in the middle of his bed, drawing the covers over her feet and outstretched legs. Next he draped a quilt around her shoulders. Finally he sat down beside her on the bed and took her hand.

"You'll be okay," he said again, stroking her hands.

"I hate snakes."

"Me, too," Blade agreed, continuing to soothe her with his hands and his voice.

"We . . . we had a servant girl once," Ruth tried to explain, "and she had an older sister who wasn't quite right—her body was all twisted and her mind was odd. She . . . she chased me with a snake when I was five, and I got hysterical. My mother wouldn't let her come back to the house anymore."

"It's all right, Ruth. Nothing is going to happen to you now. I'll get the snake out of the house right away." He started to move. The thought of the deadly viper coiled in her bed repelled him.

The room was quite cold. He hadn't bothered to heat it since he'd planned to go right to bed.

"I can't sleep in my room tonight." Ruth's voice wasn't shaking as badly as it had been.

"It's okay. You can sleep here."

"But you can't sleep in my room either. The sheets will need changing."

He smiled. "I don't intend to. I'll sleep somewhere else and I'll have Jennie change the bedclothes in the morning. Just lie down and go to sleep."

"I can't. My nightdress is in my room, and I'm still wearing my corset."

Before she realized what was happening, he'd reached out and unhooked her corset, pulled it off, and tossed it to the foot of the bed.

"You're not supposed to do that!" Her eyes were enormous. A hint of color returned to her pale cheeks.

He chuckled lightly. "I break a lot of rules. You ought to try it sometime."

"No." She looked as if he'd asked her to commit murder and mayhem.

"Why don't you go to sleep?"

"I'm afraid to close my eyes."

"I'll stay with you for a while." Blade nestled close beside her, his back resting against the solid oak of the headboard. She continued to sit where he'd plopped her, stiff as stone. He pulled her close to him. "Is this all right?" he asked.

"Yes." It was, in fact, so like the wicked thoughts she'd been having just before she'd uncovered the reptile, she wondered if he'd read her mind.

With the other hand he reached down and pulled the quilt all the way up to her chin. Then he eased her against his body, turning slightly so she fitted to his chest and hip. Immediately she tensed in shock, but quickly she began to relax. Turning her head toward him, she leaned closer and kissed him on the cheek. It was a child's kiss really, born out of gratitude and fright.

He should have let it go, but he didn't. He couldn't.

Not with how he felt. He'd desired her since the first moment when she had fainted in his arms.

He pulled her closer still.

Ruth gloried in his strength. He was so big and incredibly male, he made her feel small and delicate and wonderfully feminine. She sighed and snuggled her body even closer.

Heat shot through him. He wondered if she realized the effect she had on his body—how completely she aroused him.

"Ruth," he murmured, and his lips grazed her forehead, her temple, her eyelid. He tried to be gentle, though his thundering heart urged him to press her to the bed beneath him. He nuzzled his cheek to hers, hearing the faint rasp of his whiskers on her fair skin. He quickly lifted his head.

She wanted more. She, who had never truly known pleasure, yearned for tenderness, ardor, delight. For fire. For love.

Yet she had no idea how to make her desires known. One long finger stroked her soft cheek. His mouth trailed downward. Closer, closer. She longed to thrust her hands into his mane of hair and drag his mouth to hers.

Her heart skipped a beat.

What if he thought her ignorant?

What if he thought her wicked? Then his lips took hers.

Blade was amazed that a woman who had been married as long as Ruth knew so little about kissing a man. Hadn't that nitwit of a husband taught her anything? The little closed-mouth smack she gave was hardly better than what a five-year-old presents to a dottering grandfather.

But the body cradled against his definitely belonged to a woman. She groaned and opened her mouth to him. He realized within seconds that Ruth might not have been well educated in the school of lovemaking, but she was a very fast learner.

They moved together, body crushed to body, lips crushed to lips with a hunger that belied the brief time they'd known one another. It felt as if they'd been lovers for eternity.

Flames licked at Blade's gut with a heat that stunned him. He wrenched his mouth away from hers, though his body cried out to continue, and gulped a shaky breath of cold air.

Stop, he shouted at himself. Think!

He'd only meant to comfort her a little. Dear God, a few more minutes and there'd have been no stopping either one of them. He knew women. He knew how close to the edge she'd been, knew he could have taken her then and there if he'd forced the issue, knew she'd have willingly been his to take.

Stop!

He disentangled himself and sat up.

Ruth's face was flushed with passion and her full breasts heaved beneath the thin lace of the chemise. But her eyes looked desolate.

"I didn't mean for that to happen," he said hoarsely, struggling to gain control. "I didn't mean to upset you. I just wanted to take your mind off the snake."

"You certainly did that." Her voice trembled.

"Yeah," he said dryly. "Mine, too." He forced his legs over the side of the bed. "Look, it's getting late. We need to get some sleep. Will you be okay if I leave you?"

"Could you stay till I fall asleep? I think I can sleep now."

"Yes. Sure." He lied as he straightened the covers. Once again he settled himself down next to her, but this time there were three layers of blankets separating their bodies . . .

"It's too cold for you to be on top of the blankets," Ruth protested.

"Right now the cold isn't my problem."

She lowered her eyes in embarrassment. And he silently cursed himself. Ruth's upbringing was a hell of a lot more genteel than most of the women he'd been with the past few years. He needed to keep that in mind. But he truly wondered how long he'd be able to resist her. Her innocence—despite several years of marriage—proved to be a powerful aphrodisiac and combined with the passion he sensed in her, it was deadly.

For a moment he said nothing.

Then he turned down the lamp, and thinking he'd perhaps lost his mind, he separated the sheets and crawled in beside her. But he kept on his clothes. His shirt and trousers might suffer a few wrinkles, but his conscience would be clear in the morning.

Ruth tried to remain very still. She couldn't remember ever being so nervous. How exceedingly foolish. Only moments ago she'd pressed her hip against his groin, thrilling at the evidence of his desire. Now she was nervous because she was lying four inches away from him in the double-size bed.

She took a deep breath and tried to steady her heart. "What would people think?" she giggled nervously.

"The very worst. Now go to sleep."

*   *   *

The morning teased Blade's slumbering brain. It nudged him and he slapped it away, curling closer to the warmth cuddled against him. He inhaled deeply, the fresh scent of rain washing down on wildflowers, and he dreamed of meadows in the springtime.

A young girl ran ahead of him, laughing and calling for him to catch her. Her hair was long, and it glistened in the sunlight; she was wearing a filmy chemise made of moonbeams. He caught her, and tumbled to the grass with her, and kissed her madly, and passionately loved her.

But when he raised his youthful body from hers, he saw near her head a huge, deadly, diamond-backed rattlesnake coiled to strike.

"The snake!"

Blade bounded from the warmth of his bed, from the comfort of Ruth's body caught so close to his, and was out the door before she woke up. He stumbled down the stairs and threw open the door.

He looked at the bed.

Then he picked up the matchbox and struck a match, carefully lighting the bedside lamp.

"Son of a bitch!"

The bed was empty, the snake gone.

He thought for a moment the snake had indeed been alive and had crawled off after he carried Ruth from the room.

Frantically he looked around the room, hunting for the viper everywhere. The room was empty.

He walked out into the hall, heading for the kitchen, his thoughts on the mystery of the disappearing rattler.

The kitchen door gaped open.

Blade slowly walked to the door and shut it against the frigid morning air. The wind, he noticed absently, was blowing quite hard. The weather had changed as he'd thought it might. He picked up a stick of wood and some kindling to start a fire. Then he made a half-hearted search of the rest of the house, but the snake was nowhere to be found.

"He evidently walked out, and forgot to shut the door." After that small bit of sarcasm, he set to making coffee. He needed a strong jolt of caffeine to clear his fuzzy brain.

He was on his second cup of the fragrant brew before he realized that whoever came into the house to remove the reptile had discovered that neither he nor Ruth had spent the night downstairs.

"Damn." He sighed. But while this development might lead to gossip, it at least was not life threatening—unlike a live rattlesnake.

"Methinks you have more to worry about, boyo, than a tarnished reputation." He made a mental note to see about new locks on the doors.

He wondered if he should say something to Ruth about that little development. He thought about it a minute, and decided against sheltering her from the truth. She'd already suffered a great deal of hurt during her life because men didn't tell her the truth.

When she asked about the snake, he'd have to tell her someone had been in the house for a second time, someone deliberately wanting to frighten her. He hated to do it, but he could not erase the facts.

Tonight he'd insist that Jennie stay in the house with Ruth. And if she couldn't do so, he'd trade beds with

Ruth. He didn't want her on the first floor by herself.

A vivid fantasy of what he really would like flitted through his mind.

"Enough of that foolish stuff." He got up and pulled out the makings for pancakes. For once he felt only half interested in a big breakfast.

He was on his seventh hotcake, fairly dripping butter and maple syrup, when he finally perceived what was bothering him. It wasn't snakes, or intruders, or sex—although all three were important. What bothered him was marriage.

Or marriage to Ruth to be exact.

Because without marriage and a lifelong commitment to her, the possibility of making love with her was out of the question. And not because of her moral starchiness, or her demands. But because of his.

Gladius Blade had been brought up by parents who believed in the sanctity of marriage. Their marriage had been based on love and had been wild and joyful. His father still mourned, even after fifteen years of being a widower.

His own marriage to Ophelia had been based on her greed and his stupidity; it had been a disaster from the minute he slipped the ring on her grasping hand. Though he was actually a widower, he had been in the process of divorcing the thieving slut when she'd gotten herself killed. He hadn't mourned her for a second. Never in his life had he met a person so evil.

But it wasn't his parents' values or his own personal failure that now guided his thinking. It was Ruth herself.

She trusted him. With her whole heart and soul. He could see it in her eyes, hear it in her voice. She believed in his goodness, and since she had no one else in the world, since her own emotions weren't reliable at this time, he couldn't betray that trust. For either of their sakes.

The smell of smoke invaded his lofty thoughts. The pankcake in the heavy skillet was burning!

"Oh, hell and damnation!"

After he'd dumped the charred cake, fanned the smoke out with the open door, and cleaned the blackened pan, he decided to mix up more batter. Ruth probably would be hungry.

The one thought he managed to keep from confronting was whether he wanted to marry Ruth—to love her.

"Who said anything about love?"

"I don't know? Who did?"

He dropped a glop of pancake batter on the cast-iron stove, and with enormous effort, restrained himself from throwing the crockery bowl against the wall.

"Sorry, I didn't mean to startle you."

"This has been a terrible morning," he said shortly.

Ruth sniffed the smoky air but refrained from asking questions. Blade's mood must be even worse than her own. She retrieved a coffee cup and walked to the stove to pour herself some, accidentally brushing against Blade's arm.

"Damn it!" he growled.

She jerked away and somehow touched the hot stove. She cried out, more in surprise than pain.

All his good intentions went straight to hell.

He jerked her into his arms, his furious mouth taking no pity on hers. He consumed her. For a second she gave in to the impulse to fight him, and she clawed his hand and bit at his mouth, but her passion ran hotter than her anger.

Fire shot through her slender body, making her heart race with joy and her legs shake with a weakness she'd never before known. She threw her arms around his neck, trying desperately to get closer. Closer. Her fingers curled into the thickness of his hair and she pulled him ever closer.

She clung to him, her mouth as ravenous as his, kissing, biting.

Blade went wild.

His hands slipped over her body, touching, savoring. She was so beautiful. He writhed against her and ran his hands down over her buttocks, lifting her up to him.

He would have taken her right there on the spot but for a loud knocking at the door.

He set Ruth away from him with great reluctance. His only consolation was that she looked as dazed as he felt. She reached out to him. "Don't stop."

"Someone's knocking."

She glanced toward the door. Then she straightened her wrapper with a shaking hand and turned toward the table.

Jennie Begay waited patiently at the kitchen door. She'd knocked three times, and was happy to see the door open because she'd forgotten her shawl. "I'm here to work."

"Yeah." Blade ran a hand through his mussed hair. "Well, good. I think Mrs. McKenna has some things for you to do."

Ruth had managed to compose herself. She was sitting in the chair, however, because her legs were too rubbery to hold her. "The parlor needs cleaning," she said as if she'd done nothing in her life but direct servants. "Dust, sweep the floor, and beat the carpet. And the downstairs bed needs the linens changed. No, everything, even the blankets and bed cover needs to be removed and washed. And burn the sheets!"

Jennie stiffened slightly, but nodded in agreement.

"And I want you to sleep here tonight. In there." She pointed to the little bedroom by the pantry. "It's all made up for you."

"Do I cook?"

"Not usually. I'll do that. Once in a while I might ask you to bring me lunch when I'm working in the office. But most of the time I won't want you to do more than peel potatoes."

"Good. Then I can cook for my auntie. Tsosi likes my cooking. And sometimes Che comes by."

Jennie went off with the broom and cleaning cloths to attack the parlor.

Blade poured coffee in Ruth's cup. It had been sitting on the stove and was piping hot.

"Ruth, believe me, nothing is going to happen that you don't want."

"That's not a whole lot of comfort right now, Blade."

"It's meant to be. We can take it slow, or fast. However you wish. If you don't want me in the house—if you don't want me in your life"—he was thinking the words "in your bed" but didn't utter them—"I'll understand. I can move out to the barn."

"You'd be cold."

"I've been cold before. I'm tough. I'll manage. It would be a darned sight better if I'm uncomfortable than if you're unhappy."

She shook her head. "No. I won't force you out of your bed." She looked straight at him. "This has never happened to me before. My body has never felt this way before, so . . . hungry."

His eyes blazed hot.

"I don't know how to behave," she whispered. "I mean, I know how I'm supposed to act. I've always followed the rules and it was easy. I've never had any desire to stray. Till now." She absently ran a finger up and down the side of her coffee cup. "Did I put sugar in this?" She dipped her fingertip in the cup and then stuck it in her mouth.

He swallowed a groan.

"I don't really know you, Blade. How can I even be thinking such thoughts?"

"Listen, damn it, this isn't Saint Louis. You're not seventeen and I'm not twenty. We haven't known each other long in terms of days, that's quite correct. But our relationship hasn't been made up of visits once a week when I sit on your front porch swing and sip lemonade, and making clever conversation for a mannerly half hour. We live together."

She nodded, sipping her coffee, unaware if she'd bothered to add the sugar.

"We live together. That means I see you in the morning in your robe and slippers and you see me at night when I need a shave. We share every meal. We share our day-to-day work and discuss many of our thoughts. We've already gone through a tragedy together, and now we're trying to sift through the pieces of it. We've put up with more than one week's ration of problems." He told her then about the snake being taken from the house.

She shook her head in disbelief.

Blade lowered his voice. "Let's get back to the real problem—us. I've seen you naked, Ruth. You've seen me stripped down to my drawers. You've seen me aroused, felt me against you. That's not what happens normally, I agree. But it's already happened to us, and we can't go back and pretend it hasn't."

"I don't know if I love you!"

"I don't know if I love you, either. Not yet. I like you a lot. You're the smartest woman I've ever met. You feed me, you make me laugh, you make me crazy with wanting you. And you say nice things about my artwork."

She chuckled.

"Right now I want to protect you. That's why I'm telling you that the person you are in the most danger from is me."

"I guess I should go type then," she suggested gravely.

"This is Sunday. Take the day off. I need to ride over and talk to an Indian I know, but I'll be back about one. If you're game, we could try another picnic. I promise I won't throw you down on the blanket and savage you."

She thought for a minute, then looked up at him through her lashes. "Can we sip lemonade and make clever conversation for a mannerly half hour?"

His laughter brightened her mood. He left her to grapple with the pancake batter and went upstairs to change his rumpled clothes.

He left the house feeling bright in spite of the few restless hours he'd slept, but his cheery mood darkened when he spoke to Tsosi at the barn. The young Navajo listened with a blank face when he was told about the snake incident.

"Do you have any idea who could have put the snake in Mrs. McKenna's bed?

"No."

"Can you think of a reason why somebody wanted to scare her with a coiled snake?

"No."

"Did anybody come out here last night while we were gone?"

"No."

"Are there extra keys to the back door?"

The boy shrugged, and walked off to saddle Blade's horse without another word.

Blade wanted to kick the stable wall down in frustration. Even the damned horse knew the kid hadn't been straightforward with him. But he did nothing, because he could think of nothing to do except get on the roan and leave. He couldn't force Tsosi to communicate with him. Even though they had gotten along as friends for two years, he was abruptly reminded just how much of an outsider he was to the Navajos. It often took a lifetime for people to learn to trust each other.

It wasn't until he was almost out of the yard that he heard Tsosi talking to his mother. He didn't understand any of the language but he definitely understood the tone. They were arguing quite violently about something. Finally the boy turned and stomped toward the barn. Moments later he appeared again on the back of the big black. He rode without saddle or bridle, yet he bested any rider Blade had ever seen. He rode with the wind, part of the animal beneath him. And today both were utterly wild.

Blade almost followed him. But instead, he decided to go with the original plans. Joseph Bemish had given him the name of an Indian who'd spent time with the prospector who'd been Phelan's original guide. Blade remembered meeting the man on several occasions. Maybe that was the place he should start from. Maybe then he'd have a glimmer of what Phelan called a treasure.

Besides, he wanted to spend the afternoon with Ruth. Out in the open where they could be alone, but not so far away from civilization that he might again rekindle this morning's passion. He hoped to cool that for the time being. Or so he told himself.

The temperature had dropped during the night, and the wind had begun to blow. He'd noticed the change earlier, but his mind had been occupied with thoughts of Ruth. Now, still thinking about Ruth, he hoped the afternoon picnic wouldn't have to be canceled. They both needed a respite.

Actually the ride was pointless. The man's cabin was empty, probably for quite some time.

"Phelan, what in the hell did you find that was so important you risked your life for it?" Blade yelled the question to the pine trees.

The wind seemed to have blown away its fury by the time he got home. By afternoon the sun had warmed the breeze and the weather was extremely pleasant.

Ruth was waiting. Her lightweight coat hung over the back of a chair.

"Why don't we walk?" he asked. "I've been in the saddle all morning. A walk would do me good."

He picked up the basket and opened the door for her.

She wore a simple lavender wool dress that made her look deliciously feminine, and Blade approved of her choice. There was an amethyst brooch among his mother's jewelry he'd always loved. He'd give anything to pin it on Ruth's lacy collar and kiss the pulse on her neck as he did so.

Blade had been raised around women who wore rich clothes and exquisite jewels. He wished he could give Ruth such finery. He realized she seldom wore jewelry of any kind and most of the clothes she wore, while of good quality and excellent workmanship, were plain, severe in design.

Except for her undergarments. Those were luscious. He wondered if she recognized the types of lace and decoration her former seamstress friend had used on her lingerie. They were fit for the dowry of a sultan's bride. And no one deserved them more than Ruth.

His willful mind wandered to what she had on beneath the lace and lavender dress.

"Where shall we put the blanket?"

For a second he thought her voice was part of his fantasy, and he couldn't believe his luck.

Reality intruded when he tripped on a tree root. He straightened quickly and looked around at the slopes, the meadows, and the mountains.

"Up there," he told her, pointing to a spot on the next hill that offered a good view of the snowcapped mountains and of the house. "Be careful you don't sit on a cactus."

"You're joking!"

"Nope. See that little stickery fellow there? I sat on one of those when I first got here. I was in a hurry for my lunch as usual, and didn't watch where I parked my backside. Phelan nearly rolled on the ground laughing."

The plant in question was only ankle high but possessed quite a few lethal thorns. Ruth gave it wide berth.

"I'll watch myself," she said gravely. "Did you really sit on it?"

"Yes, ma'am." He tried to avoid her laughing eyes. "Now what's for lunch?"

"Lots of stuff," she said playfully. "Bread, cheese, apples, pickles, some dried beef, sugar cookies, and half a cherry pie."

"Hertha Bird at the Yellow Canary tried to sell me a mince pie. Your brother ordered one a week, so I've eaten enough mincemeat to last me a lifetime. I like cherry better so I bought that. "

"Good. I hate mince pie. It tastes like medicine."

"Give me a couple of those sugar cookies." He snatched them out her hands, squeezing her fingers as he did so. "I'm a hungry man."

She looked at him coolly. "I also brought us a couple bottles of root beer."

"Love root beer." He leaned over and kissed her lightly. It was on the tip of his tongue to tell her he loved her, too. The thought startled him so much he sat up straight and stuffed a piece of bread in his mouth. At least he couldn't make a careless remark with his mouth full.

Hell, if he didn't watch what he was doing, he was going to find himself in real trouble.

10

March weather in Flagstaff constantly changed. The cold, windy spell had passed. For the past three days it had been warm and springlike. Ruth had taken her daily walks with only a corduroy jacket over her clothes, and she had luxuriated in the sunny warmth, knowing with absolute certainty that winter hadn't yet ended.

She endeavored to spend at least two hours each afternoon outside the house, away from the typing machine. She felt the same need to exercise that she'd had after Farley's death, when she'd walked the streets of St. Louis till her shoes needed new soles. Walking soothed her hurt and confusion.

Although she experienced moments of deep sadness each day over Donal's death—and the unresolved conflict between them—she was able to put it in perspective. She'd loved him as blindly and fiercely as a small child adores an older hero. She'd depended on him for support after their parents died, and for the spurts of attention he'd given her thereafter. But now she understood what she hadn't been able to see in the past.

Much of Donal's affection was contingent upon her doing his bidding, working on his projects, simplifying his life. Not that he didn't love her. He did, in his own way. But he loved her best when her life centered on him. It had always been that way. When she chose to marry Farley and create a life of her own, he'd dismissed her like a bad servant.

That, too, saddened her, but it also made tolerable the unresolved problems between them. Unless she'd been willing to become his drudge again, their problems probably wouldn't have been resolved.

She tried not to think about how much her relationship with her husband had echoed the one with her brother. She wasn't quite ready to be that frank with herself. Yet she saw the similarities and knew that one day soon she'd have to confront them.

Sometimes Jennie accompanied her on her walks, but more often than not she went alone. Once Marie Manyhorses went along for part of the excursion, and told her some Navajo lore. Once as she walked she met Tsosi coming back from someplace and he stopped and talked with her.

The only person who didn't walk with her was Blade. Since that fateful night when she laid in his arms, and the fiery episode in the kitchen the following morning, he seemed to avoid her, often leaving early and returning to the house late. And he appeared quite preoccupied, more often than not working till late in his office.

Ruth was glad Jennie had moved into the house. It

made her days less lonely. And it gave her less time to
dwell on Blade. She understood part of her attraction
to Blade was his protesctiveness. His aura of security
was seductive because she was so vulnerable. But part
of it was due to her own curiosity. Would his lovemaking be as glorious as his kisses?

She was thankful Jennie arrived when she did. Jennie, more than Ruth's own high standards, kept her
from straying.

Jennie was a hard-working young woman, sweet
tempered and quite good company. And her sense of
humor was a bonus.

With Ruth's help, she'd turned the little bedroom
off the pantry into her own cozy retreat. Then she convinced Ruth to take the time to redecorate her own
bedroom.

After the snake incident, Ruth declared if she was
ever again going to be comfortable in the downstairs
bedroom, she would to have to make some changes.
Her efforts started out small with the linen and then
moving the bed, but quickly the project avalanched.
Between the two of them, she and Jennie borrowed furniture, lamps, ornaments, and bedclothes from other
rooms and made a complete change.

They located the attic after Blade mentioned its existence. The steps had been hidden behind the floor-to-
ceiling double doors in a closet in the back bedroom
Blade used as his office.

It was the first time she'd ever been in his workroom. She'd seen some of his pencil drawings in a
sketchbook, but nothing prepared her for his office. It
was about twelve feet square, with a pair of long, narrow, double-sashed windows in the outside wall. Blade

had removed the fancy curtains to make the most of the northern exposure. And he had placed the large, flat-topped desk at an angle to the windows so the true north light would come over his shoulder as he worked at the drawing board.

He'd rigged up an easel-like contraption and could slant the drawing board however he needed it.

Evidently he had the same nocturnal habits her brother once had because he'd placed lamps in spots where he could take advantage of light. A well-used ash chest of drawers—five feet high with deep drawers on the bottom, and smaller drawers on top—had been placed to the left of, and at right angles to, the desk. And a lamp sat atop the chest exactly at the point where it would cast its glow on the drawing board.

The chair, a comfortable swivel model that tilted and had casters, looked quite new.

Noticing the oriental charcoal brazier resting between the two windows, Ruth nudged Jennie.

"Blade can heat the room, his coffee, and his snack all with the same fire. And it's safer than that monstrous kerosene heater in the other office."

In Ruth's estimation, open flame on the hardwood floor probably would have been safer than the battered dinosaur in Donal's office. She refused to touch the thing, preferring to typewrite with frozen fingers.

Now she cast a speculative glance at the brazier. Maybe she could use it on the cold days when Blade wasn't working.

The office was orderly. Vellum field drawings had been carefully rolled and pigeonholed on shelves against the east wall. Ruth knew she should go on up to the attic, but she was overcome with curiosity. She simply had to look at some of Blade's drawings! She'd lived too many years with archaeologists not to be nosy, and she wanted to understand her brother's last obsession.

It didn't require much snooping to find what she wanted. After all, Blade's workroom had everything properly labeled and stored. The colored drawings of the site at the present time had been placed neatly in the bottom drawer of the chest.

Drawn on heavy ivory paper, they were renderings of the excavation as it progressed from one stage of discovery to another. The drawer above it held colored drawings of how the site must have looked hundred of years before, a full-fledged community, alive with people.

The third large drawer, the uppermost one, held pencil drawings of numerous sizes, some on drawing pads, some on cheap paper, and others on vellum. Sketches of modern Indians, mostly from the surrounding area, filled it. There was as wonderful portrayal of Che on the supply wagon that had been drawn on a length of brown paper from a shop in town.

Jennie squealed with delight when she saw it.

Ruth had picked up a small notebook from a table setting against the wall near the attic doors. As she absently flipped through the book, she found herself staring at her own face, laughing and joyous. It stunned her.

She looked so spirited and vibrant. So beautiful. Did he honestly see her that way?

The attic awaited them. "We'd better quit peeking at Blade's secrets before he catches us."

Reluctantly, Jennie returned the drawing of Che to the drawer.

Ruth opened the wide doors and found the stairs.

"Let's go exploring! There has to be some good stuff in the attic."

And there they discovered paradise. It was apparent to them that everything Donal and Blade had considered inappropriate for bachelor living had been hurriedly stuffed into the attic. Not to mention family treasures and odds and ends Mrs. Phillips had wanted stored.

The women spent hours poking around the dim loft like a pair of schoolgirls, unearthing old hats, boxes of clothing, odd pieces of furniture, bric-a-brac, curios of every sort, an expensive sewing machine and a trunk crammed with fabric, plus all the stored memorabilia of Amanda Phillips's tragic lifetime.

The first thing they hauled down was the sewing machine. It was a bit of a wrestling match but they lugged it over to Marie's cabin, along with the material Blade had purchased for Jennie. Marie, it seemed, was quite adept with the treadle machine. Then they raced back up the stairs to continue their adventures.

"Look at this bustle." Jennie held up a haircloth fashion necessity of the previous decade.

"Why are you whispering?" Ruth asked.

"I feel guilty."

"Why? We aren't stealing anything. We're just borrowing. Blade said most of this stuff was downstairs when he moved in. He and my brother needed more space and less frilly doo-dads, so they hauled everything up here. You and I are just moving some of it back down."

"I still feel guilty," the girl said. "It's so beautiful and there's so much of it. Should we be touching it?"

"Right now we're leasing the house and all of these things. Would you like this washstand in your room?" Ruth pushed a dusty covering aside to reveal the pretty stand.

Jennie gasped, her eyes filled with wonder at the marble-topped mahogany washstand with a hand-painted tile splash board and brass hardware. The tiles nearly matched the quilt she'd chosen for her bed.

"Oh, could I?"

"Certainly. And I think this pitcher and bowl go with it. See the lilacs? Now, how are we going to get it down the steps?"

"Blade," they said in unison, and laughed. After only a few days they were becoming close friends.

Ruth gave Jennie the heavy mahogany bureau in her room and replaced it with a lighter-colored birch dresser with leaf-carved handles, glove boxes on the sides, and a wishbone-framed mirror. A pottery cat preened on the top of the dresser, reminding Ruth of the brief time she'd owned a pet.

She'd packed away the dark velvet and satin crazy patch quilt under which the snake had reposed and had chosen instead a heavy white woven coverlet with a deep fringe. The heavy burgundy velvet drapes had been replaced with a natural color rejah silk hung over white lace curtains. A dainty bowl of Belgian-beaded violets sat on the fruitwood lady's desk in front of the window.

The bedroom had lost its somber, gloomy opulence and had an aura of airiness and light.

"I might not live here very long," she told Jennie as they put goose down pillows into starched cases, "but

I'm going to enjoy myself while I do. This is the prettiest bedroom I've ever had."

Now that her bedroom and Jennie's were to their own special tastes, Ruth was ready to get back to her routine. She'd typed all morning on a particularly difficult and messy bunch of papers, promising herself the reward of a lengthy stroll after she ate.

She dressed herself to go out right after her midday meal, carefully smoothing and repinning her hair. The morning sun had been bright and she thought it would be another wonderful day to walk off some of her frustrations. Blade had again left for parts unknown before she'd awoken.

She scowled at her reflection in the dresser mirror. Romance apparently didn't become easier as a person grew older. She felt as muddled and frivolous as she had at age fourteen when she'd had a mad infatuation for the grocery delivery boy who came to Aunt Minnie's house.

Aunt Minnie wasn't really her aunt; she was a distant cousin of Ruth's late mother. That was the last year Ruth stayed with Aunt Minnie—the summer of the grocery boy—because Aunt Minnie's husband died the following winter and the older woman moved from St. Louis to Charleston to be with her son, and sadly they'd lost touch.

The light in the pretty room suddenly dimmed and, frowning, Ruth looked toward the lace curtains. A heavy cloud buildup was approaching from the west.

"I knew the nice weather wouldn't last." She was disappointed, as she'd looked forward to the few hours away from the typing machine. "I'll go walking anyway. I'll just wear a coat and keep an eye on the clouds."

Her mind flitted from one thing to another as she dressed in a simple pongee shirtwaist and the rose brown skirt that went with it.

A tapping on the bedroom door alerted her to Jennie's presence.

"Come in."

"There's a man here to see you, Mrs. McKenna."

"A man? Who is it?"

"I do not know," Jennie said. "He didn't say his name. He just said to tell you. He's in the parlor."

"He's probably selling brushes, or corsets. Thank you, Jennie. Tell him I'll be right there."

"Should I fix some tea?"

"If it's a drummer, I don't want to encourage him to stay."

The girl started to leave, then hesitated. "Mrs. McKenna. Che is here today."

"Did he bring the man out from town?"

"No, he came first. He came to visit my auntie."

Ruth hid a smile. Since Jennie came to the ranch, Che managed some excuse to visit about every other day. "If you've finished in the pantry, you can go on over. And you don't need to hurry back. As soon as I finish with the man in the parlor, I'm going out walking."

"Good afternoon," she said briskly as she walked to the parlor door.

She hesitated when she realized the man looking out the front window was the same slender fellow with thinning hair she'd noticed at the hotel in Flagstaff last Saturday night. "Do I know you?"

"Yes, actually you do, Mrs. McKenna. We met a number of years ago on an archaeological expedition. I

believe it was the last one your brother and your husband worked on together."

Ruth disliked him immediately. There was something about his oily manner that made her want to run
to the dining room and count the silver. She decided
instantly to stay right in the doorway instead of enter-
ing the parlor.

"Oh?" Her tone held a definite chill.

"I'd like to talk to you about that expedition." His
smile displayed long yellow teeth.

"Why?" Ruth knew immediately she wasn't going to
like what he had to say. Her stomach tensed. Apparently little good had come from that fateful expedition
which had estranged her from Donal.

He looked a trifle insolent, but quickly masked the
expression. "Can I sit down?"

"Is this going to take long? I have other things to
do." She didn't bother to sound polite. All she could
think of was how she wanted to air out the room as
soon as he left.

"It won't take long." His voice was peevish. "The
altitude makes me dizzy."

She wasn't sure she believed him, but all she needed was to have him keel over on the floor in a heap.
She wished she'd asked Jennie to stay till he went
away and wished Blade would come home. "Go
ahead," she said gracelessly. "Sit down, but please
hurry and tell me the purpose of your business. Like I
said, I have things to do."

"Yes, your ladyship," he said sarcastically as he lowered himself into one of the Roman chairs. "Anything
you say, your grace."

Outrage jolted through her like a thunderbolt.

Before the man had his backside settled comfortably on the seat of the Roman chair, Ruth grabbed a walking cane—the same one she'd appropriated from the train—from the hat rack in the entryway and descended on him like a goddess of war.

"How dare you speak to me in such a manner, you insolent whelp! Get out of my house this instant!"

He recoiled in astonishment. A cowardly man through and through, he cringed away from the cane, certain she was about to bring the instrument down on his head. "I'm sorry," he sniveled. "Don't beat me!"

"Get out!" She poked the cane at his ribs to emphasize her words.

He scrambled to his feet, twisting away from the cane, and tripped. His feet slipped on the edge of the oriental carpet, and he groveled about on all fours.

"Get up, and get out! I don't have to deal with the likes of you."

"Wait! I have something to tell you."

She took a deep breath and calmed her temper. Slowly she moved the cane away and let him rise. But the blue fire in her eyes menaced him.

He was approximately her height, and weighed ten or so pounds more than she, but Ruth had the advantage.

She was furious. And she held the cane.

He dusted himself off indignantly, as if he was the offended party, and said in a disgruntled voice, "My name is Orlie Taswell. Did your husband ever mention me?"

"No."

"I came to your house in Saint Louis several times to see him." He waited to see if that meant anything to

Ruth and when it apparently did not, he continued, "We talked about the expedition. We talked a lot."

"Which expedition?"

Taswell backed a step or two toward the parlor door, in case he needed to beat a hasty retreat.

"The Indian mounds. The last expedition Doctor Phelan and Doctor McKenna worked on together, when there was some trouble about a missing journal."

Since that was a hurtful subject for Ruth, she hardly wanted to discuss it with this bad-mannered worm. Yet she did wonder how he knew about the bad blood between the men. She had thought it was a private matter. The tense knot in her stomach alerted her to more unpleasant news.

"I came to the house after Doctor McKenna died, but you'd sold the place. I had some trouble finding you. Did you get a packet of papers I sent you?"

"What are you talking about?"

"A big packet with your name on it. I went over to your apartment to see you but you'd already left. Did you get it?"

"What . . . ? Wait, maybe I did."

He waited expectantly. "Well, did you read it?."

"No. I didn't. The messenger came while I was packing and I stuck it in something. A box or a trunk. Is this important?"

He looked stunned, then utterly violent. "You dumb bitch . . . !"

The end of the cane jabbed him right in the belly button. He gasped and doubled over.

"Get out!"

The door flew open, and Taswell was propelled out onto the porch before he had a chance to fend her off.

He jerked himself erect and found himself facing twin blue flames. He'd never seen a woman so angry. His wife had been a weepy, chicken-witted slut who had feared his violence till he deserted her. His mother wasn't much different. Orlie Taswell had never encountered a strong-willed female in his life.

"Wait," he yelled, hoping the sound of his voice would intimidate her.

It didn't. She stepped out onto the porch brandishing the cane like a sword.

"Doctor McKenna was paying me!" He'd reached the end of the porch and was fishing down with his foot for the step.

Ruth stopped. She didn't understand exactly what he was saying. Or perhaps she didn't wish to understand, but her interest was titillated by the mention of pay. Toward the end of his life, Farley had grown very tightfisted with his money. Why, when he nearly let them freeze before ordering coal, would he pay a louse like Taswell? She was almost afraid to know.

"Doctor McKenna paid you?"

"And I want more money. That's why I sent the envelope to you. You can pay me now."

"You can't be serious. I don't know you, and I don't especially like what little I do know. What on earth would I pay for? Do you perform some type of service? Why did Farley pay you?"

"The journal."

"What journal? What are you talking about?" Her patience was wearing thin and her anxiety rising. She hissed with exasperation and advanced on him. He skittered down the front steps, stumbling once, but not quite falling.

"Your brother's expedition journal." He backed several steps across the yard. He realized with a sudden flash that she was going to be furious with the information he was imparting. And she still held the cane. He slinked farther back.

The journal.

Donal Phelan's journal.

She blinked, and swallowed. There was a loud ringing in her ears.

"No." It couldn't be true. She didn't believe it. She must have heard wrong. Yet her quivering insides told her that her hearing was perfect.

The sun skittered behind a cloud and Ruth felt as if a light had been blown out in her life. Had Farley lied?

"You knew," Taswell was saying. "You were in on it, too. You covered for Doctor McKenna."

"No. I don't even know what you're telling me. I don't understand what you're talking about." But she did.

"You're lying, goddamnit! You just don't want to pay me . . . But if you don't, I'll ruin your husband's sterling reputation!"

She was down the steps after him, and he was running as fast as his legs could go—across the yard and over to his rented horse. He could hear her yelling behind him.

"Stop," she screamed. "Tell me the truth!"

He didn't stop. He ran like hell, hauling himself up on the nag and bolting for town.

He was furious that he'd failed so miserably at this little extortion attempt when the other one had kept him so comfortable. Who would have thought the bitch would have been so tough? After all, Dr. Farley McKenna, renowned archaeologist and author, had been the easiest mark he'd ever known.

As he raced toward town he tried to think clearly, to figure out how to approach her again. He wondered if she'd shoot him if he went back to the house. He couldn't believe she'd fought him so fiercely. That old fart McKenna had folded like an accordion when he put the bite on him.

The memory gave Taswell a laugh. Scholarly types were so damned dumb at times. They had lots of book smarts, but no common sense. Any stooge knew when he bought stolen goods, he paid more than once. The hotter the item, the longer the installments.

It had been sweet while it lasted! Too bad it was over. He'd extorted a small fortune from McKenna. All for a little boost to a mediocre career. Hell, McKenna never had it in him to be a respectable archaeologist. He was too lazy to work at it, to go out in the field and sweat, to get dirt under his fingernails. All he wanted was to sit in his armchair and pontificate.

Better give it up, Taswell told himself. There were other towns and other suckers. But it irked him that McKenna was due to make another payment when he'd conked off. The money that planted the old coot probably should have gone to him—Taswell.

He guessed a man in his racket should expect a few bad days. Sometime the con got hoodwinked just like the dupe. So it was time to cut and run. Maybe he'd go south for the rest of the winter.

But Ruth McKenna's attitude stuck in his craw.

Maybe he'd stay awhile longer—safely out of the way of the lethal cane, of course—and harass her a bit.

Pay her back for humiliating him. Give her a little scare. Show her she wasn't so tough, after all.

Ruth couldn't remember exactly how long she'd been walking, or for that matter, what direction she'd been walking in, but she did know she was getting cold. She chastised herself for forgetting her gloves.

The sun, which had played hide-and-seek with the clouds for quite a while, had now disappeared behind the gray cloud bank, and the temperature had dropped. In her first furious spurt of energy she had fled the house to walk off her incredulity and anger. *It cannot be true.* She said these words over and over as if they were some lifeline to the past. But the faster she walked and the farther she went, the more she saw the sense of what that vile man said. As well as all the things Donal had said the night she'd married Farley.

What if it were true? What if that vermin had indeed been paid for Donal's journal?

For a long time, Ruth had convinced herself that Donal had not even kept a journal on that particular expedition. But he had always kept a detailed site journal on every expedition he'd ever been on, exactly like the one she was now endeavoring to transcribe.

Somewhere in the vague recesses of her memory, she conjured the picture of Donal making entries in a ledgerbook during that summer. What if he had? What if he had kept it up as he always did—day-by-day entries on the project, detailed measurements and odd sketches, weather information, comments on findings at the dig, with a brilliant theory thrown in now and then? If he had a site journal, and it disappeared as he'd insisted it had, had Farley stolen it?

No. She remembered being told by several witnesses that Farley had been ten miles away on the night Donal said the site journal was stolen.

But *she* had been in camp, in her brother's sleeping quarters changing the sheets on his cot, straightening up his mess as she had done a hundred times in the past.

Dear God, had Donal thought she had stolen the damned thing?

It all fell into place then, like the pattern of a checkerboard. She remembered with crystal clarity coming out of the doorway and seeing Orlie Taswell loitering nearby. She'd even spoken to him as she passed.

A much younger Orlie Taswell. A student. He must not be as old as she was; but now he looked fifteen years more than his age, with his thinning, grayish hair and sallow skin.

Had he stolen the book? He must have.

Somewhere during her walk, she'd accepted the fact that a journal had existed. The thought sickened her. All the lies, the hurt.

Donal had not misplaced it in his monumental mess. It had indeed been stolen as Donal had sworn.

Could Farley McKenna possibly have purchased it from Taswell? Ruth had always thought of her husband as an honorable man. But where was the honor in buying stolen research material? In publishing it as one's own?

Then an even more unpalatable thought assailed her.

What if Farley had masterminded the theft? A man so lacking in integrity as to publish stolen material surely might be low enough to plan its theft.

Farley's book about the expedition had been his one great claim to fame. It certainly had enhanced his reputation in the academic world. His professorship at the university was secure, as was his comfortable life. He'd enlarged upon his original theories in articles. He'd even been asked to lecture at other universities.

Ruth naturally assumed he'd want to go back into the field, to further his research. But he declined, first claiming conflicting schedules, then frail health.

Now she wanted to scream at her gullibility.

"I've got to find the envelope! Maybe some answers are in there."

The wind suddenly gusted off the mountains. Ruth drew her coat around her. She looked about, trying to get her bearings. She was somewhere in the pines and had no idea where.

"I'm lost." She laughed bitterly. "Apparently I've been lost for a long time."

Looking left and right, she quickly climbed an incline. The clouds were so thick and dark, she couldn't see the mountains. She closed her eyes and stilled her fears, feeling that her body was facing west. The meadows were also west. Once she got there, she knew she could see the big house. She hurried in that direction.

She buried her cold hands deep in her coat pockets and tried not to think of the gloves and scarf she'd left in her bedroom. Just as she tried not to think about the fact that her entire marriage to Farley could well have been a fraud.

Her skirt caught on a spiny cactus and she stopped

to detach it. The wind whined as it blew through the pines. Beneath her feet the pine needles grew slick from the increasing moisture in the air. Ruth skidded more than once, then slowed her pace. She had to be sensible. If she fell and broke a bone, she knew she might very well die from exposure before someone found her.

Blade.

"I haven't thought about him for more than an hour." More than anything in the world, she would have liked to see him come riding over the next knoll. As if on cue, she heard the sound of a large animal moving through the woods toward her. Blade.

She nearly shrieked in dismay moments later when an elk appeared not many yards away. The tawny animal was far bigger than a cow, bigger than most horses, which it more closely resembled, with its long narrow muzzle. And it was definitely male. The beginnings of a new set of antlers, which would probably grow into a rack seven feet across before rutting season, were visible above his perked ears.

She didn't utter a sound, she didn't move, except to breathe. The huge beast honored her with a mere glance as it lumbered on toward a more important destination, his cream-colored rump shining like a beacon in contrast to his brownish-orange coat. She guessed she wasn't enough of a threat for him to notice, much to her vast relief.

She started to walk again, down a hill, around a bend. The direction felt right and she prayed that her instincts were correct.

She didn't see the dark shadow in the trees until it was upon her.

In the first instant she thought the elk had returned to trample her. Then a black cloth flew over her head and a steely arm clutched her around the neck, squeezing, choking.

She couldn't breathe or see. A scream started deep inside her, but was crushed, strangled.

She brought her boot down sharply on what she thought was foot. The arm jerked away from her neck. She fought the shroud which blinded her. Her assailant shoved her and she stumbled, still clawing at the cloak of darkness over her head. It slipped, allowing her a glimpse of light. She saw feet and pine needles, and . . .

Pain.

Her attacker knocked her along the jaw, and she skidded, flailing her arms to keep her balance. She smelled the strong scent, the bark, the pitch, just before her head was rammed into the tree trunk.

She heard a voice as she fell. But she couldn't make out the words. Couldn't even tell if it was male or female. Couldn't think of anything more than the pain along her jawbone and cheek, and her desperate need to get the cloth off her face.

With fingers stiff as much from fear as the blowing wind, she tugged at the dingy rag. It snagged, hung up on the tree bark she leaned against. She bent forward, almost toppling over with the effort. The fabric slipped down to the ground.

The black-clad shape of her ambusher ran into the trees. A light fog touched the earth, and a peculiar icy mist clouded Ruth's vision. She wanted nothing more than to shut her eyes and rest, but she could not. She had to get back to the house, to Blade.

Using every ounce of strength she had, Ruth pushed

herself up off the damp earthy bed of pine needles. She touched chilled fingers to her aching cheek. It stung, and there was a trace of blood on her hand when she glanced at it. Stepping away from the meager shelter of the Ponderosa pine, she took her first step toward home.

It had begun to snow.

The front door was unlocked. In her haste to put the unpleasant scene with Orlie Taswell out of her mind, she'd rushed out and forgotten to lock it. Ruth went inside and closed the door behind her.

The hall was almost dark—the gloomy winter afternoon had robbed it of light. The house was empty. Jennie had gone off to spend the evening in the company of her handsome suitor, Che, and Ruth didn't expect her to be back early from Marie's cabin. With the weather change, perhaps she wouldn't return at all.

Ruth stopped in the hallway and took a deep breath to settle her nerves. The house was warmer than it was outside. Evidently Jennie had filled the kitchen stove with wood before she left. There was no fire in the fireplace. No lamps had been lit. The parlor was dark and unoccupied. Ruth didn't bother to remove her coat and hat. Instead she went quickly down the hall to the bathroom to wash her grimy face and hands.

One lamp had been lit in the kitchen, but it had been turned down very low, so the room was shadowy. Jennie had probably decided Ruth would be back late from her walk and didn't want her to trip in the dark. Jennie was a good girl.

The beef and vegetable soup they'd put together earlier simmered on the back of the stove. Ruth was thankful about that. She didn't think she was up to cooking tonight but she knew a bowl of soup would warm her.

She touched her cheek and groaned. "I wonder if I'm going to be bruised?"

A cold compress, she decided, would help her face.

She took the last few steps toward the bathroom feeling more weary than she could ever remember. Who could have attacked her?

Her fingers tightened on the glass doorknob, and she gave the door a shove.

At that moment Gladius Blade rose out of the hot, pine-scented bath he'd just taken. He was as naked as the day he was born.

11

The moment she saw him standing up in the big white bathtub, clutching a huckaback towel in one hand, his face frozen in astonishment, her mind went blank. She couldn't stop staring at him.

He was so big. So muscular. So breathtakingly male. Her breathing stopped. Her heart, however, threatened to explode.

Blade regained his senses first. Stepping gingerly over the edge of the tub onto the braided rug, he reached behind her and closed the door.

"It's drafty," he said hoarsely.

Ruth nodded stupidly. A hurricane could have blown through the place and she wouldn't have felt it.

He wrapped the towel around his hips, more to control his wayward body than for modesty. The coarse huck towel hadn't been made for such purposes, and it immediately threatened to fall off if he dared to breathe hard.

"My God, what happened to you?" he asked as he noticed the dirt, and chunks of bark on her clothes and the vivid scratches on her cheek. A purple bruise was forming along her cheekbone. Her hat was wildly askew, her hair drooped, and her coat sleeve had been torn at the seam.

"What?" She couldn't remember the question. Her eyes strayed to the knotted towel, fascinated by how the knot loosened every time he exhaled.

"You're a mess! What happened?"

She continued to look at him with glazed eyes.

He was frightened—something horrible must have happened to her. Blade quickly pulled the towel from his hips and dried off the few remaining water drops from his bath, then shrugged on his robe. It was a ratty old brown thing, threadbare and rumpled, and the tie belt had long since disappeared. It gave a pretense of propriety, but barely covered more than the towel.

"Ruth, did you fall off a horse?"

He realized immediately how idiotic the question was. Ginger had been in her stall when he returned from the dig.

He took her by the shoulders and was studying her face. She mustered all her effort and shook her head. "No," she croaked. "I was attacked."

"Good God!" He swept his dirty clothes off the seat of the chair and sat her down. Then he unpinned her hat and removed it. Afterward he began to unbutton her coat.

Her color was high, he thought from the cold and the wind.

"Are you hurt, Ruth?"

"My cheek . . ."

"Yes, I see. Anywhere else?" All he could think of was rape.

She swallowed and shuddered. Her hands rose to her throat. "He had his arm around my neck and I couldn't breathe. The cloth was choking me."

"What cloth?"

"Over my head. He threw a heavy cloth over my head. He jumped out from behind a tree and threw something dark over my head. It caught around my neck and choked me." She unfastened the buttons of her high collar.

"Here, let me help." Relieved that her injuries were not more serious, he leaned over and undid the coat all the way, and then reached up to the shirt-waist. He could see by Ruth's nervous gestures that she still suffered a choking sensation, although neither coat nor blouse was tight at the neckline. In his desire to help relieve her distress, he forgot how inadequate his own robe was, until she reached out and touched his chest.

She laid the palm of her hand in his auburn thatch and followed the hairline down to his stomach.

He straightened quickly and pulled the robe closed, knowing she didn't realize how her touch affected him.

The water from his bath made its final slurping gurgle down the drain, startling them both.

"Would you like a bath? I remembered to heat more water."

"Yes." She sighed.

Blade fetched another huckaback towel and wash-cloth from the shelf, and began to fill the tub. "How about a sponge?"

"That would be marvelous. Are there any rose-geranium bath salts left? I think I could lie in the hot water and soak myself for hours."

"I'll get your wrapper," he said gruffly. The vision of Ruth stretched out in the big tub had just flashed into his mind, and so he wanted to leave the bathroom immediately.

He grabbed his clean pair of drawers from the shelf and made his hasty escape.

Across the hallway in her bedroom, Blade carefully lighted the lamp and placed it on the dresser. This was the first time he'd been in the room since he carted the heavy bureau out for Jennie. He was amazed at the difference Ruth's redecorating had made. Removing the dark, opulent furnishings and ornaments, replacing them with delicate furniture and light fabric, had definitely improved the room's appearance and mood. He liked it, he decided. The decor reminded him of Ruth—open, natural, and honest.

He knew at that moment he intended to make love to her.

He pulled on the soft fawn-colored underdrawers and buttoned them. After crossing the room and closing the drapes against the snowstorm blowing outside, he stripped the coverlet from the bed and folded it over the quilt rack. Then he neatly turned down the soft sheets and went to the wardrobe for her wrapper.

He chose a silk negligee the color of a summer sunrise. His fingers touched the exquisite Irish lace on the collar. Ruth would look like a goddess in it. He wanted to place the gown on her soft shoulders—and he wanted to slip it off again.

He felt like a schoolboy on the brink of his first sexual encounter. Anxious, alive, and excited, aware that life would never be the same.

He hesitated.

There would be no going back once he walked in that door. She would be his.

Good or bad, both their lives were about to change forever.

Did she want him? He remembered the stroke of her fingers on his naked chest only moments ago. A lover's gesture. He knew she needed him. He remembered her fiery kisses a few days before. There was no doubt in his mind that she felt the same desire he did.

For the first time in his life, Blade recognized how much more of a chance a woman took than a man. It wasn't just pregnancy, but the whole idea that a man could walk away from a woman's bed with no more on his mind than buttoning his fly correctly. But with Ruth, if he walked back into the bathroom with her robe in his hands, he'd made a commitment. In his heart he'd as good as admitted he loved her.

He poured a small amount of her rose and lavender potpourri into a saucer and put it on the nightstand. Then he drew his robe around him and stepped forward to meet his destiny.

The sweet-smelling water lapped over her pink skin. She languished in liquid bliss. *I love him.* The thought came from nowhere.

When the door opened, she didn't open her eyes, didn't look up. Didn't feel a twinge of embarrassment about lying there covered only by clear petal-scented water.

She knew what was going to happen.

She'd known the moment she walked in and saw him naked. He was wonderful.

She gave one scant reminiscence to poor unfortunate Farley and then forgot the wretch.

Blade didn't say a word. After setting her robe down on the chair, he picked up her hairbrush and stepped toward the tub. Pin by pin he freed the thick satin twist. Stroke by stroke he touched her heart, her soul. Then slowly he looped her hair up, securing it with one pin so it wouldn't fall in the water, and reached for the sponge.

Bending one knee to the rug by the tub, he watched her for a long silent moment. She was as exquisite as a mythical goddess, a water sprite, a mermaid. He trickled the warm fragrant water down the back of her neck and over her shoulders, first one side then the other.

She sighed appreciatively, her mouth forming a tremulous smile. After dipping the sponge deep into the tub, he brought it slowly up the curve of her belly to her waist. Her lashes opened and her eyes gazed at him in sapphire-blue wonder.

"Blade," she whispered.

He bent his head to touch the pulse at the base of her throat with his lips. "Love," he said softly. "My beautiful love."

He brought the sponge to her breast. She sat up straight and turned her mouth to his. With more subtlety than he'd ever known in his life, he grazed her lips with his own. Her arms came slowly out of the watery warmth and wrapped around his neck.

The sponge floated off by itself and bumped against the cast iron edge of the tub. Then he lifted her from the bath and reached for the towel. The cotton cloth felt coarse in his hand, rough against the velvet of her skin. He dried her back and legs slowly, savoring every inch.

He carefully stroked her bruised cheekbone, swearing to himself to avenge the scoundral who hit her. Then he turned his attention to her breasts and stomach.

She watched him, the diligence with which his hands sought every moist droplet. Desire blazed through her, and her knees fairly buckled. Her hands caught the lapels of his robe. She smelled a piney scent on his body, heightened perhaps by his zeal.

Ruth thrust herself forward. His arms enfolded her. The old raggedy robe rubbed against her breasts and she groaned.

With tremendous willpower he pushed away from her.

"Wait." He reached over and pulled out the one pin securing her hair. The silky mass rained down her shoulders and back. His big hands caught in the strands, relishing the texture. Then he turned to the chair and picked up her robe.

"Oh!" She was astonished to see the gift from Elizabeth Malcolm, her dear old friend in St. Louis, the gift which had been given with the hope that Ruth would find love again and marry.

"You belong in clothes like this," Blade said as he draped the gown on her. It was perfect.

He picked her up in his steely arms and carried her to her bed. She smiled into his hot brown eyes, wondering if every woman considered it impossibly romantic to be carried in the arms of her man. Leaning forward she caught his earlobe in her teeth. His mouth sought hers, then Blade dropped his arms from under her knees in order to hug her more tightly. She slid down the front of him, delighting in the rigid evidence of his ardor.

Later, in the magical shadows of the fairy lamp, they shed the few pieces of clothing that covered them, and lowered their heated bodies to the cool linen sheets.

Their mating was more than Ruth hoped for, more than Blade imagined. It was beauty, and joy and glory. It was merely the beginning.

"I'm hungry," Blade whispered.

She roused herself from the sweet oblivion of love-making. "Already?"

"No, not that. Not yet. I'm food hungry."

She dropped back to the pillow and squeezed her long lashes shut. "You are a very strange man."

He swung his long powerful legs over the side of the bed and reached for his drawers. "I know." He grinned. "Do you want something to eat?"

"No." She pulled the quilt up to her chin. She watched him pull on his underwear, marveling at his splendid body. "Well, maybe."

"Maybe, what?" Blade knew her gaze was on him as he dressed, and savored the stirrings of revived interest.

"Maybe I'm hungry," she answered, smiling.

"Didn't you have some soup on the stove?"

Her smirk slipped into flustered distraction. "No . . . the soup! I forgot the soup!"

"The soup is fine. I'll go get us some and we can have a picnic in bed. Wait for me."

"Forever," she murmured when he left the room.

* * *

It snowed all night long.

During the course of the night Ruth discovered Gladius Blade had strong appetites for things other than food. She discovered she also did. And she ascertained that pleasure came in many ways, for Blade incited ecstasy every time he touched her.

"Are you going to sleep all day?"

She stretched and peeked at him from lowered lids.

"If that quilt slips down any lower, this coffee cup will fall on the floor, and I won't be responsible for my actions."

She rubbed one hand over her sleepy face, wincing briefly when she touched her sore cheek, and challenged him by inching the blanket lower.

"Woman! I mean it!" He plunked the cup on the nightstand, ready to pounce on her in a minute.

"All right." She pouted, her eyes sparkling with pleasure. "Hand me my robe. No not that one—the warm blue one. This is the coldest house I've ever been in."

Blade saw her toss down the covers from the reflection in the mirrored doors on the wardrobe. Where had this wonderful, passionate wench come from? Only a few days before she'd been starchy and repressed, her behavior as staid as the clothes she wore. She'd intrigued him then. Now, she drove him wild.

He turned and caught her wonderful body to him in a powerful hug, his head buried deep into her tousled hair.

A few minutes later, Ruth rushed into the kitchen wearing her wool robe over a union suit and carrying a pile of heavy clothes. She had forgotten her modesty of a week ago. At the moment all she could think of was getting warm.

"I have no intention of dressing in that frigid bedroom." She shyly began to dress, her back to him, the wantonness of her actions finally hitting her.

"Where on earth do you plan to wear all those clothes?" Blade asked innocently.

Her partner in debauchery had no idea how dramatically her train of thought had switched tracks. He felt good, no, wonderful, about their night of love. He was obliviously preparing breakfast.

"Upstairs. Where else?" she snapped.

"Are you telling me you plan to use your typing machine today? In gloves?" He was certain she was joking.

"I'm a typewriter," she answered sarcastically. "Of course I'm planning to use the typing machine."

She sounded very much to Blade like the prissy Easterner who had walked into his kitchen the first morning she arrived. He wondered what bee was in her bloomers. Naughty thoughts buzzed through his mind.

He glanced over to where she was sitting and frowned. Their thoughts were not as one. She did not look delighted with the world. It occurred to him right then that he might never comprehend the workings of a woman's mind.

With stiff movements, she pulled heavy stockings over the leggings of her union suit and reached for a stack of petticoats. Her mouth was puckered tight.

"Wait a minute. Put your robe back on and have your breakfast." He plunked a hot plate down on the table, wondering how the naked wanton who'd teased him a short time ago had turned into this prune.

At that moment the wall clock struck ten.

"I don't believe it!" she gasped in horror. "I never sleep this late."

"Hell, it's no wonder you needed a little extra sleep after the romp you had last night. I'm worn out, too." He quickly regretted his words.

Her head bowed and her cheeks went scarlet. Tears of mortification welled in her eyes.

"Hey, I didn't mean to hurt you." He reached out to touch the bruise that stood out so vividly on her cheek.

"You didn't." She turned her face from him. "I'm simply not up on the appropriate way to act with a man I spent the night romping with. I'm sure I'll learn."

He simply picked her up, pulled the rocking chair up to the stove, sat down, and plopped her in his lap.

He rocked her quietly for a long time. Finally she sighed and relaxed against him.

"I'm sorry," she said, her words muffled by his chest.

"I don't want you sorry, or sophisticated, or even witty and bright, Ruth. I want you happy. I want you comfortable with me. I want you to be yourself. What we did last night was wonderful. It meant more to me than I know words to tell you."

She nodded against him.

"I don't want you to go upstairs today. I want you to stay down here with me. I want to cuddle you, and kiss you, and take you back to bed again."

"I want that, too," she said softly. "But I have to do something upstairs. It's important."

"More important than us? Than our future?"

She thought a moment before she answered. "Not

more important than the future, perhaps. But I think I must find it so I can have a future."

"What is it?"

"I forgot to tell you. The packet that man was talking about. Orlie Taswell was his name. He came to see me yesterday." In retrospect she saw why she had been so vague. The moment she saw Blade's handsome body, all other thoughts had been wiped from her mind. "He showed up right after lunch."

"And?"

"It's a long story. May I first have my breakfast?"

When she was settled again close to the stove with her breakfast plate and coffee cup close at hand, she told him about Orlie Taswell's visit.

"The bugger!"

"I know he planned to squeeze me for money," she said. "He told me so." She ate another fork full of scrambled eggs and some toasted bread. "There is no money, of course. Apparently he'd already gotten it all. I barely managed to make ends meet this past year."

"This Taswell's a lying bastard . . ."

"I don't think so, Blade. Oh, I think he's all sorts of despicable things, including a cheat and an extortionist. I want to believe he's a liar, too." She sipped her coffee, then set it down. "But I just feel in the pit of my stomach he was telling the truth about that journal. Donal insisted he'd kept a site journal and Farley stole it."

"My God!" Blade jumped to his feet. "Farley McKenna was the colleague who accused Phelan of stealing research?" Until that moment, Blade had never connected Ruth's dead husband with Phelan's academic and financial problems.

"Farley did that, too? Is there no end to his perfidy?"

Blade sat back down. He took her hand and kissed it. "I'm not sure if this is connected, Ruth. But now it makes more sense than it did when I first heard about it. The reason Phelan couldn't get the financial backing he needed for this expedition was because of some malicious rumors and accusations spread in the academic community against him. Phelan's financial options had suddenly dried up like dead springs."

Ruth stopped eating, sickened. "No wonder he hated me."

"You?" Blade was astonished. "Farley did all the dirty work, didn't he? Why would your brother blame you? I'm sure he didn't hate you, Ruth."

"Yes he did, and with reason. Or he thought he had a good reason. Don't you see, if I had done what he believed I did, my sin was even greater than Farley's. I believe Orlie Taswell might have made it look like I'd stolen the journal for Farley. And that I then married him to cover up the deed." She stood up and went to the sink with her plate.

"Farley published his book using Donal's research and theories. He dedicated the book to me. And he even sent a copy of it to Donal."

"That certainly must have been like salt ground into Phelan's hide."

Ruth sat back down in the chair. "It must have hurt him bitterly to think I'd betrayed him."

Blade could only nod his agreement. Phelan's career, his pride, and his love for his sister had all been trampled by McKenna's misdeed.

"When Farley died so suddenly," Ruth continued, "I didn't even know where Donal was. I'd had not one communication with him since the day I married. Mrs.

Malcolm convinced me to set aside my bad feelings, and my pride, and try to locate him."

"I'm thankful you had a friend like her." He noted that a normal color had returned to Ruth's face. The bluish-purple bruise staining her cheek was a testament to the trials of the past day. Yet he still thought her the most beautiful woman he knew.

"She thought love of family was more important than pride—I think there was some tragedy in her life and some problem that was never settled." Her expression grew sad. "Like mine with Donal. Anyway, I visited his lawyer. A college friend from Harvard. He's about the only person left in Saint Louis who kept in touch with my brother. That's how I found out about the dig, and about this house, and how to get here. Donal had sent him a very enthusiastic letter. I wrote, but Donal didn't answer. At the time I was very hurt. I felt abandoned. Now, I don't blame him."

"He didn't know you were coming, did he?"

"No. I didn't write a second time. I was afraid he might forbid me to come. Mrs. Malcolm had passed away quite suddenly. I had nobody left in Saint Louis. And no more excuses to stay there. I packed up my belongings and bought a one-way ticket."

"You're very brave, Ruth."

"No . . . very afraid."

"Maybe that's the same thing."

"Blade, I have to find that packet Taswell sent me."

"I saw it. The morning after you arrived. You'd been looking in that big green trunk for your mourning clothes. You took the package out and gave it to me to hold. It had your name on it. I didn't know your name till then." He didn't tell her the kind of woman he'd thought she was that morning. That information had better wait till later. "You handed it to me instead of putting it back in the trunk because you said you wanted to read it later."

"I forgot to read it. Where on earth could I have put it?

"Did you put it in your dresser?"

"I think I would have found it when I moved my clothes from the bureau we took to Jennie's room."

They spent a chilly hour looking in her bedroom, pulling out the trunk and searching through its contents, and even venturing up to Phelan's office before the arctic air chased them downstairs again. It was only by accident that Blade found the packet in one of the kitchen drawers.

"How did it get there?" Ruth asked.

"I have no idea. Either one of the town women put it here after the funeral, or Jennie did."

"Let's open it."

"Wait. I have a better idea."

"What?" she asked suspiciously, seeing the mischievous spark in his brown eyes.

"Wait here. I'll be right back."

A short time later she heard a thumping and bumping on the stairway and stole out of the warm kitchen to investigate.

Blade was hauling a double-size mattress down the stairs.

"Very subtle, Mister Blade," she said.

"It's not what you think." With a certain amount of difficulty, considering the tables, bric-a-brac, and odds and ends littering the hallway, Blade lugged the wide mattress into the parlor.

He'd already lit the logs in the fireplace, so a bit of the chill had been taken from the room. After a little furniture rearranging, he positioned the mattress directly atop the rug in front of the flames and dashed back up the stairs for bedding and quilts.

"There," he said, when the mattress was neatly spread. "Now we can read in comfort."

"And what if Jennie comes back to the house?" she asked with some asperity.

"Ruth, we're snowed in, and it's still snowing. I can't even see the cabin from the kitchen window. Jennie won't be back till tomorrow. I guarantee you."

She tossed the brown paper-wrapped packet down on the mattress and plopped ungracefully down beside it. She said nothing, but held her hands out to the fireplace to warm then. She didn't know if she was annoyed at Blade or at herself. Or if she was simply furious with Orlie Taswell for spoiling the remnants of her affection for Farley.

Blade toted in the kitchen wood box and filled it high. Outside the storm shrieked and howled its fury; it was worse than the night before. Inside the fire popped in a brilliant blaze of orange sparkles. The room was bright and cozy. Behind her Blade closed and locked the parlor door. Ruth wished they could shut out the world forever, the hurt and misunderstanding.

The mattress dipped when he knelt on it. She looked steadily into the hungry fire, but the pulse in her neck jumped when he touched the amethyst stain on her cheekbone with his soft lips. He took her hand and laid it on his chest, observing the flame jump into Ruth's eyes when she felt the rhythm of his heartbeat. "I'm here for you," he whispered. "I'll help you any way I can."

Slowly she unwrapped the array of papers.

On the top was a letter from Taswell in a somewhat delicate handwriting explaining the contents. In a way, the graceful scroll added an extra affront to the substance of the note. Orlie Taswell was an educated man. As well as a conniving rogue.

In painstaking detail, Taswell wrote about the expedition's final days. He outlined the plot to steal the journal and the actual acquisition. It was clear he was proud of the deed.

He told what he still had in his possession, and he explained that he expected Ruth to continue to keep up the payments Farley had made, to keep quiet.

The last line read, "Or I'll ruin your dear husband's illustrious reputation."

"I cannot believe he thought I'd countenance this," Ruth said.

"He did not know you, my darling. He'd only met your husband."

"We did meet," she told him. "He saw me around the dig all summer. He knew, everyone knew, how devoted I was to Donal. How could he even think . . . ?"

"Wasn't Farley courting you that summer?"

"Toward the last of the summer, yes. It was sort of a whirlwind thing. I mean we'd known each other for three or more years, but he hadn't paid much attention to me . . . ."

Blade hurt for her when he saw the dawning of realization that McKenna's courtship had been part of the plan to separate Phelan from his valuable journal.

Her eyes filled and the end of her nose got red, but she displayed no other sign. She riffled through the rest of the papers that had been a part of Taswell's cruel batch.

The title page scrawled in Donal Phelan's unmistakable writing was on the top. A few parts of the original journal came next, accompanied by a number of copies in Taswell's dainty writing. There was a list of payments for segments of the journal. But most damning of all was a note from Farley McKenna addressed to Orlie Taswell. It told of a date and time when Phelan would be away from the site. Farley mentioned he'd also made arrangements to be away. And it warned Taswell to keep an eye out for Phelan's "nosy little sister, for she can either destroy us, or be of great use to the plan."

"I think I hate him," Ruth said hoarsely. "He never loved me. He just used me the whole time. He and Taswell must have had a big laugh over that."

"I guess Farley didn't laugh long," Blade commented. "From the dates on these extortion payments, Taswell must have begun to bleed him a short time after you were married."

"Do you think it was Taswell in the woods?"

"Maybe. You humiliated him yesterday. You didn't cave into him like he expected. You didn't give him any money."

She nodded. "I should have taken that cane to his head."

"God, I love strong women!"

She poked him in the stomach. "Watch yourself, big guy. The cane is just out in the hall."

He wrestled her down to the mattress and kissed the tip of her nose.

"Ruth, that package of papers is evidence against Taswell. You said he worked on archaeological digs. If word of the theft and blackmail gets around, he won't ever work again." He leaned back and looked down at her. "Unless you intend to keep everything hushed up. To protect Farley's reputation."

She sat up so fast, she knocked him onto the rug. "What reputation! He was a snake! A cheating, lying snake!"

"Okay, calm down. I was only asking what you intended to do."

"Farley ruined Donal's career without compunction. Donal had been his friend for years. Maybe because they were both from Saint Louis, I don't know. Donal was a far better scholar. He was smart and creative." She waved her hand, as if brushing McKenna away.

"I must try to clear Donal's name. I'll write to his lawyer, to Harvard, to the Peabody Institute. To everyone I can."

"I'll help, Ruth, any way you want."

"Hold me. Tight," she begged. "Kiss me."

Beyond their safe warm nest of fire and love, the temperature dropped alarmingly and both human and animal inhabitants sought safe shelter. No one ventured far beyond the confines of a heated room for three days.

In the ornamental parlor of the enormous sandstone house, Ruth and Blade lounged and loved, played and ate, slept and teased and loved all over again. It was enchantment.

12

When Jaspar Bird peered in the doorway of the Yellow Canary and spied his sister standing by the stove warming her hands, he almost lost his nerve. The moment he felt that old familiar apprehension tighten his innards, he nearly changed his mind and walked on by. He might have done so if she hadn't turned around and spotted him.

She waved him in with an impatient gesture, her mannish face set in the same expression of jeering contempt she'd shown him since childhood.

Reluctantly he stepped inside, deciding that now was a hell of a time to have second thoughts.

Jaspar feared Hertha. He had been afraid of her as long as he could remember. She'd been older, stronger, and disgustingly robust. He was small, sickly, and delicate from birth. She lorded over him constantly, so he avoided her as much as possible.

Today, however, he'd braved the wind and the melting snow to seek her out, though he did come close to losing his nerve at the last minute.

He sought her for one reason only—he needed her help.

Except for Hertha, the Yellow Canary was empty. Jaspar personally thought she was stupid for braving the weather and the long, icy walk down the hills into town for the few nickels she'd make that day. But Hertha had maintained a rigid schedule at work and nothing could stand in her way.

"Cold out," he said, as he removed his hat and heavy striped scarf. The moment he spoke he wished he hadn't.

Hertha couldn't help wondering how this asinine nincompoop had managed to be born into the same family that had spawned her. The question had plagued her since the day of his birth.

"Do you want some breakfast?" It was more of a command than a question.

"That would be good." He hated the whine in his voice.

As she sailed off toward the kitchen, he nervously pulled off his gloves and removed his topcoat. He'd rehearsed what he'd wanted to say to her until he thought it was perfect. Yet now he wavered as he always did when forced to confront her.

"Pour your own coffee!" Hertha hollered from the kitchen.

Although he preferred hot chocolate, since coffee gave him heartburn, Jaspar did as he was told. Giving in was easier than arguing with her.

He guessed he'd been born yellow. From the very first he'd been puny, bumbling, and weak. A spineless numskull, according to his father. A chicken-hearted dimwit, according to his sister. Luckily, his mother hadn't lived long enough to see how ineffectual a man he'd turned out to be.

God, he hated asking his sister for help. It was like sticking a hot knife in his own soft underbelly and twisting.

Hertha Bird watched her brother mumble to himself from the kitchen door. What a jerk. He must be in real trouble to come here, she thought.

She slapped the breakfast plate down on the table in front of him. The little bugger jumped like a scared rabbit. Disgustedly, she turned to the bakery display.

"You want some pastry?"

"Apple pie would be fine. Unless you have bread pudding." He knew she always had bread pudding made.

After she banged a bowl of bread pudding on the table, she plopped herself down in the chair across from him. "So, why are you here?"

"I need your help."

"Is that right?" she asked sarcastically.

Jaspar felt his stomach tighten. He wished he hadn't eaten the spicy sausage on his breakfast plate. It was sure to give him problems later. "I'm not in trouble," he said defensively. "Not exactly."

Her expression showed she didn't believe him.

"You remember Donal Phelan?"

For a second Hertha looked nonplussed. Whatever she expected Jaspar to say, that wasn't it. Then she frowned disgustedly. "Of course I remember him, you fool! He only died a week or so ago!"

Jaspar's hands grew sweaty. He'd only just begun his

spiel, and already she'd taken command of the discussion. Why did every conversation between them end up with her in charge?

"I know, dear. Ah, I'm sorry," he mumbled, confused and upset, "What I meant was . . . ah, he told me he found a treasure . . ."

"He told you?" she asked sharply. This was something she had not heard. Oh, there had been talk about gold right from the first when the archaeologist moved his expedition to Flagstaff. But she had no idea Phelan had actually talked to her brother about it. "When?"

"Ah, before he died."

"When? Exactly?" Her sharp eyes were bright with curiosity. Could it possibly be that Phelan had said something to the fat little twit?

"Ah . . ." Jaspar cleared his throat, and stuck his finger in the tight collar that suddenly seemed to be squeezing his throat like a noose. Hertha had never appeared quite so interested in anything he had to say. It frightened him a bit. Being so long accustomed to her scorn, he didn't know how to handle recognition.

"When?" she snapped.

"Damn it, I'm trying to remember." His voice was so whiny it shamed him. He made a great issue of clearing a frog out of his throat, then spoke in a much deeper tone. "It was at night. The last time he was in town, I think. We was having a drink over at the Woodbine . . ."

"Who?" she demanded.

"Phelan. And me." He hesitated. "And Blade." Jaspar didn't think it would hurt if he let her think they'd been sitting together, talking, sharing a few drinks. He liked the idea of male camaraderie but had just never gotten the hang of it.

She wasn't sure she believed him. The idea of Jaspar and Donal Phelan having anything remotely like a real conversation flabbergasted her. Donal Phelan had been an intellectual, a genius in fact. Gladius Blade was an artist, a professional illustrator she'd been told, and a gentleman. Why would such men talk to her brother?

She squinted at Jaspar. Was there something more to him that she didn't see? She stood up and cut a large hunk of mince pie, giving herself some time to ponder the situation. Jaspar did have an uncanny sense about buying and selling property and businesses. He had no scruples, of course, but that was one trait they shared.

"What did Phelan tell you?"

"He said he'd found a treasure . . . an ancient treasure on a bed a' diamonds."

Hertha's expression was priceless. It was hard to believe that so plain a woman could be set aglow. "Diamonds?"

"And he said some things about gold, and about the treasure being better than the stuff in Egypt." Jaspar didn't tell Hertha he'd heard most of this from other men talking and wondering after Phelan left the saloon. No sense spoiling the one time in his life she'd looked at him with something close to affection.

The front door opened and Cecil Sholes slouched in for his breakfast.

Ruth sat on the mattress in the parlor before a warm fire admiring her naked toes. Ankle to neck she was clothed in a warm pearl-gray union suit that fitted snugly over every curve of her body. Sighing with pleasure at the warmth toasting her bare feet, she watched the orange flames that swayed like a Gypsy dancer to violin music.

What had happened to her? To plain, stodgy Ruth McKenna who'd arrived on the train with a pile of belongings and an even larger heap of fears? To poor, dear Ruth who'd been so bloody proper all her life? To Ruth who'd never even known the thrill of a passionate kiss!

"I'm in love! Madly, wildly in love!"

Blade was the most wonderful man she'd ever met. He was perfect. She quickly remembered his Irish temper, his fondness for scandalous oaths, his occasional moody silences. Well, perhaps he wasn't a completely perfect man. But he was certainly a perfect lover. She wondered if all women in love shared the same sentiment.

The door opened behind her and in walked Blade, clad in a chestnut-brown union suit which fit his mighty form like a glove and made her blood run hot. God, what a man! She adored looking at him. Who would have ever thought that long underwear could be so erotic?

He pulled her up into his arms, and she pushed her soft breasts against his hard chest, her hips against the rigid proof of his passion. He kissed her; she made little animal noises of delight. Within moments they sank to the mattress, savoring the spell.

A sharp sound from without jarred them apart.

Ruth tried to sit up, her heart pounding. "Someone's coming!"

"No." He dragged her down again, his tongue tasting her throat.

"It's Jennie." She struggled against him. For the first

time since they had made love, she felt guilty about what she'd done.

"No," he said again, holding her firm. "It was a branch on one of the trees. The snow load broke it. Don't be scared, Ruth. I promise you nothing is ever going to hurt us."

She found his lips and kissed him fiercely, willing his words to be true.

Hertha slopped food on the plate for Sholes. By the time he'd been served, a stranger came in, and she fixed an order of sausage, biscuits, and fried potatoes for him. Then Grover scurried in. Hertha wanted to scream. It was the first time in more than thirty years she actually wanted to talk to her weasel of a brother, and she was fighting off customers. Sometimes life wasn't fair.

"Where's Myrtle?" Sholes asked good-naturedly.

Hertha didn't give a damn if Myrtle was frozen in a snowbank. "Sick."

"Too bad."

"You eating today?" Hertha's question was directed at Grover. Generally he was so hungover he couldn't look an egg in the eye.

"Sure am. Think I might try a piece of pie, too. What kind ya got?"

"Try the mincemeat. The Yellow Canary is famous all over the territory for the mincemeat pie."

"I think I will. Say, does it have a little drop of whiskey in it?"

Hertha merely smiled. The expression made her eyes squinty and emphasized her triple chins. Grover nodded and turned his attention to the stranger.

Jaspar had swilled all the coffee his bladder could hold and had gone out to the backhouse. He still needed to talk to his sister, and he had an upcoming meeting with a potential buyer for Sam Waverly's store. "I've got an appointment, but I'll be back for lunch," he said. "Could you make me some potato soup or something easy on my stomach?"

In the restaurant's front room, the stranger introduced himself to Grover as Orlie Taswell from St. Louis and parts east. They shook hands and chatted affably for several minutes. When Hertha served Grover's meal, Taswell was sitting at the table between Grover and Sholes talking and joking as if they were long lost friends.

These men didn't interest her much. A bunch of losers, she surmised. She lumbered back to the kitchen to check on the savory venison stew she had simmering on the stove. Her cranky mood from the bad weather had improved dramatically since Jaspar's visit. She decided a black molasses pie might just be what her customers would like. She added a stick of wood to the stove.

Out front the men didn't say much for a while after she returned to the kitchen. Instead, they swilled coffee and slogged down the food. Grover ate the pie with relish. It had enough spirits in it to last him awhile. If old lady Bird wasn't so goddamn homely, he'd propose.

"Do you fellas know anything about a place out a little north of here? Ranch house where some folks from back East are digging up Indian relics?"

Sholes spilled his coffee. He'd given up pretending he was too religious to drink the stuff. A man living a life of danger and intrigue needed something potent to keep him going. Sholes couldn't handle booze, but drinking coffee made him feel strong and manly.

"Heard of the place," Grover answered noncommittally. He glanced nervously at his partner.

So his informant had been correct. Taswell decided the dime he'd given the Indian kid who hung around the depot had been ten cents well spent. Now all he had to do was cast out the bait and reel these suckers in.

He needed help in his little scheme to pay back Ruth McKenna. He was a hustler from the big city. A St. Louie slick, as wily and wise as the best of them. But here in the sticks he was a bumbler. He hated to admit it, but he required the aid of these local yokels.

Taswell figured these particular deadbeats could be hired for two bits a piece. He'd offer more, sweeten the pie, sprinkle on a few lies. But he had them, sure as apples had worms.

It amused him that they were trying to outfox a cagey fox like himself. After all, he'd put the squeeze on the highly esteemed Professor Farley McKenna for over three years, bled the old fraud dry, and then kicked dirt on his grave. He wasn't about to be hoodwinked by this pair of back-assed country thugs.

He smiled his most polished smile, the one he'd practiced in front of the mirror. He looked like a real stooge. The elbow-bender in the ratty suit marked him for a pushover right away. The other clod, the big dumb one, followed along like a little yellow dog.

"I need a couple of good men to take me out there."

"You interested in old Injun stuff?" Grover asked.

"Naw. I'm interested in money."

Sholes nearly wet all over himself in excitement. Here he was, all worried because Lawyer Vanderdam was angry at their failure to find the treasure map, and somebody else was wanting to hire them. By God, folks everywhere was trying to hook up with him and Grover. Made a man feel important.

Grover was a bit more hesitant. And a hell of a lot less trusting. He spotted Taswell right away as a swindler. He just hadn't decided if he was to be the dupe or the accomplice. He waited for Taswell to continue.

"Woman out there owes me something."

"Injun woman?" Sholes asked.

"No." Taswell would have liked more coffee but he didn't want the old battleax who ran the joint to be listening in on his pitch. "White woman."

Sholes opened his yap to volunteer every bit of information he knew about Phelan's newly arrived sister, but Grover swiftly kicked him in the kneecap. He gasped in pain, sucking in a few bread crumbs that had been nesting in his beard. He began to cough.

"A woman in these parts owes you something?" Grover reminded Taswell. He ignored the series of scowls Sholes was shooting at him. He'd already figured out that Sholes was all bluff and bluster.

"Yes." Taswell continued. "She's the widow of a professional associate. McKenna's the name. She appropriated some rather valuable papers that belong to me."

"A treasure map?" Sholes asked.

Grover gave serious consideration to murdering Sholes right then and there. The only problem was the penalty—it was a tad steep in the West for that sort of crime, so he held his clenched fists tight to keep them from encircling Sholes's skinny neck. He'd simply inform Vanderdam about the oaf. Let Vanderdam murder him.

Taswell looked startled. "No. Not a treasure map. Why would you think a foolish thing like that? All there is at an archaeological site is old bones and broken pots. Mrs. McKenna has a scientific journal that belongs to me. I want it back."

"Did you ask her for it?" Sholes inquired.

Taswell was beginning to find conversation with this dolt quite tedious. All he wanted was to give Dr. McKenna's widow a lesson in manners. If he couldn't squeeze her for any more cash, he wanted to hurt her a little. "Yes, I asked her for it. And she attacked me."

"What?" Grover couldn't imagine the starchy young skirt he'd seen at Phelan's funeral doing anything the least bit violent.

"That's right," Taswell said self-righteously. "She chased me down the stairs with a weapon." He didn't mention the weapon in question was an old man's walking cane which she'd poked at his belly button. That didn't sound especially menacing. Taswell figured these men would automatically take his words to mean a gun. After all, they were out here in the wild West.

Hertha Bird brought a bunch of fragrant ginger cookies out to the display case.

"Hey, Miz Bird, how 'bout a warm up?" Sholes asked eagerly. "I could use another cup of coffee."

"I have a better idea," Grover said quickly. "Why don't we mosey on over to the San Juan? I could use a little liquid heat in my veins."

"What about the boss?" Sholes sounded very concerned. "Won't he be there this morning?"

"He's home in bed with a head cold."

"Oh." Sholes looked pleased. Vanderdam made him very nervous.

"You men work for somebody?" Taswell inquired.

"Yes," Sholes replied.

"No," Grover answered at the same moment. He hesitated a second. "We were doing some odd jobs for a fella, but he ain't payin' us no more."

"Bullshit!" Hertha Bird bellowed as she plodded into the cafe with coffeepot in hand. "Somebody paid for these here meal tickets and it weren't you worthless diddlers."

Grover stood up in a huff and walked out the door. He had no intentions of arguing with the old bat. A man just couldn't win with the likes of her. If Taswell was interested in his services, he could tag along.

Jaspar didn't wrap up his business until nearly one. By then the lunch crowd, which hadn't been large because of the weather, had more or less dwindled away by the time he sloshed through the melting snow to have his appointed meal with his sister.

He'd anticipated a plain meal to settle his belly—he'd practically begged her for the simple food he could tolerate. So he almost cried aloud when she plopped a bowl of thick, spicy venison stew in front of him. The acid in his stomach was churning, and he wondered if he could keep down his sister's stew.

"You got some soda crackers?" he asked weakly.

"Stomach still botherin' ya?"

"Yeah."

She banged a plate of crackers beside the stew bowl.

"Wonder where the hell you got the golly-wobbles, brother. Me, I gotta cast-iron gut."

He downed a few crackers and begged some milk. She brought him back some milk toast as well. He could have kissed her, except he thought she might break his jaw if he tried.

Hertha helped herself to his stew while he sipped the milk and stirred his spoon around the soggy toast.

"So what did you want to tell me about Phelan's treasure? Yer sure there is a treasure?"

"The woman knows where it is."

"What woman."

"His sister!"

"Don't you get sharp with me, Jaspar Bird."

"I'm sorry, dear. I'm just tired. Did I tell you I sold Waverly's store? Got a nice tidy little chunk for it."

"Good." Hertha wasn't interested in some crummy little store, or any other business venture of her brother's. She had her mind on bigger things. Donal Phelan's treasure. She fancied herself in diamonds. All these years of putting up with her sniveling brother were about to pay off, and the possibility of ending up with Donal Phelan's treasure especially tickled her. "What about the treasure?"

He hated to say it. It galled him more than her spicy food. But there was no choice. "I need your help."

"How?" She didn't even try to keep the greedy glint out of her eyes. She fairly drooled avarice.

"You know I'm not very good around animals." Jaspar paused. "The woman walks every day. Probably out to check on the gold. I thought I might take her and chat a bit . . ."

"Abduct her?"

"Yes!"

"You're a wimp! She'd kill you!"

"She would not!

"The hell she wouldn't! Some fella in here for break-fast said he went out there the other day and she took a shotgun after him." Hertha believed in embellishing a story for her own purposes.

Jaspar turned the color of putty. He put his spoon down in the remains of the milk toast and shoved the bowl away. A shotgun? Why were all the women he met so depraved? "I need your help." He sighed.

"You want me to snatch her?"

"No, you big ox . . ." As soon as the words were out he knew he was a dead man.

But Hertha was so intent on the prospect of possessing diamonds and gold she did nothing but thump him on the head. She'd never considered herself a vain woman before, but the thought of diamonds dripping from her ears, fingers, and throat appealed to her on the most narcissistic level. She hardly put any effort into her swat.

Jaspar blinked hard. Hertha's thumps could generally dislocate a man's teeth. This one merely crossed his eyeballs. "Sorry, dear. What I meant to say is, I want your help to hire somebody to pull off the nab. After all, you're so much better at dealing with people than I am."

The barn had a wholesome earthy scent that made a man feel in harmony with nature. The horses had been fed for the evening and were swishing their tails contentedly in their clean hay-strewn stalls.

He stepped into the dark shadows. She was waiting.

He pulled her into his strong young arms without a word. She pressed her eager, trusting body against him.

He was tired. He'd gotten little sleep the night before. The ride out from Flagstaff was a long one even on a swift horse, and he was making the trip nearly every day now.

It was becoming harder and harder for him to stay away from her. It was better for her to be here than in town, he knew, but he was killing himself trying to be with her. And he had to see her, to touch her.

"It won't be long," he told her, "and we can be together." Yet he didn't know how they'd manage. He wouldn't let her go back to working for Miss Bird. The older woman was stingy and cruel to the girls who worked for her.

No, it was better that Jennie stay here at the ranch for the time being. Blade and his woman were treating Jennie better than anybody had since her own mother died.

His hands told him the girl had gained a little weight. She was being well fed. Mrs. McKenna had found her some material for new clothes, and Marie had sewed them for her. She looked pretty. She laughed more and talked more than she had in many months. She was happy, he could tell.

Better he keep making the ride out to see her. He was strong and resilient. He could live with a few hours less sleep.

He reached in the pocket of his denims and took out a folded square of paper. "This is for you."

Her dark eyes sparkled in the shadowy light. She gasped for joy when she unwrapped the silver earrings.

He helped her put them on, complimenting her gravely about the beauty of the silver on her pretty ears. She giggled and kissed him boldly.

"I can't stay long," he told her. "I'm driving a team down to Prescott tomorrow."

"When will you come back?"

"Two, maybe three days."

She nodded. "The days will be long."

"I know, my love. But soon we'll be together. I'll find a way." Even as his mouth touched hers, he wondered how he'd ever find a way to support the two of them so they could marry.

At the San Juan Saloon, Grover was sitting at a table in the corner drinking heavily. Sholes had left for the night. Orlie Taswell had just walked out the door. In his beer-fuddled brain Grover tried to figure out why Taswell vexed him.

Oh, he understood perfectly well that Taswell was a crook in spite of his bullshit about scientific journals and native relics. One shyster could always smell another one.

What grated on Grover's mind was that he couldn't spot the scam. He was sure Taswell wanted more from the Widow McKenna than a few papers. But what? He didn't buy the notion that Taswell hadn't heard of the treasure. But why hire him and Sholes?

He shrugged and swallowed more brew. Well, whatever tricks Taswell had up his bunghole, Grover was soon to find out. He might not trust the slicker, but he and Sholes had agreed to ride out and see the woman.

"Then I'll know fer suurrrre," he slurred. With that

final thought, he laid his head down on the table for a little rest. Nobody paid him any mind. It wasn't the first time he'd passed out on the table and it probably wouldn't be the last.

"What in the hell did you do?" Che demanded of Marie.

The only sound in the cabin was the tea kettle hissing on the back of the cookstove.

"I asked you a question? How could you do something so stupid?"

Marie Manyhorses was stunned that the boy she'd welcomed into her home numerous times had suddenly turned on her like a wild mountain cat.

"Don't talk to my mother like that!" Tsosi was as surprised as his mother. And while he inwardly agreed with his friend's point of view, he couldn't tolerate such disrespectful behavior to her.

"And you? My friend," Che sneered. " Why didn't you stop her?"

Behind him, Jennie was in tears. She was the one who'd mentioned the incident to her suitor, and she sincerely regretted doing so. Che seldom became angered, but he was a fierce opponent when he did.

Tsosi was out of his chair in an instant, facing off his furious companion. He wasn't quite as tall or as broad shouldered as Che, but he was powerful and tough from years of hard labor. And he wasn't in the least intimidated by the one person whom he considered a brother. They'd been pals for years. This wasn't their first disagreement.

"I didn't know she planned to use the snake to

frighten the white lady. She told me she'd seen the
raven drop it in the yard, and she thought it was a sign
of some sort because the snakes are hibernating. But I
didn't know she took it over to the house. Or put it in
the woman's bed."

"The old man told me Phelan's ghost was spreading
sickness, and that's why I got sick," Marie said sullenly.

"No," Jennie spoke up, her voice tremulous. "Auntie, all he said was he'd heard people were talking
about Phelan's ghost walking."

"He wanted you to think the ghost sickness was on
you," Che concluded. "So you'd get rid of Blade's
woman."

"Why?"

Jennie was certain Che was correct, but she couldn't
understand why Moses Bigboy made the long trek to
the cabin just to trick her aunt.

"Jaspar Bird," Che said.

Tsosi flung himself back in his chair and scowled at
his work-worn hands.

"Jaspar Bird came walking his horse into town late
one night last week," Che continued. "I was working.
Fixing the wheel on one of the wagons. He came into
the stable and told me his horse had thrown a shoe.
From the looks of things, the horse had also thrown
Bird and kicked him a time or two, I think. That little
fat man sure is scared of his own horse."

They chuckled, and the tension in the room abated a
little. Jennie wiped her tears away. Marie settled her
quilts around her. Only Tsosi remained edgy.

"He asked me lots of questions about Mrs. McKenna. And about Phelan's work. I think he believes the
story about gold the white men are telling around

town. Finally, he offered me some cash to do a job for him."

Tsosi exchanged glances with his mother.

"What?" Jennie asked.

"I don't know," Che said honestly. "My boss came in. He'd been over having a couple beers with his brother. Came by to see if I needed any help with the wheel. Bird said to shoe the horse, and then he took off so fast he was almost running."

He sat down on a chair and was silent for some time.

"If Jaspar Bird believes the rumor about gold, he thinks Blade's woman knows where to find it." To Che's way of thinking, Ruth belonged with Blade just as Jennie belonged with him. Nobody in the cabin questioned that. "Last time Bird wanted something, it was Sam Waverly's store. Sam Waverly died. Now he wants something Mrs. McKenna has. Information. Or a paper."

"Maybe he frightened old Moses Bigboy into coming here," Jennie offered. "Moses lives on a piece of Jaspar Bird's land."

Che nodded. It sounded reasonable. He looked at Marie, but she said nothing. Tsosi got up and poured himself a cup of tea.

"Stay away from Jaspar Bird," Che told them all. "He will only hurt us. He has an evil heart."

13

The charcoal brazier sat by the window like a squat Buddha emitting a steady current of warmth. The room was now bearable, almost comfortable.

"At least I can stand to type without gloves on!" Ruth said.

"I wish you'd mentioned how frightened you were of the kerosene heater. I'd have moved the brazier into your office days ago."

"And what would you have done for heat?" she teased.

Blade met her banter with a scorching look. "I'd have thought of something."

It still amazed her that he could make her heart race with one look from across the room.

"I'm going to be gone this morning, but I should be back by noon. Can't miss lunch, you know."

She laughingly agreed.

"Is there anything you need before I go?"

It was on the tip of her tongue to say, "you," but her shyness prevented her. Yet he saw the look on her face before she lowered her lashes to look down at the papers on the desk, and he was across the room in three steps and caught her fiercely against him.

"Ruth, I can't believe what's happened to me," he whispered into her hair, "what's happened to us. I can't get enough of you." His hungry mouth claimed hers. And then he put her away from him. "If I don't leave now, we're liable to shock Jennie when she comes up with your tea."

It took her a few dazed minutes to recover from his presence, to slow the thumping in her chest. Loving Blade was the most wonderful, terrifying thing that had ever happened to her. Yes, she admitted it. She was mad about him! And he was equally crazy about her.

There had been little mention of a future beyond the completion of the dig. She tried hard to tell herself she was very modern and didn't require a commitment from her lover, but the thought didn't ring true, so she simply ignored her fears. She lived wholly in the present, and at the moment, her present job was typing up Donal Phelan's notes.

All the odd bits and pieces of paper her brother had amassed with his numerous impromptu notes had been sorted through with painstaking care. The notes had been typed, each on a separate sheet of paper. Then the material had been indexed according to subject matter and filed.

Knowing Donal as she did, Ruth suspected he would have eventually added most of the miscellaneous fragments and trivia to his personal journal. Her glimpses into other notebooks from previous digs had told her

Donal kept a fascinating account of his adventures.

Donal had kept a meticulous handwritten record of his expeditions, each in a separate bound ledger. Every artifact, fragment, bone, tooth, projectile point, and so forth was listed in detail with its exact location, date, and time of discovery. The official report dealt only with facts about the dig, and though these facts were no doubt important, they were largely interesting only to other scholars.

But the personal diaries held a sort of enchantment for they were the record of how Donal Phelan thought, on all sorts of subjects, of how his mind worked. Ruth hoped to compile all the data she'd typed into a final record of his last quest.

Moisture suddenly filled her eyes, and she dabbed at them with a hanky. Sometimes the knowledge of his death hit her hard. Shuffling the papers, she went back to work.

Donal Phelan was a thinker and a supreme investigator. As often as not, his mind bridged the actual facts he had uncovered and moved to the possibilities. He allowed himself to see the entire fabric of the situation instead of merely the various threads made it up.

His theories were wild, often revolutionary—more times than not much too far ahead of his time to be accepted. But, dear Lord, they were enthralling! And she knew, without a doubt, that archaeologists, historians, and other scholars all over the world were anxious to read what the mad Irishman had dreamed up this time.

Ruth had already read through the site journal. So had Blade. They agreed on one obvious fact—nothing within that fact-filled tome indicated Phelan had found a treasure. Not one reference pointed to anything out of the ordinary for such a dig, anything that could classify as a treasure.

Yet the man had gone to town in a mood of barely controlled excitement, and had announced to anyone who stood still long enough to listen that he had discovered a treasure.

Neither Ruth nor Blade believed Phelan had lied. Granted, he'd manipulated the truth on many an occasion to get what he wanted, but the night at the Woodbine Saloon, he wasn't asking for a thing.

"So that leaves all this . . ." Ruth sighed with a wave of her hand over the stacks of paper she'd filed. And to the half-completed diary which represented a portion of her brother's musings.

Until now the diary had been in the safe . . . not because of its great value but because she couldn't abide reading it. She had needed to wait till the raw edges of her grief healed over before she could endure sharing his thoughts.

In spite of the warmth from the oriental brazier, Ruth's hands were cold and shaking when she opened the cover page.

Yet within moments she'd settled down in the rickety old chair and began to see the excursion to the Arizona Territory through her brother's vision.

She'd read only a few pages of Donal's detailed account of his decision to see the pueblo ruins at first hand, when she laid her head on the desk and cried. Farley McKenna's scheme to rob his longtime friend and colleague had cheated her out of this whole experience. He and his cohort, Taswell, maliciously violated the relationship she had with her only relative.

When she wept out her anger, she felt curiously cleansed. The ugly past had no more power over her. She would compile the last personal journal and see that it got published if she had to pay the printing costs herself. This was Donal Phelan's last brilliant legacy. This would prove that he'd been victimized by a so-called friend. This would show the academic world that they would be proving his theories for decades to come.

As she absorbed the chronological account of everything Phelan had done, the people he talked to, the Native American myths he'd investigated, his personal thoughts, theories, "what ifs," and hopes, Ruth saw her brother not through the eyes of a worshipful child, but through those of a mature woman. She vowed never to let this last, final diary out of her possession.

She planned to type it up in manuscript form, adding all the compiled notes where they fit, but the diary itself would be stored in her trunk with her dearest treasures to pass down to her children.

That thought gave her a moment's qualm, but she hustled it into a corner of her brain to take out and examine at a later time. She read on.

Her full attention was snagged by an entry made the first spring Donal had spent at the Phillips ranch.

Tramping through a mountain meadow west of the house. Meadow boggy due to spring runoff. Stepped in spongy spot—and sunk. To my knees! Claylike mud sucked at feet and legs like quicksand. Thought I was sunk.

Ruth giggled at the word. She could imagine him wallowing in muck, mired to his knees, and more than a bit worried he was about to be swallowed up.

Saved by a granite boulder at the edge of sinkhole. Wrenched myself out. Managed to save my boots. But lost my pipe.

It wasn't until he got back to the house, toting his filthy boots, that he realized he'd literally stumbled into something wonderful and special.

Thank God I cleaned my own boots instead of asking Marie to. Vanity was its own reward, so to speak. Found traces of ash and charcoal.

Phelan went on to explain how he'd gone back to the meadow with tools and workers as soon as it had dried out enough. He unearthed what he concluded to be the remains of a prehistoric earth dwelling that had been dug at least two feet into the ground, then domed with timbers and covered with clay mud mixed with sticks, leaves, grasses, and whatever else was at hand.

In my mind I see the dwelling resembling the pit houses of the Picts in Great Britain.

Ruth had been too young to accompany Donal on the trips he'd made abroad while he was still a student. By the time he was in his late twenties, Donal had decided America was his universe to investigate.

Ruth stood up and went to the head of the stairs and called Jennie.

"Would you check on the chicken? I don't want it to get too dry."

"I already did. It's in the warming oven. What kind of potatoes do you want?"

"I think all the big ones are gone, so let's cut what we have in small pieces and simmer them with bacon, onions, and green beans. Do you want me to come down?"

"No, I finished dusting. I'll get lunch if you'll let me spend the afternoon with Auntie. She's lonely."

"That's fine." Ruth turned to go. "Jennie, does Marie want to come back to work at the house?"

"I don't think she does. She wants to go back out to her home. That's all she talks about. Ever since she got sick."

"Is she feeling any better?"

"Yes. But not real good yet."

Confident that Blade's appetite for food would be satisfied when he returned, Ruth went back to the more interesting topic of her brother's journal.

Donal lamented because he did not have an artist along to draw the pit house he found. He made a few meager sketches himself, but described beautifully things he discovered—blackened fragments of a cook pot which had originally been formed inside a basket, bits of charcoal, broken sections of timbers, and the tattered remains of a storage basket that contained a handful of red-and-white-speckled beans. And two gourds, one empty and one with seeds and the pithy remains of gourd meal.

The bottom of the dwelling stood on about six inches of decomposed ash.

The next entry surprised Ruth.

How old is Sunset Crater?

Donal apparently had done some research on the San Francisco Peaks, and in his usual fashion, found the existing material lacking.

The experts agree all the mountains and hills in this volcanic field are the same age. I disagree!

Ruth could see Donal's mind spinning a new theory. No wonder he refused to leave the area. But what exactly was this idea? Did it concern only the Sunset cinder cone, or did it deal with the ancient inhabitants?

Donal launched into an elaborate explanation about the flora and vegetation of the area, and the time it took for a desert to become fully alive again after a volcanic eruption. In spite of the fertile mulching done by cinders and ash, centuries passed before a desert—unlike a jungle—returned to normal. Starting with lichen and ending with mature trees, vegetation eventually replaced the rock, cinders, and ash, but the time span was substantial.

Prehistoric people lived in the valleys of the San Francisco Peaks before Sunset Crater erupted.

Farmers raised beans, maybe corn, and gourds. The gourds still grow wild around here. The beans survived . . .

Ruth laid the journal down on the desk, a wayward thought teasing her brain. Where had she read something else about beans?

Hurriedly she rifled through all her typed notes that might pertain to speckled beans but found nothing.

"Maybe it isn't written down. Maybe somebody told me."

She glanced at the brazier and saw that the charcoal was nearly gone. It would be safe to leave.

"Jennie," she called. She ran down the stairs to find the girl.

Since the morning was clear and sunny, Jennie was outside hanging sheets on the clothesline.

"Jennie, I want to talk to you!"

The girl swung around, startled, looking faintly guilt-faced. "Yes?" she asked as she reached in the woven basket for a pillowcase.

"About beans. Were you the one who was telling me

about the speckled beans grown in this area by the pre-historic people who once lived here? You know, people like the ones who lived in the dwellings out at the dig?"

The normally friendly girl became silent, her face stony and expressionless.

Ruth had been so caught up in her own thoughts, she didn't notice the change, didn't feel the tension. She bungled ahead before she realized Jennie had turned from a friend into an antagonist.

"What's wrong?" Ruth asked when she eventually noticed the change in the young girl's manner.

"I don't talk about the Ancient Ones." She turned her back on Ruth and reached for another sheet, shaking it with a snap.

Frankly, Ruth was amazed and a little hurt. After a moment's consideration, she realized she'd blithely stepped over good manners and cultural bounds and trod upon Jennie's beliefs.

She could almost hear her brother's scathing remarks.

"This looks like a good morning for a walk," Ruth said finally. "Come with me. Let's play hooky."

"I have work."

"You work for me," Ruth teased gently. "And I say it's time for a break. I'm tired of being cooped up with the typing machine."

Jennie had far too good a disposition not to be infected by Ruth enthusiasm. She relented and agreed. "I'll get my things."

Moments later she emerged from the house with a native woven blanket of the Gray Mountain pattern draped around her shoulders and wearing the bright red gloves Ruth had knitted for her.

"They fit," Ruth said, pleased to see her effort acknowledged.

Jennie held up her small hands for inspection. "I never had any before."

"If I'm going to drag you around the countryside, the least I can do is see that you don't freeze." She noticed that Jennie still wore the shabby blouse and skirt she'd arrived in, but she usually changed to one of her new dresses when Che came to visit.

Ruth had hoped to discover the meadow where Donal had found his lone pit house, the one he'd written so eloquently about. They walked into a meadow but she was certain it wasn't the one Donal had written about, for there was no large granite boulder, and no evidence of excavation.

For some reason she felt awkward about asking Jennie questions about the area. She'd already blundered once. She liked the girl and didn't want to alienate her. How did her brother manage to be friendly with the natives and still run a dig? The thought almost popped out of her mouth but she caught it in time. She preferred to wait and ask Blade.

It wasn't long before she spied something that caught her attention. It looked like a hogan, the Navajo dwelling, except it was small, only about eighteen inches high.

"Oh, look! Isn't it precious! Let's go see." She was on her knees in front of the tiny structure before she noticed Jennie was not with her.

"Come here," she called.

"No!"

"Why not? I want you to tell me what this is." She reached her hand toward it.

"No! Don't touch it! Come away!"

The urgency in Jennie's voice sobered Ruth. Slowly she stood up.

"Come away. It's a burial. We're supposed to leave it alone."

Ruth discovered she'd trampled thoughtlessly on another Navajo custom, inadvertently, perhaps, but rudely just the same. There was still a lot she had to learn about the variety of cultures in the West.

Blade rode up to the house as Ruth put the finishing touches on lunch. "Something smells great. It's a pleasure coming home to a hot meal."

His eyes said more, but Ruth turned her head. Jennie was outside taking down the wind-dried sheets. Ruth had no intention of parading her private thoughts in front of the girl, and she tried not to think about the fact that Jennie already knew that she and Blade were lovers. But she did enjoy the girl's company, and she hoped that Jennie would continue to stay.

"I want to talk about beans," Ruth said suddenly.

Blade had the lid off a pot and was examining the contents. "So this is what's tantalizing my soul."

"What?"

"Beans . . . and potatoes, and things."

"No, not those kind of beans. Donal's beans."

"Now don't you start."

"Start what?"

"Telling me that some handful of beans is wonderful . . . a real 'find.'" Blade started dishing up his food. "Is Jennie eating with us?"

"I don't know. I upset her this morning. Asking about beans, actually. About the prehistoric people."

Blade nodded. "Not a popular subject in all cultures, my love."

"So I discovered. What about the speckled beans?"

"Some were found at the excavation site. Your brother danced, and laughed and yelled. I think he called them a treasure. Like the stone-scrapping tool he found a few days earlier. And like some of the pottery." He frowned. "Calling ordinary things a treasure was a failing of his."

"I know. Did he find other beans?"

"No."

"Were you here when he found the pit house?"

"The one he fell into in the meadow? No, that was before I got here. He filled it back in, you know, so he could concentrate on the other site. But he planned to go back there later."

"He found beans there."

"Really? He said he didn't find much of anything—nothing conclusive, that is."

"When did he find the beans at the site?"

Blade was savoring a tender bite of the roast chicken. He set his fork down and buttered a piece of corn bread. "Last year. Just before it got hot, I think. May, maybe June."

"You don't remember anything else he called a treasure."

"Your brother found at least one treasure a week. I do remember that a few weeks later, he began to take a serious interest in the wooden beams we were finding at the site. By that time the weather was blistering," he continued. "And the number of field hands was limited because the bank account was low. So he and I were out there with the rest of them, stripped down to our denims . . . sweltering, trying to get those damned things out so he could examine them."

Jennie came in and dished herself up a plate. Blade made a little small talk with her for a minute. Jennie left, Ruth continued their original conversation. "Did you remove the wooden beams?"

"In spite of the heat, and my cursed temper, we moved the blasted things. They were heavy as hell and had been there for centuries, but he needed them right that minute."

She nodded. "Donal was driven by desperate urges to find answers to the past. So at some time in the future, truth can be defined."

"What does that have to do with speckled beans. Or timbered beams for that matter?"

"Connections. Missing links between times, places, and civilizations."

Blade reached over and covered her hand with his larger one. "There are so many facets to you. And each one has a brilliance and intensity all its own. You are the most magnificent jewel . . . a true treasure."

She didn't brush aside his compliment but accepted it with the honesty it was given. He prized her. She was dazed by her own feelings. She placed her other hand on his. Her voice was soft and tender, "You are the only person in my entire life who hasn't thought I was plain, ordinary, and efficient."

"They're all blind."

They were holding hands when Jennie came back into the kitchen. Ruth had forgotten to fix the plate for her aunt. So Jennie slipped in and dished it up herself.

They didn't need her right now, so she left without saying anything. She knew how they felt. She hoped Che would come tonight.

"I want you."

His words ignited a fire in Ruth's loins hotter than anything she'd ever experienced. Her legs went weak. Her moist lips parted in anticipation of his touch. She nearly moaned aloud.

He stood and walked slowly toward her.

The room crackled with tension.

Everything in her demeanor beckoned him closer. He excited her wildly, beyond anything she had ever imagined. Even if she'd wished to resist, she couldn't have done so. But she had no desire to deny him. Her body clamored for his touch. She yearned toward him, aching, burning.

"Please," she whispered. She was being swallowed up in flames.

He drew her to her feet in front of him.

"Please what, my darling?" He towered over her, a bold, brawny man, a mountain of hard flesh. He radiated danger.

Yet she had never felt safer. Placing both hands flat on his chest, she rubbed her palms up to his shoulders and back down again over his flat belly and lower.

He groaned. "Ruth!" He grabbed her hands and imprisoned them.

"Now how can I touch you?" she teased. Her breath warmed the spot on his throat exposed by his open collar. She wiggled her hips provocatively against him, proving she was quite capable of touching without the use of her hands.

"You drive me crazy."

"And me, my darling. I'm driving us both crazy."

He loosened his grip on her wrists, and she immediately threw her arms around his neck plunging her hands into his hair. He pulled her tight, lifting her off the floor and against him, finding her hot hungry mouth.

With a groan he swept her into his arms and into her room. Blade kicked the door of her bedroom shut, laid her on the bed and came down on top of her, unable to get close enough. He needed her against him, her mouth devouring his, her hands as wild as his own.

The impact stunned him. Each time they came together it was more intense than the times before, more powerful, more fulfilling. He wanted her for all time.

For so many years he'd wondered if he'd ever find a woman to truly love. One who would inspire him, inflame him, love him as passionately as he loved her. His answer lay in his arms.

Later they sat in the middle of Blade's wide bed surrounded by Phelan's journals and the papers Ruth had typed.

"Now you see why Donal was so excited about finding those speckled beans at the expedition site. They linked the inhabitants of the site with the people who lived in the pit house—before Sunset Peak erupted!"

Ruth flipped through several pages to find a marked passage in her brother's personal journal. "See, right here he says that the ash layer at the bottom of the pit house was very similar to the one the pueblo was constructed over. Okay, everybody figures the volcano is older than the pueblo. But they also figure that when Sunset Peak blew, it destroyed everybody and everything in its path."

He nodded. "That makes sense, seeing the lava flow. Nothing could have survived it."

"But Sunset Peak is a cinder cone," she mused. "Built up over many years—as much maybe as a hundred. What if we were prehistoric people living in the area the first time it erupted? But we were far enough away not to have been caught in the main blast. What would we have done?"

"Got the hell out of the way, if we were smart!"

"Yes. We would have moved at least as far as we considered a safe distance."

"But we still would have had to eat."

She grinned and gave him a little poke. "Even a thousand years back, you're still worrying about your stomach."

"That's not all. But yes, people would have been very concerned about eating. However, there is no way the people who lived at our dig would have had enough water to grow the type of things the people here grew."

"Maybe, maybe not. Right here it says ash which isn't too deep promotes growth that wouldn't have been normal otherwise."

"So?"

"So, if we moved as far as we could after the first blow, and still grew beans and whatever, then little by little we would have noticed we could extend our fields out farther and farther away from the volcano."

"There was more than one eruption."

"Right."

"So we picked up our household goods and moved again," Blade said, getting into the spirit of her game. "To the outer edges of our fields."

She nodded. "And each time the volcano rumbled and spewed, we moved again. Eventually we would have gotten as far as Donal's dig."

"Aren't we too old and decrepit by then?"

Ruth made a face at him. "Okay, our children or grandchildren. You know what I mean."

The idea of their children and grandchildren proceeding through life in an orderly fashion—no matter what century—excited him. His mind wandered.

Ruth was so caught up in creating history she didn't notice Blade's reaction. "But Donal evidently knew it would take more than two handfuls of beans—the one at the pit house and the one at the dig—to convince the academic world. So he started to look for other links between the two sites."

She rubbed her nose absently. "That's when he became so interested in those timbers you complained about. Especially the ones at the bottom of the pueblo."

One glance at Blade's dazed expression had her snorting in disgust. "Are you listening? I'm being brilliant."

"I'm listening." But his mind was still on the possibility of the children they might someday create between them. He decided the idea had great appeal.

"But did you hear?" she persisted. "You usually have something to add."

"What do you want me to say?"

"Something about the similarities of the beams at the bottom of the pueblo . . ."

"They were heavy."

She ignored that as if he hadn't spoken. ". . . and the broken sections he found at the pit house."

"I didn't see them."

She was annoyed. "Blade, *you* were here. I wasn't! You were able to hear all his theories—and don't tell me Donal Phelan didn't talk about them because he was never quiet about anything! He talked all the time! I need to know what he said." Her voice rose perceptively. "To put this manuscript together properly, I need to know what he was thinking. How he connected the people at the pit house and the ones at the dig."

"Damn it, Ruth, he didn't tell me. Or if he did, I don't remember. Or I didn't listen." Blade's temper rose to meet hers. "You're right, he talked all the time. But I was leading my own life, doing my own work. I didn't wait breathlessly for him to spout some brilliant theory. Maybe I should have—but I didn't know he was suddenly going to drop dead."

She flung the journal at him. It whizzed past his ear and struck the headboard with a bang.

They were both stunned, ashamed at the flare-up.

"I am so sorry," she whispered.

He scrubbed a hand across his face. Then he wrapped an arm around her waist and hauled her against him, holding her till they were both calm.

"Ruth, your brother never came out and said he suspected the people at the pueblo he was excavating came from this meadow. Not to me."

"I believe you. Maybe it's wishful thinking on my part, hoping he left one final legacy."

"And maybe you're correct. I know this winter he got very interested in Hopi legends."

"Hopi? I thought the local people were the Navajos. Jennie's people."

"The Hopis were in this country first. Then the more warlike Navajos came and drove the Hopi people away, for a while. The Hopis came back. The mountains around here are sacred to both tribes."

She leaned back and listened.

"Ruth, I wish I had listened better. I do know Phelan had a little kachina doll depicting the friendly spirit the Hopis believe lives on Sunset Crater. He showed it to me when he returned from a trip to the mesas.

"I also know the Hopi leave prayer sticks at shrines hidden on the mountain, and out in the lava flow."

She reached over and picked up the journal, turning pages well past where she'd read earlier. She looked at the last dozen or so entries he made. She turned back a few pages, and stiffened. "Blade, look!"

The legend of the fire god: the people of a corrupt Hopi village were told of an unusual light seen on the mountain.

"When was that written?" Blade asked.

"January."

"That's when he went out to the mesas."

The people were warned the light was coming to destroy the evil ones. But most of the people ignored the warnings and continued to gamble in the kivas. A few of the good people listened. They gathered their families and possessions and escaped in time. Soon the sky darkened and a large cloud of ash swept over the village, and destroyed all who remained.

"So, according to Hopi legend, some people got away."

"Yes." Ruth began to gather up the journal and the papers.

"What are you doing?"

"I want to walk out in the meadow. Get the cobwebs out of my brain. See if I can fit this together better. I know you planned to be gone this afternoon."

"I got sidetracked." He flashed her a smile. "Are you putting those back in the office?" He wanted to read the journal, but he didn't want to explain why. He wasn't ready to tell her about his past. Not quite yet. But soon. If he was going to ask her to stay with him— to marry him—he wanted no secrets.

"Now that I realize how valuable these are, I'm going to put them in the safe. Even with new locks on the doors, I don't trust the bums who have been around lately."

She was daydreaming. Sweet dreams. Walking across the meadow, fully clothed, wide awake, watching a white wispy cloud traipse across the blue sky. She was daydreaming of Blade, of his touch, which ignited fires of desire and satisfied her passion, yet which left her ravenous for more.

A raven's noisy clamor brought her back to earth with a thud. She had just left the man's warm bed and all she could think about was climbing back into it. What had happened to her?

Where was the practical Ruth who put her house in order each day before she went to work? At this moment she was supposed to be working. She'd walked out through the meadow to look at it from the hill, to think about Donal's theories about the beans found in this meadow being related to the beans found at the pueblo, not to think about Blade's hands working magic on her body.

She needed to put Donal's thoughts onto paper in an intelligent, thought-provoking manner so that other academicians would give them consideration. The only way she could do that was to study the lay of the land, to picture the bean fields as if they actually existed, and to present his words and ideas as if she truly believed them.

She did believe them. Donal Phelan had been brilliant. The world deserved to know his theories.

She was nearly all the way across the wide meadow when she discovered she'd forgotten her notebook. Thoroughly annoyed with herself, she marched back to the house.

If she could keep her mind on her work for just a short time, she could finish the typing. Then all she'd have to do is organize the manuscript, retype it, and send it off.

And go on from there.

Ruth had spent a tremendous amount of effort trying not to think about what came after the manuscript was sent. As she strode back across the meadow, she decided the time had come to face her future.

She had been so terribly scared when she left St. Louis on her journey to the Arizona Territory, so afraid of Donal's reception.

She shook her head in amazement.

What actually had happened to her had been worse than anything she could have imagined. But she had come through it remarkably well, mostly with Blade's help. Yet her own courage had been part of the process of coping.

She sighed. She'd coped with tragedy and survived. Her fortitude would help her over the next hurdle—leaving Blade.

It was agony even thinking about it.

Like slashing her heart to ribbons.

She loved him to distraction. She knew beyond a doubt she'd never love another man the way she loved Gladius Blade. She could never love that way again. But she was a realist and knew she could expect nothing beyond the moment, nothing beyond the brief precious time of their sojourn at the ranch. He'd made her no promises. She'd asked for none. She accepted their relationship for exactly what it was—golden moments exceeding her most audacious dreams.

She was simply grateful for Blade. He'd rescued her. He'd loved her. He'd set her free. He'd given her a priceless gift she'd cherish for all time. It was glorious. A moment out of time.

A chill touched her spine. Parting with him would be the hardest thing she'd ever forced herself to do. But she could do it because of him. Because of the love he'd given her, the passion he'd given her, and the strength. He'd given her back her self-esteem.

He'd given her love beyond anything she could imagine. And with that he'd given her independence. She no longer needed a man to cater to for her identity. Blade loved Ruth McKenna exactly the way she was. He loved her heart, her spirit, her intelligence, and her character. He saw beauty in her. He saw glory.

He took her love and gave her freedom.

She knew she'd be able to leave, maybe for Los Angeles to seek a job with a progressive employer like Joseph Bemish's brother. She knew now she could take care of herself.

Crossing the meadow lost in thought, she did not notice the horses cresting the hill above the house.

She walked into the shadowy entry hall and sprinted up the stairs. Her day didn't seem quite as bright as it had been, but she refused to be depressed by her decision to leave Blade when the right time came. She told herself she'd prize their love more since she'd admitted their story must come to an end.

The notebook she wanted lay beside the typing machine on the desk in the neat office, open to the last entry she'd made. It occurred to her that her own adventure might be of interest to other people. She just might write an article or two about her journey west. Maybe a magazine or newspaper would publish it.

A noise from the next room interrupted her musing. She thought she was alone in the house and wondered if Jennie had returned. Her heart began to thud. What if the intruders had come back?

She looked around for something to defend herself with, and saw a piece of lava rock on the bookshelf. Too bad her trusty cane was downstairs on the entryway coat rack.

She hefted the rock. It was heavier than she expected. Then she crept into the hall toward Donal's room. The instant she stepped into the bedroom doorway, her mind went blank. Blade knelt in front of the open safe, clutching her brother's journal in his right hand.

Her throat went dry. Anguish squeezed her heart. Had Blade also betrayed her?

"What are you doing in Donal's safe?"

Despair stabbed him in the gut.

He knew even before he looked at her that she would never believe any explanation he gave. He'd lied to her, more than once, and the lies had come back to strangle him.

He rose slowly to his full height. He couldn't remember hurting so bad.

Still holding the journal, he turned to face her. His dark brown eyes looked bleak.

"Ruth, there are some things I haven't told you."

14

An aching pressure built in his chest not unlike what he'd experienced as a young man when he had learned of his mother's fatal heart attack.

"Ruth," he beseeched.

Her face was a hard mask of disbelief.

"There are things I need to tell you."

"How did you open the safe?" Her voice was like shards of glass.

"I know the combination. Your brother gave it to me."

"Why? He never allowed anybody but me to touch it. It belonged to our father, and Donal was sentimental about the heavy old thing. Why would he give you the combination?"

There was nothing to do but tell her. Yet at this moment it seemed he'd waited too long. His explanation would sound like a whitewash job. He knew it would be very hard for Ruth to listen to his excuses and

not believe he'd made love to her just to have access to
Phelan's secrets. Especially after she'd discovered the
way Farley had used her.

"I should have told you sooner."

But the trouble was Blade had been so caught up in
the wonder of their lovemaking he'd forgotten all else.
He'd been wild and blind because of her. And obviously very stupid.

"Tell me!" she demanded, her eyes were chips of ice.

"I love you."

"Damn you!" She turned away, her anger crumpling
into a slag heap of pain.

He reached her in three steps, his hand closing over
her rigid shoulder.

"Don't." She shrugged his hand away.

"Let me explain."

She turned her back to him. "Go ahead. I'm sure
you'll have a terrific explanation."

"Will you look at me?"

He hardly recognized the woman who regarded him
so dispassionately. Her face was pinched, her eyes dry
and dull. "This will take some time," he told her. "Why
don't you sit down?"

She chose the straight-backed chair nearest the door,
as far from Blade as possible.

He laid the papers he'd been holding on the bedside
table. Then with a shake of his head he faced her.

Ruth and Jennie had straightened up the mess in the
room and packed away all of Phelan's clothes. The
room wasn't immaculate, but at least it was clean
enough for people to sit down.

Blade turned and walked over to the window, looking down on the trees and yard below. The chickens

pecked greedily at vegetable scraps Jennie was tossing into the chicken yard. "Seamus Blade is the name of the investor who financed the past two years of this archaeological expedition."

He turned just in time to see her reaction. She cocked a brow questioningly.

"My father."

"The man who bought the story of Coronado's gold?" A fine thread of sarcasm glittered through her words.

"Yes." Blade was surprised how her shaft pierced him. He walked to the quilt-covered bed and sank down onto it.

"How did you find out?"

"I was there at the time the financial deal was made."

"You knew your father was being duped?" She was incredulous. Anger, hot and swift, replaced the merciless calm.

Blade wondered how he could explain a relationship between a father and son who had never had any affinity. The father had no comprehension of the man his son was and made no attempt to learn. And the son couldn't, and wouldn't, communicate with a father who held him in such contempt.

"Let me tell you a few things about Seamus Blade. He's shrewd and smart and lucky as sin. He's an Irish immigrant who found his pot of gold in Colorado. He made a fortune while other men around him received only blisters and backaches for their efforts.

"With my mother's quiet encouragement, he got out of the mines before he died in them like some of his friends did. He went to Denver to become a respectable member of the community. And he made several more fortunes speculating and investing. He's the most fortunate man I ever met when it comes to taking financial risks and winning."

Blade ran his hand through his thick auburn mane. "Yes, I knew Phelan was bullshitting the old man about knowing the exact location of Coronado's gold. But my father doesn't seek out my advice about his investments. I'm an artist, and to his way of thinking that means I'm strange. He isn't my most ardent admirer."

"Because of your difficulty in communicating with your father, you let him be cheated," she surmised. "For revenge?"

A wave of heat flushed Blade's cheeks. Anger rolled through him like violent thunder down a mountain canyon. "Can't you understand? He wasn't cheated! It isn't the money that matters to him—he's a very rich man. It's the thrill of adventure he's after. The speculation, the risk. The chance to test his phenomenal Irish luck one more time. All this meant to him was another treasure hunt."

He thought a moment and continued. "And if he did take a dumping, I didn't see that it would hurt him much. He could do with a bit of humility now and then."

She shifted uncomfortably on the chair. Donal Phelan and Seamus Blade sounded as if they were well matched. But what about Gladius Blade?

"So how did you get here?" She recalled Blade's words about his father not trusting his advice. Why would he send his son to watch over the dig?

"I'm part of the package," he said disparagingly. "The calf that was sold with the milk cow."

"What does that mean?"

"Your brother went to San Francisco after his eastern backers withdrew their support. We've now decided that was because of your husband's influence." Blade couldn't help pointing that out. "Phelan needed another financial speculator to invest in the project, and he needed one fast or the venture would go under. Apparently, he got turned down flat in San Francisco. But he was as tenacious as a bulldog, so he kept looking, following all sorts of crazy leads. He truly believed in this expedition, and he wasn't going to let it die."

Ruth couldn't sit in the chair and watch him any longer. It hurt her to hear about her brother's dreams, almost as much as it made her ache to find out about his disillusionment. She stood and went to the window.

"Once Phelan unearthed what he needed to know about my father, the rest was simple. He followed us. And he conveniently showed up at a club where we were having a drink, then made a big show of telling us he was looking for a money man to fund a treasure hunt. And an artist to document the find."

"That's quite transparent." She turned to look at him, her eyes searching his rugged face.

"I thought so, too, at the time." He stood up and took a step toward her. But he didn't want to scare her off. "I would have preferred a more subtle approach myself, but the obvious one worked fine on the old man. He bought the story right there and couldn't wait to force his money on Phelan."

"And your services?"

"Yeah." Blade laughed mirthlessly. "It was the first

time my dear old dad ever said I was a good artist."

"When did Donal discover you didn't believe his pitch?"

"About two minutes after my father jumped into the deal. I wanted Phelan to know right from the start that I didn't trust him worth spit, and I was only coming along to guard the Blade investment. But I said nothing to my father. I learned a long time ago to keep my opinions about his business affairs to myself. He's the businessman. I draw foolish pictures."

Years of hurt and bitterness hung in the air like dark thick smoke.

"Blade . . ."

"What?" His voice was raw.

She didn't know what to say, so she said nothing. Right now her sympathy wouldn't bridge the gap between them, and she didn't want it to. She needed honesty from him, nothing less.

"What did you think after you got here?"

"It was still winter when Phelan and I first arrived. A long, hard winter. You could say we got to know each other very well before the spring thaw came. We did make one or two trips out to the dig so I could get the layout down on paper. It was fairly primitive out there at the time. Your brother has accomplished a hell of a lot in the past two years."

"You sound like you admired him."

"I did. Right from the first few days after we arrived in Flagstaff. Obviously he was a professional, even though he approached my father like a carnival shill. Eventually, I invested some of my own cash in the project. Phelan was a complicated man, Ruth. He could be as difficult as a spoiled child when things didn't go his way. But I think he was one of the finest archaeologists in the country."

"Why didn't you tell me this when I first came? I don't see any reason for the evasions and dishonesty."

"In the beginning, when you first got here, I simply didn't think it mattered. I expected you to leave right away. What good would it have done you to know about the investment?"

Her stance shifted impatiently.

Blade forced himself to go on.

"My motives for being here had changed somewhat by the time Phelan died. I was no longer simply watching how he handled the old man's investment. I'd just received word from my youngest brother that Poppa had a stroke."

He looked up when he heard her inhale. "He's okay, but rather depressed, and my brother wanted me to convey some good news to him down in Tucson about this little treasure hunt."

He walked to where she stood. "I'm sure this will sound infantile to you, but I wanted to impress my father. I have done nothing but cause him problems the past ten years. For once, there was something I could give him besides problems."

"What do you mean by problems?"

"If you had read the file Phelan had compiled about me and kept in his desk, you'd know."

"I did read it. It extolled your reputation as an illustrator."

"You only read what I wanted you to see. That night after the funeral when you went up to your brother's office—when the book fell off the shelf and hit you in the head, and knocked you unconscious for a few minutes—you had the folder in your hand. I came in and removed what I didn't want you to read."

She felt a thick tension rising in her. "What?"

"There was a detective's report about my arrest for the murder of my ex-wife and her lover."

Blood thumped loudly in Ruth's temple. She couldn't believe what she was hearing. Without thinking she backed a step away from him.

"I was acquitted," he went on smoothly as if he hadn't noticed her response, as if it hadn't pierced his heart. "I wasn't anywhere near the accident—I really believe it was an accident, by the way. But the lawyers and the publicity of that sordid mess were costly to my father. Not to mention having to buy back all the pieces of my mother's jewelry Ophelia had stolen and pawned. It was painful for all of us. The whole family. My father hadn't wanted me to marry Ophelia in the first place. Said she was after his money. Naturally I didn't listen."

Ruth smiled and nodded. She understood completely. She hadn't listened to her brother about Farley McKenna, either.

"There's a simple explanation about why I took those papers. I was attracted to you, Ruth. Right from the start. I didn't want you to know those things about my life. About the fiasco of my marriage. About my wife and her lover robbing my family. About my being drunk all the time. About a prostitute being my alibi. I'm even embarrassed to tell you now."

She didn't say anything.

"All those papers are in my dresser drawer. You can read them if you want to. I don't want any more secrets between us now."

She merely stood with her arms folded over her

chest and watched him. "Is that why you're in the safe? Because you wanted everything open and honest between us? Or because there's something more in the safe about you?"

"The reason I was in the safe is because I wanted to do something for my father. I've searched through all of your brother's papers. Despite the fact we don't see eye to eye about most things, I wanted to do something for my father to help him recover at least a part of his investment. To help him regain his health. I had hoped to find something in the journal."

He stepped closer and put his hands on her arms, silently pleading for her to understand him. "I wanted to find the treasure."

"What?" She jerked away from him as if he was poison and strode toward the door.

He caught up with her before she reached the hallway.

"You're lying, Blade!"

He turned her toward him, desperate for her to believe him.

She struggled against his strength. "There is no treasure!"

"Damn it, he found something! And I want whatever it was!"

She writhed and twisted, fighting to be free. "You used me. Just like the rest of them!"

"No! I love you! I'm crazy about you, can't you see?"

"Let me go! Don't touch me." She turned and headed toward the stairs. Stopping on the landing, she looked at him, taking a deep breath to calm herself. "I'm riding out to the dig. I'll be back by dark."

"You can't go by yourself, Ruth. The woods are crawling with treasure hunters. Remember the guy who attacked you the day of the snowstorm? Someone out there might hurt you."

"I'm going." She hurried down several steps. "How can strangers possibly hurt me any more than the men I've loved and trusted?"

When Blade went out to the stable, she'd already saddled Ginger and left. The big black was also gone.

Jennie came out of Marie's cabin with a few tin cans for the trash heap.

"Is Tsosi around?"

"No," Jennie answered. "He rode off this morning in that direction." She pointed to the south. "He didn't say where he was going."

"When he comes back, will you have him come over to the house to find me? I need to talk to him."

She nodded and walked off. He'd started back to the house when the cabin door opened and Marie called his name.

"How are you feeling today?" he asked.

"Okay."

She didn't look okay. Blade thought she looked tired and worried. Deep, dark circles ringed her eyes.

"Will you hire men to dig?" she asked. "Springtime?"

He realized suddenly how remiss he'd been. So much had happened since Phelan died, and so much of the time he'd been preoccupied with Ruth. He hadn't bothered to discuss his plans with the people who depended on him for their livelihood. He felt ashamed of himself.

"No." He studied her worn face. "When Mister Phelan died, the archaeology project ended. All I do is draw the pictures, remember?"

She nodded impassively.

"Mrs. McKenna is reading through her brother's writing about the excavation. She's going to make a book from his notes." He wondered how much Marie understood. "She should be finished in about a month. Are you going to be looking for another job?"

"No. I go home."

He realized she meant she'd go back to the reservation.

"That's good. I appreciate all you did for Mister Phelan and myself. I'll have some money ready for you when you go. You can take the chickens and the cow with you. Is Tsosi going home with you or is he going to look for other work in town?"

She didn't answer immediately, and Blade thought she might not know her son's plans.

"If he decides to go home with you, I think he should take the horses. Maybe we can find him a couple mares to start another herd. The black has good blood."

She nodded, starting to say something, then changed her mind.

Theobald Vanderdam sat his mount like a calvary officer. Through his spyglass he watched his two underlings and their new associate, Orlie Taswell. Hostility raged through him.

While his cold was better, he still had a deep raspy cough and he definitely was not thrilled about traipsing all over the countryside in the wind. But he had to get rid of Taswell.

The sun had come out and melted most of the snow, yet the ground was soggy and the wind was raw. Vanderdam's disposition couldn't have been worse.

Grover and Sholes, the simpletons he'd hired to search for Phelan's illusive plunder, had so far fumbled every attempt they'd made. They'd taken his money, gobbled his food, swilled his booze, and had now wandered off with their new buddy in pursuit of another undertaking. Or so he was told.

He didn't believe it for a minute! They were after his gold! Taswell planned to steal his fortune!

Vanderdam fingered the shotgun in the scabbard. The booty was his. No two-timing double-crossing dimwits were going to cheat him out of his prize. He urged the horse forward.

Ruth rode like the devil was chasing her. Her mind was in utter chaos. How could she have possibly fallen for another man who lied to her?

Fleeting remnants of Blade's touch haunted her, and she rode blindly, paying little attention to where she was going or where she had been. Ginger, who had spent a pleasant winter in the stables with plenty of food and very little exercise, soon grew tired of the game of chase. The mare was ready for Ruth to get off and take a hike as Phelan had often done, but Ruth urged her on.

Caa-rackkk!

From somewhere above her there was a wild yell and a shot.

Ginger jumped a foot or so and nearly threw her. If she hadn't been an experienced rider, Ruth would have sailed over the horse's head onto the ground.

Ruth hauled on the reins and with more than a little effort got the wild-eyed animal under control. Who on earth could have been shooting a gun? She touched the spooky mare with her boots and moved her quickly up the trail, away from whatever fool was playing with his weapon. Suddenly there was a pounding of hoofs. Riders were coming up behind her. Two men. Maybe more.

The indignation that had rushed into her turned to fear. She was alone, wasn't certain where she was, and after all, this was the wild West. Cowboy and Indian country. Who knew what evil lurked behind the sagebrush?

Scoffing at her overactive imagination, she nonetheless hurried the mare behind an outcropping of weathered lava rock partially hidden by a scrubby leafless aspen.

She sat with her heart pounding madly as three horses thundered past her hideout and raced up the next bluff. The sound of hoofbeats dwindled slowly and faded in the distance. Her heart continued to pound.

A curious raven swung low overhead, then flapped his ebony wings and flew onward. She let out a shaky sigh and looked around. No one was within view.

With more stealth than she ever considered possible, Ruth urged the horse back into the open, and turned back toward the ranch. The animal seemed to sense her haste. She trotted swiftly along.

Warily Ruth searched the landscape, her head turning often to look behind her. In her fright, she'd failed to notice any of the riders who'd dashed past her. Perhaps one of the horses was black, but she wasn't even certain of that. Why hadn't she listened to Blade?

Blade had lived in the West a lot longer than she had, and he knew about these pirates who were searching for the imaginary trove her brother had bragged about. He knew how dangerous greed was when it controlled a man's reason.

She'd been mad when she left the ranch house. Outraged at Blade, so she'd gone off to pout. Perhaps to punish him as much as to think out her future plans.

A bad mistake, she thought, possibly deadly.

From his perch on a higher hill, Vanderdam watched through his spyglass. Even knowing them as he did, he was awed at his hirlings' mindless incompetence. He halfheartedly wished he'd brought along a rifle instead of a shotgun. He'd be doing the world a favor by blowing them out of their saddles. But, of course, he needed the shotgun. He wanted Taswell close. He wanted no slipup.

The woman moved down one slope and up the next knoll, pushing the little mare at a brisk pace. Vanderdam felt the unanticipated whim to urge her on. She had spirit. Nerve. Gumption. He admired such qualities.

But, of course, she was his enemy. She held the key to his golden door. He couldn't let her stand in the way of achieving his goal.

Ruth stepped up the pace.

Although she neither saw nor heard anything to alert her to imminent danger, her razor-sharp instincts told her she was in jeopardy. Somehow she knew the three men who had barged past her moments before had turned around and were drawing near. A sense of foreboding caused her slender body to shudder. Why were these men after her?

There could only be one answer: Donal's imaginary treasure.

"Am I going to die because of some stupid, arrogant joke?" She urged the little mare to hurry. Surely her life couldn't be snuffed out like a lamplight just when she'd found a fine man to love. And love him she did.

Blade! Help me!

Ginger was a gentle horse, one bred for leisurely strolls among the wildflowers on sunlit days, but she had a good heart, and a great deal of sense. She heard the rider before Ruth did. She leaped forward, heading as fast as she could toward the safety of the stable.

He moved quickly into her path, so quickly she hardly noticed his presence. The obscene barrels of the shotgun pointed directly at her slim middle. From where he sat atop his horse, he could easily cut her in half with one blast.

"Oh," she said softly.

Tsosi Manyhorses had just crested a low-rising hill when he spotted Theobald Vanderdam training his spy-glass on a rider approaching him at a fast clip. It took the young Navajo a full minute to recognize the rider as Ruth McKenna. From where he watched, it seemed to him that Vanderdam meant to intercept the woman.

That didn't set well with him because he liked Mrs. McKenna. She'd been kind to him and his mother. She was a good woman, yet Tsosi knew it wasn't wise for a Navajo to interfere in a white man's business. He sat quietly on the black, pondering the situation. He was a patient man.

It was growing late and the sun was dipping low

over the ponderous mass of mountains. Sunbeams danced over the snowcapped peaks and glittered against the blue afternoon sky. A swirl of wind tossed brilliant sparkles into the air and they fell like a shower of diamonds back onto the snow.

Tsosi waited. Even when Mrs. McKenna stumbled into the draw where Vanderdam intercepted her, even when the lawyer pulled a shotgun on her, Tsosi kept his peace and waited.

Abruptly, all hell broke loose.

Behind the woman, riding hell-bent for leather, came three crazy men. Elbows flapping at strange angles, overcoats flying behind them, the three rode like Lucifer was on their tails. They rode mindlessly, shouting their fool heads off, unaware they were heading into a trap.

As they approached the draw where Vanderdam held the woman hostage, the lawyer suddenly raised his weapon and fired.

Tsosi's heart stopped. He saw Ruth fall. And then he heard a man's scream. Ruth rolled on the ground and began to scramble swiftly away from the horses.

Ginger bolted, heading down the hill to the barn. Tsosi stilled the black. Ruth was not dead, he realized. Apparently she wasn't hurt.

He looked at the other men. The horses were frantic, wild with fear and the desire to flee. They plunged and twirled, frenzied and savage. The men hung on tenaciously, trying to control their mounts.

One man, the one Tsosi had seen at the house the day it stormed, had a slash of blood on his face. More blood appeared on his shoulder. Evidently the blast of the shotgun had barely caught him at all. Any closer and it would have blown his head apart.

Tsosi turned his attention back to see if Ruth was all right. His eyes had only strayed a second or two.

She was gone! She had disappeared into the background while he watched the others.

She acted on instinct. She'd been educated, taught conventional behavior and proper etiquette, but nothing she'd learned had prepared her for such a murderous attack. Instinct alone guided her steps.

Ruth clawed and writhed her way out of the path of the pawing hoofs. The beasts were insane with fright, caused both from the ear-shattering blast of the shotgun and the extreme apprehension of their riders.

Once she'd removed herself from the immediate danger of being stomped to death beneath the deranged horses, she'd seen her chance for freedom in the few seconds of pandemonium and confusion. Grasping at the whim of fate, she fled north to the low cover of tufted vegetation and the shelter of pine trees.

The ground was slick with snow-dampened pine needles and she skidded once and nearly fell, hitting one knee on a hidden stone and plunging her hand into the pungent earth. Her fingernail ripped through the tip of her riding glove and broke. For a fraction of a second she was immobile in a sea of dread and pain, but the shock passed and she righted herself to push onward in her frantic race to freedom.

Tsosi also chose that moment to move. Spurring the black forward, he raced after Ruth while the other men were caught in their momentary chaos. He scarcely made it. Another minute or so and Vanderdam could have caught him. The lawyer would have had no compunction about killing an Indian.

The sun slipped behind the San Francisco Peaks. The air cooled quickly without the sun's heat. The pastel hues of evening stained the western sky, darkening the looming mountains.

The softness of twilight was a deceptive sham, for the danger had not disappeared with the light.

Tsosi followed Ruth up the higher slopes and into the darkness of the pines. A foreign sound, distant but distinct, caught his keen ears and drove him to halt the black sharply against a clump of brush.

A doe with a spotted fawn frolicking behind her stopped and delicately tested the air. Tsosi waited patiently. He heard the sound again. This time he identified it as metal. Not a deer but a man. Vanderdam.

"Which way did she go, boss?"

The words echoed loudly in the stillness of sundown.

"Shut up, you fool!"

Ruth heard the men's voices as she lingered behind the camouflage of a Ponderosa pine.

Cloaked in the curtain of dusk, she stopped to rest and regain her stamina. Enveloped in the deep shadows, she was relatively safe if she could force herself to remain in one place long enough to allow the men to pass.

The urge to run gripped her as the men grew closer.

She felt like a timid little fox at a foxhunt. The hounds were baying at her back, nipping at her heels, driving her into the ground. Her only weapon was her wits.

"She's got to be around here somewhere."

"Keep looking."

"What am I lookin' for? I cain't see me own nose in the dark."

"Shit! That hurt! Next time tell me when a branch is going to hit me."

"Are we goin' back to town tonight? I'm hungry."

"Let's ride down to the ranch house. She's probably gone back there."

Ruth clenched her whole body tight in an effort to remain still. She was pressed against the pine tree like part of the bark. The sharp odor of pitch stung her nostrils. She wondered if she'd ever see Blade again.

In an hour or so he'd begin to worry about her. After all, she told him she'd be home by dark. He'd make allowances for the journey and her anger. But in an hour it would be clear something was wrong. He'd search for her. She knew him well, knew he'd brave the cold night to hunt for her. He'd probably send Tsosi into town for the sheriff. If she could only hold on another hour she felt she'd be safe.

Safe in the shelter of Blade's strength.

So she waited, and a short distance away Tsosi also waited.

He'd spotted her just before Vanderdam and his flunkies rode on by. Two of them. Grover and Sholes. Even in the cover of darkness they were easy to spot. Tsosi wondered what happened to Taswell. Not that he cared one way or another, but he was curious. Vanderdam had shot only once which meant that unless the lawyer had slit his throat, Taswell was still around. He needed to keep that in mind.

Suddenly she knew she could wait no longer. She'd go mad if she stood motionless another minute. She turned from the meager screen of the pines and staggered down the hill. Her legs were numb from standing in one position for so long, and from shock and fear.

Weak and shaky, her limbs couldn't hold her. She pitched forward and tumbled head over petticoats down to the bottom of the slope. She made the sound of a frightened rabbit the instant before she clipped her jaw on a boulder.

He saw her run and fall. He was after her in the blink of an eye, in the haste of desperation, knowing without reason or information but by pure gut instinct that the lawyer and his henchmen would be back at any time. He scooped her up and threw her over the saddle, mounting in a fluid motion and spurring the black to run.

Any other man would have headed to town or at least to the ranch, but Tsosi could feel the breath of his enemies tickling his spine. He turned the horse, out of Vanderdam's path and cautiously avoiding any place Taswell might be hiding.

He rode past the ebony dunes, past the cinder cone of Sunset Peak, into the depths of the once liquid lava flow, then he hauled the woman from the horse.

She was breathing normally and showed signs of awakening at any time. He had to hide her quickly, before she came to. Awake she'd be difficult and bossy—white women always were.

With stealth and unbelievable agility, he carried her into the sharp, savage, perversely beautiful river of rock. No other man would risk being maimed on the perilous fragments of fire.

"You'll be safe," he told her inert form. "If you don't move."

Without another word, he stole away.

Not until he was mounted again and trotting toward home did he realize he had a choice. He could ride back to the ranch and tell Blade where to find his woman. Or he could ride into Flagstaff and tell Jaspar Bird. Bird had already offered him Sam Waverley's herd of horses for information about the woman. He'd probably give him more than that for rescuing her from Vanderdam's shotgun.

Tsosi wanted the horses. He wanted to build a herd as big as the one his father once owned. He considered his choices as he rode. Then he wheeled the black toward Flagstaff, to see Jaspar Bird, and all those horses.

15

Ruth woke up in the bowels of hell.

At first she was only aware of the icy cold. Her body seemed utterly frozen and she thought for a moment she was lost in sleep, dreaming some foolishness about being laid out naked on a huge, hard slab of ice in a frigid wasteland.

Something far more appalling became clear—she came to recognize that she was in fact conscious.

It wasn't a dream. She had a reason to be cold, to feel a hardness under her, to see the world as black. A metallic taste filled her mouth. Fear—at its most elemental level. No nightmare, however ghastly, could have terrified her so completely.

Instantly, she began fighting back her terror. Fear—she kept reminding herself—and the accompanying panic were her worst enemies. Far worse than the people who abducted her.

She forced herself to be calm, taking several deep

breaths in the process, and opened her eyes wide. And when she felt the panic dissipate, she peered slowly around her.

The world was black. Pitch-black. Every direction she looked was as black as a moonless midnight, as if she'd somehow been transported to the very innards of a coal mine and dumped on some melanic pile of rock. She studied the ebony dreamscape, thinking at first she must be hidden in a cave or a mine shaft. All the horror stories of people being lost in caves or falling into mines and going mad from fear came quickly and maliciously to her renegade mind. She wrestled with this new dragon till her good sense once again won out for at least a few minutes.

A moaning gray lament whispered past on a draft of freezing air. Wind. Ruth shivered in spite of her warm clothing.

"I'm outside," she told herself aloud. "Not hidden in a cave or a shaft. I'm out in the open."

She reacted to that knowledge with a tremor of dismay. She was outside, unprotected, exposed. She had no idea of her location, and wasn't certain how or when she might escape, but she knew without question she'd be incredibly cold before she reached home.

If she reached home.

With hands that shook more from fright than the wintry exposure, she groped timidly around. She'd been aware from the moment she became conscious that she was resting on a bed of rock. It was far too hard to be anything but stone.

When her gloved hands detected the twisted thrust of jagged lava stabbing upward at her soft body, she gasped in horror.

"Noooo!!!" she screamed. Panic swamped her. She was lost in the lava field!

Bolting to her feet, she scrambled like a crab off the rock, pitching forward abruptly. Throwing up her gloved hands to protect her face, she plunged downward over a ledge.

She collapsed in a heap a mere two or three feet from where she'd stood, but she had toppled hard and jarred herself badly. Her coat sleeves were torn, her leather gloves mutilated. Her chin had grazed a stone.

A heavy blanket had wrapped itself around her ankles. Not knowing of its existence, she had tripped and fallen. She sat a moment, breathing heavily, trying to think. Slowly she pulled the blanket from around her feet up to her chin. It was wool, and smelled faintly of horse, but it was very warm.

It became clear to her that trying to move around in the razor-sharp lava spill in the dead of night was not only irresponsible and stupid, it was futile. The black nightmare of rock and fragments oozed for hundreds of yards. She had no idea where she sat within its confines. Even in the light of day it would take time, adroitness, and a good sense of direction to escape.

"So here I sit," she decided, trying to find a spot that was out of the wind and reasonably comfortable. In a way her spill had been providential because it gave her a small amount of shelter from the gusts of wind that blew in concert with howls from coyotes all night long.

It was the longest, coldest, most terror-filled night of her whole life. Only the thought of getting back to Blade pulled her through.

How could she have doubted him?

How could she have allowed the treachery of her late

husband to color her belief in Blade? Farley's crimes had been committed with malice of foresight. Blade had acted to correct an oversight. Would she have an opportunity to tell him that she loved him, believed in him? The night wind held no answers.

He'd expected her home before dark. Ruth wasn't the type of woman who lingered outside after dark. Dusk had come and lengthened gracefully into twilight, with evening rushing fast upon its heels. Blade had gone down to the kitchen and started dinner, more to keep himself occupied than because he was hungry. For once in his life the thought of food held no appeal.

After Ruth had stormed out of the house, he'd tried to work in his office on a particularly difficult set of colored drawings, but he could not stop thinking about her and their terrible argument.

He ruined the drawings, and in a flash of violent rage, he swiped them off the drawing board. The paper tore, and he grabbed it furiously, mashing it into a ruinous ball, throwing it onto the floor. Then the fury that bolted through him left at the same lightning speed. And his energy left with it. He slumped in his chair, defeated.

He'd lost her.

Ruth was the best woman ever to come into his life and he'd ruined their love. Why? To save his pride? To make a few bucks? To get a pat on the back from an ornery old man who had always thought he was a worthless son, and probably always would?

He'd gone downstairs because he feared he would destroy his whole office if he didn't. He figured he'd do a lot less damage in the kitchen than around the irreplaceable drawings.

With that notion in mind, he admitted to himself , something he'd never before realized—that his work was important. His drawings of this archaeological excavation were crucial to scholars being able to understand the prehistoric people of the Arizona Territory. Now that Phelan was gone, the drawings were the key to future scientists returning to challenge the man's theories.

Blade believed in himself as an artist, and Ruth had been fundamental to his new sense of worth.

The niggling thought of her being lost was a dagger in his heart.

"She's just late," he told himself, trying to keep his eyes off the kitchen clock. He'd kept listening for the sound of her horse coming into the yard, and when dark shadows turned to blackness, he'd begun to worry. Then he'd heard the horse. Ginger. He'd taken a lamp and started toward the barn to meet her, maybe to patch things up. Then his stomach dropped. Ginger was riderless. Every horrible thought imaginable entered his brain—she was hurt, she was lost, she was dead. He'd called Jennie from the cabin to help him catch the frantic mare. It had taken them both to calm her enough to lead into the stable.

"Where's Tsosi?" Blade had asked. Tsosi had a way with animals. Blade wanted his help. With the mare. With the search.

"He's not home," Jennie had told him. "Auntie is worried.

It wasn't until they'd cooled down the mare that Blade found the splatter of blood on her flank.

Blade could not have imagined a night more wrought with agony, suffering, and fear, if he'd spent a lifetime doing so. Every possible worry, suspicion, and fantasy haunted him. With each minute that passed, a new and more morbid fiction taunted his thoughts. He realized then thc true curse of a creative mind. Because whatever notion teased his anguished brain, he immediately visualized it in gruesome, colorful detail.

Activity was his only savior, and so from the moment he realized Ruth was missing, he'd searched for her.

He simply had no choice.

Into the night he hunted and explored, probing the empty countryside with a lantern in his hand. He groped his way up every hill and down every gully until he was weak from lack of sleep, lack of food, and fatigue. Sometimes he walked when he thought he might be able to see better on foot than mounted. He would have crawled on his knees in hell, if he could have found her.

But she was nowhere to be found. It was as if she'd vanished from the planet. When he finally admitted hope was exhausted, he turned his horse around and rode to Flagstaff. Perhaps Sheriff Cameron could succeed where he had failed.

Jaspar Bird was already in bed in his rooms at the back of the office he kept near the armory, when the persistent rap sounded on his door. He had treated himself to a plate of beef pot roast at the hotel dining room that evening and his stomach was giving him fits. He had been up taking soda several times, so he'd barely settled down to doze when the pounding woke him.

He tried to ignore it, but he wasn't a man who could refuse the summons of another person. He was far too cowardly.

He padded sourly across the room, a candle in his hand, and had to throw the bolt before he could open the door.

He stood there in his red nightshirt and bare feet, peering out into the darkness. Jaspar swayed in the breezy doorway, his candle flickering, wondering if he was about to be attacked for the money he had hidden under his lumpy mattress. Then he recognized the young Indian.

"Tsosi?"

"I have the woman."

The slight breeze puffed and the candle flame went out. Jaspar scrambled back into the room for a match. He heard the door close and knew the boy had come inside. It annoyed him that an Indian would dare enter his house without an invitation, but he did little more than scowl into the darkness. After all, Tsosi was taller than he, younger, and whipcord strong.

The match flared, and the odor of sulphur stung his nostrils. "What did you just say?" Jaspar demanded.

Tsosi observed the potbellied little man with something close to aspersion. Bird postured like a rooster, despotic and huffy, a man above other men. And yet there he stood, pretending to be a tough man, in a funny red sack stretched so tightly over his paunch that his belly button looked like a doughnut hole. A smile hovered on Tsosi's normally stern mouth. Jaspar Bird was utterly comical.

"I have the woman," Tsosi repeated.

"What woman?"

"The white woman. Ruth McKenna."

Jaspar stared at him stupidly. "You have her where? Outside?"

It had been a rough day and Tsosi was weary. He wished he'd just taken Ruth back home to Blade. Why hadn't he thought of doing that earlier when he had the opportunity?

He wished he was sleeping in his own bed instead of trying to talk to this fat fool. But it was too late to change his mind now. He'd already awakened Bird.

"Some men chased her."

"What?" Jaspar didn't think he was hearing correctly.

"They chased her and tried to kill her. She hid. I found her."

"Where did you put her?"

Tsosi was far too smart to reveal everything to this little coyote. Bird couldn't be trusted. The only reason Tsosi even tried to deal with him was the promise of Sam Waverly's herd of horses.

He simply looked at Bird, knowing the white man couldn't stand the scrutiny.

"Is she safe?" Bird blustered.

"She's safe. For now."

"What does that mean?" Jaspar tried very hard to sound formidable.

"She's safe." Tsosi wasn't in the least intimidated.

Jaspar snorted and snuffled and made throat-clearing noises.

Tsosi simply waited.

"Well, we've got to do something!"

Tsosi offered no suggestions. He'd done his part. The rest was up to Jaspar. So he waited.

"Now."

When it became apparent to him that the boy had no intention of telling him what to do next, Jaspar blustered a little more and then came up with the solution. "I need to tell Hertha. She'll know what to do."

While Tsosi waited, Jaspar dressed and began to rehearse what he'd say to his sister. Even though they'd agreed to throw in together to search for the gold and diamonds Phelan told him about—Jaspar had now begun to believe the little fable he'd spun for his sister—he still was intimidated by the woman. Habits of a lifetime were hard to break.

Finally, fully dressed in a suit and tie, he picked up his derby hat, blew out the light, and walked to the door.

"Hertha is helping me on this project." He made it sound as if this was another of his important business negotiations. "She'll know what to do about the woman."

Tsosi didn't care about Hertha Bird. All he was interested in was Sam Waverly's herd, and he was beginning to wonder if that wasn't more trouble than it was worth. For the very first time he began to have qualms about Blade's reaction to his part in Jaspar Bird's project. He didn't especially like what he was thinking. Blade had been a good friend to him, and he felt as if he was betraying him.

Approaching Hertha on a sunny afternoon in the park was no treat, and in the dead of a winter night it seemed downright dangerous to Jaspar. In fact, it took him several minutes to calm her at being awakened so late at night. However, greed did triumph.

Tsosi, who hung back by the door out of simple

good sense, was awestruck at what the middle-aged woman looked like without her corset. In her nightgown with her hair stringing down, she was a sight! To his eyes all white women were pale and a little strange looking, but Hertha Bird looked dreadful.

"We need a wagon," Hertha said. "It's too far to walk and I ain't riding a horse. Go hire us one."

"Yes, dear."

"Not you, you idiot. The Injun." She cocked her head at Tsosi. "You, boy. Bring a wagon and team down to my restaurant in a half hour. Can you tell time? I wanta pick us up some food before we go. And I need to leave a note for Myrtle."

Tsosi turned silently and went out to his horse. If he was lucky he'd find Che to rent him the wagon. Otherwise, he'd have to do a lot more explaining than he cared to do. Even though he was well known at the stables, Tsosi wasn't too certain the owner would let him have a team without a good reason, or without cash money.

And he was damned sure he didn't want to explain how he'd abducted the white woman and had hidden her in the lava flow. If he did, he'd be tossed in jail before old lady Bird got her corset on.

Jennie had just made tea and was trying to calm her frantic aunt, who was now almost hysterical about Tsosi not returning home, when the cabin door was wrenched open and three men, all packing guns, burst in.

Marie Manyhorses uttered a feeble shriek and slumped back in her chair in a dead faint.

"What do you want?" Jennie's voice shook more than her hand on the cup.

"Where's the McKenna woman?"

"I don't know," she gulped. She did manage to set the teacup on the table, then wished she hadn't. It was the only weapon she had.

The lawyer—Jennie knew him from town—pointed the shotgun directly at her middle. "Where is she?"

Jennie went cold from fright, but she answered the question bravely. "She didn't come back from her ride."

"The horse is here," the smaller rumpled man said.

"The horse came back without her."

Vanderdam lifted the shotgun a little higher.

The girl gasped audibly but did not panic. "The horse had blood on it."

"Where's Blade?"

"Looking for her. He left at dark. He hasn't come back. He's still searching."

"What about the boy?"

"Tsosi?" Jennie shook her head. "He left this morning."

"Where did he go?"

"Sam Waverly's place."

"What's an Injun doin' there?" Grover asked.

"Takes care of the stock for Jaspar Bird. He never came back. Auntie is scared for him." She glanced at her aunt. "She's been very sick. She's worried he might be dead."

"Good riddance," Sholes mumbled. "One less redskin is fine with me."

Vanderdam turned his head slightly. "You, Sholes, go over and search the house. Look for the woman. And the map."

Sholes scowled belligerently at Vanderdam's back, but he left without comment.

"Grover, go search the barn and the yard."

Grover also left without a word.

Vanderdam smiled at Jennie, his pale eyes narrowing. "And you, my little Navajo flower—I have plans for you."

Fear clawed at her gut, but Jennie didn't flinch when he touched her.

"On second thought," he said, chuckling, "you're not clean enough for my taste. Go over to the big house and fix us something to eat. Hurry up, before I change my mind."

His cruel laughter hung in the midnight air long after she'd fled.

Tsosi was in luck. Che was unhitching a team from the supply wagon when he walked into the stables. No one else was in sight.

"What are you doing here?" Che asked. He and Tsosi had yet to resolve their differences. Che wondered if Tsosi had come to make peace with him.

"I need a wagon."

Che just shook his head and began to care for the animals.

"For Bird."

Che turned quickly and looked at him, his posture stiff, waiting for an explanation.

"Bird and his sister want to take a ride. They sent me for the wagon."

Che went back to what he'd been doing. He wondered why his friend was out in the middle of the night trying to rent a horse for people neither of them trusted. He came up with several explanations, none of which he liked.

Finally he walked over to the water barrel, filled the dipper and offered it to Tsosi. "Tell me," he said.

Reluctantly Tsosi took the dipper and began to explain. Che didn't say anything until he finished.

"I didn't think you were so stupid."

"I want those horses. So I can take my mother home to live. So I can be a man."

"You're going to be one dead Navajo if you aren't careful. Then who will take care of your mother?"

"I've earned those horses. I've cared for them since Waverly died. Bird promised."

"Bird's promises aren't worth piss!"

"What should I do then, just go home?"

"If you do that now, Bird and his sister will tell the sheriff you took the woman. Then you're dead."

Tsosi looked very unhappy. "What do I do?"

Che thought a minute. "You take the wagon down to the restaurant and leave it. Then you and I can ride out and find Mrs. McKenna before the Birds get out there. If we take her home safe, the sheriff won't have to know."

"The Birds won't tell?"

"They'd look like crooks."

Tsosi gave it a lot of thought. "I'll lose the horses."

"That's better than getting hanged by a white mob."

Tsosi didn't like that idea at all. He walked to the stable door and stared out at the dark street. Finally he nodded. "Okay."

"Good," Che said. "Now all you have to worry about is Blade breaking your neck."

* * *

Sheriff Cameron answered the door with surprisingly good grace considering the time. He stood there in his faded red longjohns with his hair sleep-tossed and his eyes bleary, absently scratching his backside.

"What's wrong?" he asked Blade.

"Ruth McKenna is missing. She went out riding this afternoon and didn't come back. After dark her horse came home—with a splash of blood on its flank. I've been searching since then"

Cameron nodded. "Guess we better go take a look. You heat up the coffee while I get my clothes on. Get the venison roast out of the icebox and fix us some sandwiches. It may be a long day."

"I hope not."

"Before we ride out, I want to stop by and see Jones, my deputy. He can round up a search party in the morning and ride out to help."

Hertha Bird packed an enormous basket of food and pastries while her brother wrote a note to Myrtle, the girl who waited tables. Myrtle was instructed to go get Toolie, the assistant cook, and have him fill in for the day. Hertha might plan on being a rich woman by nightfall but she had no intention of losing two bits in sales while she was out fortune hunting.

"Is the wagon out there yet?"

"I think I just heard him drive up out back."

"Good. We need to get moving. Is he driving us?"

"I don't know. Do you want him to?" Jaspar tried to keep the begging note out of his voice. He desperately wanted the Indian kid to handle the team, but he was afraid to tell his sister.

"I don't want to take a long trip with someone who sits like a stump, and grunts like a pig when I talk to him," Hertha said, her mouth pursed up.

"Well, he does have a horse." Jaspar couldn't hide his disappointment.

"Good. He can ride his own horse. He can leave right away and meet us."

"Yes, dear. That's a fine idea. Except for one thing?"

"What?"

"He didn't tell me where we were going?"

"You idiot! Did you ask him?"

"Yes." He sounded very indignant. "I asked him twice."

"And what the hell did he say?"

"Nothing. He didn't answer me. He just looked at me like . . . like an Indian."

"When are you ever going to learn how to treat these people?"

Jaspar didn't answer her. He just looked at her, unblinking, the same way Tsosi had looked at him.

"Well, goddamn it, go ask him again! And get an answer this time!"

"Yes, dear."

"Don't call me dear, either, you worthless twit!" Hertha thrust the basket at him. "Put this in the wagon." She headed back to the storage room.

"Aren't you coming?"

"In a minute." She took out her keys and unlocked a cabinet.

Jaspar got an uneasy feeling.

"Hertha, what are you doing?"

"You know what I'm doing, Jaspar."

"But why?"

"That Indian knows about the McKenna woman. He knows about the treasure. And he knows about us."

"My God, sister . . ."

"Didn't you learn anything? Papa said don't ever leave witnesses. Jaspar, that boy is a witness."

"But I promised him Sam Waverly's horses for helping us."

"I don't care what you promised him, Jaspar. That's between the two of you. I'm just planning on fixing him a little breakfast. Maybe a piece of pie." She took down the mortar and pestle and reached for a small bundle of herbs.

"What about the treasure?"

"We'll get it. The woman will take us to it."

"Are you sure, sister?"

"I'm going to have Donal Phelan's treasure. I deserve it."

Tsosi couldn't believe his luck. He'd gotten rid of Jaspar and Hertha Bird without having to make up an excuse. All he did was promise that silly Jaspar he'd meet them out at the lava flow at sunup.

By the time the sun rose, he and Che would have ridden out to the lava field, and rescued Ruth McKenna. She'd be safe in her bed by the time the Birds got out there. Tsosi felt better right then than he'd felt all night, but when he stepped in through the door of the livery stable, he realized his luck had run out.

Standing beside Che, getting ready to ride out was Sheriff Cameron. With him was Gladius Blade.

"What are you doing here?" Blade asked.

Tsosi wasn't a good liar, so he stuck with the truth. "Came to see Che."

"Ruth McKenna is missing," Blade told him. "We're going out looking for her."

"You boys might as well ride on out with us, seeings how you're still up." The sheriff checked his canteens, and went over to fill one from the water bucket. "Blade packed us some food."

"Sure," Che said. "We'll help. Just let me saddle up."

Tsosi looked furtively at his friend, wondering what he should do. Che seemed to be ignoring him.

"Yeah," he answered finally. "I'll help look.

The Birds were on their way within minutes, the unfamiliar wagon swaying as Jaspar raced toward the edge of town. For once his fear of all things remotely connected with horses did not assert itself. In fact, the sensation of leather reins in his hands and the breeze in his face made him feel incredibly stalwart and adventurous.

Besides, Hertha was more frightened of the speeding wagon than he was. That in itself made him feel six feet tall.

They made excellent time because the horses were fresh, and the main road out of Flagstaff north was dry because it was heavily traveled.

It wasn't till they'd taken the turn off between Sam Waverly's place and the Phillips's ranch on the road Phelan had used to haul in supplies to the dig that they began to have trouble. Part of the road was on a dry wash that flooded whenever it rained and became a bog when it snowed. The wash hadn't completely dried out from the latest snow, and the wagon slowed to a crawl, barely avoiding getting stuck.

When they reached the first incline, Jaspar reached for the whip. Within short order, the pudgy little man realized he loved the whip. It gave him a great feeling of power to snap the thongs over the horses and have them do what he wanted. That, of course, was his downfall.

They went up a hill too fast and the wagon bounced at the top and began to sway precariously. Since Jaspar didn't know what else to do with the dangerously swaying wagon, he laid the lash down hard, and the horses jumped in pain. The back of the wagon fishtailed off the side of the rough road, bumping the outer wheel against a rock, and careened sideways down the steep incline.

Jaspar was pitched sideways from the wagon like a bouncing ball.

Hertha, screaming as loud as her mighty voice could bellow, was hurled over the seat into the back of the wagon with a tremendous plop and an ominous renting of corset stays.

The frenzied horses lurched forward, running from fear of the wagon. When the back wheel hit some big rocks with a violent crack, the hub smashed, the axle broke, and the wagon tipped sideways.

The tired horses jerked and strained, rolling the wagon on its side. Finally the animals stopped. It was mere luck they hadn't been badly injured, and they shuddered and trembled, breathing heavily. But they stood still and waited for a person to free them from the tangled harnesses.

The large, elaborately packed lunch basket bumped out of the wagon and split, pouring its contents out on the ground.

Ruth must have dozed, although she had no recollection of doing so. In fact, she'd made every effort to stay awake. But once she raised her head from the blanket that protected her from the night's iciness, she noticed the moon had come up and was shining benignly over the hellish, turbulent, picturesque scenery. She no longer feared this fiendish spawn of nature—she knew she'd escape when morning came—but nevertheless she held it in deep respect.

Sometime later she detected pale tentacles of light in the eastern sky. Moment by moment the heavens changed, from charcoal to slate to smoke. From indigo to plum to mauve. From carnation to peach blossom. Like a miracle, daylight unfolded.

She held her breath at the spectacle. Had anything ever been so beautiful?

"Oh, Blade," she murmured without being aware she even spoke. "It's so wonderful to be alive!" She waited patiently until the dawning was complete before she shrugged off the wool blanket and stood up to study her prison of stone for the quickest way to escape.

There was no quick escape. It took more than an hour. Her skirts were a hindrance, as was the blanket she refused to leave behind. She picked her way carefully around snags, over gaps, down veering slopes and up out of dips, through buckles, twists, and burrows.

Once she fell, catching a small but deeply rooted

bush and so avoided plunging into a stony gorge. She rested, shaky and scared.

And then she saw it.

Hidden from anyone who wasn't planted in the exact spot where she sat . . . a cave.

Not merely a cave, an enormous bubble, actually, caused when the molten lava had begun to cool. From where she sat, with the rising sun shining directly into the opening, she saw the sparkling crystal prisms glistening back at her. Her whole body tingled. It was Donal's cave of diamonds!

She had no doubt. This was the discovery he'd raved about shortly before his death.

Slowly, carefully, heart thudding with every move, Ruth inched her way forward.

The cave's entrance yawned before her about three feet from top to bottom. And inside were ice crystals, exquisitely brilliant in the golden light of sunrise. She peeked in.

And felt a wave of disappointment.

"I can't believe I was so foolish," she said angrily. Yet somewhere in the recesses of her private thoughts and dreams, she, too, had hoped her brother had found a treasure. Spanish gold, or something equally magnificent, some counterpart to the splendors of Egypt.

Donal Phelan's treasure did indeed rest in the caves. But just as his bed of diamonds was a mere crystal formation of ice, his archaeological trove was a half-dozen clay pots filled not with plunder but . . . beans. Dried speckled beans.

"Oh Donal." She laughed, crying at the same time. "Only you would brag about beans."

And yet she knew in her heart he considered the

beans a treasure. Perhaps even the red pots were a treasure. They were the link!

The beans offered proof of his fledgling theory about the link between the pit house and the pueblo. The same prehistoric tribe—or their children—who had lived at the pit house in the meadow, had eventually migrated as far as the big pueblo.

The Hopi legend could have been based on fact. And whether anybody else believed him, Donal had proven the idea to himself. She saw the prayer sticks in the cave, ancient and partially deteriorated.

"This must be an offering," she decided, "from the people who survived to the Fire God."

After sticking a handful of the age-old legumes in her coat pocket to prove that she'd found them, she again began to pick her way across the river of rock.

She stopped only once, to mark in her mind the way back to the cave. She planned to share it with Blade.

When at last she climbed up the final hill and stepped from lichen-covered lava to plain brown dirt, her blue eyes glistened with tears. "Now I can go home," she said.

"Not quite yet, girlie." Hertha Bird stepped out from an enormous broken boulder at the top of the hill. Her jacket was split out the side, her face was scratched, and her hat was askew. She looked like she'd been stomped by a buffalo.

In her hand was an old but quite deadly-looking pistol. "You're gonna find us the treasure."

16

They didn't talk much as they rode. Their only objective was to put as many miles between them and Flagstaff as they possibly could before daybreak. Each man seemed caught up in his own private thoughts.

All of Blade's reflections were about Ruth. He was no longer tired. Indeed he'd felt a new spurt of energy the moment he received help from the others. They all knew the area even better than he did, and in the light of day they'd be a first-rate search party. When daybreak came, he was certain he'd find her.

Sheriff Rand Cameron spent quite a bit of his time pondering Ruth McKenna's disappearance. Perhaps it had nothing whatsoever to do with her brother's untimely—and suspicious, to Cameron's way of thinking—death, but the sheriff wasn't taking any bets on it.

Cameron thought he'd check the dig first. That's where his deputy and the rest of the men from town would meet them later in the morning. If they hadn't found her by then, they could spread out and search the countryside.

Tsosi rode the black harder than usual. He was more worried than he'd ever been in his life. Was he going to be accused of kidnapping? Now that he'd given it some more thought, he wondered if that wasn't exactly what he'd done. At least, according to the white man's laws.

A tremendous shudder ripped through his young body when he thought of the hanging tree on Cherry Street. He wondered if he'd be decorating that horrible place before nightfall.

He also wondered what would happen when the sheriff caught up with Jaspar and Hertha Bird. How would they explain being so far out from town? Especially when the whole town laughed about the two of them being so afraid of horses? Tsosi knew that Hertha, at least, and maybe Jaspar, too, would toss him to the dogs to save their own hides. Was that tall tree his fate? He longed to spur the black and run.

Yet he didn't dare leave the group of riders. To do so would immediately put the blame on him. He just hoped Mrs. McKenna didn't awaken from her bump on the head and decide to walk through the lava in the dark. Or freeze to death.

Surely she had found the blanket he left. If she woke up, that is. He looked covertly at Che, but the predawn sky was still quite dark and he knew Che hadn't noticed his glance.

The sky on the eastern horizon lightened perceptively although stars still hung beyond the mountains to the west. There were a few billowy clouds in the serene canopy of heaven, puffy and white against the dove gray background. The world was on the verge of awakening, and few people in town had more on their minds than a hearty breakfast and the day's work ahead. But the riders knew better. Each, in his own way, prayed to sidestep catastrophe and come through unscathed. With relief and also anxiety, they watched the sky lighten.

"Cameron! Look over there! To the left!"

Over by a clump of brush about halfway up the hill was a peculiar mound that did not resemble a rock or an animal, but a human body. Blade's stomach tightened.

At first he thought it must be Ruth. Who else could it be? But as he rode closer, he decided the still figure must certainly be that of a man. And even though the morning light was gray and still somewhat dim, he was certain the body on the ground was dressed in black, not the brown riding outfit and winter coat Ruth had worn when she left the house.

They all slowed their horses and approached with a certain amount of caution. After all, this could be a trick. Highwaymen had been known to pose as accident victims. Cameron checked his pistol as he rode. Blade touched the stock of his rifle. Minutes passed.

"God!"

It was light enough to see well now, even though the sun had not peeked above the mesas to the east of them. Orlie Taswell lay sprawled on the ground in a crumpled spread eagle. His eyes were open in an expression of utter astonishment. One side of his cheek was peppered with buckshot scratches and there was a bloody tear in the shoulder of his jacket. A black-handled stiletto—slim and wicked as hell— thrust up from the vein in his throat, and pierced the ground beneath him. The earth was dark with blood.

"Looks like he barely had time to gurgle," Cameron observed. "Wonder who did this."

"That lawyer," Tsosi answered. "Vanderdam."

Cameron frowned and cocked his head. "Is there something you didn't tell me, son?"

"I was coming from feeding Sam Waverly's horses." Tsosi hesitated, the image of the hanging tree in his mind, and then went on. "For Jaspar Bird. I saw Vanderdam shoot at him." He pointed to Taswell's body.

"Anything else?" Cameron inquired quietly.

Tsosi nodded. He knew he better tell everything now. Maybe he could still escape jail—or worse—if he told Sheriff Cameron before they ran into the Birds.

"He wasn't dead then. The lawyer's horse moved."

"Tell him," Che said.

Cameron's head jerked around to Che, then quickly returned.

"He had the woman."

"What?" Blade bellowed the word. "Why the hell didn't you tell me before?"

"She got away. She fell off her horse when the shotgun fired, and she ran." He pointed in a direction.

Blade moved his horse. He intended to go after Ruth before another minute passed.

"They chased after her."

Blade reined in the roan. "They? Who the hell are 'they'?"

"A couple of drifters named Grover and Sholes," Cameron answered. "They been hanging out with Vanderdam at the San Juan a lot lately. I had a suspicion they was up to somethin', but I didn't know what. Figured they'd show their hand sooner or later."

"If you were suspicious, for crissakes, why didn't you arrest them?" Blade demanded.

"'Cause they hadn't done nothin' yet."

"They sure as hell have now."

"Yeah, and we need to keep a sharp eye out for 'em from here on in. But our first problem is finding Mrs. McKenna. Where did you say she went, Tsosi?"

He pointed in the direction Ruth had fled the evening before. "She ran up there . . . but she isn't there now."

Blade made a growling sound. Even Che looked faintly alarmed.

"I know your people put a lot of importance on storytelling," the sheriff said patiently. "But fer the love a' God get to the point."

"She's in the lava flow," Che said. He wasn't certain how much more Blade could take before he exploded. Better to get the talking out of the way and get to riding again.

"How the hell did she get there?" Cameron queried angrily.

"I took her," Tsosi answered.

"Are you in on this, too?" Blade demanded of Che.

"No," Tsosi explained. "He didn't know till I got to town. I hid her from those men. The lawyer and the others. I thought they might kill her if they found her."

"We were going to ride out and get her when you came in the stable," Che said.

"Well, let's go," Cameron grumbled. He had a lot more to say to Tsosi, but right now it would be easier to handle Blade if they rode on. Pronto.

Fury raged through Blade. He felt like jerking Tsosi off his horse and stomping him into the dirt. He wanted to grab him by the throat and shake him till his eyeballs bulged and his teeth clattered. He wanted to do more, but he was too damned mad to think of what.

God Almighty, he could hardly stand the thought of her alone all night in those hellish rocks. He prayed that she was safe, that she'd stayed where the boy had left her and not wandered around in the dark.

Had she been warm enough?

He wracked his fear-dazed mind trying to recall exactly how cold it had become during the night that had just passed. He ran a weary hand over his face in frustration. How was he going to live until he found her?

A few minutes later they reached the crest of a hill and spotted the wreckage of a wagon that had tumbled down the slope on its side. They raced down to the wreck, certain they'd find someone injured in the debris. But no one was there. However, a large amount of food and a violently smashed basket lay strewn around some rocks.

"Leave it," Cameron said. "Let's find where the horses went. Maybe those folks are on the horses."

Blade noticed the look Tsosi shot at Che. He opened his mouth to question them, but at that moment shots rang out, thudding into the wagon bed in front of them, splintering the wood to slivers. Che slid off his mount, and the other men followed suit immediately, hunkering down behind the protection of the upturned wagon. There they waited.

"Who are those people?" Che asked.

Three men were riding toward them hell-bender style, wild, crazy bastards from the looks of them. Guns upraised, coats flying, they galloped down toward the wagon. The men behind the broken freight truck simply watched. A shotgun blast split the morning air above their heads with a thundering blow. Somewhere a bird squawked angrily.

"Son of a bitch!" Cameron snarled. "Does anybody know who are they?"

"Vanderdam," Blade said calmly and raised his rifle. He hoped Donal Phelan was roasting his nuts off in Hades right now because of his stupid treasure story. One foolish lie had caused inconceivable harm.

"Let me do it," Cameron said. "Then it'll be official." He raised his Colt and rested it on the wagon.

The men galloped closer, running as if they expected to fly over the top of the uptilted wagon. Cameron waited. They all waited, weapons ready. Vanderdam raised the shotgun again. Cameron took aim and squeezed the trigger, and his companions grabbed their ears as the percussion from the shot blasted out.

A ringing filled Blade's head, and he could smell the acrid odor of gunpowder choking the air.

Vanderdam jerked backward slightly. A small red hole appeared right above the bridge of his nose. He continued to rush forward. Cameron raised the Colt again.

Vanderdam suddenly lurched sideways, flopping off the horse with a sickening thud. As he fell the men caught sight of a red skirt, a frothy petticoat, and a small brown foot.

"Jennie!" Che screamed and dashed out toward her, mindless of the danger from the other men or Vanderdam's oncoming horse. But Grover and Sholes were no danger. Their exploits had ended like a burst balloon.

Vanderdam was still midair when Sholes threw his hands in the air. "I surrender, Sheriff," he yelled. "Don't kill me. I got a family."

"Shut up, you asshole," Grover snapped, but he, too, raised his arms.

"Climb down from those horses, pronto, and don't make any sudden moves," Cameron told the men. "I'm cranky this morning, and I'd rather leave you here for the varmints to pick at than tote you back to town."

The crooks climbed down slowly, carefully. Evidently they were convinced that Cameron would gun them down if he was provoked. And since their boss lay on the ground with a hole in his head, they had a right to believe the sheriff was as mean as he was pretending to be.

Che held Jennie in his arms, speaking to her softly, trying to quiet her fears. The breath had been knocked from her when she fell, and she'd bitten her lip. Che used his shirttail to staunch the flow of blood, all the while assuring her that she was all right.

Grover and Sholes nearly went to fisticuffs trying to outconfess one another. Grover admitted knifing some cowboy in Abilene, and Sholes insisted on telling everyone that he'd deserted his wife and five children. They bragged proudly that they were the ones who Blade caught breaking into the house. Sholes relayed in detail what they ate.

However, it was Vanderdam, they both insisted, who put the pig sticker in Orlie Taswell's jugular.

"Slicker than shit," Sholes said. "Sombitch never even saw it comin'."

"Because of the treasure," Grover told them. "He thought Orlie was after his treasure."

"But he weren't," Sholes explained. "He didn't know nothin' about the gold. He was after the woman. Tryin' to spook her an' all. 'Cause of some kinda papers she stole from him."

"Taswell had been blackmailing Ruth's husband for several years," Blade informed the sheriff. "When McKenna died, Taswell thought he'd milk Ruth for some cash. He picked the wrong woman."

"She took a weapon after him," Sholes offered righteously.

Blade snorted. "She poked him in his chicken chest with a walking cane. And ran him off the porch."

Cameron laughed loudly.

"I think Taswell might have been the one who attacked her in the woods, though. The afternoon it started snowing. Unless it was you bozos."

"She was attacked?" Cameron wanted to know. "Why don't folks tell me these things?"

Sholes and Grover denied any knowledge of an attack on Ruth. They even managed to sound sincere.

"I believe them," Blade said. "I can't imagine why these two would want to harm her. She doesn't have any money."

"They chased her yesterday," Tsosi mentioned. "I watched from a hill."

"She has the map!"

"What map?" Cameron ask Grover. He snapped a handcuff on him, pulled it through a wagon wheel, and secured the other end to Sholes. Both crooks protested furiously at such cruel treatment, but the sheriff seemed unmoved.

"The treasure map," Sholes said, as if the entire world knew of its existence."

"There is no map," Blade and Cameron replied together.

"Che, is Jennie fit to ride?"

"Yes."

"Let's go then. We've got a lady to rescue."

More than ten minutes passed before anyone spoke. They rode with a single purpose, to find Ruth.

"Who was in the wagon?" Jennie asked.

"The Birds," Tsosi answered.

"Both of them?" She sounded incredulous.

"Yes."

Cameron wheeled his horse around and stopped.

"Is there more you need to tell me, son?"

Tsosi looked taciturn. Seconds passed before he answered. Tension rose. Even the horses felt it.

"They know where she is."

Tsosi's words were quietly spoken, but they couldn't have had more impact if he'd shouted them.

"Jezuzzz!" Cameron snapped. "Why didn't you tell us before?"

"Those men started shooting at us."

"Let's get the hell up to those rocks."

Blade knew what Cameron was thinking. The Birds were notoriously, laughingly, frightened of horses. Yet not only had they hired a wagon to take them cross country in the dead of night, they'd also climbed upon the horses after they'd rolled the wagon. They were in a desperate hurry to get someplace. And that place was where Ruth was hidden.

They rode steadily, fiercely, eating up the miles beneath the horses' strong hoofs. After a while, they rode past the dunes and cinder cone and eventually could see the lava flow.

Blade relaxed a bit at the sight, but he soon tensed up again as he tried without success to find Ruth somewhere within the river of molten rock.

"She's not here," Tsosi said as they moved close to the spot where he'd carried her in the previous night.

"What?!!" Blade's grip on his emotions was unraveling by the minute.

The boy pointed to the torn wool blanket that barely showed over the side of a weathered piece of basalt. Whether it had been accidentally dropped near the side of the lava flow or purposely draped over the rock, nobody knew.

"I left that blanket with her," he explained. "Way over there."

"So she got out." Blade's growl was one of relief and terror.

"The horses were here," Che said, examining some nearby hoofprints. "The ones from the stable."

"So they have her." Blade's voice sounded bleak.

"This horse manure is fresh," Cameron said. "They didn't leave too long ago. Do you think they went to the dig?"

"That's my guess."

"They're city folks, pure and simple. It'd take something powerful important to get them outta town."

"Treasure," Tsosi told them. "They thought the woman knew how to find the treasure."

"Jaspar told us to scare her away," Jennie put in. "Moses Bigboy came over and talked about ghosts. Marie found the snake."

"The snake!" Blade cried. "I forgot about the damned snake!"

"Let's go find Miz McKenna," Cameron rumbled.

"Then I wanta get all this down on paper. I hear-tell folks make good money writing novels. Think I might try my hand at it."

Heading due north they left the lava flow, and began to slowly circle a bit to the east. The land changed abruptly. The cinders which had littered everything began to dwindle and show the sienna red sandstone lying beneath.

The tall pines thinned out only to be replaced by junipers. At first the junipers were full and luxuriant but very soon the effects of wind and drought showed on the bent, withered, and scrubby bushes.

In the violet distance, sandstone mesas jutted upward like silent sentinels, watchtowers of the ancient land. A few remnant clouds breezed lazily across the sky.

"This is all Phelan's fault," Cameron told them. "If he hadn't teased poor old dumb Jaspar about finding diamonds and gold . . ."

"He didn't mention gold," Blade maintained. "Just a treasure set on a bed of diamonds."

"Shiiiit . . ."

"Doesn't make much difference now." Blade wondered as he spoke if it would make a difference for Ruth. "Do you think they killed him?"

"My gut says yes," Cameron answered. "It never felt right that Phelan just keeled over. Doc told me there are ways to cause a man to have a heart attack." He was silent a minute. "Can't imagine Jaspar knowing 'em, though."

"Men aren't always what they seem to be," Blade said. "Women either."

"That should be my next campaign slogan," Cameron

grumbled. "Okay. Let's prepare for the worst. Let's go in thinking they're killers. Like they're the same brand a' scum we got tied up to that wagon back there. Let's catch 'em first and talk after."

No one spoke.

"If we ain't prepared, we might be dead before the day is done. And Mrs. McKenna, too." He was silent a minute, then gave a little chuckle. "And if it's all a mistake and those two ain't guilty as sin, I'll apologize real pretty for hunting 'em down like varmints and hauling 'em back to jail."

They walked the last half mile on foot to avoid making noise.

"The horses came this way," Che said. "I recognize this hoofprint."

They left their own mounts tied to some bushes some distance from the overlook, and moved stealthily to a position shielded by a gnarled juniper, some scrub brush, and a few winter-grayed weeds. It wasn't much of a shelter, but it was enough.

They saw the two stable horses, heads hanging from fatigue, standing unattended on the flat below.

The pueblo had been situated on a long finger of sandstone that jutted out into an enormous bowl-shaped basin that was sheltered on two sides by surrounding flat-topped mesas. The juniper-strewn ridge stood high above and descended down to the pueblo site from the west.

The pueblo was an impressive sight to anyone who looked at it. But on this particular morning, it presented Cameron and his rescue party with a monumental problem.

The prehistoric people who had originally populated

the once-proud dwellings had built their structures far enough away from the ridge to eliminate the possibility of a sneak attack from any would-be enemy.

Unfortunately, at that moment, the person who desired to creep up on the unsuspecting folks down at the ruins was Sheriff Cameron.

He raised his field glasses and studied the area, then silently handed them to Blade.

"Hell." He dropped the glasses. "Where are they?" He handed the glasses back to Cameron. "Any ideas?"

"Maybe inside one of the rooms. But which one? You wanta see?" Cameron asked Che.

The young Indian took the glasses. After a moment he lowered them but continued to stare at the ruin.

Tsosi reached for the field glasses and looked, then passed them back to the sheriff. Nobody noticed Jennie's scowl.

"I see Hertha," Che said suddenly. "Look down there." He pointed to one of the smaller chambers on the southeastern side of the ruin.

"That's the last room Phelan excavated," Blade said. "Where is Ruth?"

"Apparently she's alive," Cameron said. "It appears to me that Hertha is sitting on something, a camp stool maybe, just outside a doorway. So it's a damned good bet Mrs. McKenna is inside. Diggin' for buried treasure, I'd guess." He handed the glasses back to Blade. "What do you think?"

After a moment, Blade nodded. "It looks like she may have a gun. How are we going to keep her from using it?"

"Let me think about that a minute. Let's move back a little ways so they don't spot us. I didn't see Jaspar, but he's bound to be pokin' around someplace. Jennie, why don't you pass out the sandwiches while I'm thinking?

Ruth tried her best.

On the uncomfortable ride out to the dig, she had explained to Hertha Bird and her posturing brother about the reality of Donal's treasure. About the pots of beans in the ice-filled lava cave. She even offered to show the bean-filled red pots to them. She might as well have talked to a corpse, for all the good it did her.

The big woman had slapped her silly.

The blow caught Ruth across the same cheekbone that had recently healed from the bruise she'd received in the woods the afternoon she was attacked. Hertha's whack hurt like the devil, and started a fire of hostility burning in Ruth.

"Phelan had a treasure!" Hertha screamed.

The words rang in Ruth ears. And Jaspar parroted them foolishly, "Phelan had a treasure."

For the rest of the ride, they'd harangued her about the existence of the treasure, which grew in size and splendor with every mile. As they continued their way down the incline to the ruin, she tried again to convince them about the truth of the treasure. Ruth was an honest woman, and she believed reason would eventually win out over craziness.

"It's here!" Hertha insisted. "The gold and diamonds are right here where he was digging."

Ruth shook her head in denial, trying to make the pair see the sense of her argument.

"You lying bitch!" Hertha shrieked, and shoved

Ruth off the horse they shared to the ground. "You want the treasure for yourself!"

"No."

"You can't have it," the older woman continued, "It's mine. He owed it to me."

"Who owed you?" Jaspar asked out of the blue. Until that moment he'd said nothing along the trail to contradict his sister. He was still smarting from the thrashing she'd given him for upsetting the wagon.

"Phelan, you asshole. Who else?"

"He owed you?" Ruth asked, grasping the question in Jaspar's startled query. "He owed you what?"

"The treasure." Hertha flicked her skirts coyly. "For what he did to me."

You've got to be joking, Ruth thought, but wisely kept it to herself. She wanted to keep the woman talking, needed to understand the workings of her peculiar mind. Yet she must be extremely careful. She now believed Hertha Bird was a very dangerous woman.

Jaspar was an oaf, a lout, and essentially his sister's flunky. Hertha did all the ordering, all the thinking, and Jaspar simply followed her.

Ruth was certain she couldn't count on him for any assistance, but she did think she might capitalize on his deep-seated resentment of Hertha.

"What did my brother do to you?" Ruth asked cautiously.

"He insulted me," Hertha said primly.

"He was often a rude man," Ruth agreed.

"Get one of those shovels." Hertha changed the subject abruptly.

Ruth did as she was told and soon was trying to scoop the earth from a room that showed recent excavation.

"Your brother impugned my honor," Hertha volunteered.

"When?" Jaspar asked incredulously.

"Go find another shovel, you idiot. Make yourself useful."

He pouted, but did as he was told. He was back quickly, squeezing himself into the same tiny room as Ruth because he didn't want to miss any of Hertha's story. Not that he believed her, of course.

"He scorned me," Hertha said, holding one plump hand in front of her, imagining it covered with diamonds. Ruth shoveled dirt and waited. "Donal Phelan was courting me, you know."

"He was not!" Jaspar insisted.

"Go dig somewhere else!"

"No! I wanta hear this. When was Phelan courting you?"

She took a deep patient breath. "The past few months. Words weren't spoken, a'course, but he was making the trip into town every week for his order, instead of having Che bring it."

To save money, Ruth thought.

"To see me," Hertha said.

Jaspar glanced at Ruth and rolled his eyes. She winked back. Hertha didn't notice the exchange.

"And I was giving him extra things in the order, without charging him, and bigger servings than other folks, and he stayed around to talk. He even came into the kitchen. So I invited him to my house . . ."

Ruth was beginning to feel uncomfortable. Surely Donal hadn't made a sexual overture to the woman! She was crude, homely, and didn't even smell clean. His taste ran more to the type of overpainted harlot

Ruth had recently encountered at the hotel.

"What did he do?" Jaspar asked.

"He laughed at me."

"Is that all?"

Hertha glared at her dimwitted sibling. "He told me I made a mistake. He had no intentions of marrying me, that he'd never, ever, be hard up enough to crawl in bed with a stupid cow like me."

"What did you do to him?" Jaspar asked, his voice peculiarly hoarse.

"You know what I did. I had to. He insulted me. He would have told everybody how I answered the door in my nightgown. People would have talked. Laughed. Papa said, no witnesses."

"You didn't have to kill him!"

"What are you talking about?" Ruth asked. She felt as if she were trapped in a cage with two rabid animals.

"Papa said . . ."

"Papa was an assassin!"

"Papa was a bodyguard!"

"Donal died of a heart attack," Ruth said, more to herself than these strange people who were holding her prisoner.

"Of course he did," Jaspar said. "She made him have it. She knows the kind of herbs."

Hertha smiled almost sweetly. "Papa said there were a dozen ways to kill a man and make it look natural."

Ruth plunged the shovel deep into the dirt, trying to control her horror. Was it possible that this woman, this creature who served food to people every day, had poisoned Donal?

And would likely kill her, too, as soon as it became

obvious there was no gold, no diamonds, not even a chunk of turquoise jewelry?

"I've got it!" Cameron shouted. He looked over to where Che and Tsosi shared some lunch with Jennie. "I want you two to be Indians."

Tsosi glanced quickly at Che, then back at the sheriff.

Che almost managed to mask his thoughts. Only a flicker crossed his black eyes. He nodded. "I can do that."

Blade didn't try to hide his confusion. "Would you mind explaining?"

"Well, I been wondering how to sneak up on 'em, but we can't. It ain't possible to hit that place with a sneak attack. We gotta charge 'em!"

"What about Ruth?" Blade's voice was as cold as the blood running through his veins.

"I figure she's in that room in front of Hertha."

"And Hertha has the gun."

"Right."

"And she'll cut Ruth down the minute she sees one of us."

"Not if she sees Indians."

"Goddamn . . . you may be right."

"She knows them," Jennie said. She was quite weary of doing little more than passing out sandwiches. Ruth was her friend, and she intended to be in on the rescue.

"Right," Cameron agreed. "She knows 'em up close, like at the back door of the bakery. But out in open territory, outside of town where she ain't familiar, she just might well think they're renegades."

"Are you sure?" Che asked.

"No I ain't, if you want the honest truth, but I think it's the best chance we got. The best chance we got of gettin' Ruth McKenna out alive."

Che took a deep breath and walked back to the spot where he could overlook the ruins. The path down wasn't too steep but it was littered with loose shale and a few cinders. The horses could lose their footing.

Blade came up behind him. "She has a gun. I think she'll shoot. She'll try to kill you if she can."

"Yes."

"You don't have to do it. You have Jennie to think about. I'll go in your place."

Che turned and looked directly at him. "Never saw a redheaded Navajo."

Blade laughed and shook his head. "I mean it."

"I know." Che walked back to where the sheriff waited. "I'll do it."

"So will I," Jennie said.

"No!"

Cameron ignored the girl's suggestion and Che's outburst. "You and Tsosi let your hair down and take off your shirts."

"It's winter," Tsosi protested.

Cameron looked at him with steely eyes. "Mrs. McKenna would be home in her warm parlor right now, if it hadn't been for you."

Tsosi unfastened the top button of his shirt.

Within moments they were stripped down to their pants, with their hair blowing wild in the wind. Mounted, with rifles in hand, they did look like renegade Indians.

Jennie jumped on her horse, determined to help.

"Stay at the top of the hill," Che ordered.

"Only because I want to," she answered.

And they were off, screaming and whooping. At the edge of the ridge, Jennie fired her rifle in the air.

Blade and Cameron rode hell-bent down through the brush toward the back side of the ruin, hoping Hertha and her eastern-bred brother would be too busy fighting Indians to notice their approach.

At the first blood-chilling war whoop, Hertha Bird tumbled off her rickety camp stool. Swinging her head around, she saw several bloodthirsty redskins thundering over the ridge toward her. Her one horrified glance took in the chief firing at her from the top of the hill.

She screamed, bolted off the ground, and dove into the room where Ruth and Jaspar watched in stupefied wonder.

"Indians!" she shouted.

The inhuman cries of the warriors got closer.

"Shoot them!" Jaspar wailed.

Huddled behind the other two, Ruth cowered in fear. For the past hour she'd been expecting Hertha to murder her, but she hadn't counted on being scalped by Indians.

"I don't deserve this, Donal Phelan!" she whispered, sensing her brother's invisible presence amid the ancient ruins. "And if your stupid exaggerations get me killed, you better pray I never find you!"

Hertha's gun blasted like a bolt of thunder.

"Did you get him?" Jasper asked.

"No—you hit my arm!"

Outside the tiny room, rifle fire sounded in a continuous tumultuous roar. Recklessly, one of the warriors raced along the path close to the door of the pueblo, shrieking madly.

"Fire again! Before he gets away!" said Jasper.

"I'm out of bullets!"

"They'll murder us! Scalp us!"

With meteoric swiftness, a man jumped from the top of the wall down into the room, landing lightly, weapon in hand.

Blade!

"Oh, God," Ruth moaned and leaned against the plastered wall.

Cameron burst in from of the open door, his Colt drawn menacingly. "Drop the gun! Now!"

Hertha let the empty pistol fall to the dirt floor.

"Now slowly, you two walk out, down the path."

Hertha, with her pasty-faced brother behind her, marched down the incline to the field below.

Blade didn't stop kissing Ruth for quite some time.

When he did, after he finished telling her how sorry he was, how scared he'd been, how much he loved her, they walked arm in arm down to where everyone else waited.

Jennie had collected the shirts Che and Tsosi had left up on the ridge. They had dismounted and were dressing, when Blade and Ruth joined them.

Hertha surprised them all by bursting into tears. "I loved him," she wept.

"Who?" Blade asked.

"Donal," Ruth told him. "She said she poisoned him."

"I didn't know a thing about it," Jaspar said innocently.

For once Hertha didn't bother to insult him. Tears ran down her dirty, weathered cheeks. "He owed me his treasure."

She pushed herself up astonishingly fast for a large woman and darted toward where the horses stood. Had she been less timid with horses, she would have gotten away. But the horse shied as she grabbed for the reins, and Hertha jumped away from it.

Ruth was hot on her tail. All the fear, all the horror of the past twenty-four hours congealed into one mass of fury. She'd never been so angry or so determined in her life.

"Stop! Let Cameron do it!"

Ignoring Blade's shout, Ruth threw herself bodily at the bigger woman.

The impact knocked Hertha to the ground with a mighty thump. Ruth fell with her, down and over. She grabbed hold of the front of Hertha's jacket and hung on.

Hertha rolled over and back, trying to dislodge the little mouse of a woman who was thwarting her escape. She batted Ruth with her paw up alongside the temple.

Ruth saw a second of blackness and then red and green stars, but she only tightened her grip. When she heard the sound of fabric tearing, of Hertha's jacket giving way, she grabbed for a chunk of stone. Jaspar made one feeble attempt to aid his sister. He took two steps toward Ruth as she rolled Hertha in the dirt. Blade picked up a shovel, and whacked Jaspar directly across the belly, then turned his attention back to Ruth. Jaspar folded up like an accordion, pitched to his knees and retched up his breakfast. Ruth's slender fingers curled around the stone. Hertha landed two hard blows to her shoulder but she hung onto the rock.

She raised it slowly and brought it down hard against the bigger woman's temple. A small mew escaped Hertha's lips. Then she fell backward with a clunk. She lay on the ground like a fallen log.

It was over.

Ruth was in Blade's arms, assuring him she was none the worse for wear in spite of her harrowing ordeal.

He was a hard man to convince. He'd been so damned scared for so long he needed to feel guilty about something. She let him hover and fuss a little while, but finally she reached her arms around his neck and pulled him close.

"You talk too much," she said, and then she showed him how she really wanted to be comforted.

Sometime later Cameron had finished chatting with Jaspar, who had been only too willing to tell every sordid detail of his family history he could recall.

"I thought he was our crook," the sheriff said to Blade. "Don't look like he's guilty of much except being a fool. 'Course that's for the judge to decide, not me." It was noon before they were ready to leave the excavation site.

"I don't know what the hell happened to my deputy and the other men from Flagstaff. Maybe they got lost," Cameron grumbled. "I'm deputizing you two." He indicated Che and Tsosi.

The young men nodded.

"Blade will be taking Mrs. McKenna back to the ranch for a good rest," Cameron continued, " but I'm gonna need help getting all these criminals back into town. I have an idea that the first chance that old bat gets, she's going to try to get away."

Hertha was trussed up like a holiday turkey with several strong pieces of harness from the stable horses. She was squirming and swearing a blue streak. Except for an occasional glance, nobody seemed to be paying much attention to her.

"I'll have my hands full with her. You two deputies are in charge of Jaspar and those fellas we have waiting back there attached to the wagon wheel. I'll see that you get paid for your help, including Jennie, and I'll buy you a meal in town. Too bad one of the best eating places is gonna be closed down."

Blade and Ruth followed them back down the trail. They paused by the lava flow.

"If you treat me real nice tonight," Ruth teased, "I'll bring you back here tomorrow and show you a treasure."

"You found it?"

"I found it. In a cave. On a bed of ice crystals."

"Are you going to tell me what it is?"

"No. I want you to be surprised."

His brown eyes darkened. "I can wait. I already have my treasure. You." He leaned over and kissed her.

Epilogue

Pine-scented water lapped at the sides of the bathtub. Blade lounged comfortably in the warm water, feeling utterly content. "I'm going to miss this," he said.

"There are other bathtubs."

"Big enough for two?"

Ruth merely smiled, completely engrossed with sponging his wide chest.

"I can't believe Jaspar Bird bought this place. He still thinks there's a treasure out here some place," Blade continued.

"I can't believe he convinced the judge he was innocent of all crimes, and got off with little more than a stern lecture."

"He snitched on his sister. It's hard to believe she poisoned more than one person. Cameron said he got a wire from the Pittsburgh police and it was all true," Blade said.

"If that search party hadn't reached Grover and Sholes when they did and got them back to the doc . . ."

"Damned fools, eating all that food spilled on the ground . . ."

"That pie was meant for Tsosi, you know," Ruth reminded him.

"Hertha was damned careless with her noxious pastries. Doc thinks that was what made Marie so sick."

"I miss her. I know she's happier back at her home, but she was nice to me."

"Except for the snake," Blade said.

"Well, yes. There was the snake."

"Tsosi will take his herd on out this weekend."

"I'm so glad Sheriff Cameron offered Che the deputy position permanently. Now he and Jennie can get married."

"Speaking of marriages . . ." He picked up her palm and kissed it. "Have I told you recently what a beautiful bride you are, Mrs. Blade?"

"It's been almost ten minutes."

"You are beautiful, Ruth. I love you."

"And I love you, Blade. The wedding and the reception were everything I ever dreamed of. I still can't believe all the flowers arriving by train. And Myra Bemish's wonderful cake."

After a lengthy silence, she asked a bit breathlessly, "Do you think your father will like me?"

He chuckled. "If he saw you right now, he would."

She swatted at him. He caught her hand and pulled her close, then kissed her.

"He'll love you. The whole family will."

"Do you think they'll understand about us leaving after a short visit, to take the manuscript, and the

papers Donal left with his lawyer, back to the Peabody
Institute to clear his name?"

"The Blades are an understanding lot. And they stick
together. Next to loving, that's what we do best."

AUTHOR'S NOTE

We have taken the license of moving the archaeological excavation several miles closer to the house, simply because of the time it would take to reach the site on foot or by horse.

It was actually Dr. Jesse W. Fewkes who carefully mapped and photographed the Wupatki Basin in 1896. His guide, Ben Doney, spent many years digging for artifacts and searching unsuccessfully for the Losr Padre Mine.

It wasn't until 1930 that Lionel F. Brady, a geologist from the Museum of Northern Arizona, found potshards on the surface of the ground near Sunset Crater. Excavation revealed a buried pit house that had been occupied when the crater erupted, proving that Sunset Crater was much younger than anyone suspected.

Then, by using tree-ring dating, experts were able to establish not only the correct age of Sunset Crater but also that the timbers used to build the pit houses were of the same age as the timbers used to build Wupatki. There is even conjecture that the pit house dwellers took the beams from their pit house because of the lack of timber at the pueblo site.

COMING NEXT MONTH

THE MIST AND THE MAGIC by Susan Wiggs

A spellbinding romance set in 17th century Ireland. On a cliff high above the sea, John Wesley Hawkins meets Caitlin MacBride. With true Irish whimsey, Caitlin has just grasped a white and blush-colored rose and wished for her true love. Hawkins walks into her life, but danger and adventure lie ahead before these magnificent lovers can find a happy ending.

SILENA by Terri Herrington

A powerful romance set in Nebraska in the late 1800s. Silena Rivers is on a quest to discover her true identity, with the help of handsome Wild West showman Sam Hawkins. But along the way, they find that love is the only thing that really matters.

THE ANXIOUS HEART by Denise Robertson

An enchanting contemporary novel set in London about a courageous and feisty young woman who pulls herself out of a low-income tenement building to discover the amazing world outside.

THE MAGIC TOUCH by Christina Hamlett

Beth Hudson's husband Edward, was a magician obsessed with the occult. He had always promised her that he would be able to communicate with her from beyond the grave; and two years after his death, his prophecy seems to be coming true. With the help of Lt. Jack Brassfield, Beth reopens the investigation of her husband's death and gets more than she bargains for.

AMAZING GRACE by Janet Quin-Harkin

An engaging romance set in Australia just after World War I. Grace Pritchard, a beautiful young Englishwoman, is forced to choose between two men . . . or face a difficult future alone in the male-dominated and untamed Australian outback.

EMBRACE THE DAY by Susan Wiggs

A Susan Wiggs classic. An enthralling and romantic family saga of spirited Genevieve Elliot and handsome Roarke Adair, who set out for the blue-green blaze of Kentucky to stake their claim on love.

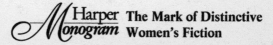

Harper Monogram The Mark of Distinctive Women's Fiction

ANALISE

Analise Caldwell was the reigning belle of New Orleans. Disguised as a Confederate soldier, Union major Mark Schaeffer captured the Rebel beauty's heart as part of his mission. Stunned by his deception, Analise swore never to yield to the caresses of this Yankee spy...until he delivered an ultimatum.

ROSEWOOD

Millicent Hayes had lived all her life amid the lush woodland of Emmetsville, Texas. Bound by her duty to her crippled brother, the dark-haired innocent had never known desire...until a handsome stranger moved in next door.

BONDS OF LOVE

Katherine Devereaux was a willful, defiant beauty who had yet to meet her match in any man—until the winds of war swept the Union innocent into the arms of Confederate Captain Matthew Hampton.

LIGHT AND SHADOW

The day nobleman Jason Somerville broke into her rooms and swept her away to his ancestral estate, Carolyn Mabry began living a dangerous charade. Posing as her twin sister, Jason's wife, Carolyn thought she was helping her gentle twin. Instead she found herself drawn to the man she had so seductively deceived.

CRYSTAL HEART

A seductive beauty, Lady Lettice Kenton swore never to give her heart to any man—until she met the rugged American rebel Charles Murdock. Together on a ship bound for America, they shared a perfect passion, but danger awaited them on the shores of Boston Harbor.